The Silver Queen
Sovereign: Book Two

Josie Jaffrey

CONTENT WARNINGS & SERIES RECAPS

There is a full list of content warnings at the back of this book, and also available at Josie's website at the link on the left below.

Recaps of the Silverse books are available on Josie's website at the link on the right below.

CONTENT WARNINGS

www.josiejaffrey.com/content-warnings

SERIES RECAPS

www.josiejaffrey.com/series-recaps

By Josie Jaffrey

Stories from the Silverse: the World of the Silver

The Seekers Series
Killian's Dead (short story prequel, free to Josie's subscribers)
May Day
Judgement Day
Winta's Day
Valentine's Day
Dark Days
End of Days

The QuickSilver Trilogy
Kill Me Quick
A Quick Study
Quick and the Dead
QuickSilver Omnibus Edition

The Solis Invicti Series
A Bargain in Silver
The Price of Silver
Bound in Silver
The Silver Bullet

The Sovereign Trilogy
The Gilded King
The Silver Queen
The Blood Prince

Silverse Serialised Stories
Dead Box
Dead Road

Silverse Short Stories
Encounters: Silverse Short Stories

Other Fiction

The Deluge Series
The Wolf and the Water

Short Stories
Broken Wings (collection)
Ring The Bell

Prologue

The Silver body was an incredible thing. Fibres knitted back together, organs were shocked from inertia and desiccated tissue healed as blood plumped flattened veins.

These powers of regeneration were inexplicable, but they were also predictable, so Charles knew when he would find Emmy awake, but still weak enough to present no danger to him.

That was the moment he chose to threaten her. He was that kind of bully.

'You're going to tell me how it works,' he said, leaning over her supine body.

The leather straps were enough to keep her in place for now, but in ten minutes' time she'd be able to snap them as easily as a human would snap spider gossamer.

She blinked up at him, brown eyes opened innocently wide. It was an expression that would have made even a gullible man suspicious.

'How are you immune?' Charles said, leaning closer to her face.

Emmy's gaze traced the lines of his brow, his lips, his stubbled cheeks. So familiar, and yet now they engendered no fear in her. Those days were gone.

'You're showing your age,' she said.

He was. His dark hair was greying at the temples, giving him the appearance of a dissolute cavalier.

'I might be getting older, my queen,' he poured disdain into the title, 'but so is your son. Now tell me what I want to know.'

Charles didn't see her move, he just felt the impact then found himself on the floor. There was blood in his mouth, spilling over his lips while tears spilled down his cheeks. The bitch had broken his nose.

Steps thundered into the room around him, and by the time he got to his feet they were already holding her down, although she hadn't freed herself from the straps. She must have head-butted him, because his blood was all over her. It stained her teeth.

And she was laughing.

1

Julia could still see the blood. The Invicti had cleared away the bodies to Empress knew where, but the stones of the square were stained the dirty burgundy of death.

It was a stark reminder of their new reality: the Red had contaminated the Blue.

'Do you think it's still contagious?' Claudia asked her.

They were peering into the square through a crack in the kitchen shutters, picking out the dark patches in the morning light. The tracks of yesterday's deeds were impossible to miss.

Marcus, a disgraced Server, had been exiled to the Red. He should have died there, but instead he'd shambled the taint of the forests back into the city, leading a wave of horror through their homes, infecting everyone he'd touched. Or scratched. Or bitten.

They were all dead now, and the Blue was defiled.

But that wasn't why Julia's stomach felt like it was in a miserable free fall. That was Lucas's fault, because she and Claudia were on their own. Julia had only realised Lucas was gone when she'd been woken at dawn by the sound of the courtyard door clicking shut behind him.

She had no idea where he was now.

'Jules?' Claudia nudged her.

'Contagious?' Julia said. 'You mean you think it's in the blood, whatever made Marcus and the others the way they were?'

'Don't you? It's like the stories, after all. It looks like everything we were told about the Red was true.'

They'd been raised on fairytales of the horror that lurked beyond the city boundary, where creatures carried blood that would kill in an instant, and a bite of fruit was a death sentence. But Marcus had still been walking, despite being contaminated, and despite the fatal injuries that had cut darkly around his wrists.

'It's not all true,' Julia said. 'Marcus and the others, they didn't exactly die, did they?'

'They weren't the same, though. Didn't you notice their eyes? They weren't right.'

'Well,' Julia said, pushing away from the window, 'I'm not going to risk going outside again.'

'What choice do we have?'

'We need to do what Alba said. We find somewhere safe to hide, and we stay there until this is over.'

The Empress had summoned Livia and her other Attendants to the Palace, and Alba had told them what that meant. It meant she was getting ready for a siege, preparing to protect her favoured humans from the ravages of the Nobles. It meant there was going to be trouble. Julia had hoped Marcus would be the start and end of it, but the city was still silent despite the height of the sun, and Livia had still not returned.

As though to confirm Julia's fears, there was a thud against the front wall of the building. Both girls turned towards it as it sounded again, louder this time, knocking pots from their shelves and leaving creeping fissures in the paintwork before the noise moved away across the square.

The fight against Marcus's kind might be over, but the fighting amongst the Nobles was just getting started.

'We can't stay here,' Claudia said.

'The cellar,' Julia suggested. She didn't want to leave the house, not with Lucas still out in the city. How would he find her again if she wasn't where he'd left her?

'We can't hide down there,' Claudia said. 'There are windows.'

'Then where?'

But they had nowhere else, and Claudia's expression betrayed that knowledge. This building, their cellar bedroom and Livia's kitchen, were the only places they had ever called home. The closest Julia had to a substitute was Lucas's rooftop, but that had been destroyed in the fighting the night before. It would be stained now, just like the streets of the Blue.

Julia returned to the window, opening the shutters a scant inch so she could track the progress of the fighters across the square, but they were moving too fast for her to follow. The figures were just flashes of darkness in rolling melees. If Lucas was amongst them, she couldn't pick him out.

'Pack what you can,' Julia said. 'You're right; we can't stay here.'

As she turned away from the window there was a crash from the hall. The front door had buckled inwards, scattering shards of ancient wood across the floor and depositing a bleeding Noble at the foot of the stairs. Julia recognised him from the box at the Nomination: one of Rufus's friends.

'No time to pack,' Claudia said, grabbing Julia's hand.

Claudia dragged her towards the courtyard door. She snatched a roll of knives from the counter as they passed, but she didn't stop. The kitchen was already shuddering with violence as the girls tumbled out into the day, crockery shattering and tables creaking into firewood behind them as the fight followed the fallen combatant into what had once been their home.

They ran blindly as dust and clamour chased them through the courtyard and into the alleys that twisted a labyrinth around the square. The fighting was louder there, in the open heart of the city between the palace and the temple, so they put it at their backs and sought out the quieter corners. It meant squeezing between stucco buildings that embraced over narrow passages, their bare feet slapping on stone worn smooth over centuries of use.

Claudia stopped when they reached the junction with the next street. Her body blocked the passageway.

'What?' Julia said from behind her. She noticed the smell - stale, rotting meat - but could see nothing past the taller girl.

Claudia flattened her body against the edge of the alley, giving Julia a clear view of the road beyond.

It was even worse than the square. The grimy marks here weren't so much stains as streaks of dried gore, laminated to the paving slabs by the sun. There were darker areas that Julia initially assumed were dirt, but then they shimmered with movement, revealing themselves to be swarms of flies.

'They haven't cleaned here?' Julia said.

Claudia didn't reply, she just pointed a little way up the street. Julia leaned forwards to follow her line of sight, and wished she hadn't. There were still bodies here, lying halfway out of doorways and windows, their fingers and teeth latched onto their companions in a macabre daisy chain that led along the street and back towards the square, to where Marcus had made his entrance the previous night.

This was his path of destruction.

'We'll have to go back,' Julia said, looking from her bare feet to the gruesome red lacquer of the street. If Claudia was right and the contamination was in the blood, then Julia wasn't prepared to walk across it.

'We could put our cloaks over it so we can cross,' Claudia said.

'We could, but it might seep through. And we don't know what's on the next street over. There could be more blood.'

Claudia looked conflicted, but she let Julia lead her back the way they had come. They diverged from their original path as soon as possible, taking a shortcut through a small garden. It looked like it had been flattened by recent skirmishes; trees were horizontal, broken branches littered the grass and the place still smelled of bruised greenery. The adjacent buildings were shaking cement from their walls, as though the Nobles fighting within were trying to bring the roof down on top of themselves.

'So, are we going to the edge?' Claudia whispered as they slipped past.

The Blue was a city that petered out towards the forest. In its centre, around the square, the buildings were multi-storeyed and well-maintained. At its outskirts, abandoned huts hunkered against the sides of ancient, unloved structures that were mouldering into the carcasses of fallen trees. The Blue was a diminished creature, an echo sitting in the imprint of a greater ghost. It was as though the outside of the city were rotting from the contamination of the Red, its citizens huddling together for protection at its heart.

'I don't think it's a good idea to be that close to the trees,' Julia said. 'Let's find somewhere between the square and the Red, but away from the fighting.'

That proved more difficult than expected. The Nobles were spiralling out from the city centre as they fought, and the girls found their way blocked more than once.

At first their surroundings were familiar, places they had worked as Servers and played together as children, but eventually they had to leave those well-trodden paths to avoid either the

Nobles' fighting, or streets that bore signs of contamination. The winding route forced them northwards into areas of affluence that were so far removed from their day-to-day lives that they felt foreign. This was where the Candidates lived, the young humans who had been selected for the honour of ennoblement. Well, potential ennoblement, at least.

Julia exchanged a glance with Claudia as they stepped off the street through an archway that was normally guarded. Beyond it was a wide, stuccoed corridor, but its far end was obscured by curtains of beads and bright materials.

They had never seen what lay on the other side.

'We shouldn't,' Julia said. 'They're probably guarding the other side.'

'I think the Nobles are busy right now, Jules.'

'They won't all be fighting.'

'Maybe not, but those who aren't will be trying to stop those who are. Come on,' Claudia said, turning to Julia with a wicked twinkle in her blue eyes. 'Haven't you always wanted to see this place?'

There was a hungry edge to Claudia's look that made argument futile. This was what she had wanted, to be a Candidate and live in this place. Given this rare opportunity to see it for herself, nothing would stop her from taking a peek.

Claudia slid her fingers between the decorative fringe and pulled its weight to the side.

The sight was more colourful than Julia had expected.

It was clear now why there had been no one guarding the archway: there was no one left alive for them to protect.

There was no going back. The palace or the temple might have been safe, but they were both situated on the square, right in the middle of the fighting. The home of the Candidates had been the only other sanctuary Julia knew.

Claudia wanted to stay and tend to the dead, but Julia pulled her away, back into the street, despite her tears. They couldn't risk the blood, or the return of whomever had killed the Candidates.

'You remember what they wrote on the temple,' Claudia whispered as they hunkered in the shadow of a staircase to regroup.

Make no more Silver.

The words had appeared on the pediment at the end of the Nomination ceremony. Humans had been drained and the writing had painted on the stone in their blood, as a warning to the Empress to stop the ennoblements that would occur after the Casting ceremony. The Nomination was just a preliminary step to that end.

Apparently the protestors hadn't been satisfied that their demands would be met, so they were ensuring their wishes were fulfilled by other means.

'You think the same people who wrote those words killed the Candidates?' Julia said, her mind rushing through the implications.

'What else could they be fighting about? They don't want any more Nobles because they think there are enough already. They think they should be drinking from humans, not making them into more of themselves.'

Julia looked at her friend in surprise and said, 'How do you know that?'

'Rufus,' Claudia said. Her Noble, to whom she was assigned as Attendant. 'I overhear things sometimes. Some of his visitors were angry about the limited number of Attendants. And lots of people died last night. That's got to have made things worse.'

Julia had seen hundreds dead, so she dreaded to think what the final tally would be. Claudia was right: if the Nobles had been worried about their blood supply before Marcus's invasion, they'd be frantic now. It was terrifying to think how many Attendants might have died, and how they would ever replace them.

'We need to hide,' Julia said, 'and we need to do it soon. If any of the Nobles find us, we're in trouble.'

'Even Lucas?' Claudia asked, her tone gentle enough to suggest she was nervous of mentioning him.

Julia bit her lip to quash the anxious churn in her stomach.

'I don't know,' she said, because she didn't want to think about it, not here in the open. 'Come on, we need to get somewhere safe.'

They tried a few houses along the street, carefully creeping from one to the next. They were all unbarred, but they were also unsuitable, either because they had already been compromised by fighting or defilement, or because their rooms weren't secure enough to be safe. An old man had taken up residence in one nonetheless, the first human they'd seen all day, but he chased them back out into the street with angry whispers before Julia could ask him a single question. The rest of the houses appeared to be deserted.

'Why do none of these places have a cellar?' Claudia whispered as they turned into the next street.

'I'm more worried about where everyone's gone,' said Julia.

The area was suspiciously empty. Julia knew where the Nobles were, because she could hear the distant crashes of their combat. She could even feel the reverberations of their combat through the pavement, but her fellow Servers seemed to have vanished.

She couldn't bring herself to voice the suspicion that was nibbling at her nerves: maybe they were all dead.

The houses started to shrink as she and Claudia moved towards the outlying areas of the city. The low roofs of double- and single-storey houses opened up the vista, giving them a clear view of the farmland that bounded the city's northern edge. The vineyards basked in the morning sun, as though nothing had changed since yesterday. Julia wondered whether its Servers were even aware of what had happened down here in the city.

'There,' Claudia said, pointing across the road to a tiny house set between two larger ones. Each of its neighbours had small windows at ground level, but it had none of its own. 'It might have a sealed cellar,' she went on. 'If they dug out the two on either side, wouldn't they have done them all? That would make sense.'

'We can look,' Julia said.

In truth, she was starting to feel a little desperate. If they went much further from the centre then the houses would begin to devolve into shacks, and the deserted streets were unnerving her. She had never seen the Blue so devoid of life, and the strangeness of it gave the place an air of anticipation, as though it were waiting to be filled with activity. They needed to find a bolt hole before that happened.

The door opened easily enough, despite the lock that would have sealed it from the inside. There were just two rooms: a kitchen that had been stripped of everything but a few bits of broken pottery, and a sitting room stuffed with foul-smelling rugs and blankets. This had not been a prosperous house.

But Claudia had been right. When Julia moved one of the rugs aside, there was a hatch underneath that opened to reveal a short set of dirt stairs that led down into a dank cellar. It, too, was small and practically empty, but it was also sealed and secret enough to serve their purposes.

'They're getting closer,' Claudia said, looking out of the window towards the thuds and crashes that were now growing in volume.

Julia joined her at the front of the house, trying to gauge the distance.

Claudia still had the roll of knives tucked under her arm, but they had nothing else with them. If they'd had time, she would have suggested checking the adjacent houses for supplies and survivors, but the battle could've been on top of them in seconds.

It wasn't worth the risk. They needed to get out of the way before the Nobles barrelled through this place.

'Come on, then,' Julia said, ushering Claudia down into the cellar in front of her before closing the hatch behind them both. She did her best to pull the rug back into position so they wouldn't be found, but she didn't waste time making it perfect. It wasn't as though the Nobles would actively be searching for them; all they were interested in was fighting each other.

And killing Candidates, apparently.

In the darkness, they had no way of marking time. It had been long enough that it felt like hours and the cellar held no more mysteries.

There was a single candle on a shelf at the foot of the cellar steps, but neither of them had any means of making a flame. It was damp underfoot, and a tentative exploration of the floor yielded only a broken bucket and a small crop of mushrooms. The space couldn't have been more than ten feet square.

'So what do we do now?' Claudia said. 'How long are we supposed to stay here?'

'I don't know,' Julia said. 'How long are they going to carry on beating the city to bits?'

'Didn't Alba say it was weeks last time? We can't stay here for weeks.'

'We won't have to.'

'You don't know that.'

Julia reached out and fumbled Claudia's hand into her own.

'It'll be alright,' she said. 'It's not much different from our cellar, really. A bit darker, and a little less comfy, but we'll be alright. It's just for now.'

The steps were drier than the floor, so after standing for a few minutes listening to silence from above, that was where Julia chose to sit.

Claudia didn't join her. She was moving around the cellar, pacing as though she were marking its size.

'Do you think Marcella's alright?' she asked.

Marcella was the goddess, the beautiful Candidate whom Rufus had chosen to sponsor. Last they had heard, he had rescued her from Marcus's hordes, but they didn't know what had happened since.

'I'm sure she's fine,' Julia said. 'Didn't Rufus say she was?'

'That was last night. What happened back there, where the Candidates live, it was recent. Don't you think?'

Julia had been trying to push it out of her mind, but she couldn't stop herself from remembering the scene beyond the curtain. It wasn't as though she was a stranger to gore, not after the horrors of the previous night, but she had been able to dissociate herself from those events because Marcus's people had been so clearly been changed from humans into something else. Their bodies had taken on an alien aspect as a result. What Julia had seen this morning had been different, because the blood spilled on the grass of the Candidates' sanctuary was just like her own. Those murdered girls might have been her and Claudia, and Julia could almost see her reflection in their faces.

She could see what might have been.

'I'd be surprised if Rufus has let Marcella out of his sight,' Julia said, 'particularly if he knew this was coming.'

'You still think he had something to do with it?'

'I'm certain he did. Have you forgotten the Nomination? He was watching the pediment too early. He was waiting for that message to be painted on the temple. He's part of this, Claud.'

Claudia shuffled over to Julia, moving carefully in the darkness, then sat down beside her.

'I know he was,' she said, 'but I can't believe that–'

'Shh,' Julia interrupted.

There was a noise, just on the edge of her hearing.

They had heard similar noises over the course of the past few hours, if that was how long they had been in the darkness, but there was something more immediate about this sound. It was percussive, like a series of detonations, but the muffling of the tone made it difficult for Julia to tell how distant it was. It could have been caused by a building collapsing a mile away, by someone fighting in the street outside, or by a rat scurrying across the hatch.

After just a few seconds, it was silent once more.

Julia wished for a window. She knew it would have made them less secure, and knew that they had chosen this house specifically because it was the only one with a dark cellar, and yet her inability to scout the street made her feel exposed.

She rose to her feet and pressed her ear up against the wooden hatch, straining to hear any remnant of the noise.

There was something. It wasn't as loud as it had been at first, but there was a soft, rhythmic sound coming from the front of the house.

'What is it?' Claudia whispered.

'I don't know. It sounds like–'

Julia fell backwards down the stairs as something crashed through the hatch. She shielded her face from the shower of rotten wood that rained down on her, which meant she didn't see the hand reaching down until it was already wrapped around her ankle. It tugged so sharply that her joints felt as though they had popped from their sockets, and then she was dragged up through the hole.

'Jules!' Claudia cried, scrambling to catch her, but she could never have moved quickly enough to stop Julia's assailant. Julia had only the briefest glimpse of Claudia's horrified face, upside down, before she was pulled out of the cellar towards the door.

But Julia wasn't giving up. She latched her hands around the broken floorboards, ignoring the splinters jamming into her palms as she held on for all she was worth.

Her ankle was tugged harder.

'Let go,' her attacker barked.

She knew it was pointless to struggle. There was no resisting the Noble, who could break her leg without breaking a sweat, but now that she'd started fighting she found it impossible to stop. She gripped the boards tighter as she kicked out with her free leg, trying to connect with a foot, or a knee, or a shin, and failing.

The woodworm-infested planks broke before her strength did. She flailed around for another handhold, but there were none to be had. Her bleeding fists clasped around rugs and rags, but nothing that would anchor her as she slid across the floor.

Julia's stomach lurched, and the next thing she knew she was up high, sitting on pockmarked stone with a view of the city spread out in front of her. It was late afternoon, and the sudden heat raised sweat from her skin after the cool dankness of the cellar.

When she registered the arms holding her in place from behind and the breath at her neck, that banished the last of the chill.

'Lucas?' she whispered, but his name came to her lips more through hope than belief. The scent wasn't right, and he wouldn't do this to her. He was a Noble, but he wasn't like the rest of them.

Or was he?

He hadn't cared enough to stay.

Curious fingers had found the silver stud in her ear, the gift that he had given her, as though her captor knew the association. Then it came to her: the sour wine smell of the body at her back, familiar and dangerous.

Rufus: Claudia's Noble, who had left her bruised and bleeding every time he'd taken her blood.

'Lucas is gone,' Rufus whispered in Julia's ear, 'and he's not coming back.'

'I don't believe you,' she lied.

She should have called him Master.

He was a Noble, after all, and she was just an Attendant, albeit assigned to someone else: Lucas. Rufus shouldn't even have been touching her, but from the way he was holding her against him, with his fingers teasing through her hair, she guessed all propriety had been cast aside while the Nobles played in the city's ruins. There was no point in pandering to him with titles when it was clear that he would do what he wanted with or without her compliance.

'I brought you here to see it for yourself,' Rufus said, pointing across the city.

She could just make out the temple roof and the pennants that flew from the top of the palace. Beyond them, at the point she guessed must be the south side of the square, a column of smoke rose into the blue sky. She could see the flames.

Lucas's rooftop garden was on fire.

'That's your building too,' Julia said. She felt numb.

'I've found somewhere better,' said Rufus, then he ripped the stud from Julia's ear.

She cried out, but his hand was over her mouth, silencing her scream.

'Hush,' he whispered. 'You don't want a pack of hungry Nobles to come looking for you, do you?'

The pain was so blinding that for a moment she didn't realise what had happened. Her vision strobed. Strange, that such a small wound should hurt so much, and bleed so freely. The blood was running down her neck, pooling in the hollow of her collarbone.

Rufus leaned forwards and licked it from her skin. His tongue was too hot, too urgent in the way it insinuated itself across the curve of her throat. She shuddered involuntarily, hating that her body betrayed her emotions so freely.

Rufus noticed, and chuckled softly at her discomfort.

'Your master has left you,' he said, 'so you'd better prepare yourself for a new one, Julia. You could do much worse than me.'

'You already have an Attendant,' she mumbled against his hand.

'Yes. For the moment.'

His words chased acid fear through her veins.

Not Claudia.

'Either way,' he went on, 'you won't be needing this anymore.'

The earring sang as it hit the stone, bouncing until it rolled to a stop in front of Julia's feet. It was dripping with blood.

She was so shaken that she didn't move when Rufus released her. There would be no point anyway; it wasn't as though she would be able to get away from him if he wanted to keep her close.

But instead he stood and stepped away, off the side of the building and back down into the city. He didn't look back.

Julia was left alone, staring at the bloodied token of Lucas's former affection.

By the time Julia made her way back to the house where she and Claudia had been hiding, it was already too late.

She couldn't move as fast as she would have liked because there was something wrong with her knee, but Rufus hadn't carried her far, only a couple of hundred yards. Just far enough to ensure that she wouldn't be able to interrupt him.

Claudia was his Attendant, after all, so he was entitled to take her blood.

Julia found her still in the cellar, sprawled on the steps with her blonde hair trailing in the dirt. The pale skin of her arms had already been bruised from weeks of abuse, but now it was broken open over one of her wrists, leaking into her cloak and over the roll of knives that lay half untied at her side. Her eyes were closed, her lips more blue than pink, but she was breathing.

'Claud?' Julia whispered, lowering herself down at Claudia's side. 'Claud, you have to wake up.'

Her friend didn't respond.

Julia drew on the half-remembered knowledge she'd acquired over years of watching Livia tend to injuries, and tried to stay calm. She needed to elevate the wound, that was the first thing, so she stretched out the injured arm above Claudia's head, resting it against the staircase's higher steps.

Next… what was next? Check for other injuries?

She turned Claudia's head from side to side in her shaking hands, feeling for a bump that might explain why she was unconscious. She prayed that she'd find one, because otherwise the blood loss was to blame, and there would be no hope then.

There was no bump, but Julia's fingers came away wet from Claudia's scalp; there was a small cut. She had hit her head after all.

Julia's eyes watered with the relief of it, and from the anxiety that Rufus might still have taken too much blood, but then Claudia breathed out something that might have been words.

'Claud?' she said. 'Did you say something?'

'I'm alright,' she whispered.

'No, you're not.'

'I slipped.'

'Onto Rufus's teeth?'

'On the steps,' Claudia said. 'Afterwards.'

She didn't meet Julia's eyes as she spoke, and her complexion coloured with the same bewildered shame she had worn after her first encounter with the Noble. He'd bitten her then, too.

'Please don't tell me he's not that bad,' Julia said. 'Not again. I don't think I could stand that right now.'

Claudia pushed herself up into a sitting position, wincing as she adjusted her bloody arm.

'It looks worse than it is,' she said. 'Look, it's not even bleeding anymore. I'm sure it was just an accident.'

Julia gave her a sceptical look.

'Accidents happen,' Claudia insisted.

Julia remembered the blood pouring from Marcella's hand after the Nomination ceremony, and the bite that still scarred Claudia's neck. She saw the knives on the steps, nearly released from the material in which they were wrapped, as though Claudia had tried to pull one free.

'Rufus seems particularly accident-prone,' she said.

Claudia's nod was resigned. The ripped flesh of her wrist was a deliberate affront, and they both knew it.

Julia brushed the hair away from Claudia's face and kissed her forehead, pressing her lips to her friend's skin with the solemnity of an oath.

'We have each other,' she said, wrapping Claudia in her arms.

'What happened?' Claudia murmured into Julia's hair. 'To you, I mean.'

'I'm fine,' said Julia, squeezing the earring that she still held in her bloodied fist. Her palm stung with splinters. 'He just wanted me out of the way.'

Claudia leaned back from the embrace, pushing Julia's hair away from her neck.

'You're bleeding,' she said.

'I'm fine,' Julia repeated, but the words were hollow. She knew that today had only been the beginning of their pain.

For the Nobles, there was always more blood to be shed.

2

Blood is a strange thing.

Throughout his long life, it had held many meanings for Cam. When he'd been a child, it had been nosebleeds and fistfights, first a curiosity and then a badge of honour. In his human years, it had become symbolic of life and death in the births of children and the fatalities of battle, but it had always been a source of fear.

Until the day he had turned Silver. Then, it had become pleasure. Everything about it was laden with exoticism, from the heady scent to the way it felt in his veins, fizzy and regenerative, making him laugh with its energy.

Blood had been nothing but life. There had been power in that: the invulnerability of being almost deathless.

Except something had changed. The balance had been tipped. With the contamination of the Red, and latterly of the Blue, blood had regained its fearsome nature. One drop could make him mortal, with all the vulnerability that entailed.

This should have worried Cam, but as they neared the trees that circled the city his main concern was how little it concerned him.

He suspected he knew why: there was someone waiting in the Red for him, someone who carried the blood that he should fear, and Cam couldn't wait to see him again.

'Why didn't you bring your own damn horse?' Tommy asked. 'I gave you a perfectly good one.'

'I told you: I was in a hurry. And Hades is not "perfectly good". He's an utter bastard and you know it.'

They'd raided the stables before they left the square, taking as many horses as they could, but most of them had been either injured or spooked by the inundation of Weepers the previous night, so there hadn't been enough. There were fourteen Invicti and only ten horses, so some of them were having to share.

Tommy was riding with Cam, but Cam had taken the reins and Tommy was sulking about it. It wasn't like him to be petulant; in fact he was usually the grown up of the group. That was how Cam could tell he was anxious.

'I feel like a child,' Tommy said. 'I'm the bloody Secundus. Why can't I ride with Viv? She is my wife, after all.'

'Because she's pregnant. Her horse is already carrying two. Do you want to crowd her, in this heat?'

'I should at least be at the reins,' Tommy protested.

'You don't know the Red like I do.'

That ended the argument, as Cam had known it would. Tommy's heart hadn't really been in it; he was just looking for a distraction because he hated not being in control. But Cam had spent centuries in the trees, learning their paths and dangers, so he was leading this rescue mission. Tommy might have had seniority over him, but for now Cam was in charge.

They dismounted when they reached the fence that marked the edge of the Blue. Cam's landing was accompanied by a distant crash from the direction of the city, but that wasn't unexpected. The Weeper attack was bound to make the Nobles erratic, with all the blood donors they had lost. Cam had anticipated that there would be violence. In fact, he was surprised the rest of the Nobles had remained civil this long.

'Trouble?' Viv asked.

'Lorelei can handle it,' Tommy said as he handed Viv down from the bay mare she was riding. 'There are more than enough Invicti left in the Blue to deal with a few scuffling Nobles.'

On Cam's advice, they had brought only the strongest Invicti with them: the ones who were old enough to have known Emmy. Their squad needed to understand the importance of what they were doing, but the Silver who didn't remember their queen would think she was just a fairytale, because that was what Laila had wanted them to believe.

Laila, the Empress of the Blue, and one of their strongest Silver. At least she had been, until the previous day, when she'd drunk contaminated blood and had been turned human. Cam regretted that he wouldn't be in the Blue to see how that turned out, but not enough to make him wish he were staying behind.

'Lorelei could probably manage them all on her own,' Viv said. 'I'm not sure she needs anyone's help.'

'That's probably what she thinks,' Tommy said, his grumpiness creeping into his tone.

'She'll lead them well,' Cam said to him. 'You chose a good Tertius. You know that. She can hold the city with the rest of the Invicti.'

They'd left their comrades with Lorelei to face the invasion that was coming to the Blue from the northwest, from the mountain enclave that Cam was setting out to infiltrate.

Lorelei would need soldiers who were the exact opposite of Cam's party. She needed young Silver who would fight for the Blue to their last breath, because the city was all they had ever known, and because they couldn't imagine a world in which it didn't exist. They'd give everything just to make sure nothing changed.

For the Invicti who surrounded Cam, change was just part of life. They had settled in the Blue because it was the only source of uncontaminated blood, so they'd had no choice but to stay, but given the chance they would rather move on and adapt. They were always up for adventure, which was why they were perfect for this mission.

It was going to be dangerous.

'Well, what are we waiting for?' Adewale asked. 'Let's get out there. I miss the woods like you wouldn't believe.'

'Good. Maybe we can leave you in them,' said Alistair. His accent had been Scottish once, but centuries in the city had rounded it out until it resembled everyone else's. Homogeneity was the curse of the Blue, a place where the smallest variations could mark you out.

Adewale was joyfully different. His parents had been Nigerian, and he bore the rich earth tones of their skin, but he'd been born in Scotland, where he'd met Alistair. They'd been annoying each other ever since in the way that only the best of friends can.

'I know you don't mean that,' Adewale said with a good-natured grin as he slung his arm around Alistair's shoulders. 'Without me, who would you criticise? You take so much pleasure in telling me I'm wrong.'

Eveline rolled her eyes. 'Enough, already.'

'Here,' Viv said, handing round bottles of blood from her horse's packs while Eveline pushed open the gates into the woods. 'Let's have a toast from our leader.'

Cam started to look over at Tommy before he realised that Viv was talking to him. He was the one steering this squad of ancients into forests they hadn't seen for centuries. He was so used to being on his own that the concept of being part of their corps felt as though it belonged to another life, one he wasn't sure he wanted back.

He would have to get used to it, and quickly.

He raised his bottle.

'To bringing Emmy home. To reviving the Primus, and reuniting them at last. To the King and Queen.'

'To the King and Queen!' the Invicti chorused.

Cam poured a libation onto the threshold of the Red, then they drank their bottles dry. There was no point in conserving their contents; the blood they carried wouldn't last long in the summer temperatures.

'Alright,' Adewale said, clapping his hands together. 'Let's get this rescue underway.'

None of them saw the figure watching them from the moss-covered ruins of the city's outskirts. It lurked behind a fallen tree, waiting for Cam to close the gate after the last horse and then, moving silently on the soft ground, it followed.

'No, you've got it all wrong,' Alistair was saying. 'You can't stack those logs so tight. The fire won't be able to breathe.'

'My dear friend,' Adewale said, 'your concern is touching, but I make my own fire every day. It will breathe perfectly well.'

'Making a fire in a grate is completely different from making a campfire. You can't just apply the same technique and hope for the best. How can I leave you behind in the woods if you don't even know how to make a proper fire?'

Cam dropped his face into his hands and wished he were travelling alone again. His nights had been so peaceful.

But empty.

No, he didn't want to be alone. He wanted to be with Felix, but they wouldn't reach the salt lake shore until the next day. That was where Felix would be waiting for him. Until then, Cam would have to make do with the company of his squad, but he didn't feel any less lonely when he was with them, he just felt more crowded. He had been away from them for too long.

'Hey,' Viv said as she joined him by the lean-to at the back of the cabin. He had been tending the horses, but now he was just standing there, trying to find the energy to go back to the others with a smile on his face.

'Hey,' Cam said, returning the greeting.

'Having second thoughts?'

'About the mission, no. About bringing Alistair *and* Adewale… Maybe.'

'As if you could separate them,' Viv laughed, and the sound was strident in the peace of their surroundings.

It was nearly dark, but they weren't close enough to the lake to hear the nighttime animals awakening on its far shore. In these trees, on the border of the Blue, the wildlife that remained had learned to be silent.

'Tell me what I can do,' Viv said.

'What do you mean?'

'I mean that there's something on your mind. Do you want to talk about it?'

'I'm fine. I'm just trying to work out a plan.'

Viv gave him a frank look that made it clear she didn't believe him.

'Cam, we're in this together,' she said. 'I know you're worried. We're all worried about this army, and the Weepers, and what it means for our blood supply, and the future of the Silver, but you can talk to me. We'll get through this, just like we got through it last time.'

But that wasn't why he was worried. He knew it should have been what was preoccupying him, so how could he tell Viv that all he cared about right now was Felix?

He wanted to be alone with his thoughts, and his memories, and his hopes, because tomorrow there would only be reality. He was afraid that he might have misconstrued the situation, or that Felix would see him differently when the Invicti were around him, or that their kiss on the lake shore might have meant less to Felix than it did to him.

To Cam, it had felt like the beginning of a new life, and the end of his old one. There was an awkwardness in the prospect of those two worlds colliding.

'I'd better go and prepare the camp,' he said, forcing a smile, and then he slipped away.

But when he joined the others, he found that the work had already been done. The fire was made, the cabin was being readied, and Aaron was busily stirring a pot on the edge of the fire pit while potatoes baked in the coals. Even Tommy was busy, scouting towards the lake with Eveline and Darius, while the others foraged for mushrooms.

Cam's evening routine had been usurped, so he had no tasks behind which he could hide while he let his mind roam. Still, he needed his hands to be busy so his thoughts could be free.

That was why he was carving stakes at the edge of the camp when the boy walked out of the trees towards him.

He was vaguely familiar: tall and dark, but with a lean frame that spoke of his youth. His walk was loping but hesitant, although it became more determined the closer he approached, as though he were shoring up his courage. Cam suspected the boy was exactly as young as he looked.

Eveline yelled, 'Northwest,' as the scouts walked back into the camp from the south, and the whole squad looked up from what they were doing to track the progress of the intruder.

But they deferred to Cam when he rose to his feet.

'You've come from the Blue,' he said, his voice carefully pitched so that it was loud enough to be heard by a Silver over the distance that separated him from the boy, but not by a human.

'I was sent,' the newcomer replied, his tone equally soft. He was a Noble, then.

'By?'

'Lorelei. She said you'd be expecting me.'

Cam looked again at the boy's face. He remembered Lorelei mentioning something, but he hadn't been paying as much attention as he should have been. They'd had very little time to speak before the squad had left.

'You were the one on the rooftop last night,' Cam said, finally dredging the conversation from his memory.

'And you were the one in the square, the one who killed them all.'

'You saw that, did you?' Cam said, rubbing the back of his neck with his palm. Trust Lorelei to send this kid in blind, without telling him anything about what they were dealing with. 'I think you'd better come and sit down.'

The boy's steps were tentative again as he entered the camp, but he didn't stop until he was standing at Cam's side, waiting for him to speak.

'I'm Cameron.'

'Lucas,' the boy replied.

Gods, but he was young. His youth was loud in the shaking of his hand as he reached out to clasp Cam's, in his downturned eyes, even in the way he wore his pack slung awkwardly over his shoulder so it tipped his hips out of alignment. He was young enough that he still teetered in his new adult body, like a foal trying to find its feet.

'So,' Aaron said from the fireside, 'you threw a load of Weepers off a roof, and now you think you're one of us?'

'Shut up, Aaron,' Cam said, his eyes still fixed on Lucas.

'Weepers?' Lucas looked genuinely bewildered.

Damn you, Lorelei.

'I guess we have to fill in some gaps for you. But first, some introductions. That's Thomas, leader of the Solis Invicti. You address him as "Secundus". Next to him are Viv, Eveline and Darius. Alistair and Adewale are by the fire there, and you already know who Aaron is.'

Lucas nodded to them each in turn. Adewale boomed his exuberant welcome, while Viv smiled hers.

'You'll meet the others later,' Cam said.

'Others? There are more of you?'

'Six more, fourteen total. Well,' Cam corrected himself, 'fifteen, including you.'

Lucas didn't say anything to that, but his eyes were wide.

'What's wrong?' Cam asked.

'Nothing.'

That was a lie. The boy was obviously intimidated.

'I just didn't expect so many,' he added, in response to Cam's raised eyebrow.

'Most of them are friendlier than Aaron. Don't take it personally - he's like that with everyone.'

'It's true,' Aaron admitted, 'but that's only because you're all idiots.'

Viv interrupted the bickering, ever the mother in waiting.

'Come and sit down,' she said to Lucas. 'Let's have some food, and we can get to know each other.'

By the time the others came into view of the camp, Viv had extracted Lucas's entire life story. As far as Cam could tell, he was a willing participant in her interrogation. Lucas had barely said a word to the others, but for Viv he was an open book. It was a skill of hers that Cam envied all the more because it was one he used to possess himself.

'So he's coming with us?' Tommy whispered, leaning in close to Cam as they sat by the fire. 'Do you really think that's wise?'

'Do you really think we have a choice?' Cam said. 'How can we send him back now? He followed us into the Red, despite everything Laila tells them about it. He risked everything to come here. If Lorelei thinks he'd be an asset, then maybe we should trust her.'

'But what are we supposed to do with him? He's just a kid. I'm surprised he can even hide his silver.'

'Alistair can train him.'

Tommy laughed. 'For battle? In four weeks? You're overestimating his talents.'

'You didn't see him fight, Tommy. I know he's young, but he's got something about him. He's got power. Lorelei's right: we can use him.'

Tommy shook his head, staring into the flames. 'And if it means telling him everything? Do we tell him the truth about the Weepers, and the vaccine, and the cure? Do we tell him about Emmy? That's why you assembled this little group of misfits, isn't it? Because we're the ones who know it all, down to the bone.'

It was a problem. The humans and Nobles of the Blue were taught pure mythology, while those few who were old enough to have lived through the Fall knew the real power that humanity held over them. Laila taught the humans that going into the forests would be suicide, but in truth the Silver were the only ones who had any reason to fear the Red. The humans could just walk away from the Blue, and then the Silver would have nothing. They would die without uncontaminated blood.

That was the knowledge the Invicti had protected.

'I don't know what we're going to tell him,' Cam said. 'We'll work it out.'

He stood as the triumphant foragers reached the fire, ready to make the introductions, but Viv beat him to it.

'Everyone, this is Lucas,' she said.

Six suspicious faces stared at the boy.

'Be nice,' Tommy said to them. 'He's going to be joining us on our journey.'

'So,' Viv said, jollying through the awkward moment, 'this is Linh. She's our mushroom expert, as you can see. This is her husband Gul. The big guy is Bartek, and next to him is Konrad. He's quiet, but he's a joker and an expert tactician, so don't turn your back on him for a second. Our tattooed lady is Naia and, last but definitely not least, the blonde is Zita. She's stronger than her size suggests, just so you know. She can take Bartek down, so I wouldn't push your luck by trying to spar with her.'

'Once,' Bartek grunted. 'It was one time.'

'Did you want a rematch?' Zita asked. 'Any time, little man.'

A clang cut through the argument, and they all turned to see Aaron holding a spoon poised next to his cooking pot, which was apparently serving as a dinner gong.

'If you savages are done posturing,' he said, 'then maybe you could hand over the mushrooms so I can finish up this meal I've slaved over for you. Or are you ingrates not hungry?'

Things moved quickly then. In the bustle of eating dinner, arguing over sleeping arrangements, and getting themselves ensconced for the night, there was no time for anyone to raise the question of why Lucas had joined them, or to tell him the reason for their journey.

Cam knew it was only a temporary reprieve, but it was a welcome one. He didn't need to be babysitting right now; he had enough on his mind as it was.

They were going to bring Emmy home. It would change everything, and the Blue would never be the same again.

That was the most important thing. He knew it would be as transformative to their world as the Revelation had been, and perhaps even as dramatic as the Fall, but still his excitement was reserved for someone else.

Because tomorrow would be the day he saw Felix again.

In the end, Cam carried his blanket out to the fireside. He was too agitated to sleep, and it was impossible to think clearly in the cabin, surrounded by the noisy warmth of fourteen sleeping bodies. The smell had been as thick as the air in a teenager's bedroom by the time he had finally extracted himself from beneath Tommy's feet, Zita's hair and Bartek's out-flung arm, and he was gasping for the fresh breeze.

He wasn't used to being around other people and to be presented with so many in such a small space was overwhelming. He used to love it: the camaraderie of living overlapping lives. Now it just felt intrusive.

He'd become antisocial in his old age.

'You're up,' Viv said as she joined him by the smouldering remains of the fire. It was barely dawn, but they would keep long hours on this trip. They had a lot of ground to cover.

'Couldn't sleep,' he said.

Viv cut to the chase. 'I'm worried about you.'

Cam offered her a wry smile. 'You always say that.'

'Doesn't make it any less true. You're happier. I can see that, and I'm glad, but you still seem so far away. I don't know. I thought that when you found Emmy, you'd come back to us. I thought maybe you'd be your old self again, but you're still so distant, Cam, and that worries me, because you used to be so close.'

'I know.'

'I just want the old Cam back,' she said, and the familiar words twisted open a vulnerability he preferred to keep closed.

He wanted to tell her that the person he used to be didn't exist anymore. He wanted to swear and scream his frustration that she would ask him to wear a face that was no longer his, not just because it would hurt him to play the part, but because he mourned his old self too. He wished he could be the joyful creature that had once inhabited his body, but it was gone and he was left with nothing but his mission, and the flickering hope of an attraction that was too new for him to call it love.

He wanted to tell Viv all of those things, but instead he just said, 'I know.'

It was a relief when Aaron joined them, despite his foul mood. He berated them for not reviving the fire, ranted for ten minutes about how unappreciated he was as a warrior and a chef, then clanked his cookware around so violently that it wasn't long before the rest of the squad emerged from the cabin in search of breakfast.

They ate quickly and saddled up with a practiced ease that was surprising, given their generally shambolic attitude towards proper conduct. Their fluidity was the result of hundreds of excursions together, and despite his initial discomfort Cam felt himself falling back in step. Lucas, however, was always five steps behind, and he was getting under everyone else's feet.

'Watch it, kid,' said Eveline as she swung into the saddle, narrowly missing Lucas's head with her feet.

'I'm twenty,' Lucas said. 'I'm not a kid.'

Eveline smiled, showing her teeth as she leaned down towards him. 'Well,' she said, 'I'm a thousand and fifty-nine, so I'd say you're more like a toddler to me.'

Viv glared a warning at her. 'You can ride with me,' she said to Lucas, helping him up onto her bay.

After that, Cam had trouble keeping Tommy's mind on the mission.

'You wouldn't let me ride with her,' he muttered as they pulled ahead of the other riders.

'No, because you're twice the boy's size,' said Cam. 'You would have flattened the poor horse. And anyway, it's not for long. We'll send scouts ahead on foot when we reach the continent, and then you can have a horse to yourself.'

'You're going to use the rest of the blood?'

'Yes,' Cam said. 'Most of it, anyway. It's not going to last much longer, so we may as well.'

'And are you going to talk to him?' Tommy looked back over his shoulder at Lucas. The boy had clearly never been on horseback before, because despite Viv's soothing presence, he had tensed up as though he expected the mare to buck him off at any moment.

'Dear god,' Cam muttered.

Why had Lorelei sent them this boy? He clearly hadn't been schooled with the children of the more influential Nobles, or if he had, then he'd learned nothing. The latter was the more worrying prospect.

'Are you sure this isn't a mistake?' said Tommy.

'Yes.' *No.* 'Alistair can start training him tonight. If he doesn't show any improvement over the next couple of days, then we'll send him back.'

'So are you going to talk to him or not? Someone needs to, and you're the one running this rescue.' For once, Tommy seemed glad of that fact.

'Fine, I'll talk to him,' Cam said. 'We'll stop for some food before we make the crossing, and I'll speak to him then. Happy?'

'Not easy, being in charge, is it?' Cam could hear the smile in Tommy's voice.

'Oh, stop gloating.'

'Never.'

It was going to take them hours to get over the lake. Cam had built the latest ferry for himself, so it was only designed to take one horse at a time. With ten horses and fifteen people, they'd be here all day.

Bartek volunteered to pull the ferry across on the line, for a few journeys at least. He took Konrad, Naia and Zita with him on the initial run so they could set up camp on the other side of the water. They'd get things ready while he collected the first of the horses.

The squad had settled into a familiar rhythm now. Aaron was already bustling around assembling food, although no one had designated him the chef, and Eveline was standing watch with Darius at her side. Linh and Gul had gone off foraging again and with nothing else to do, Alistair was needling Adewale about the way he had arranged his horse's packs.

'Come on, Viv, and you two as well,' Tommy said to Alistair and Adewale. 'We'll get the horses watered before Bartek comes back.' He gave Cam a significant look as they walked away. He was leaving Cam alone with the boy.

The bastard.

With the ferry halfway across the lake, they were the only two left by the landing stage. The waves lapped against the stones, reflecting the sunshine in blinding sheets of light while seagulls picked their way along the shore, teasing morsels from the tide line and screeching so the air was alive with the sound.

Cam's mind was blank. He had no idea how to start this conversation. Thankfully, Lucas did.

'I don't know why she sent me,' he said, 'and I don't think you do, either.'

'I do know,' said Cam. 'She saw what I saw. She saw you fighting like you were born to it, though I'm guessing you've had no training.'

'No. No training,' Lucas said. There was resentment in his tone when he added, 'I'm not one of them.'

Not one of the elite, Cam assumed. It didn't seem as though he had much love for them either.

'And you don't know what you were fighting?'

'Whatever the Red turned Marcus into.' As he spoke, Lucas's dark brows creased in sympathy. There was his alliance, then: he cared more for the humans of the Blue than he did for its Nobles.

Interesting.

'They're called Weepers,' said Cam. 'Look, it's complicated, but I guess the easiest way to explain it is to say that there are two kinds of contamination in the Red: one that makes the monsters, and another that kills them. I used the second kind last night in the square, which is why they died.'

Lucas was silent for a moment while he thought on that. Eventually, he said, 'So the Red's no danger to the Nobles?'

Cam laughed.

'You don't think we're monsters, Lucas?' he said. 'Because it can hurt us too, so now that you're out here you need to be careful. No meat, and unless we say otherwise, no blood that doesn't come from a bottle.'

'Where else are we going to find it?'

Of course, Lucas didn't know that humans lived in the Red. He didn't know that they *could* live out here, contaminated, because Laila had wanted them all to think they were trapped in the Blue. With Lucas's human sympathies, it would be dangerous knowledge for him to have.

He was bound to see humans in the Red sooner or later, but for now Cam sidestepped the question.

'We'll have to do without when the bottles go bad,' he said. 'Do you think you can handle that?'

'I've done it before,' said Lucas. He seemed surprisingly relaxed about the concept. It was time to rattle him.

'For two months?'

'Two *months*?'

'Two months,' Cam confirmed. 'Four weeks there, and four back, with no blood for most of that time.'

Cam watched Lucas carefully, but he couldn't pin down his reaction. He wasn't scared, that much was clear, but there was unhappiness in his expression. Something about the length of the trip was making him reluctant.

'Can you manage that long without blood?' Cam asked, because that was the most obvious cause of his discontent, but Lucas just shrugged in return.

'I've done it before,' he said, which made no sense at all because every Noble in the Blue had access to an Attendant.

'By choice?' Cam asked.

'Necessity.'

It was clear from his tone that Lucas didn't want to discuss it further, so Cam let the subject drop. One thing was clear: this boy had not had a normal Noble upbringing.

Aaron interrupted their tête-à-tête then, bringing slabs of dark bread layered with cheese and ham, the last meat they would have until they returned to the Blue. The others joined them to eat, except Bartek, who was already loading up the first of the horses onto the ferry.

It did not go well. When he was three-quarters of the way across the lake, a Weeper howled from the direction of the continent. It was too distant to be any threat, but it thoroughly spooked the horse. The mare was in the water before Bartek could get it under control, so Zita and Konrad had to swim out and persuade it over to the far shore. It had been carrying Zita's packs, and she didn't look pleased that they were now waterlogged.

'Stupid animal,' Bartek grumped as he pulled the ferry back to the island. The rest of the squad was too busy laughing to offer him any help in loading the next horse.

'We'll carry the saddlebags separately from now on,' Cam said, brushing the remains of his sandwich from his fingers, 'and I'll come over on the next trip too, in case there's another howl. There's something I want to check out.'

As he ate, Cam had been scanning the far shore for any sign of movement. The squad was making enough noise to raise the dead, and that would have carried across the water, so why was there no sign of Felix? Cam had expected to see him walking out of the trees the moment the horse went into the water, but the forested hillside was strangely still.

Something was wrong. He needed to get to the opposite shore, and he needed to do it now.

He and Bartek crossed the lake without incident, and in silence. Bartek was taciturn at the best of times, but he seemed to sense Cam's mood, and not a word passed his lips on the way.

Cam handed the horse's reins off to Naia as soon as they reached the far shore, then leapt straight from the ferry to the sloping banks that cambered up and away from the lake.

He had no time to spare.

Leaving the others to salvage their supplies, he followed the green nutmeg scent of Felix into the trees.

3

Someone was following them. Julia had once or twice caught the scuffling echo of her own bare footsteps, or the strange impression of occupied space behind them in the flicker of a shadow, or the distortion of light.

Whoever was tracking them wasn't very good at it.

She wished they had never left the cellar, but then they hadn't really had a choice. With the hatch shattered and the ground reeking with their blood like a scented invitation, they were lucky to have made it safely through the night. They'd stayed long enough for Claudia to regain a little of her strength, and for the crashes of fighting Nobles to relent, but now they needed water and food, and there was none to be had in the adjoining buildings. Julia had checked.

It was also becoming increasingly apparent that Claudia needed medical attention. For that matter, so did Julia. If they didn't get their wounds washed, sewn and treated, then things were going to turn ugly.

There was only one option: they were going back to the square.

But they weren't the only ones. After ten minutes of feeling as though the back of her head had a bullseye on it, Julia couldn't explain it away anymore. They weren't being followed coincidentally. They were being tracked.

She was sick of being scared, and she had no energy for a chase. If whoever was following them decided to attack, then she'd fight back, but she'd lose. She was already shaking with nerves, and prolonging the tension would only make her weaker. Better to get it over with now.

She waited until she and Claudia had just passed along a narrow alley trapped between two walls, then turned to face back the way they had come.

'Alright,' she said. 'Who are you, and what do you want?'

There was a second's pause before the stalker revealed herself, moving into the alley at its opposite end. Dark hair straggled over sharp bones covered with pale skin and stained with gore.

'You smell of blood,' the girl said.

Julia took a step backwards, nudging Claudia into the street beyond, then asked, 'Who are you?'

'Priscilla. Who are you?'

'Attendants already claimed by other masters.'

The girl laughed, and in her wheezing pitch Julia heard the extent of the injuries she'd suffered.

'There are no masters anymore,' she said. 'Didn't you know?'

She hopped forwards, one leg dragging behind her. It didn't seem to be causing her any pain, but it explained her inept pursuit, and why she had been tracking them in the first place.

She was thirsty.

'Claud,' Julia whispered. 'Run.'

But they still had their knives. They would not be defenceless. Claudia pressed one into Julia's ruined palm, and she closed her fist around it despite the pain.

Her eyes never left Priscilla, but Julia still didn't see her coming. One second she was twenty yards away, and the next she was pushing Julia to the ground, her teeth grazing Julia's neck. But instinct must have kicked in somewhere in that tiny slice of time, because the knife was now between them, clasped in Julia's hand, and rammed into Priscilla's chest.

The Noble collapsed, her deadweight trapping Julia's injured knee.

She wasn't moving.

'Come on,' Claudia said, dragging Julia free, 'she won't stay down forever.'

So they ran, Claudia in a wobbly stride induced by blood loss, and Julia with a limp that did almost nothing to lessen her pain. They took all the paths they'd avoided on their journey the previous day, following the most direct route to the square along streets where the paving slabs had been dented with impacts and littered with fallen masonry. Once-proud buildings had now tumbled down to block their way, so they had to scramble over brickwork that was mingled with broken finery of the kind they'd thought they'd never get to touch. The contents of all these homes was smashed apart now, and it baked in the sun.

But at least the fighting here was over. The thuds were more distant now, and more focussed. Instead of being scattered all over the city, they were coming from just one direction. Julia could guess their origin. She was willing to bet that the Nobles had all gravitated back to the square, just as she and Claudia were doing now.

Apparently Claudia had come to the same conclusion, because she pulled Julia into a recessed doorway two streets later and wouldn't carry on.

'We can't just walk into the square like this,' she panted. 'They'll smell the blood and that'll be the end of us.'

'But we need Livia's medicines.'

'If they're even still there. If the house is even still standing.'

Claudia made a good point. When they'd fled from it the day before, the Nobles had already been busy destroying the kitchen. But without Livia's medicine, Claudia's wrist was going to become gangrenous. They'd bound it up as best they could with strips torn from the bottom of their dresses, but it was seeping in a way that was concerning. It was the only one of their many wounds that looked unhealthy.

Despite her attempts to hide it, Claudia was in trouble.

Julia made a decision.

'Come on,' she said, opening the door in whose porch they were hiding. 'We're going to find what we need for cleaning and stitching, because one of these fancy houses must have a well and a sewing kit, and then I'm going to get you some medicine.'

'Jules–'

Julia put her finger to her lips and pulled Claudia inside the house, closing the door behind them.

The place was big. It was probably one of the biggest houses in the city, and it was certainly the biggest one Julia had ever been inside. A huge wooden staircase curved around the walls of the entrance hall, climbing three storeys above them, although the top floor looked as though it had fallen onto the one below. The building had taken some damage.

Directly in front of them, double doors opened into a wide space that was so large and empty that Julia couldn't fathom its purpose.

'What is this place?' she whispered.

'I don't know,' Claudia said. 'A gymnasium? Or a dance hall?'

The floors were polished wood, smoothed to a shine by wax and by the passage of a thousand feet. As Julia stepped through into the room itself, she saw tables and chairs folded up against the wall, as though they had been recently cleared from the space.

'A dining room, maybe,' she suggested.

Whatever the place was, they found what they were looking for through an unobtrusive door set into the panelling of the back wall. There was a kitchen there. A back door opened onto a communal garden with a water pump that served the surrounding houses.

A few minutes' searching located a needle and thread, some alcohol, a clean cloth, and a bucket. If they'd had more time then Julia would have laid a fire and boiled some water for their wounds, but the hearth was cold, so she would have to make do with using it straight from the well.

'I'm not washing my wrist in that,' Claudia said as Julia plunged her hands into the newly-filled bucket.

'No, you're not,' said Julia. 'You can make a fire while I'm gone, and we'll boil some water when I get back, then get you stitched up.'

'If I make a fire then someone's bound to notice the smoke.'

'Not when half the city's already burning.'

'Then we can boil some water up for you right now,' Claudia protested.

'It'll take too long. You need that medicine, but I can't patch you up properly before we have it, so you can't come with me. Right now, we just need to get me cleaned up enough that I don't reek of blood, so I can go back to the square. Please, Claud.'

The silence stretched before she replied. 'Well, you're going to need some new clothes, then. I'll go and see what I can find.'

Julia had managed to pull most of the splinters from her hands by the time Claudia returned with a clean dress and cloak, of much higher quality than the ones Julia was wearing, and a stack of bedsheets.

'For bandages,' she explained. She set them on the counter, then used one to dab Julia's palms dry. 'A couple of these do need stitches, but I'm more worried about your ear.'

'Can you sew it up?'

'I think I'll have to.'

The wound opened up again the moment Claudia started cleaning it, but it took her only ten agonising minutes to douse and stitch both Julia's earlobe and her hands, after which the blood clotted so quickly that Claudia could just wipe it away.

'They say the Nobles can smell a drop of blood from a hundred yards away,' Claudia said as she bound up Julia's hands. She was worried.

'I doubt they'll even be able to sniff it out at ten feet with all the blood that's already soaked into the square.'

Claudia looked away. 'I don't want you to go,' she said.

'I know. But I promise I won't be long.'

Julia stripped the dirty dress off over her head, and a tiny tinkling sound caught their attention. The earring had fallen out of her pocket, and now it was rolling in small circles at her feet. For an inanimate object, it was strangely insistent.

Claudia's gaze wavered between the silver stud on the floor and Julia's repaired earlobe, which still bore the mark of the piercing at its centre.

'I can put it back in if you like,' she said. 'But it's now or never.'

It was a split-second decision that Julia told herself had more to do with her shaky state than it did with her true feelings for the boy who had deserted her.

But she still said, 'Yes.'

The day was hot enough to be unpleasant, not just because of the sweat that stuck Julia's hair to the back of her neck, but because the warmth released odours from the streets that she would rather had stayed where they were. Even hundreds of yards away from the charnel piles, the stench was thick in her nostrils. It was bringing the birds into the city, a black aerial assault of creatures that were normally only occasional visitors to the Blue.

More bodies had been removed since the previous day, the blood scrubbed clean away, but fatty patches of darkness still marked their passage across the stones, and the smell of putrescence hung around the stains.

Still, perhaps it would help to mask Julia's own scent from the Nobles.

She ran into the first of them two streets away from the house where she had left Claudia. They were dragging bodies onto a cart that was already heavily laden, and they weren't doing it quickly. In fact, they were moving as slowly as humans would in this kind of heat, although of course there were none of those around. If they were sensible, they'd stay out of sight. Julia certainly intended to.

She tracked back around the corner. There were no alleyways that would let her cut past the Nobles, and the only other street that would take her in the right direction was still soaked in blood. She was about to start despairing when she noticed a stucco staircase built up the side of the house at the end of the terrace. The buildings were all flat-roofed here, and so close together that she would be able to jump from one to the next.

She might not be able to go around the houses, but she could go over them.

She had to climb three floors to get to the top. As she got closer to the square, the buildings were becoming uniformly taller and better maintained. Not many of their inhabitants had maintained their roofs, though. Where Julia had expected to see terrace gardens like Lucas's, there were only piles of discarded furniture and equipment that had been left up here to crumble in the sun. It seemed a waste, but then these residences had their own private gardens, so they had no need of the space.

Lucas would have made it beautiful.

Julia could hear voices below her: the Nobles, a man and a woman, now collecting the last of the bodies. She crept carefully along the rooftops, taking long strides to bridge the gaps between them, until she could pick out the Nobles' words.

'Gods, they stink,' said the man. 'Don't we have Servers to clear up this shit?'

'You're hilarious,' the woman said, chucking another body onto the heap.

The man cringed away, his face screwing up with distaste.

'I'm serious,' he said. 'Why the hell can't they do this? It's not like we care if they get contaminated; we only drink from the Attendants anyway.'

'Right, and how many of those do you think survived the night? You really are a fucking idiot sometimes. We're going to need all the uncontaminated blood we can get, so yeah, it does matter if the Servers touch the vaccine.'

'Alright. Fine. Unlike some people,' he said, 'I haven't had years to get used to the whole contamination, vaccine, cure thing, because *some people* thought it wasn't important that the rest of us know about it.'

'Oh, shut up with your whining. It's not like you ever left the Blue.'

'Well I'm definitely not leaving it now. It's bad enough that I have to risk touching this lot. Isn't it better for a few humans to get contaminated than for us to get cured?'

'Look,' the woman said, hands on hips, 'we've got too many Nobles and not enough humans whose blood we can drink. Which of us do you think is more expendable right now?'

The man was silent for a moment.

'Shit,' he said.

'Come on, you've got gloves, haven't you? Just shut up and give me a hand with this.'

Even with two of them, it took a while to get the cart moving. They steered it in an awkward circle and then out towards the Red, with every appearance of strain.

That was why the streets hadn't been cleaned, then. They'd run out of blood. Julia understood that much, but the rest of their conversation was difficult for her to decipher. She didn't know what a vaccine was, but it didn't sound like anything good.

The cure, however, was more perplexing. Why wouldn't the Nobles want to be cured, and what was wrong with them in the first place?

They were questions Julia couldn't answer, but they preoccupied her as she made her way cautiously towards the square. If only Claudia had been here, she could have helped her work it out. She always had been more perceptive than Julia, who wasn't even sure her comprehension of the Nobles' words was good enough for her to relate them to her friend later. She couldn't remember the things she hadn't understood.

But Claudia was waiting, and the longer Julia took to get the medicine, the longer the wound would fester. She needed to stay focussed.

The length of twelve more rooftops took Julia to an alley that was too wide to jump, but there was no staircase here to take her down to the ground. Instead, she had to jump down to a balcony at the back of the final house, which did her knee no good at all. From there the only option was a trellis that started six feet below.

She was only two storeys up, but when she leaned out to look over the edge of the balcony it seemed like a bone-breaking drop.

Claudia, she reminded herself.

She was doing this for Claudia, to stop her friend from losing her arm.

One deep breath, then Julia was sitting on the balustrade, her feet feeling for the sill between the balusters. That was the easy bit. Next, she had to turn her back to the open air and crouch down so she could grip the ledge and lower the length of her body down to the trellis.

She could feel the stitches pulling in her palms.

Her toes were just teasing the top of the trellis when her hands slipped from the balcony. It might have been that the bindings gave her too little purchase on the stone, or that her hands were too damaged to hold her weight, but either way she ended up snatching desperately at the trellis on her way to the ground.

Thankfully the wood was sturdy, since it had been used to train a plum tree to the wall. She ended up tangled in its branches, panting with terror and screwing her eyes up against the pain in her hands. It was a couple of minutes before she could even contemplate moving. She took the last few feet of the descent carefully, sparing her bad knee, and collapsed into the dirt.

More than one of her stitches had ripped open. The blood was soaking through the bandages.

So much for her chances of going undetected. She might as well have banged a drum and dressed in red.

From then on, Julia stuck to the ground as far as possible, but the gore on the streets forced her up onto the roofs again when she finally reached the block on which Livia's domain resided. The rooftops here were better tended, used for drying fruit and clothing, but they hadn't survived the attack unscathed. Blood spattered freshly-laundered sheets and pooled in corners where the movement of fists and feet had been printed on the stone. One roof had caved in entirely, so Julia had to balance along the edge of the walls to reach the next house, but she was intent on her goal now and refused to acknowledge the sickening depth of air that waited just an inch away from her feet.

In distracting herself from the drop, she fixed her eyes on the view across the square. She could see the blood-stained stone, the fractured temple, and the charred mess that had once been Lucas's garden. It dragged her on towards the end of the block, to the roof of her former home, and pulled her attention down to the remains of the square that was spread out at the end of the alley below her. She could see only a slice of it, but that was enough.

The Nobles were moving slowly. Fists slammed lazily into jaws that didn't dodge in time, and feet dragged rather than danced. The blood that powered them was no longer in their bodies; it soaked the ground instead. Others were spectating as they passed objects from hand to hand, too tired to fight themselves, but not to bet on the outcome of the final brawls.

The scene had an air of respite. The Nobles were winding down after the first round, because they needed more blood to fuel the second.

They would come looking for the Servers soon. Julia needed to get back to Claudia before that happened.

She found the hatch in the far corner of the roof, but it wasn't designed to be opened from the outside. It was wooden, and it nestled into the stone with not a single gap that was large enough for Julia to get her fingers in and lever it up. A knife would have done the job brilliantly, but she'd been in such a rush that she'd left them all with Claudia.

Stupid.

A few minutes' searching along the rooftops located a shard of bone and a promising piece of flint. The bone shattered immediately, but the flint slipped between the wood and the stone with just enough give for Julia to pry up the hatch.

To reveal yet another drop, because the ladder for reaching the roof from the room below was propped up against the wall on its far side.

Julia sighed to herself. It meant further stitches popping as she lowered herself down, and another impact for her bad knee. She diminished the latter by stripping the rooftop clotheslines to make a cushion for her fall, but she still twisted the joint uncomfortably.

It took a few minutes for her to recover, during which she surveyed the unfamiliar room.

If she hadn't been certain of the geography, she might have thought she was in the wrong house. There were three floors above the kitchen, all of them off-limits without Livia's permission, which had never been given to Julia. She could see why.

The wide room was filled with beds, tens of them, crammed in as tightly as the space would allow. Beneath them, belongings were piled neatly and with a proprietorial air that said their owners took as much pride in them as Julia and Claudia did in their tiny shelf of trinkets in the cellar.

What had Livia been up to? Julia knew that she had taken in a lot of girls, but they all had their rooms on the ground floor, or in the cellar like Julia and Claudia. No one had ever climbed the staircase in this house except Livia and her guests, so whoever was living up here must have been using the roof to get in and out.

Who had she been hiding?

When Julia was able to manage the stairs, she found that the floor below was much the same as the one she had just left, although the beds here were fewer and larger, and had been separated with sheets that hung from the ceiling, providing some semblance of privacy. Only the floor directly above the kitchen looked anything like Julia had expected it would: the space had been separated into a few rooms that Livia clearly used for sleeping and entertaining.

But Julia didn't linger, because she knew exactly where to find the medicines she needed: in the kitchen, behind the precious stash of tea that Livia kept for special occasions. She had a couple of tea plants of her own in the courtyard, and each spring she harvested the leaves carefully to dry and store in a jar for the rest of the year.

That jar was smashed now, and the treasured leaves were spread across the floor in a mess of brick dust and ash. The cupboard that had once held it was gone, along with part of the wall into which it had been set. The medicine was nowhere to be seen.

The kitchen had been completely destroyed. Everything was smashed to pieces, from the counter to the sink to the hearthstone itself. The whole room had been gutted and its contents reduced to splinters that reeked of soot and damp.

Julia didn't even know where to start looking for the medicine. The floor was so littered with shattered glass and a thick paste of spilled water and plaster dust that it would be treacherous under her bare feet. She was about to wade in nonetheless when she spotted the familiar salve pot, smashed in half and empty.

It was gone. She'd come all this way for nothing. She'd fallen off buildings, she'd balanced over treacherous falls, and she'd pulled so many stitches that even now her makeshift bandages were dripping blood from her hands to the filthy mess at her feet.

And it had all been pointless.

She couldn't accept it. She wouldn't let herself accept it, so she climbed painfully back up the stairs to Livia's rooms and ransacked the cupboards, looking for anything that might help Claudia. When her search of the first floor proved fruitless, she moved up to the next, where she found a trunk that she hadn't noticed before underneath the window. On top of it sat a bucket that was attached to a hook protruding from the outside wall. A length of rope snaking through the window connected the two, worn from long use. It looked as though the mechanism had been used to haul water up from the courtyard below. A second bucket on the floor bore a residual smell strong enough to evidence that it had been used to convey less palatable liquids down to the drains. Less palatable to humans, anyway; there were traces of blood around the rim.

The sight gave Julia hope, because it brought the room into sharp focus. She noticed the details she had missed: the dark stains on the floor, the smell of detergent and herbs, and the lye-bleached white of the sheets.

This wasn't a dormitory; it was a hospital.

She opened the trunk to find an array of medicines like nothing she had ever seen before. There was more of the salve, together with jars and pots marked with pictograms demonstrating their usages. One showed a hand spreading a paste over stitched skin, and another a swollen cut being washed with liquid. She pocketed both, along with the familiar-smelling salve, which was marked only with the letter "L".

Feeling triumphant, Julia smiled at the thought that she could return to Claudia with more than she had set out to find.

But when she lowered the trunk lid, exposing the window behind it, she met the eyes of a Noble standing in the courtyard below. He didn't look as though he was in any better state than Priscilla had been, but apparently his sense of smell was unimpaired, because he'd zeroed in on the blood that soaked the bandages on Julia's hands.

She ran.

She didn't stop to see if he was following, or to think about the best route out of the house, she just ran up the stairs to the top floor because it was the most immediate way of putting distance between them. Once there, she grabbed the ladder and slammed it into place, starting her climb to the roof just as she heard footsteps hitting the staircase below her.

The Noble wasn't moving at speed, so at least she had that on her side. She hoped he might also be distracted by the blood she was leaving behind her as her bandages smeared against the rungs, and she kicked the ladder free as soon as she reached the roof. Anything to slow him down.

Then she had a choice.

She couldn't lead him back to Claudia, but neither did she want to attract more pursuers by moving closer to the square. In the end, she jumped from the corner of the building to another row of houses that moved away parallel to the square. She had almost reached its end when the Noble made it out of the hatch, and by then it was too late to change her mind.

There was no staircase leading down from the last building, and no balcony onto which she could drop. She was trapped four floors above the ground, armed only with the shard of flint she had picked up earlier, facing down a Noble.

He jumped the gap between the terraces with such ease that Julia wondered if he had been exaggerating his injuries. Perhaps he could move at speed after all. Perhaps this was just a game to him, one that he wanted to savour.

'I recognise you,' he said, and his gaze flicked to her earlobe, where the silver stud was held in place by stitches and broken flesh. 'You're Lucas's Attendant,' he pronounced with a smile. It was not friendly.

'I'm already assigned,' Julia said, as though the Noble hadn't just told her he already knew that.

'Well, Lucas is gone,' he said as he strode towards her, 'so it looks to me like you're fair game.'

That might have been the end of things for Julia if the Nobles in the square hadn't caught her scent.

She was surrounded by them in seconds. They appeared on the roof from every direction, jumping up from the streets below or from adjacent buildings, battling each other to get to her.

Before she knew what was happening, she was swept up in snatching arms. Nausea tugged at her stomach, then she slammed into something, hard. As her equilibrium returned she realised she was lying on the ground, but the fighting continued above her. It wasn't until the rabble had thinned that Julia was able to lift her head and see that she had been carried to the square. She was exactly in its centre, where she had least wanted to be, hemmed in by Nobles who were fighting over her blood.

When the victor emerged, she was going to die.

But then something changed. It was as though the world had emptied of sound, because the hush that descended on the square was complete. The Nobles were frozen around her, the attention of each of them fixed on a single point across the square that Julia couldn't see. She pushed herself up to her knees, but her attackers were crowded tens-deep around her, so she might as well have had her eyes closed.

There were footsteps. A single set, stepping slowly but confidently in her direction. As they approached there was a murmur through the crowd, whispers and the rustling of clothing, then the Nobles were on their knees too.

The sun fell on Julia's face again. Now she could see what had so affected the Nobles: a man, topless, bloodied up to the elbows with gore that dripped onto the stones. His face was fierce but familiar, with startling blue eyes and features so fine that they might have been carved from stone and crowned with gilded curls.

He looked at the state of the square, then at Julia, and finally at the Nobles crouched on the floor around her.

When he spoke, his voice was like liquid ice.

'Would someone care to tell me what has been done to my city?'

4

It didn't take long for Cam to reach the end of the scent-trail. It dead-ended under a tree at the top of the slope. The vantage was such that someone sitting in the branches above would be able to see the whole of the lake crossing, and most of the island's nearest shore as well. It was a perfect look-out point.

'You're still here,' Cam said.

Felix dropped out of the tree, landing in a crouch in front of Cam. As he stood, he said, 'I told you I'd wait for you.'

That was true, but Felix's words seemed to have lost some of their heat since then.

'Why didn't you come out when we reached the shore?' Cam asked. Fear was starting to pinch in his stomach now, because this wasn't the reunion he had hoped for.

'I was waiting for *you*,' Felix said.

Ah. Maybe that was the problem, then: Cam had brought company.

'We're going after Emmy,' he said.

'And the Weepers?'

'Dead,' Cam replied, then added, 'Thank you,' when he remembered where he'd got the contaminated blood to bring them down. Felix had cut his hand open for the cause, and Cam could see where he had bound it closed.

It was far from the only injury Felix had sustained. His face was still mottled purple and blue from the beating he had taken in Charlestown, although it was less swollen now, and his broken ribs couldn't have had much of a chance to heal. Under his granite exterior, the woodsman would be suffering.

'I'm surprised you could even get up into that tree,' Cam said. 'Aren't your ribs killing you?'

'I've had worse.'

Cam didn't know what else to say. It had been two days, just forty-eight hours since they had last seen each other, and Felix had kissed him in a way that promised more to come. But now there was empty space between them that Cam didn't know how to close. Worse, he felt as though Felix didn't want him to close it.

But he'd had no reason to wait for Cam. Their oath was discharged, and Felix could have left if he'd wanted to, but he'd stayed. That was something, at least.

'So,' Cam said, crossing his arms over his chest, 'what now?'

'You're going back to the mountains?'

'Unless they've moved Emmy, yes. What are you going to do?'

'How many of you are there?'

'Fourteen. Well, fifteen.'

Felix raised an eyebrow, but made no other comment on the correction. 'It's not enough,' he said.

'It's what we have.'

'Still.'

'We're stronger than we look,' Cam said, a little hurt that Felix was underestimating him. Hadn't Cam saved his life, after all? More than once, as well. 'Most of us are over a thousand years old, Felix. We know what we're doing.'

'But you don't know the mountains.'

'I know them well enough.'

There was a pause before Felix replied. 'Not like I do,' he said.

The tension flowed out of Cam's shoulders.

'That sounds like an offer,' he said.

Felix just smiled back.

And then they were sixteen.

The introductions went smoothly enough, although Naia took a little too much interest in Felix for Cam's liking, and Aaron complained about having to cook for yet another unexpected person. His passive-aggressive comments seemed to elicit no reaction from Felix, but they clearly riled Lucas.

The boy had a lot of anger in him that needed to be directed, and there was no one better to do that than Alistair, so Lucas's training started that night while the others watched from their campfire on the slope above the lake shore.

'So,' Viv said to Felix, 'you met Cam on his last trip?'

'That's right.'

'When exactly?'

'When I was going through Hungary,' Cam interjected, assuming that Felix wouldn't know the old geography well enough to explain it in a way that Viv would understand.

'On your way back?'

'The way there.'

Cam didn't like the way this was going. He didn't want Viv invading the time that he had spent alone with Felix, because it had been theirs alone. Thankfully, she didn't pry. In fact, she didn't seem to pick up on the tension between them at all, which was odd because Cam could feel it drawing tighter minute by minute.

Instead, she just said, 'You saw the place where they're keeping her?'

'The outside,' Felix replied. 'One entrance, set in the stone. Sounded like there were a lot of Izcacus in there, too.'

'There were, but they'll be on their way here,' said Cam. 'They said they'd be in the Blue in a month, which means they're leaving about now.'

Lucas took a tumble by the shore, and Alistair's voice carried back to them.

'Keep your fucking guard up,' he yelled. 'You've got legs, you know, so bloody move!'

'You're getting better, boy,' Adewale called encouragingly, then he lowered his voice and said to Cam, 'We'll have to keep an eye out for the invaders while we travel. Perhaps we could eliminate some so that Lorelei has fewer to deal with.'

'No,' said Cam. 'We don't want them to know we're coming. If we see the army, we stay out of sight and let them pass.'

'How do you know they won't bring Emmy with them?' Tommy asked.

'I don't, but if it were me then I'd wait till I had control of the island before bringing her over. They're not going to risk having Emmy on the loose, not before the fighting's done. They need her.'

'Because the Primus's blood makes her immune to contamination,' Darius said.

'That's what Chloe said.'

'Well,' said Zita, 'I'm not going to trust the word of that backstabbing bitch.'

'You can tell her that yourself when we get to the Carpathians. I'm sure she'll be happy to see you again, too.'

'I doubt it. I'm going to gut her for what she did to the Queen. And Darius, of course.'

'Why?' Viv asked. 'What did she do to Darius?'

The soldier in question backhanded Zita across her upper arm.

She growled back, but to the others said, 'Nothing.'

'I'm going to gut you all if you don't stop bickering like children,' said Eveline. 'Now can we please eat before you nauseate me completely?'

Aaron dished out hot potatoes and stew thick with grains. It wasn't luxurious food, but it was filling and nutritious.

To avoid any further snark from the cook, Cam collected two bowls: one for himself and one for Felix. Aaron narrowed his eyes at that, but wisely kept his mouth shut for once.

'Here,' Cam said, offering Felix the bowl.

He took it and nodded to the wide tree stump on which he sat, a little way up the hill from the fire.

'You going to sit?' he said.

'Do you want me to?'

'Yes, Cam,' Felix said, meeting his eyes, 'I want you to.'

That thoroughly flustered Cam, but he sat nonetheless.

It might have been a large stump, but it was snug with the two of them sitting together. Their thighs were touching, and Cam could feel the heat of Felix's muscles through their clothes. It was… distracting.

'The boy fights well,' Felix said.

'Boy? He's the same age as you.' Cam laughed, but he could understand why Felix would assume that Lucas was younger.

For two people so close in age, they couldn't have been less similar. Where Felix was quietly confident and self-contained, Lucas was bubbling with the energy and insecurity of his youth. But then Felix had grown up dodging the dangers of the Red, whereas Lucas had led a sheltered life in the Blue, despite the relative deprivation of his upbringing.

'Maybe you could make friends with him,' Cam suggested. 'He could do with talking to someone his own age, rather than someone who just looks it.'

Felix half choked on a mouthful of potato.

'Are you alright?' asked Cam.

'Fine,' he coughed. 'Too hot, is all.'

'Well? What do you think?'

Felix's brow creased. 'We're different people.'

'That's exactly why I think it would be good for him.'

'We have nothing in common. It's not like you and me.'

You and me. As though there were such a thing.

'And what are we like?' Cam asked.

Felix looked down at the bowl in his hands. 'We understand each other, I think.'

'I don't know. Sometimes I don't think I understand you at all.'

Felix didn't reply, he just watched Cam picking at his food. Down by the fire the rest of the squad was laughing, resurrecting old stories from other excursions, but Cam and Felix were stuck in a silence that felt fat with the things Cam wished he could say.

He was just confused. It meant something that Felix had waited for him, that he was still here, and that kiss... But now it was as though he'd thrown up his defences to keep Cam out, as though he regretted their closeness.

'What do you want from me?' Cam finally asked. 'We both know I can navigate the mountains as well as you can, so why are you coming with us?'

'You don't want me to come?'

'I didn't say that,' said Cam. 'I just don't understand why you're here.'

Felix shrugged. 'There's nowhere else.'

That hurt, not because the words themselves were hurtful, but for everything they didn't say.

Felix wasn't here for Cam.

There was no point in pressing him further, so Cam gave up and ate the rest of his meal in silence. Felix made no attempt to start a conversation himself, so that seemed to be the end of that.

It wasn't long before bowls had been emptied and packed away, horses settled for the night, and rugs rolled out around the fire where they would sleep. The squad didn't dawdle as they turned in for the night, because they knew that tomorrow would be another early start. They knew how to conserve their energy in the field.

Cam left Felix by the stump and fetched his own blanket, assuming that Felix would sleep in the trees as he had often done whilst they were travelling together. Cam could understand that impetus to be away from the Silver, especially as there were now so many of them. He felt a measure of it himself tonight after his conversation with Felix, enough that he set his head down a little distance away from the rest of the squad.

In the darkness, it was difficult not to remember the other caravan that had stopped in this spot, the one of blood and bones. If they were still out there then it wouldn't be long before the squad crossed their path, and then they'd have to decide what to do with them. The caravans had been the joint contrivance of Charlestown and Laila, and with her now cured it might well fall to Cam to decide their fate.

If he had his way, they'd contaminate all the humans in the world with the vaccine and doom the Silver to fade out into nothing. One after another would be cured and dragged back into human lives. It was the only course of action that made sense, the only one that would erase the inequality and stop their barbarism.

It was the only thing that would stop his own destructive tendencies, which chafed in his chest at his disappointment. He wanted to punch down trees and break them apart with his fingers, just to feel the skin split. That way, maybe the pain could bleed out of him instead of coiling round and round in his stomach as though his body would never let it go.

He wanted to scream.

He wanted to cry.

But instead he stuffed the monster down inside himself and pushed his fist against his stomach to keep it there, while he prayed for sleep.

They decided to send out a scouting party the next morning, and it wasn't a minute too soon. The remaining blood was already on the turn, and it wouldn't get them far. Through the Carpathians perhaps, to the mountain lake settlement probably, and so that was the meeting point they designated. If the scouts' blood supply fell short, they could walk the rest of the way.

It would be three days' hard riding for the main squad, and less than an hour for the scouts, which was Cam's main reason for wanting to go on ahead with them. He could do with some time to himself, away from the bulk of the squad, but that wasn't what he told them.

'I've been visiting Ana and Vasile for decades, and their ancestors for centuries,' he said to Tommy. 'I can't just send a bunch of Invicti to them without being there myself. They'll panic. I have to be the first to arrive, or we don't go there at all.'

'Cam…,' Tommy sighed.

'You'll be fine. You enjoy being in charge, right?'

'This was supposed to be your mission.'

'And it still is, which is why I have to be in the scouting party.'

Tommy swore under his breath and kicked at the doused remains of the fire. 'Fine,' he said. 'Who else?'

It had to be six of them in total, because they still only had ten horses. In the end, Cam chose Eveline, Darius, Naia and Zita. He would have taken Adewale too, but they had to leave Alistair behind to train Lucas, and the two went together or not at all. In any case, the sixth had to be Felix. Cam had mixed feelings about that, but Felix was human, so Cam couldn't leave him alone with the Invicti, and anyway his horse was waiting at the mountain lake for him, along with Cam's own horse, Hades.

Reluctant though Cam was, taking Felix with them was the only solution.

'Well, I'm not carrying him,' Zita said.

Naia jumped on the opportunity too quickly. 'I'll do it,' she said, eyeing the woodsman predatorily. 'I do love them rugged.'

'Actually,' Cam said, 'I was thinking Eveline might.' She was strong and asexual, which made her perfect from Cam's perspective, but she was having none of it.

'No,' she said, looking at Felix, but she broke eye contact as soon as Cam turned to her. Then she looked again, and Cam would have sworn that there was something odd about the exchange. For an irrational second he thought Eveline might be following in Naia's lustful footsteps, but then the moment passed and she was her normal, abrasive self again.

'Carry your own food,' she said.

'I told you, he's contaminated. He's not food.'

'Then why is he even here?'

Good question.

Cam had woken that morning to find Felix asleep just a few feet away on his own blanket. He'd smiled at that, before he'd remembered their conversation of the previous night. He could only assume that Felix's proximity had more to do with protection than it did with affection, and Felix's next words confirmed that.

'I'd be more comfortable with Cameron,' he said.

'Good,' said Darius with a sneer, 'because I certainly wasn't going to offer.'

Felix might have been comfortable, but Cameron was dreading the journey. It wasn't easy, travelling at that speed. He had to concentrate fiercely to avoid hitting trees or falling over rocks, and being enveloped in Felix's scent wasn't conducive to clear thinking.

Still, they managed it without incident and reached the mountain lake by mid-morning.

Unfortunately, they were the only ones. Cam had expected the others to struggle since they didn't have his experience in the Red, but he'd been surprised when Eveline was the first of the runners to drop out of Silver speed. Perhaps the blood she'd drunk wasn't as fresh as the rest, but she was at least a day's walk away when her strength ran out. Zita, Darius and Naia were a little closer, but not by much, so Cam would have time plenty of time to smooth their path with Vasile and Ana.

He would also have an entire day alone with Felix, and maybe a night too. That was going to be awkward.

Cam came to a stop at the lip of the valley in which the lake was nestled, so the people would have plenty of time to see him approach. It also gave Felix his first glimpse of the place from its most picturesque vantage point. The sun reflected off the still water, which glistened where it was pushed into waves by the passage of a boat or the breach of a fish. The cluster of buildings that hugged its shore was decked with flowers at this time of year, all in bloom with a rainbow of colours. Cam could hear the sound of wood being chopped. Livestock ambled carelessly on the grassed slopes, and the small area of arable land was bursting with greenery.

The settlement was a bucolic idyll that soothed Cam's anxieties away.

'Beautiful, isn't it?' he said, inhaling the cool freshness of the air.

Felix slid from Cam's back and dropped their bag on the ground. Four steps took him to the edge of the escarpment.

He looked out, and Cam looked at him. The wind caught his too-long hair and whipped it across his face, but it didn't seem to bother him. His eyes were fixed on the sunlit paradise spread out beneath them.

'What is this place?' he asked.

Cam smiled and said, 'The best place on Earth.'

Ana met them at the bottom of the slope with a collection of her closest relatives, but Vasile was not by her side. He had been unwell on Cam's last visit, and although they had said their goodbyes in anticipation of Vasile's death, it was difficult to imagine that his illness had claimed him. He had always seemed so strong.

Ana must have seen the concern in Cam's eyes, because her first words to him were, 'Yes, Domnul Cameron. Vasile has left us. You missed him by only ten days.'

'I'm so sorry, Doamna Ana. He was a good man.'

'And a good husband. So we have kept his vigil, mourned him with song and celebrated his life with feasting.'

'I'm sorry I wasn't here.'

Ana reached out and took Cam's hand. 'You are kind to us, Domnul Cameron, but you have no need to bear our pain. Now, who is your companion?'

Cam took a step back so he could usher Felix forwards.

'A friend of mine,' he said. 'Doamna Ana, this is Felix. Felix, this is Ana. She's in charge of this place.'

'Doamna Ana,' Felix said to her. 'Your town is incredible.'

Ana's face creased with joy. 'Thank you, Domnul Felix,' she said. 'I hope you enjoy it here. Are you staying long?'

'We have more companions arriving over the next few days,' said Cam. 'We were hoping we could stay with you in the meantime, if it isn't too much of an inconvenience?'

'Of course not! Domnul Cameron is always welcome, as are his friends.'

'Are you certain? There will be sixteen of us in all.'

'Ah,' Ana said, with a twinkle in her eye, 'then Vasile would be pleased to know that his last work was useful. He built another hut for you, a better one, so between the two there will be plenty of space for you all. Let me show you.'

As they followed Ana around the lake towards Cam's usual hut, he was looking around for Chloe, but there was no sign of her.

'Doamna Ana,' he said, 'I sent a woman and her child your way with two horses, bringing you the gifts I promised. Did they arrive safely?'

Ana's forehead crinkled into a maze of lines. 'We've had no visitors, Domnul Cameron. When did you expect them to arrive?'

'Ah,' said Cam. 'Maybe not just yet.'

He hadn't taken account of the timing. It was less than a week since they had left Chloe and Alex in the Ore Mountains with the horses. It would take them three to get here.

'*Scheisse*,' Cam said to Felix, switching to German. 'I'm an idiot. What are we going to do now?'

'Three days at least for your riders to catch up,' he said. 'So Chloe will be halfway here by the time we leave.'

'We meet them in the middle, then. We'll only have to share horses for four or five days.'

Felix nodded.

'Apologies, Doamna Ana,' Cam said, turning back to the gerontocrat. 'We were hoping to take our friends' horses on from here. My own horse is among them, whom you may remember from my last visit.'

'That beast?' Ana laughed. 'I'm surprised you want to reclaim him. Well, if that is your only concern then we can lend you a couple of our own.'

Cam was surprised by the generosity of the offer, but suspicious all the same. Ana was a shrewd trader, and Cam suspected she would want something in return.

'That's extremely kind of you, Doamna Ana, but what can I ever do to repay you?'

'No repayment is required.'

'I insist.'

Ana didn't answer for a moment, as though she were genuinely considering his question, but Cam knew that was simply her way of being polite. She wouldn't have offered the horses had she not already decided what she would ask of him in exchange.

'Well, if you insist, then perhaps you might be able to tell people of our little town. Our usual traders have been less reliable lately – we haven't seen some for months now – and we're in need of more settlers as well.'

Cam and Felix exchanged a glance. The disappearance of the traders was concerning news, though not surprising.

'There's been some trouble on the plains,' Cam said, trying to find the right words without panicking Ana. 'That's why we're here, to resolve it, but of course we'll spread the word. The woman and child I mentioned, I think they wanted to stay, if you'll have them.'

Ana clapped her hands together and smiled. 'There, then. You have already proved a man of your word.'

She shooed some chickens out of the path as they rounded the corner of the assembly hall, and that caught the attention of the children playing between the huts at its back. Soon they had a crowd of little ones following them, while their parents tried to corral them back. They were more suspicious of Cam than their children were, because they understood what he was.

'Domnul Cameron,' said a dark-haired girl as she tugged on Cam's hand. He recognised her as one of Ana and Vasile's great-grandchildren. 'Have you brought us presents?'

'Not today,' he said. 'I'll make it up to you by bringing something just for you on my next visit. How does that sound?'

Her little cheeks flushed with the width of her grin.

'Now back to your mother, Mihaela,' Ana said gruffly, but with a smile. 'Domnul Cameron is tired from his journey.'

The children left them one by one as they approached the edge of the residential huts, where Cam's usual cabin sat away from the rest. Except now it wasn't on its own.

The new hut was twice the size, made from stone as well as wood, and beautifully finished. A chimney betrayed the presence of a fireplace, something that had been lacking from the old one, and logs had already been stacked up outside the door for him.

'I don't know what to say, Doamna Ana. Thank you.'

She smiled. 'We're pleased to have you here,' she said, with every appearance of sincerity. 'Vasile wanted to make sure that you would feel welcome, in case you ever decided to start spending more of your time with us.'

'Thank you,' Cam said again.

The offer hung in the air between them, not exactly spoken, and not exactly rejected either. It was something to think about.

'Alone again,' said Felix as he built a fire for their dinner.

Ana had apologised for leaving them to fend for themselves, but one of her granddaughters was in labour, so there would be no feast that night. Cam was glad of the solitude, or he would have been, had it not been complicated by Felix's presence.

They hadn't spoken for most of the day. Cam had people to visit, and he'd managed to stretch those social niceties until the evening. Those duties had the added benefit of taking him out of the cabin, which was as well-finished inside as it was outside. The community had clearly put a lot of effort into presenting him with a space that felt like a home, and he didn't know how to feel about that. He'd spent the afternoon thinking about Ana's offer, and apparently Felix had been doing the same.

'Would you live here?' he asked while he struck the flames to life.

Cam thought for a moment before saying, 'I don't know. I'd think about it. They've done things right here. No Izcacus, no servitude, no blood tyranny, just everyone working together.' He pondered on that as he selected vegetables from the pile that Ana's son had brought them earlier in the day. 'But I couldn't stay here now, not like this. If I were human though…'

He shrugged.

'But you're not,' Felix said.

Cam looked up and waited for Felix to meet his eyes before he spoke again. 'I could be,' he said.

'Is that what you want?'

'I don't think it would be the worst thing in the world. Sometimes I feel like I've lived long enough.'

'You'd give it all up,' said Felix, and Cam was surprised by the disbelief in his tone. He had no love for the Silver.

'Wouldn't you?' Cam said. 'Being dependent on the blood of other people to survive… We're just parasites. The problem is that we're also strong, and we abuse that power to get what we need. What kind of way to live is that?'

'But you could use your strength to change things.'

Cam shook his head, frustrated at his inability to articulate his feelings. 'It doesn't work like that,' he said. 'If you have to force people to do things, how can they be right? And even if I think I'm only using my strength to help people, there are still times when I can't control it, or I make mistakes, and people die as a result. And I'm *trying* to be a good person. What about the Izcacus who aren't? We're all just people, and everyone has an agenda, whether they admit it or not. That makes people with power dangerous, and that's not what I want to be. I just think we'd all be better off if the Izcacus didn't exist at all.'

Felix reached over and took the vegetables from Cam's hands. He'd been gripping them so tightly that he'd snapped them all into pieces.

Cam laughed wryly. 'You see? That's the kind of thing that happens when I stop paying attention. When I'm unhappy, or angry, or distracted, things happen that I don't mean.'

Felix smiled as he dropped the vegetables into a pot of water.

'At least I don't have to chop them now.'

Cam sighed and said, 'That's not the point.'

'So, what? You'd give it up?'

That was the question. Like all power, the strength of his body was addictive. Surrendering it wasn't a small decision, but after centuries and centuries of seeing what it made people into, Cam felt he was entitled to decide when he'd had enough.

'Not yet,' he said. 'Not while Emmy's still out there, and the Blue's in danger. But in the future, when all of this is resolved? I could stand to step away from it.'

Felix went still, his eyes locked with Cam's.

'You're talking about suicide.'

'No,' said Cam. 'I think I'm talking about peace. If what I want is this place, with everything it has to offer, then what I need is humanity.'

The conversation might have degenerated from there if Darius and Zita hadn't made their entrance then.

'They told us we'd find you here,' Darius said.

'Jesus,' said Zita as she looked around the inside of the hut. 'This place is a fucking dump, isn't it? It's making me homesick for our shitty bunkhouse.'

'Shut up, Zita,' said Cam, regretting the necessity of bringing them here. He hoped the riders would reach them soon, because the Invicti would ruin this place if they stayed too long.

'You two can give Felix a hand with dinner,' he said. 'I'm going for a walk.'

They let him go without comment. He paced around the lake until Felix called him back, and then the four of them ate in silence. The other Invicti must have sensed his mood, or maybe it was just that they were exhausted from their running. Either way, they finished their food quickly then spread out their blankets on the floor and went to sleep. Once they had started snoring, Cam got to his feet.

'I'm going to turn in too,' he said to Felix, heading for the ladder that led up to a half-height loft hanging over part of the room. It had been furnished with a soft mattress that was big enough for a whole family, and the thought of collapsing into it was fast becoming irresistible.

He crashed out in seconds, but it didn't feel as though he had been asleep long when a familiar scent awakened him.

'I don't think I was clear yesterday,' Felix whispered.

Cam blinked his eyes open and rolled over to face the woodsman, who was lying on the mattress next to him. It was strange to see him in such a furnished environment when all they usually had were leaves and the sky.

'What are you talking about?' Cam whispered back.

Felix reached out and ran his fingers over Cam's cheek, brushing at the stubble he'd accumulated since they'd left the Blue, then he leaned forward and kissed him.

It was nothing like the kiss they had shared on the lake shore, because nothing about it was chaste. It was hungry and determined, and incapable of being misconstrued. If it hadn't been for the Invicti sleeping downstairs then that might only have been the beginning of their evening, but Cam heard Darius rolling over in the room beneath them and pulled away.

Felix let him, but not without pressing a last kiss to his forehead.

'This is what you and me are like,' he said, and as he spoke he laced his fingers with Cam's.

They had a dreamlike quality to them, those few moments of reconnection. Cam wouldn't have believed they were real had he not woken the next morning to find Felix lying beside him, their hands still entwined.

5

'I don't believe you.'

'Seriously, he was as close to her as I am now, right Jules?'

'Yes, Claud,' Julia said.

It had been more than a week ago, but the King's return was still the news on everyone's lips. Never mind that Livia was coming home today, or that the Empress hadn't been seen outside the palace since the night of the Contamination; all anyone wanted to talk about was the legend of the King's awakening.

'His hair blazing like the sun, fists dripping with the blood of his enemies, and so beautiful it could blind you. Right Jules?'

'Yes, Claud.'

They'd spent the past week putting the kitchen to rights with the help of the other girls, who had been returning from the palace in dribs and drabs. The news they'd brought with them had delighted Claudia and bored Julia to tears. The types of tapestry, the silken cushions, the finely-crafted furniture and the jewelled walls were all intricately detailed to extremes that made Julia want to scream, just to block out the inane babbling.

The other girls had nothing of consequence to impart. They'd seen nothing and done nothing during their sojourn in the protection of the Empress, and yet their week spent sitting in a pretty room was apparently more worthy of attention than Claudia's stories of how they had battled contaminated humans, thirsty Nobles and infected wounds to save each others' lives.

Julia didn't really care, except she could see how much it hurt Claudia. The only story the other girls would even hear from them was the appearance of the King, and that was Julia's story, not Claudia's. In the circumstances, Julia couldn't blame her for milking it for all it was worth.

'My Noble told me all about it,' said Tatiana, one of the younger Attendants. 'He told me the statue was cracked open during the Contamination, and the King had been alive inside it the whole time. Can you imagine? Then he went out into the city and killed all the people who were contaminated, just with his bare hands!'

She stepped in front of Claudia as she spoke. The girls circled closely around her. Claudia was left outside the clique like Julia, with nothing to do but watch as the others listened, enraptured while Tatiana lied through her teeth.

'Come on,' Julia said, looping Claudia's hand over her arm. 'Let's go and collect the food from the temple.'

With one last, mournful look at the others, Claudia let herself be led away.

The Blue was still in such disarray that they weren't getting deliveries. So many houses were standing empty that the farms didn't even know which ones to deliver to, so instead the steps of the temple were serving as a market of sorts.

The stone had been scrubbed clean. Everything had by now, but the hot air of the city still tasted like something rotten.

At least the produce was fresh.

'They're never going to accept us, are they?' Claudia said as they turned into the square. 'You saw everything, right here, but they're happier to believe the things they make up than to listen to someone who actually watched it happen.'

'They've always been like this,' said Julia, 'and I think they're just going to get worse. They're scared, so they're biting harder.'

'But we've done *nothing* to them. And we had nothing to do with what our parents did. I mean, we were babies!'

Julia pulled Claudia closer. 'I know it's not fair,' she said.

'You're damn right it's not fair.'

'But my parents walked out into the Red. After what just walked back in, I can understand why the others are keeping their distance.'

'That's ridiculous. It's not like we're contaminated.'

And it was ridiculous, but it also made sense. Julia and Claudia had been out in the city during the Contamination. They'd actually fought contaminated humans, and while in Claudia's mind that made them heroes, Julia could understand why the other girls might decide that they were tainted by it.

Claudia understood that too. Julia could see it in the way she was winding down, her anger cooling into resignation.

'You know why they're doing it,' Julia said. 'They've made up their minds, and there's nothing we can do to change them.'

'It doesn't make it right.'

'I know,' Julia said, 'but does it really matter what they think? We know what we did, Claud. We've got the scars to prove it.'

Thankfully, that was the only mark of their adventures that they still carried.

They had both healed well. With the medicine from Livia's upper rooms, the infection in Claudia's bite had cleared up in a matter of days, and Julia's knee was as good as new. Their stitches had already come out, although for the moment Julia's hands were still bound. The skin was too sensitive for her to manage without bandages, but at least she was recovering.

She had the King to thank for that.

'Come on,' she said, 'let's go and see if there's any news.'

The temple had become a hub over the past few days. As soon as the bodies had been cleared, and the city had been silent for long enough that the Servers could believe the fighting was over, people had started to congregate in the square. That was where they had found their lost loved ones, or where they now waited for them to return. There had been hundreds to start with, milling around on the steps, but there were half that number now. Although some still went out into the streets to search for survivors, most had given up hope. It had been days since the last body was pulled from the rubble.

In her darker moments, Julia wondered whether Lucas had been among the dead.

She and Claudia were transferring their house's vegetable allocation into a basket when the gong rang out across the square. They exchanged a panicked glance; it hadn't been rung since the Nomination.

Claudia scooped up the basket and they walked quickly towards the palace along with the rest of the square's congregation. They were only a few rows back from the bottom of the palace steps, but there was nothing to be seen yet, just a lonely guard waiting out the minutes before he could strike the gong again.

The crowd's expectation felt nervous. People fidgeted, toes tapping, and so many people were whispering that it was like standing in a field of wheat in a breeze.

Two more low chimes, spaced apart at designated intervals, brought the rest of the city's inhabitants out of their homes and into the streets.

They were still so few.

The Servers used to fill the square from side to side. During the Nomination, when people had come down from the farms to join the rest of the Blue, they had spilled up the streets, into houses and onto roofs, just to get a glimpse of the ceremony.

Today, the square was barely a quarter full. People were looking around anxiously, as though they expected the rest of the city to turn up at any minute, but they weren't coming. They were out somewhere in the Red, rotting into the earth.

The gong sounded one final time, and then the Empress appeared. She was wearing her usual jewelled finery, with a beaded headdress and golden chains that looped from her nose to her ear, but they seemed to weigh on her today. She was diminished by them rather than enhanced, so they were more like a costume to hide behind than they were an ornament to her face.

She looked like a shadow of herself.

A moment passed in which the Empress stood alone in silence, then the door to the palace was opened again and there he was: the King.

If the people had arrived at the palace feeling nervous, then they left it intimidated and perhaps a little awed.

The King had an aura to him. He shone, and it was so easy to get lost in the cadence of his voice that it almost didn't matter that his words made no sense.

There were going to be protocols and processes, quarantines and quotas, and numerous other things whose meanings were opaque to Julia. What was clear was that they were all going to be tested for contamination before Attendants were reallocated and normal duties could be resumed.

It wasn't until later that Julia realised there had been no mention of the dead Candidates. She had seen none of them in the square either.

Perhaps there would be no Casting that year.

'The contamination that they're going to test us for,' Claudia said as they were ushered towards the temple with the rest of the Servers, 'do you think that it's this "vaccine" you heard the Nobles talking about?'

'Maybe,' said Julia. 'I guess we'll find out.'

'Eventually. It's going to take them hours to get through us all.'

She wasn't wrong. While the King spoke, guards had been arranging tables at the top of the temple steps. Twelve Nobles now sat at them in groups of two, calling forward the Servers one at a time. Julia couldn't tell what was happening at the tables, but whatever it was took about a minute for each person. Julia and Claudia might still be waiting when night fell at that rate; they'd been near the front at the palace, which meant they were now at the back of the queue.

'Can we just go home then come back?' asked Julia, but as she followed Claudia's eyes over her shoulder she realised that wasn't an option. Guards were walking the edges of the crowd, so no one would be leaving until this was finished.

Amongst them, Julia spotted Lorelei, the guard who had saved them on the night of the Contamination. Julia would have avoided her, because she still suspected that Lorelei had been involved in what had happened that night, but Claudia was already walking towards her.

Left with no other option, Julia grabbed the basket of vegetables and followed.

'Hi,' said Claudia.

Lorelei looked down her nose at her. 'What do you want?' she said, but then she saw Julia following behind. 'Ah, Lucas's former Attendant. Ready to be reassigned?' Her grin was not encouraging.

'Is that what's happening here?' Claudia asked.

'If you're both uncontaminated. After all, Lucas is gone, and we can't have good blood going to waste, can we?'

'Come on,' Julia said, tugging Claudia away. 'Let's go and wait our turn.'

They were almost out of earshot when Lorelei called out Julia's name. Julia's stomach clenched at the gleeful tone in her voice. It could only mean trouble.

'Why don't I help you out?' she said, walking towards them. 'Well, don't look so bloody scared. I'm not a fucking monster, you know. You don't want to spend the whole day here, so let's get you to the front of the line.'

'Thank you,' Julia said, 'but I don't mind waiting.'

'Don't be an idiot.' She smiled in a way that did nothing to dispel Julia's anxiety. 'Come with me, both of you.'

Lorelei took the lead while Julia glared at Claudia, who gave her an apologetic grimace in return. They skirted the crowd until they reached the edge of the staircase, where the guards stepped aside to let Lorelei usher them up to the temple. If Julia had been hoping they'd be stopped then she was going to be disappointed, because it looked as though Lorelei was giving the orders here.

'These two next,' she said to the men who sat behind the nearest table. A woman was waiting nervously in front of them, sucking at her finger.

Now that Julia was closer, she could see the objects laid out in front of them: thin slices of wood, a jar of blood, knives, alcohol, a pencil and book, and a few randomly-shaped objects that she couldn't identify. Two buckets under the table held more slices of wood, except these were bloody.

It was not a reassuring sight.

Julia watched as one of the men inspected the bloodied wood on his table, then added a drop of blood to it from the jar. A few seconds later, he said, 'Contaminated,' and his companion beckoned the woman forward. One of the random objects was pressed to her right cheek, and when it was removed there was a red-brown cross printed on her skin.

No more blood donations for her, apparently.

'This one first,' Lorelei said, pushing Claudia forward.

Julia watched while her friend's finger was pricked with the tip of a knife, then squeezed to coax a drop of blood onto a clean piece of wood. Again, the man behind the table added blood from the jar, then squinted down at the wood.

His deliberation seemed to take forever.

Julia wanted to shake him.

Finally, he declared, 'Uncontaminated,' and Julia felt as though she could breathe again.

'Palace?' the man asked Lorelei, and she nodded back.

A mark was printed onto Claudia's left cheek, but this time it was a circle rather than a cross, with a triangle nestled inside it.

'Report to the palace tomorrow morning,' the man said, then Claudia and her basket of vegetables were waved away.

She shot a small smile over her shoulder at Julia as she went, nodding towards the bottom of the steps. She'd wait for her there.

'And finally,' Lorelei said to Julia, 'it's your turn.'

Julia didn't want to go up to the table. Something was going on here, and she hadn't worked out what. She hesitated, but Lorelei just clasped the back of her neck and pushed her forwards.

'Hand,' she ordered.

When Julia still didn't move, the man who was wielding the printing wedges grabbed her wrist and dragged her towards the table. It was the work of seconds for the seated man to prick her finger, squeeze out the blood, mix and examine it.

'Uncontaminated,' he said.

'Oh, good,' said Lorelei. 'This would have been a bit pointless otherwise.'

'Palace?'

'No.'

The man at the table opened his book, but Lorelei took it from him and started flicking through the pages.

'This one,' she said, her finger indicating a particular line of text.

The man looked at her and raised an eyebrow. 'You're sure?'

'Just do it.'

'Name?' the man asked Julia.

She gave it, then he scribbled something in the book on the line Lorelei had indicated, while the second man pressed a wooden stamp against her cheek. But that wasn't the end of it: when it was done, he reached over with a paintbrush and added something within the circle of skin that still tingled with wet dye.

'Well,' said Lorelei as she shepherded Julia away, 'what a fucking delight this has been.'

'But who am I assigned to?' Julia protested, trying to turn back to the table. It wasn't as though looking at the book would have benefitted her, because she could barely write her own name, but she knew the knowledge was there, encrypted in symbols that meant nothing to her.

'Just be at the temple at dusk tomorrow,' Lorelei said. 'Your Noble will find you then. Trust me.'

With one final grin, Lorelei was striding back up the steps. Julia was left with only more questions, to which she was certain she would not like the answers.

But Claudia was beside her. She reached out and stroked Julia's cheek.

'What does it say?' Julia asked.

Claudia just shrugged; she couldn't read it either. Instead, she smiled and said, 'Home?'

Livia didn't come home that night. The girls waited until it was already dark before giving up and making their own dinner, but they kept sneaking glances towards the door as they worked, because no one wanted to step on Livia's toes.

The kitchen was less crowded now. Some of them, Tatiana included, had never returned from the square. The others were pretending that the missing girls had been chosen to serve in the palace, but they all knew that was a lie; Claudia would be a palace Attendant and she hadn't been told to present herself until the following morning.

They could tell themselves whatever they liked, but Julia could see the haunted look in eyes that had watched the marks go on the wrong cheek, the crosses that symbolised contamination.

No one knew where they had gone.

No one knew where Livia had gone either. She still hadn't returned when Claudia left for the palace the next morning, nor by dusk when Julia set out for the temple.

The last time Julia had made this journey, she'd pulled her cloak over her head and hidden in its folds while she'd waited for Lucas to reveal himself. This time, it was too warm for a cloak and she wasn't allowed to hide her cheek. It was her Noble's name, the other girls had said. A few of them bore similar scribbles in the centre of the circles stamped on their faces, marks that would identify them as allocated Attendants.

The thought of belonging to anyone but Lucas turned Julia's stomach.

The temple steps were crowded tonight. Every Noble in the city seemed to be meeting their Attendant at the same time, and that made for something of a scrum. There was no order to things; people clustered in whispering groups, or sat alone on the stairs, or stood still in the shadows of the temple's entablature as though they were trying to melt into the darkness.

Julia chose to sit, finding a space at the foot of the steps that was far enough away from the others that she couldn't make out their conversations. She didn't want to hear their worries. She wanted to be alone with her own.

It was some time before the first Noble arrived. When she did, it took her several minutes to find her name written on the cheek of her Attendant. After that, they came in greater numbers, laughing together with their friends.

'Found yours!' one shouted from just behind Julia, but he wasn't talking about her.

'And I've found yours,' another said from the far side of the steps. 'You might want to send her back, though. She's a bit beige.'

'Are you offering to swap?'

And so it went on. They laughed, and joked, and made it seem as though this were a game. Julia screwed her eyes shut and tried to block out their voices while she waited for it to be over.

The rush didn't last for more than half an hour. In that time, the steps had emptied so that there were only twenty Attendants left, and in another half hour just four remained.

When it was full dark, Julia sat alone.

She had started to wonder if there had been a mistake. Perhaps Lorelei had been playing a twisted joke on her, and wanted Julia to sit here all night waiting for a Noble who would never arrive. Maybe Lorelei wanted to humiliate her.

When he finally did turn up, slipping out of the darkness like oil spreading over water, she wished for humiliation instead.

'Good evening, Julia,' he said.

She was so full of rage that she couldn't speak.

'I see I'm going to have to take that little trinket out of your ear again. Surely you've worked out by now that he's not coming back for you?'

Julia cupped a hand over her earlobe, protecting the healing flesh in case he decided to rip it open again. She knew he was capable of it.

He just laughed.

'If it means so much to you. Come on, then.'

It took her a couple of seconds to get her legs working properly, and then she was up and following Rufus across the square. She walked behind him with all of the dread that had slowed her feet the first time she'd met her Noble. The only difference was that her fear of Lucas had turned out to be ill-founded, but she knew all too well that she was right to be afraid of Rufus.

They were heading towards the northern end of the square, away from the building Rufus and Lucas had shared. It was burned out now, nestled in cracked paving, whereas the houses around the palace gleamed with new stone. Julia remembered Rufus's boast to Lucas, that his ground-floor apartment was the best accommodation in the city, and belatedly realised how shallow those words had been. Compared with the buildings Rufus was now leading her towards, his old place had been a dump.

He saw her looking and smirked.

'You're going to be grateful you were allocated to me. My star's on the rise.'

Julia kept her mouth shut.

Their destination was behind the palace. It was a rarity in the Blue because the house stood alone, detached from those around it in a circle of trees and greenery. There was a garden just visible at the back, a private well in a private courtyard, and balconies that climbed from the ground to the fourth and final floor, each strewn with greenery.

Yet it was all without purpose. Where Lucas's garden had been stuffed to bursting with plants that could feed him, or cure him, or flavour his food, this place was full of botanical redundancies. Julia couldn't spot a single thing in this sea of moonlit grey that was useful, and that in itself was a statement. Rufus didn't need a vegetable patch, or a herb garden, or an orchard, because everything he needed would be provided by someone else's labour. All he wanted were pretty things to adorn his home.

'Impressive, isn't it? And it's all mine, the whole building.'

He led her through the gate set into his walled garden and up the path to a porch that was newer than the rest of the building. The place must have seen some fighting, but it had been repaired well enough that she could barely tell.

Waiting on the other side of the door was someone Julia had been praying to see ever since the Contamination. Julia's face started to slide into a smile, but at a tiny shake of the head from Marcella she schooled her expression into nonchalance.

'My Candidate,' said Rufus. 'Meet my new Attendant. You can keep each other company.'

'Hello, Julia,' said Marcella.

'You can show Julia up to her room. I have some things to arrange.'

Her room?

'My room?'

'Marcella has a room upstairs, and there's one for you next to it.' He grinned. 'I did say you'd be grateful.'

'You mean for during the day.'

That had to be what he meant. Julia had never heard of Attendants living with their Nobles, except at the palace. But then Rufus was the Empress's son, wasn't he?

'With all the trouble in the city over the past few weeks, do you really think I'd let you out of my sight? No, you can go home tonight to collect your things, but when you return tomorrow morning you'll not leave again. I mean, why would you want to?'

He opened his arms to indicate the splendour of the candlelit entrance hall, with its stone floors, its rich fabrics, and its sweeping staircase that spiralled tightly above them as though they were in a tower rather than a grand house.

It was a gilded cage.

'Well?' he said, an irritable edge creeping into his voice. 'Go on then.'

Marcella looped Julia's arm into her own and started escorting her up the stairs. Her feet were encased in embroidered slippers, which were a step up from Julia's own bare feet, but meant she had to move carefully on the polished floor. Julia could see the strain in the way Marcella held herself on the shining wooden steps, as though any slight deviation in her posture would break her balance.

The door below them slammed and footsteps moved away along the path.

Julia turned to Marcella to speak, but was interrupted by a finger pressed to her lips.

Not yet, Marcella mouthed.

The strain was in her face as well. Her features were made for smiling, with round cheeks and wide lips, but there was a downturn to them now that drew lines in the flint of her skin. Sorrow had been carved into it, breaking her perfect complexion. It was Julia's starkest warning of what was to come.

Rufus had broken Marcella. He'd broken the goddess: resilient, intelligent and controlled. If he could do that to her in the space of a few weeks, then what would he do to Julia?

They didn't speak until they were safely inside Julia's room with the door shut behind them. It was on the second floor, sandwiched between two floors above and below, so their movements could be monitored from any other room in the house.

'Julia,' Marcella whispered, pulling her into her arms. 'I'm so sorry you're here.'

'Are you alright? Has he hurt you?'

'There are worse amongst them. I'm still alive, at least.'

The Candidates. Marcella must have heard about them.

'Do you know what happened to the others?' Julia asked.

'It was the Nobles, I think. I saw them alive and then, the next second, bleeding, dying.'

'You were there?'

She nodded, dropping her head as tears pooled in her eyes. The motion pulled one free and it shattered onto the floorboards with the hollow sound of a heartbeat.

After a moment, she whispered, 'I was the only one left alive. Rufus brought me back here just in time. I was grateful for that, at first, until I'd had time to think.'

She pushed the tears away, but there was still misery in her eyes. She knew he was involved in what had been done to her friends, whether it had been done by his hands or not. For her to be the only one left alive, and for him to arrive just in time to save her, but none of the others… there was too much coincidence in that.

'And now he keeps you trapped here,' Julia said.

Marcella forced a smile.

'We'll have each other.'

It was such a horrible echo of Julia's own words to Claudia that she couldn't stop her mind from putting together the future she could expect: a life in this building, just the two of them, and she'd never see Claudia again.

'This isn't forever,' Marcella said, taking Julia's face in her hands.

Julia flinched a little to the side, trying to avoid Marcella touching the tender skin where the stud rested in her ear. Her movement just drew attention to it.

'You're still wearing his silver.'

'Despite Rufus's attempt to remove it.'

Marcella's eyes traced the hot scar on Julia's earlobe.

'He did this to you?'

'He did all of this to me. My ear, my hands. My knee too, although that's better now.'

'And Lucas did nothing to stop it?'

That was the moment that it hit home. Rufus had told her Lucas was gone. She'd heard him leave, and she'd even seen his garden burned to the ground, but it wasn't until she heard the proof that she could accept it for herself.

If he had still been in the city, he would have stopped Rufus from hurting her. He would have stopped him from ripping the earring through her skin.

'Lucas is gone,' she admitted, to herself as much as to Marcella. 'He left.'

Marcella took Julia's hands, stroking them softly, and looked down at their tangled fingers.

'So Rufus truly is your master now,' she said, 'as much as he is mine.'

Julia's skin crawled at the words.

She would never call him Master.

Livia was finally home when Julia returned that evening.

The girls were all packed into the kitchen around her chair, much like they had been in the days before the Contamination, listening to her stories while they sewed and knitted and carved shapes out of wood. They were still there when Julia returned from packing her few possessions from her cellar room.

There were no signs that Claudia had even been home.

'He was a king,' Livia was saying, 'and more than a king. He was a ruler and a guiding hand on the plough of the world. But one day, he started to grow tired of his responsibilities. It was then that an army gathered amongst his people, an army that would threaten them all.'

It took Julia a moment to realise that Livia was telling the story of *the* King, their King. She'd heard it before, from Lucas, but Livia's version was slightly different. Where Lucas had focussed on the romance of it, Livia was talking about the King's struggles against an invasion that had brought contamination into the world.

'And they said,' Livia finished, 'that one day the King would return to purge the world of contamination. So it's no coincidence that he's woken up now, just as the Red has bled into the Blue. Things might seem gloomy at the moment, but you wait and see. You'll be surprised.'

A few of the girls shuffled out then, thanking Livia on their way to bed, but others hung around with questions, or stuck determinedly to her side, as though their endurance proved their loyalty. Julia had to wait another hour for the kitchen to clear.

'So,' Livia said as the last girl left for her room, 'what was it you wanted to ask me?'

'How did you know–'

'Why else would you wait up through their blathering? Now sit, and tell me what's on your mind.'

Julia brushed the ashes away from the hearth and sat on its edge.

'Is it true?' she asked. 'Is the King really going to cure the contamination?'

'Does it matter? They have to believe in something, and they may as well believe in him. He seems a good enough sort, but then you'd know that better than most, being as he saved you.' She squinted at Julia. 'But that wasn't what you wanted to ask me, was it?'

'Not really.' Julia didn't know where to start. 'That day, when I came to the square, I was looking for medicine for Claud's arm. There was… well, that doesn't matter now, but I came here and the kitchen was destroyed, so I went upstairs.'

'Ah,' Livia said. 'And now I suppose you have some questions.'

'Yes.'

'Well,' she exhaled, 'it's probably time you knew.'

'Knew what?'

'What happened to your parents.'

Julia felt her mouth drop open. Of all the things she had expected Livia might say, that hadn't even made the list.

'I know what happened to my parents,' she said eventually. 'They walked out into the Red and they died. What's that got to do with anything?'

Livia reached over to where the kettle was now boiling on the fire and poured them both a cup of herbal tea. She was stalling.

'Your parents,' she said, 'they weren't like you. They were more biddable, more accepting of the way things are in this city, but I reckon we all have limits and they reached theirs. When I told you they had no choice but to leave you behind, that was the truth. What I didn't tell you is they weren't the only ones who left, not by a long chalk, and some of the others came back.'

'From the Red?'

'Yes, from the Red. They need somewhere to stay when they're here, and they need someone to heal them right. They come to me.'

Julia couldn't comprehend it. The idea was so big that it didn't seem to fit inside her head. There were not only people living out in the Red, people who had come from the Blue, but they travelled between the two places. They crossed the line.

'And they're not contaminated? They're not like the people we saw on the night of the Contamination?'

'They're just like you and me. They look the same, think the same and bleed the same.'

Julia stared at her.

'So my parents are…?'

'I've never seen them again. They could be alive, but they're most likely dead.'

'But there's a chance.'

Livia smiled.

'There's always a chance. The world's bigger than you know, my girl.'

6

There was a chance that Cam had chosen the wrong route. He was trying to anticipate which path Chloe would take through Hungary, but there were so many she could have picked. Add to that the possibility that she might become lost, and the permutations were endless.

But there was one constant: they all had horses to water. With the summer so dry, it made sense that Chloe would follow the Tisa river into Romania, so Cam had gambled everything on sticking close to its banks.

But it had been a week since they'd left the mountain lake, and there was still no sign of the former Silver and her son. If they'd had extra horses to run then Cam would have sent out scouts, but they needed to conserve the strength of all twelve.

Ana hadn't been able to spare them more than two horses, so although Cam and Felix each now had their own stallions, Gul rode with Linh, and Tommy had insisted on riding with Viv. To everyone's surprise, Alistair had offered to share with Lucas, so student and teacher rode together.

Characteristically, Eveline had refused to share at all, so instead she was on foot. She must have been as exhausted as the horses, but she wasn't complaining.

'Maybe they got delayed,' Viv suggested.

'By what?' said Tommy. 'The weather's clear, and we haven't seen another Silver since we left the Blue.'

'That doesn't mean they haven't run into any.'

Cam had nothing to add except his worries so he said nothing, but Felix caught his mood. He rode a little closer to Cam's side, then reached over to squeeze his thigh when no one was looking. It was probably supposed to be reassuring, but after ten days of sleeping in a pile of Invicti with Felix at his side, every touch was electric. They hadn't had the privacy to touch palms, or whisper promises, or kiss, and their affection was too new to withstand the braying scrutiny of the other Invicti.

Later, Cam told himself, *Mission first*, but still the first thing in his mind was always Felix.

They came across the camp a couple of hours later, set back from the riverside, and it was heavy with the salty aniseed scent of Alex's skin.

'Shit,' Cam said, dismounting. 'They were here.'

The ground wasn't scuffed, so it looked as though they'd been captured elsewhere then brought to the camp before the caravan had moved on, taking them with it. By the looks of the undergrowth, there had been only a few tents here, so it should be easy enough for the Invicti to manage the captors.

And maybe, if they were very fortunate, the caravan might have some uncontaminated humans the Invicti could use to refill their blood supply.

Cam cringed the moment the predatory thought popped into his brain.

'They're contaminated,' said Eveline, crouching on the ground by the tracks that led further into the trees. 'Chloe and her boy.'

'Yes,' said Cam.

'Then the caravans have no reason to take them.'

'The horses,' Felix said quietly. 'They'd take them for the horses.'

'And the meat,' said Cam, wishing it weren't true. 'They use it to keep Weepers away from their camps.'

'Then we'd better get a move on,' said Tommy.

They all mounted up, but Eveline wasn't moving. She was looking back towards the river along the path they'd just walked, alert and poised like a cat waiting to pounce.

'I'm going to check our backs,' she said.

'What is it?' asked Tommy.

'Maybe nothing. I thought there was someone behind us, and there was almost a scent, but it's gone. I'm just going to check, then I'll catch you up.'

'Eveline…' Cam said, but she was already out of sight.

He turned to Tommy.

'Does she seem off to you?'

'No more than usual. Come on.'

The caravan hadn't gone far, which wasn't a surprise since the scent trail was fresh. It didn't seem to be in a hurry. The dozen or so Silver who accompanied it obviously weren't expecting the Invicti, because Cam and the others had them surrounded before they had time to gather their weapons.

'Who are you?' said the apparent leader of the group. He was dressed like a bandit, with rough-spun clothing that looked as though it belonged on a larger man.

These were not people who were thriving, but they were still doing better than their captives. Two wagons were crammed full of people, one group half-dressed in rags and the other draped in sheets. They were all filthy. Flies buzzed around them, but they seemed to have become accustomed to the pests. They no longer bothered to swat them away, they all just closed their eyes against the worst of their attentions.

All of them, that is, except Chloe. She was a frantic ball of movement in the middle of the huddle, waving one arm over her head while she held Alex close with the other.

'You've stolen our horses,' Cam said to the Silver, nodding towards the back of the convoy where Sandor and Hades were tied to a small cart. 'And you've kidnapped our friends.'

'Well, I wouldn't say friends exactly–'

'Shut up, Darius.'

'Jesus Christ,' Chloe muttered, so quietly that Cam wouldn't have heard her if he were human. 'Did you have to bring him?'

Darius kicked his horse forwards.

'Oh,' he said to her, 'I'm sorry, would you prefer that we leave you here? If it's too much of an inconvenience for you to be rescued–'

'No one is rescuing anyone!' the leader of the Silver said, drawing a knife from his belt. 'You're all going to die, and then we're going on our merry way with our prisoners.'

'I'm terribly sorry,' Tommy said, sliding from his shared horse. 'We didn't actually introduce ourselves. How rude. We're the Solis Invicti.'

Cam could see bandit eyes roaming over his companions, looking for the telltale signs and finding them. There was the tattoo on Naia's arm, Solomon's mark on the hilt of Adewale's blade, and the sheer immensity of Bartek, whose size had spawned his own legends.

There was a pause in which he heard the leader swallow. Meanwhile, someone at the back of the wagons was swearing colourfully.

'So,' said Tommy, 'maybe you'd like to run away now?'

'But you work for the Empress,' said a woman on horseback. 'We work for the Empress. Aren't we on the same side?'

'Laila always did her own thing. But then, that doesn't matter anymore because, you see, she's human. So perhaps you'd like to reconsider running away?'

The leader squared up to Tommy in an attempt to save face, but as soon as he heard the rest of his party deserting behind him, he scarpered into the trees.

'Well,' Cam said, 'that was easy.'

'They won't all be that simple,' Tommy replied.

'Maybe not, but it's a good start.'

Chloe tutted.

'When you two are done congratulating yourselves, do you think you could get us out of here? Some of these people have been stuck in this cart for weeks.'

Most of the captives had just been tied up and thrown into the cart, but others were chained to loops in the floor. Their shackles took some time to loosen, so by the time everyone was free Aaron had already raided the supply cart and cooked up stew for everyone.

He was a bit of a softie under his vulgar exterior, if truth be told.

Once everyone was eating happily, Cam got down to business.

'Are there some uncontaminated amongst you?'

The mass of campfire diners was silent.

'They've had Silver draining them daily, you idiot,' Chloe mumbled through her mouthful. 'They're not going to just volunteer that information.'

'Right.' Stupid. Cam tried a different approach. 'I'm Cam, and I'm an Izcacus, along with the rest of my friends here. We have a favour to ask of those of you who are uncontaminated, but first let me say what's going to happen afterwards: all of you are leaving here free. I suggest that the uncontaminated should take a bit of blood from those who are contaminated, so you'll be safe from Weeper attacks, and from other roaming Izcacus in future.'

'Er, are we going to discuss that policy at all?' Tommy whispered in Cam's ear.

'No. It's the only way they'll be safe.'

'But the blood–'

'No, Tommy.'

Tommy held his hands up in surrender and stepped back into line with the other Invicti.

'A few weeks ago, I was northwest of here with Chloe.'

As Cam pointed her out, she waved cheerfully at the others, as though this were some kind of workplace orientation rather than a congregation of run-down hostages in the woods.

'We managed to rescue a group of uncontaminated humans up on the coast there, but there are more people who need our help, along with a friend who's been kidnapped by one of the groups of Izcacus. What we really need from you is some uncontaminated blood that we can bottle, if you can spare it, to help us help them.'

Some of the humans were shifting uncomfortably, exchanging looks with their neighbours through closed faces. This was not going well.

'We're not going to make you do anything,' Cam went on. 'No one has to give any blood at all, you don't even have to tell us if you're uncontaminated or not, but if you'd like to help others like you, then please come and see me.'

Cam turned away. After a few moments, the murmurs started. Some people were translating from Cam's Hungarian into Croatian or even German, so this caravan must have travelled widely, but none of the noises sounded positive.

There was no trust here.

After a few minutes, a woman stood up. Cam relaxed; he'd got through to them.

'I will donate,' she said, but Chloe threw a stick at her before Cam's smile could reach his eyes.

'Sit down, Rosa. We all know you're contaminated. I know they're Izcacus, but these guys are decent, so stop messing around.'

Under the protests of Rosa's friends, Cam could just hear Alex's little voice saying, 'You never let me throw things, Mummy.'

'Okay, look,' Cam said, holding out his hands for quiet. 'We don't need your blood. We can manage alright without it for the moment. It would help, but it's not a big deal, so don't worry about it. Eat your food, wash in the river if you want to, help yourselves from the supply cart, and if you want to sleep here then we'll make sure you're safe until the morning. After that, we're moving on, but if you change your minds in the meantime then come and see me.

'Squad,' he said, turning to the Invicti, 'set up the perimeter.'

They didn't strictly need it. One of them could have managed guard duty on their own, but Cam hoped that more bodies would make people feel more secure, so he spread four of them around the camp while the others unpacked tents from the wagons.

There weren't nearly enough for everyone, but there didn't need to be. The Invicti were used to sleeping under the stars, and half of the humans had left as soon as they'd finished eating. For the others, the forest floor was an upgrade from the hard, cramped wood of the wagons.

Cam made sure the blankets were shared, and gave away his own. Felix followed suit, and that shamed the rest of the squad into doing the same. It wasn't as though they needed the warmth.

Felix though… It might have seemed like an easy gesture to make in the heat of the afternoon, but the nighttime temperatures could be brutal. If it rained, then he'd shiver through the dark hours.

'Aren't you going to be cold?' Cam whispered to him. The others were already occupied with their own tasks, but Cam was careful with his attentions nonetheless. He was always careful.

Felix was more reckless.

'You can always hold me if you're worried.'

Cam suppressed a groan.

He couldn't. He really couldn't, not until they'd accomplished their mission and could have the privacy they needed.

Thankfully, they were interrupted by Chloe.

'So,' she said, rushing up to them with Alex in tow, 'I didn't expect to see you. I'm pleased you showed up when you did, don't get me wrong, but I didn't expect to see you so soon. And in this company.'

Her eyes slid sideways to Darius, and Felix took the hint so quickly that it surprised Cam.

'Hi Alex,' he said, crouching down to his eye level. He must have spent time around children to be so easy in their company.

'Mum let me eat a rabbit.'

'I see,' said Felix. 'Do you want to learn how to catch one?'

The child's face twisted with scorn, judgmental in the way that only very young people can be.

'Pfff,' he snorted. 'Rabbits aren't so fast.'

'Maybe not when you were Silver.'

Alex considered this seriously, then nodded his head with the kind of solemnity that is usually reserved for royalty or executions. Or a combination of the two.

'Thanks,' Chloe whispered to Felix as he grabbed his bow and led Alex into the trees. He smiled back, and a fault line cracked across Cam's emotional control. He wished he were going with them.

'You'll have to deal with the company, I'm afraid,' Cam said to Chloe. 'I don't know what happened between the two of you, but Darius is a good soldier.'

'Oh, I know he is. It's just that, well…' She fiddled with the whorls of hair that tickled the top of her ear.

'Well?'

'I haven't told him about Alex.'

Cam looked at Darius, and then at the back of the little boy walking away by Felix's side. Alex's skin was the deep dark of Darius rather than the copper of Chloe, and now that Cam thought about it, that disdainful expression of Alex's was exactly the same one he so often saw on Darius's face.

'Him?' Cam whispered.

Chloe nodded.

'Well, Jesus, Chloe. You have to tell him.'

'I'm going to. I meant to. You know, he wasn't even supposed to be out here and it just kind of happened, and then he never came back. Then I got cured and held captive, which seems to be happening more than it should at the moment, and–'

'Wait,' said Cam. 'You're telling me that Darius was up in the Northwest near Charlestown, what, five years ago?'

'Six.'

'Now that, I didn't know.'

As he spoke, Cam watched Darius setting up tents on the other side of the fire. He could think of only one reason why the man would have been visiting the coastal settlement with which Laila had formed an alliance.

If Cam was right, then they had another traitor in their midst.

Eveline returned at nightfall.

When Cam asked if she'd found anything, she just shook her head and joined the others by the fire, but she seemed confused and frustrated. She may not have found the person who was following them, but Cam was willing to bet she'd found something else that had worried her. He'd have to find a quiet moment to ask her about that.

Alistair had been training Lucas in every bit of his spare time, so they were sparring in the firelight while the rest of the Invicti watched, together with a fair number of the humans.

'He really is good,' Tommy said as he joined Cam at the edge of the crowd.

'Yes.'

That was another thing to worry about. The boy was just twenty years old, and yet after only a weeks' training he had started to fight Alistair as an equal. These last few days he seemed to win their bouts more often than not, and that just shouldn't have been possible. Once they had blood to spare and could add in speed, he was going to be unstoppable.

Who was this kid?

'You seem concerned,' said Tommy.

'Aren't you? I mean, look at him.'

Lucas had grappled Alistair into a headlock, and was now kicking his legs out to bring him to the ground. Despite struggling to the last minute, the trainer eventually tapped his submission on Lucas's arm.

But Alistair never submitted. Ever.

Tommy shrugged. 'It happens. Every now and then, someone turns Silver and seems to gather in power that isn't their own. You remember what happened with Emmy.'

'But Lucas wasn't turned. He was born.'

'Well. It happens.'

'Does it?'

'He's an asset. It seems like a good deal to me. I don't know why you're worrying about it.'

Neither did Cam, really. He could pretend that he was concerned it would be too much for Lucas, that just because he was physically prepared for a fight didn't mean he would be mentally, but that wasn't it. It just made him uneasy.

'Why don't you turn in?' said Tommy. 'We'll take the watches through the night. Get some rest.'

'Alright. Thanks, man.'

'Maybe we'll have some fresh blood tomorrow. You never know.'

But Cam wasn't hopeful. The humans had only eyed him with suspicion throughout the evening, which graduated to open hostility when he spoke with Chloe.

She knew who was contaminated and who wasn't, but he didn't ask her for that information. Instead, he kept his distance from her as much as possible in an attempt to engender trust.

Felix, however, was doing the opposite. He and Alex had returned with half a dozen rabbits to add to the evening's meal. Of course, only the contaminated humans could eat them, or those who wanted to be contaminated.

Well over three quarters of them tucked into the morsels happily.

Three quarters of the humans now contaminated.

They swapped horses the next morning. Cam tried to insist that Chloe should keep Hades, since he was so attached to Alex, but she'd obviously had time on their journey to get acquainted with the horse's less savoury habits because she was having none of it.

Hades greeted Cam by stamping at his feet and trying to bite his ears, so their lack of affection for each other clearly remained mutual.

The squad took four horses from the ones that had been abandoned by the bandits, leaving the carts and the rest for Chloe's party. They were a little wild, but still much better behaved than Hades, and their addition meant that everyone in the squad now had their own mount. They could push harder on the remainder of their journey.

'I spoke to Darius,' Chloe said to Cam while they were packing up the camp.

'I can see that.'

Darius had been following Alex around all morning, uncomfortable in his skin as he tried to play the father. Children were a rare thing for the Silver, so none of them had much need of parenting skills, and Darius was showing his inexperience.

He offered Alex a rock, which was rejected with disdain. Next came a flower, then a flint, then a leaf, all of which were ignored in favour of Alex's current occupation: digging a hole in the ground with a stick. Finally, in desperation, Darius offered Alex his knife, which was snatched up with eager hands.

'Excuse me,' Chloe said to Cam, slipping away to avert the imminent catastrophe.

He watched them for a couple of minutes, the strange collection of people who together made a family. It had already changed Darius. There was a softening of his sharper edges, tinged with awkwardness, and at the same time a thread of fierce anxiety made his movements jerkier than normal.

He was not a man in control, and that made Cam wonder. Was it because this wasn't something Darius wanted, or precisely because it was? Was he worried about breaking this fragile happiness he'd attained without earning it? Did he want to protect his new family, or just escape it?

There was no telling from his expression, and when the two groups finally parted so did the family, Chloe and Alex to the mountains and Darius with the Invicti.

Cam had remembered the promise he'd traded to Ana. He'd asked Chloe to tell the remaining humans all about the mountain lake while they'd sat around the fire the previous night. For lack of anything better to do, most of them were going to follow her there. How many would stay with her until the end was anyone's guess.

The real surprise was that four of them had woken Cam that morning, so early that the sun was still rising, with offers to donate a bottle of blood each. Felix had done the honours following Chloe's approval, and now they had a small stash to get them through the next few days. It wasn't enough to achieve anything except a little scouting, but he was grateful for it nonetheless.

'Do you think she'll contaminate them all?' asked Tommy as they rode towards Slovakia.

'I hope so.'

'I can't believe you mean that. You're not that stupid. If we're going to contaminate every uncontaminated human we come across, then what are we going to drink?'

'And if she doesn't contaminate them, what's going to happen when they meet a bunch of Weepers? Was it better when the world was covered in them, instead of the vaccine?'

Tommy smiled wryly. 'Better for whom, Cam? Us or the humans?'

'Because that's how you see it. How about the many or the few? Is it better for every uncontaminated human to be at risk of becoming a Weeper, or for us all to live human lives? We could rebuild, then. No Silver, no Weepers, just people.'

Tommy looked almost offended by the suggestion. Cam could understand why; this wasn't the way the Silver thought.

'You're talking about genocide,' said Tommy.

'Am I? Or am I talking about destroying a privilege that most of us weren't even born with?'

'And those who *were* born to it?'

Cam shrugged. 'We all still profit from other people's suffering.'

'Because we need to so we can live.'

'No. So we can live *as Silver*.'

But Tommy just shook his head and kicked his horse on until he was riding alongside Viv. He was never going to understand where Cam was coming from, because his beliefs were rooted in millennia of dominance. The Silver were superior, that was accepted as a given, and they had to be sustained. There was no other option.

But Cam had expected that attitude. After all, it was hard enough for him to contemplate surrendering his own strength. The thought of the Silver doing it *en masse* was inconceivable.

'You're talking to the wrong people,' Felix said softly.

Cam sighed. 'I know, but I don't think there are any right people.'

Discussing his views with a man who was not only leader of the Invicti, but was also expecting his own Silver child... Well, Cam might have chosen a better audience.

'I understand,' said Felix.

Still Cam felt lonely in his opinion. He was the only one of his kind willing to restore the world to its old shape, even if that did mean sacrificing the Silver in the process.

Another week's travel took them through Slovakia and into Czechia. They ran into two more caravans, one of which forced a fight. That didn't last long, not with the blood the Invicti had salvaged from the first.

Cam's speech was the same every time, although Tommy had made him promise to stop encouraging the uncontaminated to contaminate themselves. He did as he was asked, but fed them big, game-filled meals courtesy of Felix's bow, then sent them all after Chloe. If the meat didn't do the trick, then he trusted that she'd ensure they were all exposed to the vaccine.

Each time, the squad was gifted enough blood to send scouts at speed to find the next caravan. The squad followed the scent trails through the trees, directing their route along paths that their scouts had marked to the next campsite, until one day they caught up with Konrad to find that he was waiting in a clearing alone.

'They're gone,' he called as the Invicti rode out of the trees.

'If this is a joke–' said Tommy.

'No joke,' Konrad said, showing them his empty palms as though the inhabitants of the caravan might have been hidden up his sleeves. 'They're just gone.'

The detritus was spread out behind him. Tents had collapsed, the fabric ripped where tent poles had been pushed through them, and the remains of fires had been kicked around in multiple scuffles. There were no horses, but there were echoes of their presence in the turned-over carts and broken traces at the edge of the camp.

'Weepers?' Cam asked.

'Maybe, but there's no blood,' Zita said. 'If there were Weepers, there'd be blood.'

'And we've heard none,' said Adewale.

'Also,' said Alistair, 'Weepers would explain why the humans were missing, but not the absence of the Silver.'

'All good points,' said Tommy. 'But what's your alternative explanation?'

Cam went looking for the hunks of meat he had learned to expect around the caravan camps, and found them in abundance. These people had been prepared for a Weeper attack, and given the amount and freshness of the bait they had laid, there was no way the creatures would have made it past the boundary.

'Two suggestions,' Cam said as he returned to the clearing. 'Either this is the work of the Silver to the northwest, or the Weepers are getting clever again.'

It had happened once before. During the Fall, before the Invicti had eradicated Weepers the first time around, they'd adapted. They'd realised that people only hid from them when it was dark, so they'd started sacrificing their eyesight to attack during the day. They'd realised that they could overpower the Silver if they coordinated their attacks, so they'd lost their fear of them. In the end, they'd been meticulous enough to set traps and reap their rewards.

But when these new Weepers had been spawned over the past few months, that sentience hadn't returned with them. If it was coming back now, then they were all in trouble.

'Shouldn't we have crossed paths with the army by now?' said Aaron. 'Aren't they supposed to be invading? I thought you said they'd be in the Blue in four weeks.'

'That's what they said,' Cam said.

'Well, it's been three, so either your hearing's shit or their maths is.'

Zita slapped Aaron on the arm, narrowing her eyes at him in rebuke.

'No,' said Cam, 'he's right. We're travelling in opposite directions between the same points. We should have run into them a week ago.'

It had been bothering him too these past few days.

'We can't have missed them,' said Adewale. 'We've scouted every path for miles.'

Darius came back into the clearing from its northern edge.

'They went this way,' he said. 'Clear tracks, and recent.'

'How many?' said Tommy.

'Lots. The whole camp, I would guess, and some horses. Probably others who forced them to leave too, because what other reason would they have to abandon everything here?'

Cam hesitated for a moment, crouching down to follow the marks in the dirt. There were crushed bones, brittle from the fire, but no blood.

'You think it was them?' said Viv, close at Cam's side. 'You think the army came and grabbed them?'

'No. They wouldn't all fit in this clearing. We'd have seen more disturbed ground.'

'Then you think the army's been delayed?'

Cam shrugged.

'Maybe things didn't go the way they wanted them to in the Blue. Or maybe they heard we were coming and decided to fight us first. I guess we'll see when we get there.'

The fear bubbling at the back of Cam's mind was one he didn't want to acknowledge. The only way the army would have any idea of the Invicti's movements, or the outcome of events in the Blue, would be if someone from the city had told them so. The likeliest suspect was one of the Invicti themselves, which made him think of Darius, but if he'd been up in Charlestown like Chloe said, then that meant he'd been working for Laila, not Charles.

Didn't it?

Someone had brought about the Weeper attack, someone aligned with Charles, someone who wanted to soften up the Blue before the army attacked. That person had to be working from inside the Blue.

Or inside Cam's squad.

'Well,' said Tommy, 'it might not have been the army, but someone's been through here. Let's find out who.'

As he mounted up to follow the others, Cam was preoccupied by his thoughts and by protecting his toes from Hades. He didn't notice that Felix wasn't at his side when he rode out of the clearing, nor did he notice the bird lifting into the sky from the tree line. There was a roll of paper tied to its leg, stained with green.

7

The stain wouldn't wash off. Julia had tried everything over the past fortnight: scrubbing it with alcohol, rubbing it with ash soap, and coaxing it with fat, but nothing would make it budge.

It didn't matter anyway, because it was too late now. She was assigned, and taking the mark off her cheek wouldn't change a damn thing. Still, her skin felt dirty, because she was branded with his name.

The wrong name.

She saw it in the mirror every morning, because Rufus had made sure she would. She'd never really seen her reflection before, except distorted in water and metal. In the clarity of the three mirrors with which her room had been furnished, it was difficult to avoid her deficiencies. She was mediocre in every way, and somehow that made her less than normal.

Until the stain on her face.

She'd scraped the skin until it bled. He'd smelled the blood and licked it clean.

It was the only time he'd taken her blood himself since that day on the roof, because usually he liked Marcella to do it for him. He liked the goddess to bring it to him, a thimbleful at a time.

Julia sat on her bed while she waited for the door to open.

It was the same every morning. She rose with the sun, because she still hadn't got out of the habit of lighting the fire in Livia's kitchen, and then she washed in the bowl of water that stood on the neat dresser against the wall. There was a comb there too and ribbons for her hair, because Rufus liked her to look neat.

Then she'd make her bed, pulling the crisp sheets into place. They were so white that Julia would have imagined they'd never been bloodied if she hadn't known that her wounds broke open every night and bled into the fibres. The stains were there now, under the blanket, hidden away beneath the blinding fabric.

Then she waited for the goddess to come and open her veins.

The afternoon would be spent tidying the house, then sitting on the first floor with Marcella, sewing or knitting with empty heads and silent mouths.

Because he could hear it all, so reliably that Julia was starting to believe he could even hear her think.

When the goddess came into the room, she walked softly. Her slippered feet were a whisper on the floor.

They didn't say "Good morning" anymore. No morning was ever good in this house. Instead, the goddess said, 'Are you ready?', and Julia nodded in return, offering her arm for the sacrifice.

The goddess's hands were practised and clever. They found the veins that wouldn't bleed too much, and pricked a hole just large enough to fill the tiny goblet before clotting closed it. It had taken her a week of soaked cloth and stitches, bleeding out the animation from Julia's body, but she was practised now. They were both practised, and numb.

There it was: the quick stab, the cup, the slow drip.

Familiar, and yet so distant it seemed as though it were happening to someone else.

'Do you wonder where he'll go from here?'

Julia's voice was a whisper, but she knew that the goddess had heard from the way she stilled.

'How he'll make this worse for us,' Julia went on. 'I wonder if one day he'll ask you to bring more than my blood.'

'Julia, I–'

'I wonder if he'll ask you for the silver in my ear, or a piece of my skin, or a slice of my flesh. And I wonder if you'll do it, because neither of us really has a choice.'

'Of course we have a choice. I'd never do that to you.'

Julia looked down at the cut in her vein.

'So you do this because you want to. You bleed me because, what? You like the feeling of power it gives you? Like he does?'

'How can you even ask me that?'

'You said we had a choice.'

The goddess took the cup away, and Marcella pressed a rag to the wound.

It was easier to think of her that way, bifurcated, half goddess and half Marcella, because Julia couldn't reconcile the girl who kept her company with the ethereal creature that demanded her blood every morning. Better that they should be two people inhabiting the same body, one for each role, torturer and nurse.

'Will I see you downstairs?' Marcella asked, gathering her tray of blood and blade.

Julia nodded. She would be missed if she didn't come, because Rufus liked her to watch.

First though, she waited for the bleeding to stop.

By the time she joined Marcella, Rufus had already left.

'Was he angry?' she asked.

'Yes, but not with you. He's gone to the palace.'

'Oh?'

'Because Claudia asked to visit you.'

Julia would have sworn that her heart stopped beating in that moment. It had been weeks. Weeks without Claudia, without any company except Marcella's, without any news from outside the walls of this prison.

'And?'

Marcella smiled. 'The Empress agreed.'

Despite Rufus's protests, which detained him at the palace, Claudia arrived within the hour. There were just the two of them left in the house, Julia and Marcella, because apparently Rufus hadn't had the time to find someone to babysit them. So when Claudia arrived, they had her to themselves.

Which was just as well, given her reaction on seeing Julia.

'Empress,' she breathed as she wrapped Julia in her arms. 'What's happened to you, Jules?'

'You know what's happened.'

'They told me eventually. Is this what I looked like for all those weeks?'

Julia looked down at the bruises and cuts marching up and down the veins of her arms. She could feel the weakness in her step, and see the concavity of her stomach. It mirrored the hollow eyes that stared back at her from the mirrors in her room. She was always tired now, and eating had become a chore. She neglected it and didn't care, because part of her hoped she'd waste away.

If she were a ghost, then at least she could walk through the walls of this place and fly away.

'Come and sit,' Marcella said to them both, because she could see that Julia needed to. She was kind that way.

'Here,' she said once Claudia and Julia were settled on the sofa. 'Have these.'

She handed over a box of biscuits, fine and buttery, too fine for Servers to eat.

'If Rufus finds out they're gone–'

'They were a gift from him. Here, take them.'

As soon as Julia's fingers closed around the box, Marcella glided from the room and closed the door behind her.

She and Claudia were alone.

'Jules…'

There were tears in Claudia's eyes.

'I'm alright. It's not so bad. The house is gorgeous, and I have Marcella.'

'And you look like you're dying.'

Julia waved her hand dismissively and said, 'You're so dramatic,' but her wrist felt as though it were floating. She'd often had that sensation these past few days, as though parts of her were starting to detach themselves from her control.

Claudia caught her hand and pulled it into her lap.

'Your fingernails are almost blue.'

'I'm cold.'

'We're in the middle of a heatwave.'

Julia looked out of the window. She could see the heat rising from the earth, distorting the straight lines of the palace walls.

'Oh.'

Claudia shuffled closer, until she could wrap her arm around Julia's shoulders and pull her into her warmth.

'You can't stay here,' she whispered. 'He'll kill you.'

'He might,' Julia conceded.

Claudia rubbed at her arms, as though she were trying to urge warmth back into them. All Julia could feel was the abrasion. There was no warmth to be coaxed from her bones, but Claudia wasn't giving up.

'Eat the biscuits,' she said, 'and while you do I'll tell you all about the palace. Alright?'

'Alright.'

Julia hadn't thought she was hungry, but as she raised the first biscuit to her lips, saliva started pooling behind her teeth. She could smell the sweetness of the honey, carried on the richness of the butter. The first bite dissolved on her tongue and rolled around her mouth like cream, the impact of the sugar so strong that her cheeks ached with the watering of her mouth.

This was the kind of food that would make even a Noble weep.

She ate them all, all six of them, one after another, while Claudia spoke.

She told Julia about the room she shared with another Attendant, who had been there for a decade. That was all she divulged of the woman, so Julia gathered they weren't good friends. She was probably just as prejudiced as the girls from the kitchen, and so not worth Claudia's concern.

But the story got interesting when she started speaking about her duties, because apparently she was rarely required to donate her blood. The common word around the city was that the Empress was a traditionalist: she liked to drink from the vein, and she liked to do it at every meal. That was why the palace always needed so many Attendants, or so they said, but Claudia's experience didn't bear that out.

'They've called on me only once, and not for the Empress, for one of her guards instead. They've got loads of us in the palace, all fed the best food and kept from having to work in the kitchens, but none of them ever seem to have more than a single mark on them. It's like they're deliberately letting us recover before we're called again.'

'Maybe they are,' said Julia around a mouthful of biscuit.

'Maybe.'

Julia licked the last crumbs from her fingers and put the box aside.

'I spoke to Livia before I left,' she said. 'Did she mention it to you?'

Claudia shook her head, her expression rueful. 'I haven't been back. I didn't even see her.'

'You should.' As she spoke, Julia looked Claudia squarely in the eye, trying to convey the importance of her suggestion.

'What have you heard?'

'It's more what I saw. The upper rooms.'

'You asked her about them?'

Julia nodded.

'And?'

'I was right: it is a hospital.'

'Then why keep it hidden?'

Julia leaned closer to her friend, so close that her lips touched the shell of Claudia's ear. 'She said she treats people from the Red.'

'No,' Claudia breathed, covering her mouth with her hand as though she were truly scandalised. 'Not the contaminated, not Livia. Are you telling me that she's responsible for Marcus, for the Contamination, for all of it?'

'No. Empress, no. I'm telling you the people who come to her don't seem to be contaminated at all. They're like the ones they led away from the square after the testing. There's nothing visibly wrong with them.'

Like Julia, Claudia struggled to assimilate that information. She sat silently for moment, her fingers fidgeting in her lap.

'But the Red,' she said eventually. 'And we saw what happened to Marcus when he went out there. We saw what he turned into.'

But of course neither of them actually had. They'd seen Marcus ejected from the Blue, seen him cross the boundary, then weeks later they'd seen what he'd become. They knew nothing of that intervening time, so they couldn't say exactly what had caused him to turn into the creature he had been when he'd died.

'Do you remember his wrists?' said Julia.

'You mean the cuts?'

'They were all the way round, Claud, like someone had done it deliberately. Maybe someone wanted to bleed him. Maybe that's important.'

Claudia pursed her lips, thinking, then said, 'Maybe someone was keeping him tied up, and he pulled his way free.'

That would explain it. The wounds had been deep and dark, but dry, as though they were old. They could have been rubbed into his skin over weeks of struggling.

'It doesn't change anything,' said Claudia.

'What are you talking about? This is what we've been waiting for. All that listening at windows and sneaking around Rufus's rooms, it was all to get this information. And Livia had it all along.'

But Claudia didn't seem reassured.

'My parents could still be alive out there,' said Julia.

'Your parents who abandoned you. We've been over this, Jules. If what you're saying is true, if they really could have just come back into the Blue whenever they liked, then that makes what they did to you worse, not better.'

'We don't know everything. There could be a reasonable explanation. Livia didn't tell me the whole story.'

Claudia pouted, as she always did when they discussed Julia's parents. She'd never made a secret of the fact that she didn't think they deserved Julia's goodwill.

'Talk to Livia,' said Julia. 'She'll tell you.'

'That there are people still alive in the Red? Alright, maybe I could accept that, but how would we live? It's huge, Jules, and we'd have to fend for ourselves. Even if it wouldn't kill us immediately, we'd give up everything we have here for a wet forest. We wouldn't survive that.'

But what Julia heard was, *I wouldn't survive that.*

Unlike Julia, Claudia was happy now. She was an Attendant in the palace, with a grand room and decent food, in the company of royalty. She didn't want to give it up because she didn't feel as though there was anything that she needed to escape.

Julia was the only one who still wanted to run away.

She forced a smile.

'So, you're enjoying the palace?'

Claudia's eyes lit up, as though she were imagining it in front of her eyes.

'It really is beautiful,' she admitted.

'And what about the King?'

Claudia's voice dropped to a whisper as she said, 'I've seen him. Sometimes, when I creep down to the kitchen at night to sneak a sweet from the pantry–'

'Claud! You don't.'

'Oh, no one minds. But sometimes he's there in front of the fire, just watching the flames. He smiles when he sees me, but he looks like he's far away, if you know what I mean. I think he's sad.'

'Why?' said Julia. 'Do you think Lucas's fairytale is true? Do you think he really did lose his love, and that he's waiting for her to come back to him?'

Claudia smiled, but with a twist to her lips that turned her expression into regret.

'I really wish it was,' she said, 'but then where is she? If his love had to come back for him to wake up, then where is she? And if she is back, why would he be unhappy?'

Julia echoed Claudia's sad smile.

'Well,' she said, 'it was a good story.'

Claudia might not have been donating much blood at the palace, but she'd clearly made some new friends, because Rufus returned to the house that lunchtime in a foul mood. He told Julia that weekly visits had been approved between her and Claudia, the next one to occur at the palace, and then he locked her in her bedroom. There was no escaping it without breaking the slats that covered the window, which Rufus would hear.

She wasn't much inclined to escape right now anyway. Claudia's reluctance had put a dent in her plans to leave the Blue, and she was still feeling weak and tired enough to appreciate the opportunity of an afternoon nap.

That was how he caught her sleeping.

He must have moved silently through the house, or Marcella would have intervened. That was what Julia told herself as Rufus's hand fastened over her mouth. Marcella wouldn't have let any harm come to her.

But the goddess would. The goddess would have held her head down so he could reach the vein, because Julia was Rufus's Attendant after all. She was his entitlement, and the goddess was his right hand.

'Shh,' he whispered in her ear. 'I'm not going to hurt you.'

They were words she couldn't believe, particularly when the force of his hand had already broken the inside of her mouth against her teeth.

'You think it's cruel of me to take your blood, but it's only so little each day, and I ask my Candidate to take it instead of me so you'll be more comfortable. Isn't that a kindness? Isn't that better than biting through your skin?'

Julia felt the sweat prickling cold along her spine. He was always dangerous, but this was different. The edge in his voice had her legs twitching with the need to run, but he'd covered them with his own, and both her hands were held fast in one of his. She was going nowhere.

She could smell the wine on his breath, even though it was still early. He often drank, but not like this. Not so much before the evening, not so his eyes were pink with it.

'But perhaps he never bit you. Perhaps you've never felt what it's like to have Noble teeth in your neck.'

He took his hand away from her mouth, but she kept it shut.

'That's not an answer.'

His hand was on her cheek now, fingertips tracing the stain on her skin. It was reverent, as though he were marvelling at the paint that granted him possession over her blood. As though it went beneath the surface.

Julia closed her eyes, squeezing them shut against the helplessness that was coiling hot in her chest. She wanted to scream, but his hand was back over her mouth now. It wouldn't do any good anyway, because there was no one here to help her.

'Perhaps he did bite you,' Rufus slurred. 'Maybe you even enjoyed it. You might not enjoy this so much, I think.'

As though he wished it would hurt.

Julia had tensed in the second it took for his teeth to reach her neck. Maybe that made it worse, because she'd never felt pain like it. It screamed in her veins, and then she was screaming against Rufus's hand, working her lips pointlessly against his grip on her jaw.

It seemed to last forever, but it could only have been a second or two, because she hadn't taken a breath.

His tongued laved her broken skin.

'The mark on your cheek is pretty,' he said against her throat, 'but I always like to leave my own. And unlike him,' he added, flicking the silver in her earlobe, 'I'll never leave you.'

Tears were streaming out of Julia's eyes now, though she couldn't tell whether they were from pain, fear or misery.

This was her life in this house, a life of bloody sheets and veins drained in the silence, and somehow the silence made it worse. If she could have screamed, then maybe it would have broken the spell, but the back of her throat was acid from straining against his hand and trying not to vomit with the pain. When he finally took it away from her mouth, she could do nothing but breathe into her shaky tears.

His weight left the bed, and then her hands and legs were freed.

She didn't move.

A smear of perspiration cooled around her lips. The skin over her wrists was cold and clammy, and her dress stuck to her thighs, but she couldn't tell whether the sweat was hers or his. That was how entangled they'd become in that torrid embrace, so she didn't know where she'd left off and he'd begun. He'd invaded her skin, burrowing into it, and leaving the sour scent of his body spread over hers.

She could feel the echoes of his fingertips digging into her jaw.

He hesitated at the door, leaning heavily against the frame as he made his way out of the room.

'You should know that I meant it, Julia,' he whispered. 'I'll never leave you.'

Julia couldn't move.

She hadn't moved all afternoon, all evening, all night, but time had moved. It had slipped away in strobing slices of light and dark.

She remembered him leaving her here. She could feel the warmth of her blood chilling on her shoulder as it seeped into her pillow.

She was segueing in and out of consciousness.

There was a flash of Marcella. Or the goddess – there was pain – but no, it was Marcella, a needle in her hand.

Julia would have laughed if she'd had the strength. Always sewing, sewing, so regularly that she almost wondered whether girls of the Blue practised the skill in fabric just so they could use it in skin.

Another slice of time gone, and then it was light again. Had it ever been dark?

If she looked down, she could see her hands crossed over her chest. They were still marked with the half-moons of his nails, seeping, scabbing and hot.

The room smelled of salt and damp.

There was a creak from the other side of the room, and if Julia could have moved then she might have flinched. Then there was a face, dark and rich and soft like curves of furrowed earth, inviting.

A smile.

'You're awake,' Marcella said.

Julia opened her mouth to answer. Her lips cracked, splitting down the middle. She could taste the blood.

'Don't try to talk. Here.'

As she spoke, Marcella patted at Julia's lips with a damp cloth, wiping away the tightness that had collected on their surface. A few moments later she used another rag to drip water into Julia's mouth.

'I'm sorry I wasn't here. They called me over to the palace. I didn't know, or I would have come. I'm so sorry. If I'd been here…'

Julia's throat was still bone dry, so she did the only thing she could, and raised an eyebrow.

Marcella looked down at her hands.

'You're right. If I'd been here, I wouldn't have done anything to stop him. I wouldn't have been able to stop him, but I wouldn't even have tried.'

She raised her eyes to Julia's as she spoke her next words, as though she meant to confront the truth of them, but they came out as a whispered confession: 'Because I'm scared.'

The corner of Julia's mouth twitched up in sympathy. She was scared too. She was going to die in this house, with a monster for a Noble, and no one would lift a finger to stop it. She'd known it by the end of her first day in this place, and she'd cried with the fear of it.

She would have cried now if she'd had any tears left in her.

But Marcella never cried. She knew what her end would be – Julia had seen it in her eyes and in her dark philosophy – and yet she had always kept misery at bay with a rigid column of inner strength.

It had collapsed now. She was bending under the weight of it.

'I would have come to you sooner,' she said.

Julia flailed a hand free from her chest, grappling unsuccessfully for Marcella's. She wanted to touch her. She wanted to tell her that she understood.

Marcella caught Julia's fingers in her own and raised them to her lips, kissing the knuckles as though she owed Julia benediction, rather than the other way around.

'I'm so sorry,' she said.

* * *

It took days for Julia to regain her strength.

If she knew one thing for certain, it was that she never would have made it without Marcella. Marcella, the goddess, had been her recovery. She sat with Julia day and night, so determinedly that Rufus didn't object when she dragged in her mattress from her own room, so she could always be within reach.

That worried Julia a little in her moments of lucidity. The damage must have been worse than she'd realised, so bad that Rufus no longer took her blood. If he'd ever discussed that with Marcella then Julia didn't know about it, but she suspected that the goddess would have refused if he had asked.

Because the goddess had changed. She no longer demanded sacrifices, she only offered cool water, whispered reassurances on breath sweet with fruit, and warm hands over her fevered skin.

There was singing too. It was low and soft, like the rumble of a purring cat, and it reverberated through Julia in the gentlest of caresses. Something about the tone seemed to set her body back in order, soothing the sharp edges of her pain and letting her find the sleep she so desperately needed.

Marcella's presence became so welcome that even the scent of her skin could comfort Julia. The breeze from the window would catch a wisp of her perfume and bring it to the bed where Julia lay, and she'd feel something release in her chest. It unlocked the last of the tension she was holding, because she knew she was safe as long as Marcella was close.

This must have been what it felt like to have a mother.

'Twelve of us left,' Marcella was saying, 'out of so many. Twelve Candidates left.'

She often spoke to Julia, and Julia knew this because the sound of the low voice by her bedside was so familiar, but she couldn't recall the previous occasions with any clarity. This was the first time that she had heard anything beyond the murmur of the words, the first time that their meaning had registered.

She tried to clear her throat, but it felt like it was packed with sand.

'Here,' Marcella said, scooping Julia into a seated position with one arm while she offered a glass of water to her lips with the other.

Julia could only manage a few sips before her head fell back against Marcella's chest. She was lowered back down to the pillows, and her eyes closed themselves once more.

'Easy,' Marcella whispered. 'There's no rush. I'm right here. I'm not going anywhere.'

But Julia was. She had to be.

She had always wanted to leave the Blue, hadn't she? She'd been waiting for the proof she needed that the world outside the city was safe for humans, and Livia had given her that.

But she'd waited too long to act. She should have left the moment she'd had the news from Livia, but she'd wanted to speak to Claudia first, and part of her had been unwilling to accept that Rufus would bleed her to the point of death. The part of her that believed everyone was basically decent had clung naively to the hope that he would prove her wrong, and that everything would turn out alright in the end.

But she had forgotten that he wasn't human.

She'd let herself hesitate.

She'd waited until Rufus had locked her away in this place, from which there was no escape.

But there was a chance.

Through those last days of recovery, as she was finally able to sit on her own, and drink, and eat, and speak, the one thing that kept Julia going was the thought of her visit to Claudia.

She had to be well by then. She was expected at the palace in four days' time, and she couldn't be late.

8

The army was late.

It was only just leaving the mountains now, nearly four weeks after Cam had expected it to do so. It should already be arriving in the Blue, but here it was, weaving through the same narrow pass he and Felix had taken on their first journey to Charlestown together.

At least Lorelei would have plenty of time to prepare for the attack.

'Mind your feet,' Cam whispered as he came to a stop on the ledge that overlooked the pass.

Felix dropped carefully to the ground, then placed their pack gently on the rock at his feet. The fall of the smallest stone might alert the passing army to their presence, and they weren't here to be seen. They would observe silently, then report back to the others.

Cam had insisted on scouting the route to the mountain stronghold himself, because he was the only one of the Invicti who knew where it was. One final caravan had provided the blood he needed to make the trip, but enough only for him. He was glad of that, but he couldn't have said whether it was because he felt this mission was his to finish, or because he wanted some time alone with Felix.

Because of course he had carried the woodsman with him. Everyone had assumed that he would, including Felix himself. Apparently the other Invicti viewed them as a matched set now, like Adewale and Alistair.

Only Cam knew how different their relationship actually was.

101

The early summer had banished the thick dusting of white that had made their first trip this way so perilous. Without the snow blanketing the ground, it was easier to track a course towards the peaks. Their stepped tops were still difficult to reach, for a human at least, but once scaled they provided an excellent vantage point. When Cam and Felix lay on their bellies and peered over the lip of their perch, they had a clear view down at the hundreds of people weaving their way along the path below, accompanied by wagons and horses and covered carts.

It was so dry that it was difficult to believe this was the same spot they had visited weeks ago. What had once been a landscape of white and dark was now a landscape of rock and dirt.

And smells.

The thaw had revealed carcasses that had been preserved in the ice, and the gorge below them was steeped in the scent of decay. It rose with the heat of the day, impregnating the thick air with unwelcome memories of the deaths that had occurred in this place. Cam remembered the alcove they had found between the teetering piles of rock, the snow cave and the bodies inside. Perhaps those scents were mingled in the thick palate of the place, or perhaps the lynx had taken the bodies away as soon as they had defrosted.

Maybe the Weepers had instead.

As they'd travelled further towards their destination there had been fewer caravans, and those that they'd found had contained fewer uncontaminated humans. Perhaps that was unsurprising, given how many Weepers they were hearing on this side of the continent.

But they hadn't actually seen any. They heard plenty, but none approached them.

A howl echoed through the pass then, and both army and watchers stopped walking and turned towards the sound.

A few minutes later, a horse galloped back along the line from the vanguard, pushing its way past the convoy until it reached a small mounted group directly below Cam and Felix's lookout point.

'It's the scouts,' the rider said, his voice echoing around the canyon. 'The creatures have them backed up against the crags.'

'Send in the contams then.'

Cam didn't recognise the man who had spoken, so he couldn't have been that old. In fact, Cam didn't recognise any of these people. If they were Silver, then they were new.

Lorelei was going to tear them to pieces.

'We've tried that,' the rider was saying.

'Well?'

The man was riding with three other men, all of them dressed in shirts that looked as though they were stained with dried blood. The rest of the army wore clothes that were pummelled to the yellowed grey colour that was as clean as most fabric got out here, but these four wore the bloody dye with pride, as though it were a badge of honour.

Or perhaps a mark of rank, because now the rider seemed ashamed to be bringing unwelcome news to the blood-shirted man.

'The creatures are keeping their distance,' he said. The angle was too steep for Cam to see the rider's expression, but his voice sounded like a cringe.

'What? What do you mean?'

'They're avoiding the contams. They're targeting the Silver instead.'

'But that's not possible. They've never attacked us before.'

He was definitely not old, this man. He couldn't remember the Fall. He couldn't remember what it had been like then, when the Weepers attacked everyone indiscriminately, when they'd planned and trapped. He couldn't remember what it had been like the last time they'd got smart.

The people around the riders were starting to panic. If Cam could hear their conversation from all the way up on his rock, then the soldiers surrounding them on the path certainly could. There were mutterings, and the horses were picking up on the atmosphere too. They nickered uneasily, shifting their weight from foot to foot as though they wanted to run.

The man realised his mistake, and scrambled to reestablish his authority.

'The contaminated blood will end them,' he said, raising his voice so the words would carry, but then he added in a harsh whisper, 'Tell them to shove the meat in the creatures' faces themselves, if that's what it takes. We're not going to be delayed again.'

The rider turned and raced back the way he had come, through the pass to the east. He must have relayed the message, because it wasn't long before the column moved off again, taking their war to the Blue.

'Is she there?' Felix whispered in Cam's ear.

Cam just shook his head.

He'd been watching the line, looking at the shapes piled in the back of every cart and wagon, and inspecting the gait and rising scent of every figure who passed beneath them.

Emmy wasn't here. If she had been, he would have picked out the sweetness of her fragrance even amongst all the others, even surrounded by the aroma of decay.

And if she wasn't here, there was only one place she could be.

It took hours for the army to clear the pass. Cam and Felix didn't move until it was gone, except to extract paper and pencil from the pack. Cam listed off the army's assets – horses, machinery, soldiers, weaponry, hierarchy – in case they got the opportunity to send a message back to Lorelei. That way, at least she would know what to expect.

One thing was clear: the Blue was going to be woefully outnumbered. There had been hundreds of Silver. *Hundreds*.

How so many could have existed in this place without them ever knowing was beyond Cam. The sheer numbers... How had they bred so many, and so quickly?

But they were unprepared for the sort of opposition they'd be facing in the Blue. The ragged line of soldiers was untrained, poorly disciplined and young. So young. Many of them looked like they were only just in their teens, and yet still they were being sent into battle.

Charles's focus had clearly been on amassing numbers rather than ensuring the effectiveness of the fighters he had. It was an old failing of his, and one that would end badly for him. The Invicti were skilled, and they were used to fighting large numbers of ill-prepared enemies. After all, they'd fought the Weepers for years.

Still, they were out of practice, and some of them had never seen battle under the relative peace of Laila's rule.

'Shit,' Cam muttered as they watched the last stragglers trail out of view.

'Problem?' Felix asked.

'No. Maybe. Shit, there's a lot of them, isn't there?'

'Did you see the catapults?'

Cam dragged a hand down his face and groaned. 'Yes.'

They were compact things, but they'd be devastating to the Blue. A few well-aimed fire strikes would level the old wood-framed buildings surrounding the square before the invaders ever set foot over the boundary fence.

Not that it would be any good at keeping them out. After all, it was made of wood. *Wood.*

The truth was that they had never expected an attack, not like this.

If Cam wanted to save the Blue, they'd have to get back there, with Emmy, before the fighting started. And it was still at least a day before they could expect the other Invicti to arrive in the mountains.

'But no Emmy,' Felix said.

'No.' There was at least that to hold onto. 'She's still here somewhere, so let's go and find her.'

They crossed the tracks of the army as Cam carried Felix over the mountains and then south, following the western edge of the range towards the stone door where Cam had first picked up Emmy's scent.

But they crossed other tracks too. These joined from the southwest, as though they had come up along the mountains from Austria.

'The caravan?' Felix asked.

He was kneeling down in the leaf litter with Cam as they tried to parse the marks into some kind of sense. Whoever had come this way, they hadn't been subtle. There were broken branches along the length of the path, and hoof prints had sunk into the wetter ground.

'You mean the one from the clearing?' Cam said. 'You think Charles's people have been kidnapping caravans?'

'It would explain why he has so many Izcacus, and why there are so few caravans near here.'

'Partly, maybe. But it can't just be that. And why bring them all the way south and round the mountains instead of coming through the pass to the north like the army did? Unless they were trying to avoid getting in the way, I suppose.'

'Makes sense.'

'But look,' Cam said, trying to puzzle it out, 'they wouldn't just take the horses through the door we saw last time, would they? Would they even fit? And that army had carts and equipments and all kinds of other stuff that would be too wide. There has to be another entrance.'

'Well then?' said Felix, looking at him expectantly.

'Alright. Let's follow the tracks and see where they take us.'

At first, it seemed as though they were heading for the entrance they already knew about, and Cam's excitement started to dim, but they soon diverted south. There was another path here, one that was now well-trodden, but that Cam would have sworn hadn't existed on their last visit. It skirted around the face of the mountain, rolling over its foothills before descending into a valley hidden between two peaks, then disappearing into a cave as it curved back into the rock.

There were fences here, and crude buildings. The fields were empty now, but troughs and stables bore the evidence of their former use.

'This is it,' Cam whispered as they slipped between the trees. 'That's how we get in.'

Felix set up their camp at a decent remove from the cave entrance while Cam went back to mark the path for the others. He left his blood on bark and leaves, cutting open his hand again and again, and watching it heal each time. The Invicti would be able to follow the trail to him as easily as if it were painted in neon, but so could any other Silver, so he stopped near the entrance to the cave and rinsed his hands in a stream before returning to Felix. The last thing he wanted was to lead the enemy to their hiding place.

Which was an excellent one. Felix had done them proud. They couldn't have a fire, for obvious reasons, but he had built a shelter in the lee of the mountain out of dry branches and fresh ones filled with wide sprays of leaves that he had cut from the canopies that surrounded them. It was practically invisible amongst the other young trees that were growing up against the stone, and if Felix hadn't been standing right next to it then Cam would have thought it was just another group of saplings.

'Nice shelter,' Cam said as he approached. 'So, I've laid the tracks. But, um, I guess the others won't get here till tomorrow. So. Yeah.'

Alone again. For the first time since the mountain lake, alone.

Felix smiled and looked down at his feet.

'What?' Cam said.

'You ramble when you're nervous.'

'I'm not nervous. Well, I'm nervous about the army, I guess, and rescuing Emmy. There's a lot going on right now. Are you saying I shouldn't be nervous?'

The smile was still on Felix's face, but there was a twist in it now, a pinching of the lips that turned it into rue.

'You shouldn't be nervous about me,' he said.

'I'm not,' Cam replied, rubbing the back of his neck, then he stopped himself as he became conscious of the gesture.

'Okay,' he said. 'Maybe I am. But this isn't really the time for this talk. Tomorrow's the big day, or maybe the day after. We're going in. We're going to get her out. We need to focus on that right now. It's the most important thing.'

He was rambling again, the words coming thick and fast, but if he didn't convince himself that this was a bad idea then he'd give in, and it wasn't the time for that. Not while Emmy was still in there, while they were camped on the enemy's doorstep, with the Invicti due to arrive within the next day.

It just wasn't the right time.

Felix took a step forwards, reaching out to take his hand.

'Cam…'

'It's not that I don't want to. It's just that we need to be on guard.'

Felix took another step, closing the distance between them, then his hand was on Cam's cheek and his lips were a whisper away.

'You don't need to be on guard against me,' he said.

'Not you,' said Cam, but he didn't pull away. 'Maybe we should–'

Then Felix was kissing him, and Cam's thoughts were so scrambled that he couldn't remember why he'd thought this was a bad idea. His fingers were tangling in the thick strands of Felix's hair, clasping at the back of his head to urge his lips forwards.

As it turned out, Felix didn't need any encouragement. As soon as Cam responded, Felix steered him towards the shelter until his back was up against the rock face by its side, then trapped him there in the frame of his arms.

'Felix…'

'You don't need to fight it.'

Fighting was the last thing Cam wanted to do right now, and interrupting their kiss was second to last, but Cam had heard something.

It sounded again in the next moment, distant but louder this time, a noise like the cracking of branches underfoot.

'Shh,' said Cam, putting his hands on Felix's chest to push him back.

Felix leaned away, looking over his shoulder as he searched for whatever had disturbed Cam. He wouldn't be able to hear it though – the noise was too far away and Felix's human hearing was too weak.

'Someone in the forest,' Cam whispered. 'On the other side of the valley. We need to be careful.'

Felix nodded, instantly switching from seducer to scout.

'I'll take first watch,' he murmured. 'You get some sleep.'

All business, no play.

Cam didn't argue, partly because he was exhausted from the run to the mountains, and partly because he didn't want to show his disappointment.

He crept into the shelter and lay along its length, noting with some regret that it was narrow enough that the two of them would have had to curl up against each other in order to fit in the space. That might have been nice.

But instead of joining him, Felix sat in the entrance at Cam's feet and, pulling the branches closed over the doorway, peered out through a small gap between the leaves.

After watching him for a few minutes in silence, Cam closed his eyes and tried to uncoil himself enough to sleep.

The Invicti arrived early the next morning. They must have ridden hard through the night, because they were much earlier than expected.

Cam had just woken Felix up with a kiss and had been looking forward to seeing where the morning might take them. He groaned.

'What?' said Felix.

The Invicti were making enough noise to wake the dead. Cam was surprised that Felix couldn't hear them already, but he seemed genuinely confused. Perhaps there was still some chance that their enemies might not have heard them thundering into the valley.

'The others are here,' said Cam.

'You're sure?'

'Yes. I can hear Alistair complaining about the way Adewale's tied his saddle's girth.'

'Damn,' said Felix, smiling as he pushed Cam's hair back from his face. 'I had plans.'

'Oh, god. Don't say that.' Cam started to scramble backwards out of the shelter. 'Look, I've got to go and meet them. Just...' He leaned back in for one last kiss. 'I'll be back. But can we keep this to ourselves for now? Please?'

Felix just shrugged and smiled.

'Alright. I'll be back.'

Cam found the Invicti about a mile away, crashing through the undergrowth along the centre of the path and making absolutely no attempt at stealth.

'Is it possible for you to make any more noise?' he said softly. 'You do know that their base is just inside this rock face, right?'

He pointed, and thirteen pairs of eyes followed his finger.

Thirteen.

Someone was missing.

'Where's Eveline?' he asked.

'Bringing up the rear again,' said Tommy from the saddle. 'I think she's getting paranoid, but it keeps her happy, and someone's got to do it. What's wrong with you today?'

'I'm trying to retain the element of surprise.'

'Well then you should have left your bastard horse with Chloe,' said Zita. 'He keeps trying to eat bits of me.'

'Blame the Secundus. He's the one who gave him to me.'

'Well, you can take the little shit now.'

Zita threw Hades's halter to Cam, who caught it before the horse realised what was happening. That was something of a relief, because it meant that Cam was one step ahead of his stomping hooves. He managed to jump up into the saddle before he sustained any injuries.

'This way,' he whispered, then led them back to the camp.

Felix was standing by the shelter when they arrived, but he'd clearly just been to the stream to wash. He was wringing his shirt out into the undergrowth, tendrils of damp hair framing his face and dripping onto his naked chest.

'Dear god,' Naia murmured from behind Cam, 'thank you for your bounty.'

'You're gross,' said Zita.

'Yeah, he's contaminated, you know,' said Konrad, ever practical. 'Keep it in your pants for once.'

'Won't, can't, don't want to,' said Naia, then she kicked her horse on ahead so she was the first one to reach the shelter. 'Well, hello handsome,' she said as she dismounted.

Felix nodded a greeting at her, and for a moment Cam was a little worried, but then Felix's eyes found his, and he smiled. It was a small twitch of his lips, just enough that Cam could tell it was meant only for him, and it settled the jealousy that had threatened to creep up from the pit of his stomach.

He hadn't realised that he'd become so possessive.

'So,' said Tommy as he helped Viv from her horse, 'this is your entry point?'

'The entrance we saw on our last trip was to the north,' said Cam, 'but this one is larger, and seems inactive now that the army has gone. We haven't seen a single person, although we heard someone patrolling on the other side of the valley.'

'Have you approached?'

'No. We need to send in a scout. I think we should scout the rest of the mountain too, because there may be other entrances we've missed. It's your call from now on, though. I got you here, but the raid's all yours.'

'Oh good.' Tommy grinned. 'I was hoping you'd say that. Gul and Linh,' he said, turning to address the dismounting Invicti, 'you scout up the mountain from the north, Zita and Bartek from the south, Alistair and Adewale from the west and Naia and Konrad from the east. Make sure you're back by nightfall. Darius, intercept Eveline on her way back and scout the valley. Aaron and Lucas, you set camp. Cam and the human can stay behind to help.'

'Felix,' Cam said.

'And what about me?' said Viv. 'I hope you don't expect to leave me behind.'

'Oh hell no,' Tommy said with a smile. 'You and me? We're going in there.' He nodded towards the cave. 'Ready?'

Viv pulled a couple of knives from her horse's saddle and holstered them in her belt.

'Ready.'

* * *

It was strange to be the one left behind.

Cam could understand it, because he'd been away long enough that he didn't have a natural partner in the squad, and because he'd already done his fair share of scouting.

Still, he felt left out.

Aaron was busy as usual, preparing food for dinner whilst muttering angrily about how much easier it would be if they'd let him light a fire. Felix had helped Cam settle the horses and was now preparing shelters for the rest of the squad. It was a generous gesture, but Cam suspected it had more to do with getting out of earshot of Aaron than it did with any genuine desire to ingratiate himself with the Invicti.

That left just Lucas and Cam, now at a loose end, sitting around the area that would have been a campfire if it hadn't been too dangerous to light one.

Cam could feel his impatience scratching beneath his skin. He wanted to get this fight done, to find Emmy, and get back to the Blue before it was too late.

And he wanted Felix.

'So what are we doing out here, exactly?' Lucas asked, picking aimlessly at the grass. 'Some kind of raid?'

It took a moment for Cam to understand what he was asking. How was it possible that Lucas still didn't know why they were here?

'Has no one told you?' said Cam.

'Everyone's been a bit busy.'

'Alistair hasn't told you?'

The boy shrugged one shoulder. 'We train. We don't chat.'

'Oh.'

Cam should have been paying more attention to him. He'd passed him off to Alistair for training and expected that Viv would pick up the rest of the pieces, but that wasn't how it worked.

Cam had been the youngest for long enough to know how it felt when you were left to work everything out for yourself.

'I'm sorry,' he said. 'I didn't realise that the others hadn't told you. This must be a bit overwhelming.'

'At first. That place where we stayed in the mountains... I didn't realise that people lived out here. I'd suspected it, but until then it hadn't been real. I didn't understand that at first, after what you told me about the contamination, but Viv explained it.'

'And what did she tell you?'

'The truth,' said Lucas. 'The things you tried to talk around.'

The words hit home hard, but the boy was smiling and his tone was gentle. He was sympathising rather than accusing. That threw Cam more than the prospect of having to explain himself.

'It's all the wrong way around,' Lucas went on. 'We're the ones who should be afraid out here, not them.'

'Except the uncontaminated,' said Cam.

Lucas nodded. 'Except them. So there's really only one thing to do if there's a human you care about, isn't there? Contaminate them.'

As he spoke, his eyes drifted sideways towards Felix. If Lucas had noticed their relationship, then Cam wondered how many of the Invicti had worked out how close they were.

But then Lucas didn't look at Felix with their prejudice. He didn't see a contaminated human like the rest of the Silver did. He didn't see him as a creature from whom he couldn't drink. He just saw a person.

There was common ground between them there.

'You have someone you care about, then,' said Cam.

'It's why I didn't want to come. I had to leave her behind.'

'Wait, you didn't want to come? I thought you volunteered for this. Lorelei told me you wanted to join the Invicti.'

That clearly confused Lucas. He tried to hide it, looking down at his hands as he threaded a blade of grass between his fingers, but Cam still caught the crinkling of his forehead.

'I did want to join,' he said after a moment. 'I wanted to see the Red for myself, to find out how much of what I'd been told was true, but I never told her that.'

'She must have heard it from someone else then,' said Cam.

'Hmm. Maybe.' Lucas's gaze was still fixed on his hands.

'But if this isn't what you wanted–'

'It is. The timing was bad, that's all. Forget about it.' Lucas forced a smile.

'Alright. But look, don't go contaminating all the humans you care about just yet. There might be another way.'

That caught Lucas's attention. He was watching Cam carefully now, his gaze flicking over his face as though he were searching for signs of deception. There would be none.

'What do you mean?' said Lucas.

'I mean there might be a way to wipe out the contamination completely. It's why we're here.'

'To find an antidote?'

'In a way. Did you ever hear the story of the Gilded King?'

When the scouts started to return, pair by pair, they joined the others on the ground. It felt a little odd to sit in an arbitrary circle around a fire that didn't exist, but it had become their evening habit over the past few weeks, so they stuck to it.

Those scouting the sides of the mountain had found no additional entrances, just a few vents that were too narrow to admit a person. Eveline and Darius had found trails suggesting that the smaller entrance was the only one currently in use, which bore out the evidence Tommy and Viv had found in the cave mouth.

'There were broken things,' Viv was saying to Cam. 'Nothing useful left behind. It looked like they'd cleared the place out.'

Tommy had called the two of them away from the others after dinner, gathering them just within the tree line so they could watch the cave while they planned their approach.

'But we can get in that way?' Cam asked.

'The entrance was blocked off, but a few decent hits should clear it.'

'We'd alert them with the noise.'

'Yes,' said Tommy, 'but if they're all on the other side of the mountain then we'd still have the initiative. This is a back door built as a staging area for the army. They won't be expecting us to approach from this direction.'

Cam nodded. It made sense.

'We saw them on our way here,' said Viv. 'The army.'

'Did they see you?' Cam asked.

He got a withering look from Tommy in response. 'We're not amateurs.'

'There were a lot of them,' said Viv.

'I know,' said Cam. 'I was hoping we could get this rescue mission finished quickly, so we could be back in the Blue in time to help Lorelei. If not, then I counted them as they went by, so if we find enough noncontam blood in there then maybe we could at least send a messenger back to the city, so she knows what to expect.'

'It won't help,' said Alistair, joining the three of them under the trees. 'They had siege weaponry.'

'And she needs to know that, so she can make sure they never have the chance to use it.'

'Or we just tell her to move. Take the King and leave.'

Cam turned to look Alistair in the eye. 'And abandon the Blue?'

It was a plan that he hadn't thought the other Invicti would ever consider. In truth, it was less radical than his own plan to break the walls down and let everyone be contaminated, even the Silver. But in his plan there was no aggressor other than the vaccine, and in his plan no humans would die.

What Alistair was suggesting was very different.

'We can't just abandon the people.'

'Cam's right,' said Tommy. 'We need the uncontaminated blood. Where would we get it from if we lost the Blue?'

The others nodded along, but that wasn't what Cam had meant at all. He'd been thinking of saving lives, not their blood supply.

Still, the end result was the same, even if their logic followed different paths. They wouldn't be abandoning the city.

'We can send Lucas back with the message,' said Alistair, dropping his voice. 'He's good, but he's the least seasoned of us.'

'If we find the blood,' said Tommy.

'Yes. If we find the blood.'

They dropped the subject then, but Cam could feel the unspoken words in the silence as they watched the mouth of the cave. He could see the thoughts percolating through Tommy's mind in the twitch of his brows, the quick squint of his eyes, and the tilt of his lips as he put a plan together.

If their enemies under the mountain had access to uncontaminated blood – which Cam was sure they would – and if the Invicti could defeat them and secure that supply, then there was more at stake than just a message.

If they had the blood, then there would be no need to return to the city at all. They could ask Lorelei and her squad to bring the King here, and leave the Blue to its fate.

They could leave the entire city to die.

9

The city was as silent as the grave when Julia set out for the palace that morning.

Rufus had absented himself, presumably so he could pretend the visit wasn't happening, so Marcella was the only one there to say goodbye. Julia tried to keep it light, but something must have shown in her voice or in her expression, because Marcella caught her hand as she was stepping through the door and pulled her into a hug.

'I wish I had something to give you,' she whispered in Julia's ear.

'You could come too.'

Marcella put her hands on Julia's cheeks then kissed her forehead.

'My best chance is if I stay here,' she said. 'Your best chance, too.'

She was right. Rufus would come looking for his Candidate if she went missing. He'd track her through the city, into the Red if he had to, anything to get her back.

Julia was more replaceable. If she was lucky then he might just let her slip away.

'Goodbye,' she said, 'and thank you.'

Marcella smiled tightly. 'Be careful.'

The short walk to the palace felt like miles. It was the first time Julia had left Rufus's house since she'd arrived weeks ago, and everything felt too open. The breeze on her skin was like an assault, the sun too bright, and the scuff of her bare feet on the paving stones reverberated around the streets in a way that felt wrong after the muffled silence of inside.

She'd forgotten what it was like to be outdoors.

The sound of the wind disorientated her. The shine of the sun against stucco white buildings blinded her. The soles of her feet were so soft after walking on only polished floors and carpet that the little rocks and spiky plants of the city dug into her flesh.

It made her feel vulnerable, hobbled by the weeks of insulation and isolation. Whether it had been deliberate or not, Rufus had rendered her weak.

And in this state she was proposing to leave, into the Red, just when she needed to be at her strongest.

She hesitated at the bottom of the palace steps, but she could already see that the guard at the top was expecting her. His eyes stroked down her stained cheek, then he reached out to open the main doors for her. She had to run up the stairs in order not to keep him waiting.

A Server was waiting just inside.

'Miss Claudia's guest?' she asked.

Julia nodded.

'This way.'

It should have been a relief to be inside again, but instead Julia simply felt more exposed. The entrance hall across which the Server led her was double height, supported by columns inlaid with marble and slabs of other coloured stones that Julia couldn't name. Everything was buffed to a high polish then dimly lit. Oil lamps set in alcoves flickered violently in the draught, making Julia wonder whether several had already been accidentally extinguished. The shiny rock was smooth and cold under her feet, too cold even for this heatwave. The place felt more like a tomb than the temple ever had, despite its recent incumbent.

Julia suspected that the atmosphere bothered her escort too, because the woman hurried across the wide space to a door in the corner, then slowed her pace as they entered a series of low-ceilinged rooms. The temperature was much more pleasant here, and it warmed further as they processed through the palace until they finally reached a small sitting room that opened into a courtyard filled with plants.

Functional plants: herbs, peppers, tomatoes, and every kind of climbing fruit. Claudia was amongst them with a watering can, tending the beds and picking off bugs. She was so engrossed in her ministrations that it was a moment before she noticed Julia.

Julia's escort cleared her throat.

'Jules!' Claudia called, abandoning her watering can. 'You're here! Come and see our garden.'

Her smile faltered the moment that Julia stepped out into the sunshine.

'What happened?' she said.

Instead of trying to explain, Julia pulled her hair away from her neck, exposing the messy spiral of stitches that still marked her skin.

'Come and sit,' said Claudia, taking her hand to lead her to a bench amongst the herbs.

Julia checked they were alone before she spoke.

'I'm leaving.'

'But you only just got here.'

'No, Claud, I mean I'm leaving the city. I'm going into the Red.'

Julia had expected protests, but Claudia just nodded as her eyes alighted on the ruined flesh of Julia's neck.

'How bad was it?' she asked.

Julia couldn't look at her friend's concerned face, because the sight was making tears well in her eyes – how pathetic, to cry with pity for yourself – so instead she looked over Claudia's shoulder at the butterflies flitting around the tomatoes.

But that hurt too, because it was so like Lucas's terrace. It all reminded her of what she had lost, and what more she was about to give up.

'I think that I almost died,' she whispered once she had pulled herself together. 'I think Marcella saved me.'

'I'll come with you,' said Claudia.

There was determination in her tone, but a question too.

'No,' Julia said. 'You're happy here. And you're safe here, aren't you?'

'They look after me.'

'Then you're staying, but I can't. He'll kill me, Claud.'

'And Lucas? Your parents?'

'They're not why I have to leave.'

They both watched the butterflies for a moment before Claudia spoke again.

'When?'

'Today. If I go back there, it'll be another two weeks before I can leave, and I just don't know if I'll make it. Maybe he was making a point with this,' she said, waving at her stitches, 'but maybe not. Maybe he didn't mean for me to survive.'

Claudia looked like her heart was breaking, but her response was unflinching.

'Then you've got to go. Right now. You're going to need food, water, clothes.'

'Shoes.'

'*Definitely* shoes. What else? Some of Livia's medicine, maybe?'

Julia shook her head. 'No time to make another stop.'

'I've got some in the kitchen. Come on.'

The other end of the courtyard led straight into the kitchen. It was a good time of day – too early for lunch but too late for breakfast – so the place was empty. It was also painfully familiar. Everything about the layout mimicked Livia's kitchen, only it was four times as large.

'Strange, isn't it?' said Claudia. 'This is where she learned to cook, so when she left and had her own kitchen, she laid it out the same way.'

'You talked to her, then?'

'Why do you think I'm telling you to go? She promised that they were fine, the people who came back from the Red. If she says it's alright, then I believe her.'

'It'll still be dangerous though.'

'That's what these are for,' said Claudia, opening a drawer to pull out the roll of knives they'd swiped during the Contamination. 'You have everything you need in here: filleting, gutting, stabbing. There's even a bread knife.'

Julia didn't quite know how to respond to that, but she took the bundle gratefully and followed Claudia around the kitchen as she packed a bag with food, medicine, and bladders of water and wine.

'I can fetch some extra dresses from the laundry. I don't know where you're going to get shoes from, though. We don't have any here.'

There was a noise from the doorway.

Julia watched Claudia's eyes widen, then turned to see the King standing at the entrance to the courtyard, tapping his fingers on the doorframe. The sunlight picked out the gold in his hair, but all she could see was the ice-blue of his eyes, freezing her in place.

There was a heavy but empty moment before he spoke, a moment in which it felt as though the world might end.

'You shan't need dresses,' he said.

'Your highness,' said Claudia, but he wasn't finished.

'No. You want shirts and trousers. And if you need shoes, you'll find them in the guardhouse.'

Julia couldn't believe that he would help her. It took her a few seconds to accept it, and a few more to find her words, by which time he was already standing in front of her.

'Why?' she said. 'Why would you help?'

'You might say that I have something of a fondness for rebels.'

He smiled, a tiny gesture that was barely more than a twitch at the corner of his mouth, and yet it lit up his eyes. He seemed more human in that moment, as though he were remembering his past.

Julia knew that he must have had one, of course, but when a mythical figure comes to life it's difficult to imagine them ever existing in the same way that normal people do, with relationships and history that fit around them. Just like everyone else, the King had a context into which he fitted, it was just that unlike everyone else, his context no longer existed.

He was lost.

His voice was faraway when he spoke again, his eyes unfocussed over Julia's shoulder.

'The things we do here in this city, they happened once before, although not so darkly. Back then we caged people with the truth, rather than with lies. That was my vision. That was the vision of my forebears: reciprocity, balance, symbiosis. We had something to offer you, a mutual exchange, and it worked. It preserved our races through the Fall. But now,' he said, his eyes lingering at Julia's throat, 'we force our agenda and take without giving. We demand, as though we are entitled, and so we foster rebellion, because there is no logic to it.'

'Logic?' Julia repeated, unable to follow his words.

'We are not moral creatures,' he said. 'Do you understand?' Then he laughed softly as though he had told a familiar but favourite joke. 'Because of course, morality is irrelevant. What people care for is natural justice, that's what stability requires, but there's no justice in this place. This isn't the path I would have chosen for us.'

'I'm sorry, I don't–'

The King waved his hand.

'No, I apologise. I find myself speaking in riddles these days, because no one remembers what came before. It's simply that this city is not as I left it. It has become corrupted, and I understand why you would wish to escape. This is not your fight, but I see that you are caught up in it, as surely as you were the day I met you.'

Julia would never forget that day in the square, the King walking godlike through the fallen Nobles, but she'd expected him to forget her the moment he'd turned away.

'You remember me?' she said.

'I do. I won't stand in your way if you want to run, but you had best be prepared to run into trouble. Perhaps your friend, the midnight biscuit thief, might see her way to stealing another tin from the pantry for you. You can blame it on me.'

Claudia blushed beetroot, but the King's expression was soft. She had been right: he didn't mind at all.

'In the meantime,' he continued, 'I have a job that will require the full attention of the guards, so if you'll excuse me. Stay safe, little rebel.'

'Thank you.'

'For what?' The almost-smile twitched at the edges of his lips once more. 'I was never here.'

Claudia couldn't follow Julia out of the palace, so they had to say goodbye in the courtyard. It was brief and awful, with each of them trying not to make the other cry. If they'd cried, someone might have asked why, and if they'd delayed, then Rufus might have come looking for Julia. Either way, everything could so easily have fallen apart.

It was simpler to slip away.

Trying to hide the bundle Claudia had given her, Julia had walked silently from the back of the palace into the yard at the back of the guardhouse. Now she was hiding behind some kind of shed, watching while she waited for the guardhouse to empty.

'What now?' came a voice from inside.

'New orders.'

A lot of swearing followed, then a lot of footsteps. None of them came through the yard. Still, she waited another ten minutes, counting the six hundred seconds, just to be sure.

Then she couldn't put it off any longer.

With a quick glance around, she emerged from her hiding place and ducked inside the building.

The corridor she entered was empty. An arch to her left led into a wide room that looked to be a common area. To her right a half-open door revealed a dormitory filled with beds. It smelled of teenaged boys, mud and lanolin. Julia had been privileged to be raised in a house populated solely by women, so her exposure to the kind of funk that pervaded the guardhouse was limited, but the odour was unmistakeable. She wouldn't find what she needed on this floor.

The stairs at the end of the corridor beckoned.

She was halfway towards them when she heard the front door opening. There was nowhere to hide in the bare hallway, so her only options were upstairs or into the dormitory. She chose what seemed like the safer option, running back to scramble under the nearest bed. She dragged her bundle in behind her.

It was only after she was facedown in a pile of miscellaneous laundry that she thought to check for obstructions. Still, there was enough room for her to squeeze between the dirty clothing and the mattress and there was no time to choose a different bed.

'Lori?' a voice called from the direction of the common area.

Footsteps marched her way, making no attempt at stealth. That was some reassurance, at least. Julia might have her face pressed into a soldier's sweat-stained shirts, but at least the one out in the hall hadn't worked out she was here.

Yet.

'Lori?' he called again, from the base of the stairs.

There was a groan from the floor above. 'What the fuck, Santos? I've been out all night. I said don't fucking disturb me.'

'I know, but the King needs everyone, he says. Some kind of drill, he says. I told him you'd been out all night–'

'You did *what*?'

Feet hit the floor upstairs, followed by a clattering that didn't sound good.

'On patrol,' said Santos. 'I said you were on patrol. That's all I said.'

'Are you a fucking child that I need to tell you this again?' the woman said as her footsteps thundered down the stairs. 'You don't. Fucking. Volunteer. Information.' Each word was punctuated by a slap, to Santos's face Julia guessed, and then she recognised the woman's voice.

Lori. Lorelei.

She'd nearly walked upstairs and into Lorelei's bedroom, just as she was trying to escape the Blue. The fear of it turned her stomach. It was some minutes after she'd heard Lorelei and Santos leave before she was finally able to extract herself from under the bed.

At least she knew the guardhouse was definitely empty now.

The stairs were sturdy under her feet, but they still creaked as she let them take her weight. Everything above ground level creaked here: the floorboards, the bannisters, even the walls. She would have been found in a second if any of the guards had still been here.

The top of the staircase opened into a dormitory much like the one below her, but the rest of the floor was crammed with rooms for one or two people. A further set of stairs climbed to another storey, and probably another storey above that, but Julia didn't have time to explore. She didn't need to, because this was where she would find what she needed.

There were a hundred tiny clues that women lived here: hair ties, oils, a picture on the wall, the scent of vanilla in the air, daggers with hilts shaped for small hands, a single dress in moss green hanging from a hook by the window. There was a row of hooks there, but all the others held cloaks and belts, with a line of boots arranged against the wall beneath.

Julia dropped her bundle onto one of the beds and went to the boots first. Most of them were too big, but she eventually found a pair that fit. They were more elaborate than she would have liked, with knee-high skins that tied closed with thong wrapped criss-cross around the calves, but they'd certainly protect her feet. She'd probably sweat to death in this weather, but at least her ankles would be safe from snake bites.

Guessing that the guards were unlikely to be suspicious of items going missing in this shared space, she decided to confine her raiding to the dormitory, taking a little from each of the folded piles of clothes arranged under the beds. There were socks, trousers and shirts, together with a sling bag that would serve to carry her provisions.

She shrugged out of her dress and changed quickly into the strange male garb. It was odd to feel fabric rubbing between her legs, but she supposed she would be grateful of it when she was sleeping in the trees. The boots felt even stranger, and they took a long time to secure, so long that she worried the guards would return while she fumbled with their straps. She wobbled in them at first, getting used to the extra weight on her legs and the sensation of soft ground sticking to her feet.

Then she was nearly ready.

Mindful of the cold nights, she grabbed a short hooded cloak that belted across the middle to give easy access to weapons slung at the hip. There were plenty of those to choose from, but Julia took only a few of the smaller blades: two for her belt and the other to strap to her thigh. She only needed them for their sheaths; after all, she had knives enough of her own.

One final addition caught her eye as she was packing her dress and provisions into her bag: a short crossbow tucked into the shadow of several larger ones that were stacked in the corner of the room. She'd never used a weapon like it before, but her food wouldn't last for long, and she'd need to learn to hunt if she was going to survive in the Red. She couldn't rely on the help of the people she hoped to find.

They might not even be out there.

She might never see another living person again.

She pushed the thought away as she stuffed a bundle of crossbow bolts into her now-full bag and tied it closed. The weapon itself hooked onto a loop at the back of her belt, nestling on her hip against the bag she slung across her shoulders.

And that was it. The only thing left for her to do was walk away.

Julia slunk out into the alleys behind the guardhouse, tracking east and north, away from the palace and Rufus's house. She couldn't have been more conspicuous in the city: a figure too curvy to be male, and too short to be a guard, dressed in clothes she had no business wearing and armed to the teeth.

If she looked as awkward as she felt, then she'd better stay out of sight.

She'd decided on her route to the boundary with some hesitation. The less populated streets to the north of the city would be the safest way to the trees, but also the longest. She'd have to skirt the edge of the vineyard to avoid having to circle the lake, where Servers worked all day every day, fishing in its centre and planting rice at its edges. The vineyard would be the quieter option at this time of year.

And it was, but not quiet enough. She had pulled up her hood as she made her way through the streets, but in the fields that just marked her out: a spot of darkness moving amongst the vines. Heads turned her way as Servers tended the roses at the ends of the trellises, but none of them approached her. There were murmurs though, and she knew her passage had been noted.

She could only hope that the Servers would assume she was a Noble, because then they would keep their knowledge to themselves.

That wasn't what really worried her, though. The bulk of her anxiety was directed at the dry ground at her feet, where a new path had been carved into the grass. It hadn't been there last month, before the Contamination, but now hundreds of footfalls had worn it bare.

She wasn't the only one who had come this way recently, not even nearly. Maybe that would hide her tracks, but maybe it meant she was walking into trouble. Either way, it was too late to turn back now. The trees were already looming overhead, and the coolness of the shade was calling her onwards.

'No, not like that,' came a voice from the forest.

Julia looked around for cover, but the vines were strung too thin to hide her. After a few frantic seconds, she ducked to the side and crammed herself between the trees and a stack of cut logs, just as two Nobles walked along the path and out into the vineyard.

'Look,' one of them was saying, 'you've got to tie the loop so it tightens when the rabbit runs into it. See?'

'Can't they just catch their own food? I mean, for Christ's sake, they're taking up enough of our time as it is. It would be so much easier if we could just… you know.'

'And you know why that's not an option. Try again,' said the first, handing something to him.

Julia waited until they were just dots in the distance before creeping out and onto the path that led into the trees. The boundary fence was just around the corner, taller and better maintained here than in the south, presumably to keep the animals away from the crops.

The path ended at a gate that was barred with a beam too heavy for Julia to lift.

She nearly turned back then. It was the first time she'd even thought of giving up, but it wasn't simply that the fence seemed impossible to scale. No, the problem was what the fence represented. It was the barrier, the boundary, and the point of no return. This was the threshold that she'd seen Marcus cling to that day when he'd been ejected from the Blue. This last step was the significant one, significant enough for him to let the guards break his arm rather than voluntarily cross the line over into the Red.

This was where it all changed. The obstacle in front of her just made it that much more appealing to walk away.

But Rufus would have noticed that she was missing by now. She had been due back from the palace an hour ago at least, judging by the position of the sun, and he'd already be looking. If he found her, she had no doubt that he'd make sure she wouldn't escape again.

So she turned back to the gate and gritted her teeth. She would find a way to the other side.

In the end, the squirrels found it for her. There were two trees leaning towards each other over the fence about a fifty yards from the gate. The animals were fighting over the intertwined branches, or playing. It was difficult to tell which.

Julia's scramble across was less dignified, and it cost her some of the newly-healed skin on her palms, but she made it up one tree and down the other relatively unscathed.

She was concentrating so hard on not falling that her feet touched the leaf litter on the other side of the boundary before she had time to remember what it meant.

It should have been terrifying. She'd been planning this day for years, and dreaming about it for even longer. She'd wondered all her life how it would feel to have the soil of the Red under your feet, seeping its contamination up into your body. When she was a child, she'd thought the air would smell sharper, like yeast and rotting fruit, and that the world would be painted in different hues. It had seemed so distant for a land that was so close.

In that respect, the reality was anticlimactic.

Everything seemed the same. The earth was the same colour, and the air smelled just as damply rich. The grazes on her hands bled into the bark and the dirt had worked its way into her skin, but she wasn't a monster yet.

She was in the Red, and nothing had changed.

It was late afternoon by the time Julia reached the edge of the trees. She'd walked quickly through the forest, following the path, but staying only just within sight of it. She could do without another close encounter with the Nobles.

Then the trees opened out ahead and she saw the fence.

She wasn't sure what she had expected to find at the end of the trail, but it wasn't this. Perhaps she had expected the woods to go on forever, covering the rest of the world in the shade that was denied by the city, but when the path led out into just more fields it seemed disappointingly mundane.

The rail fence ran in both directions as far as Julia could see, up and over the horizon at shoulder height following the edge of an endless patchwork of crops and grass. Some enclosures held livestock – cows mostly, with some sheep and pigs – but the rest were filled with people, backs bent over row after row of fruit and vegetables.

For a moment, Julia thought she'd found a new settlement, but then she saw the Nobles walking around a group of huts at the centre of the fields. They were easy to spot, because they were the only ones without Xs daubed on their cheeks.

She'd found the missing Servers.

She was about to slink back into the trees when a bell rang out from the direction of the huts and the Servers stood from their work. Those in the field nearest to Julia had been harvesting strawberries, but now they abandoned their baskets and started walking towards the centre, where the Nobles were already counting them as they left the fields.

But there was one figure who hadn't moved.

Julia thought she had hidden herself well in the trees, but her movement must have caught the Server's eye because the girl just stood on the other side of the fence, staring straight at her.

It was Tatiana.

'Run,' the girl said, so softly that it barely covered the distance between them.

Julia saw the blood then, two imperfect lines circling Tatiana's wrists. The cuts were red and fresh, skin rubbed raw, and they were mirrored on her bare ankles.

'Run across the water,' she whispered. 'Go now and never come back.'

Julia didn't stop to ask questions. She just ran.

10

Tommy was running through the raid plan for the fiftieth time when Cam excused himself from the group. There was still an hour or so until they started their approach, which gave him just enough time for a quick wash in the stream. He wasn't particularly in need of it, but he told himself it was a good idea to minimise his scent for stealth purposes. In reality, his motives were less laudable: he'd seen Felix sloping off in this direction a few minutes previously and was hoping to catch him with his shirt off again.

But Felix wasn't at the stream. His green nutmeg scent crossed the water and carried on around the side of the mountain, weaving through the trees in the direction of the smaller entrance. Cam kept expecting to see him around the next trunk, but as he followed the trail closer and closer to the stone doorway, he started to become concerned.

Had Felix been captured?

There were no signs of a struggle, but that didn't mean he hadn't been taken. He could have been knocked out and carried, and the woods were full of enough different scents to bear that out.

Cam's feet moved more quickly, rushing to keep up with his senses as he zeroed in on the scent, stronger now, so strong that Felix had to be close. Felix and one other, who smelled of straw and horsehair. He could hear voices now too, low murmurings, not more than a couple of hundred yards away.

His instinct was to rush in, but he made his steps slow, because something wasn't right here. Although Cam wasn't yet close enough to hear his words, Felix's voice didn't sound distressed. It sounded confidential and persuasive.

'Alright,' an unfamiliar voice said. 'I'll tell them. You'd better go.'

'Don't worry about me.'

'Felix, no one worries about you. No one cares. You're fucking human. Or did you forget?'

'Why do you think I'm doing this?'

Cam had crept close enough to see them now, but he didn't know how to decipher the scene.

Felix was far from being a prisoner. In fact, he looked like he was talking with a friend, or at least an acquaintance. Cam could tell from here that the other man wasn't human, because he wasn't hiding his silver.

'Whatever,' he said. 'I'll see you tomorrow. Same time?'

Felix nodded, then walked back towards Cam as the Silver disappeared in the other direction.

Cam didn't approach, he just waited until Felix had walked close enough to see him, then crossed his arms over his chest to draw his attention.

Felix didn't seem surprised to find he had an audience, nor did he seem embarrassed to be caught speaking with someone who must be their enemy.

He said, 'You saw that?' as though his betrayal had been nothing more than an interesting flower or a passing bird.

'I did,' said Cam. 'Do you want to explain it for me?'

He stopped right in front of Cam, so close that he'd had to tilt his chin up to meet Cam's eyes, but there was no aggression in his closeness. His expression was gentle.

'Do you think I'd betray you?' he asked softly.

'Who is he, Felix?'

'Do you?'

Cam took a step back. 'I don't know. I barely know you.'

Even to Cam the words sounded harsh, but he couldn't unsay them. He wished he could, despite his doubts, because Felix's next words had too much distance in them, too much hurt.

'He's someone I knew from Charlestown,' he said. 'He tracked me here from the stone door, recognised my scent. I was unlucky.'

'So?'

'So I lied. I told him I was looking to trade hides and meat, like I used to.'

'And tomorrow?'

'He wanted to talk to the others before agreeing. That's all.'

Cam tracked back through the overheard conversation, matching the pieces together.

It all fitted. If Felix was lying to him, then he was doing it convincingly.

Still, he'd have to tell Tommy. If there was any chance that their raid was compromised, then the Secundus needed to know about it. This was Emmy, Cam's friend, their queen. There was too much at stake for him to ignore it.

But it was just a suspicion after all, and Tommy wouldn't react well. Cam couldn't say how far he might go. Felix was just a human to him. Just a useless, contaminated human. Tommy would see him as disposable, but to Cam he was increasingly essential.

Right now, he was more than a friend and less than a lover. But next week, next month, next year, one day, he might be everything. Cam could feel that easiness between them stretching into the future, and it filled his stomach with a sharp surge of joy that he couldn't tamp down.

He could crush it though, if he did the wrong thing now.

Shit.

He didn't know what to do.

'Don't let this be it,' said Felix.

'I don't want it to be, but you know what this looks like.'

Felix took Cam's hand and placed it over his heart, pressing it against his chest. He held Cam with his eyes, ice blue on rich brown, and they spoke for him before he said a word.

'I would never betray you.'

Cam could feel Felix's heart thudding beneath his fingertips, the regular rhythm strong and sure. Its steady rate urged him to believe what he was hearing, and he wanted to, so much.

In the end, his instincts made the decision for him.

Without him even wishing it, his gaze trailed down from eyes to cheek to mouth, following the curve of Felix's lips, and Felix took the cue.

The kiss sealed a pact between them, as surely as the Silver oaths they'd sworn on their way to Charlestown.

But Cam had forgotten all about that. In the urgency of the past few weeks, he'd stopped questioning why Felix would have that ancient knowledge. He'd forgotten the arcane press of palm against wrist. The only touch he cared for now was the press of Felix's lips against his own, and the texture of his hair beneath his fingertips.

Eveline was the first into the cave. She'd insisted, and when Eveline insisted there was no point in arguing, so the others waited in the trees for her to give the all clear.

It seemed to be a long time coming, but then Cam always felt this way when they were on mission. He was more a scout than a soldier if he was honest about it, because he'd always been better at observing than he was at fighting. He was strong, like all of them, but it was a strength he didn't like to use.

After what felt like an age, Eveline appeared at the cave mouth and waved them inside. They left Lucas and Aaron in the trees, but Felix had insisted on coming into the compound. Cam was the only one who cared enough to object, but Felix wore him down with stories of his prowess in battle. Cam had reminded him that he was still missing a tooth from the last time they'd infiltrated a group of Izcacus, but Felix had laughed it off.

He was nearly as stubborn as Eveline.

'My squad left, Cam's right,' Tommy reminded them as they approached the entry point, bodies low and knives drawn. 'Bartek to Eveline at point, Linh's squad rear. Eyes open. Go.'

They separated as grass gave way to dirt, which gave way to darkness as they stepped into the cave's overhang. The ground was strewn with hay and straw, presumably left behind from its previous inhabitants, but otherwise there were few obstacles except the stones at the back of the space that blocked their path into the heart of the mountain.

That was why Bartek was in the vanguard. It took him only seconds to roll the boulders aside, despite the fact that it had been days since he'd had any blood. He and Eveline slipped into the dark corridor beyond and the others went to follow.

But the defenders weren't where they were supposed to be. They weren't on the other side of the mountain at all. They were here, right behind the entrance, as though they'd been expecting an attack.

Cam glanced over at Felix, but he seemed just as surprised as everyone else.

He couldn't have done this. He wouldn't.

'Rear, form up!' Tommy shouted. 'Left, right and point, forward!'

'Got you,' Linh shouted in response.

There were about twenty of the defenders at Cam's rough count, more than the four Invicti in the rear squad would normally handle, but he didn't question Tommy's orders. The Secundus knew what he was doing.

Cam jinked around their attacks and plunged into the corridor beyond, dragging Felix along at his side as they left Linh to cover their backs.

Ten of the squad entered the mountain. Ten of them to find Emmy.

The rough-carved stone quickly gave way to tunnels of concrete and wooden props. It was a mishmash of old mines, transport tunnels and new excavations, and it made Cam feel supremely insecure. He didn't think of himself as being claustrophobic, but the dirt and dust dropping steadily from the ceilings was enough to convert him.

After a few hundred yards, when the sound of the fighting behind them had become muffled by distance, the tunnel split in two.

'Stick to your sides, Bartek with me,' Tommy said.

Cam's squad split right as ordered, and Eveline joined them.

Five and five, into the darkness.

It was slower going than Cam would have liked. He trailed one hand along the dirt wall so he could feel when the nature of the tunnel changed. Suddenly there was polished stone under his fingertips, too lush for a hole in the ground like this, and then he knew they were getting to the heart of the place. Light seeped into the darkness in ten steps, and in twenty he could see its origin.

'Eveline and Darius rear,' he whispered. 'Felix centre, Zita to me.'

The squad formed up silently around him, but when they reached the hall at the end of the tunnel they saw they weren't the first. The space was lit by mirrors and vents, making it brighter than it had any right to be. There were felled Silver here, another ten, each with injuries that would incapacitate for hours without killing.

It took skill to do that.

'The Secundus,' Zita said.

Tommy had beaten them to it. There were two more passages leading off the opposite side of the room, and Tommy's squad would have taken the left, so Cam took the right.

And ran straight into trouble.

There were doors set along the sides of the tunnel, metal and solid, but decaying and warped. Most of them were standing open to reveal empty rooms beyond, but a few were closed. They had to check each and every one because that was the whole point of the sweep: to search the place until they found Emmy. Unfortunately, the defenders had anticipated their tactics and set their ambush accordingly.

'Shit,' Zita gasped, caught off guard by the Silver hiding behind the door she had just opened. He was little more than a boy, so she put him down easily with a quick blade to the eye, but with doors now opening on both sides of the corridor they found themselves surrounded.

'Put your weapons down,' said a man from the back of the crowd.

When Cam picked out his face, his heart sank. He was the man from that morning in the forest, and he was looking straight at Felix, eyebrow cocked.

But Cam wasn't prepared to give up that easily, and neither was Zita. She launched herself at the man, screaming like a missile, scrabbling at his face until it caved in beneath her fist with a sickening crunch. The other defenders just stared as she rode his body down to the ground, then removed her dripping hand from his skull.

The defenders were just kids. Untrained, unseasoned, they were too busy watching the first fights to anticipate the ones that were rapidly approaching them. Zita hadn't even paused. She leapt onto her next victim while Cam threw his knife at one defender and took the another down with a quick twist of the neck. Behind him, Darius had already crushed two skulls and was working on this third. In seconds they were standing in a circle of bodies while Felix and Eveline looked on with what might have been admiration.

'Are you two going to help at all?' said Darius, wiping his bloody hands on his thighs.

'Maybe.' Eveline shrugged. 'When you need it, if I feel like it.'

'You three,' Cam said to the Invicti, 'take point. Check out these other rooms.'

While they did so, Cam turned to Felix.

'We're going to talk about this later,' he said, pointing down at the unconscious form of Felix's acquaintance.

'He knows I lied to him,' Felix said, with every appearance of regret. 'The sooner we leave the better.'

'Come on then.'

They cleared five more corridors before their path brought them to another hall where Tommy and his squad were taking down the latest group of defenders.

'Doesn't this seem a bit easy to you?' said Alistair as he dispatched the last one by cracking his head open against the floor. 'I was expecting a little opposition here, but all these are is a bunch of wee bairns.'

Alistair's Scots tended to emerge when he was anxious.

'How many have you taken out?' Tommy said to Cam.

'Fifteen, give or take.'

'So that's twenty at the cave, another fifteen for us, and ten here. Sixty of them down with not a single scratch on us. What are we missing?'

'Why are you surprised?' said Zita. 'We're the Invicti, so of course we win.'

Cam shook his head. 'Not like this.'

'Alistair's right,' said Tommy. 'They're sending out the kids to slow us down. They're buying time.'

'For what?' said Adewale.

'Contaminated blood,' said Felix.

Eveline made a dismissive noise and the other Invicti followed her lead, turning away.

'No, listen,' said Cam. 'He has a point. They know they can't beat us, so they'll try to weaken us first, with blood. They'll try to cure us, or make us cure ourselves. It's what Laila's people tried in Charlestown when we were getting Chloe out.'

Bartek exchanged a look with Darius.

'They wouldn't,' the big man said.

'Of course they would,' said Darius.

'But we're not killing any of them. Not properly. They'll be fine tomorrow. It's cheating if they're trying to make us *dead* dead.'

'I don't think they're playing,' said Cam.

Zita pulled her hair back from her face, streaking the blonde with blood. 'Then we won't either.'

The squads had split again to explore the remainder of the tunnels, and when they reconvened there was only one area left to search: the western side of the mountain, closest to the stone door. That was where they found the rest of the defenders, all gathered in the mouth of a single side passage that led down into the rock.

They found the missing leaders there too, shirts stained red with blood, guarding the doorway.

'Let me go first,' said Felix as they peered around the corner towards their destination.

'No,' said Cam.

'If they use contaminated blood, it won't hurt me.'

'It's a good plan,' Tommy said to Cam.

But Cam couldn't entirely trust him, not yet. He told himself that was the cause of his reluctance, but actually he was equally concerned that sending Felix out would make him a target for all of the defenders. He wouldn't last a second, and while Tommy may have been prepared to sacrifice him, Cam wasn't.

It was already too late, though. Felix had stepped out into the passageway, and the defenders could see him now. He didn't rush; he just strode slowly down the tunnel as though he were strolling in the trees.

Maybe that was what confused the Red Shirts, or maybe they could tell he was human and so assumed he presented little risk to them. Perhaps that was why they simply watched him approach, but Cam didn't miss the movement of Felix's hands as he walked. The shapes he made were hidden in front of his body, but Cam could see his elbows signalling gestures from behind.

'Something's wrong,' he whispered.

'Give him a second,' said Tommy.

The first Red Shirt was watching Felix carefully, but he didn't move to attack. In fact, he didn't move at all until Felix was standing in front of him, when he reached out a hand.

They shook.

'That doesn't look right,' said Bartek.

Cam was starting to think the same. He felt as though a pit were opening up in the bottom of his stomach, because the whole situation held unmistakeable echoes of the events of that morning, when he'd seen Felix's clandestine forest meeting.

But then Felix moved. He pulled the Red Shirt forward by his clasped hand, while thrusting a knife up under his chin and into his brain.

The Red Shirt hadn't been expecting it, that much was clear, because otherwise Felix would never have been able to overpower him. The other defenders were already rushing forwards to take Felix down, but they'd knocked over their hidden cache of bottles in the confusion, so now contaminated blood was slicking the stone floor.

That was the moment the Invicti had been waiting for.

'Go!' Tommy shouted.

The Red Shirts had scrambled over each other to reach Felix, but they divided as the Invicti approached, leaving just one with his hands around the woodsman's throat.

Cam brought the attacker down. A single blow to the head was all it took, a movement so fluent that it was practically automatic, but it took the Red Shirt to the ground and slammed his open head wound into the blood that puddled around their feet. When the defender scrambled back up to his knees, he was as human as Felix.

Felix nodded his thanks, but Cam was already turning away towards the onrush of Silver. He'd deal with Felix later.

The defenders were relentless. The Invicti had them contained for the moment, but these fighters were of a very different calibre from the young ones they had already faced. They didn't fall easily, and when they finally did, they held back enough energy to propel themselves away from the pool of contamination beneath them.

They might have struggled, thirteen Invicti against thirty-odd Red Shirts, but the blood had started to slide down the sloping tunnel now, chasing the defenders back along the corridor they were protecting. The Invicti followed them closely, stepping through the mess as though it couldn't cure them in a second. It was a risk, but that passage was where they would be keeping Emmy, so that was where they needed to be.

Then things started to go wrong.

Zita took a hit to the jaw and her feet flew out from under her. Naia caught her before she could hit the ground, snatching Zita out of the air when she was just inches away from the blood, but that left Naia unable to protect herself from the knife that found its way between her ribs. It would heal eventually, but with no blood to support the healing, her fighting form would be compromised.

Unfortunately, the incident also telegraphed their lack of blood to the Red Shirts.

'They've got no blood!' one of them shouted, then their hands were at their belts.

Cam had wondered why none of the defenders were moving at speed, and this was the answer: they'd been saving their precious blood supply because they didn't know that the Invicti had none. If they'd used up their blood early, they would have left themselves open to attack if the Invicti had flasks of their own.

But they didn't. After weeks of travel they had nothing left, and now the Red Shirts knew that. They could revel in their advantage.

Tommy and Darius managed to snatch bottles from the two closest defenders while they were raising them to their lips, which helped to even the balance a little, but still left them with tens of supercharged Silver whom they weren't fast enough to counter.

'Left!' Tommy shouted as he punched two Red Shirts away from the wall, clearing a path down into the passage beyond, but no one was free to take the opening.

Eveline was nowhere to be seen, but Cam could hear fighting around the corner, back the way they had come. It sounded like she was tied up for the moment. He was busy himself, battling desperately to keep the defenders away from Felix, but he wasn't going to be able to hold them for long without some help.

There was none to be had though. Naia had been pinned against the opposite wall by two defenders while a third barrelled towards her. Konrad was there in time to stop the attacker and get her free, but that left Zita fighting four at the edge of the pack. The rest of the Invicti had similar problems. Bartek was working with Darius to take out the middle of the group while Linh and Gul were back-to-back in a circle of defenders, and although there were three Red Shirts at their feet already, not all of them had been cured.

None of the Invicti had hit the floor yet, but at this rate it wouldn't be long before they did.

There was a cry then from the direction they were fighting towards. For such a brutal battle it had been eerily silent, so when the scream came it cut through the air, deadening into the crush of bodies between the rock walls.

The Red Shirts turned like sentries, giving a couple of the Invicti the openings they needed to bring their combatants down. Even that wasn't enough to regain the Red Shirts' attention though, because now they were streaking away from the Invicti, flooding down the sloping passage, through the terminating doorway and beyond.

'So,' said Adewale, 'should we be worried about that?'

'What do you think?' said Alistair.

Bartek snorted derisively. 'They're cowards.'

'Are we all here?' Tommy asked, looking around the squad. 'That wasn't one of us crying out?'

'…twelve, thirteen, and Felix,' said Viv. 'All accounted for.'

'Then let's find out who it was.'

The passage ended in a sharp left turn that took the Invicti into a series of chambers hollowed out from the bare rock. This wasn't like the stone-lined corridors they'd chased the young defenders through, places that looked like they were a legacy of industry, travel and entertainment. These rooms were quite different, ancient beyond ancient, with an arcane air that sent a shiver along Cam's skin. It was damp here, and cold. The puddles along the edges of the chambers exuded the reek of algae and mould.

This was nothing more than an adulterated cave system.

The clamour drew the Invicti on through the complex. The screams had stopped now, but there was a whimpering sound beneath the thud and crush of combat, rendered all the more worrying because of its plaintive edge.

The bodies of the Red Shirts were piled up around the entrance to the final chamber. When the Invicti finally pushed their way in, Cam realised the destruction they had seen outside was just overflow. The chamber itself was little more than a cell, big enough for a high cot and nothing else. Standing on top of it, surrounded by the Red Shirts she'd incapacitated, the Queen stood with her hand wrapped around the throat of the last defender.

'Emmy?' said Cam.

He had to ask, because she looked nothing like herself. Her body had been stripped back to skin and bones by deprivation, and her eyes were wild in her face. Blood ran from her fingers and her mouth where she'd clawed and bitten her way through the defenders.

Alone.

On her own, despite her visible frailty, she'd taken out twenty full-strength Silver.

There was a gasping from the man whose throat she held. Cam looked at him properly for the first time.

It was Charles. He was older, yes, and human now, just as Chloe had said, but it was him. Diminished, cowering on his knees as the Queen squeezed her bloody fingers into his skin, but undeniably Charles.

'Emmy,' Cam said again, trying to draw her attention away from her prey.

She didn't reply.

'Emmy, he's human. He won't hurt you.'

'He has,' she whispered as her grip tightened.

'You'll kill him.'

Her eyes met Cam's then, but there was no hint of recognition in them. They were as empty as water as she said, 'Good.'

After that, there was only the soft crunch of cartilage as her fist closed through the flesh.

The journey back to the camp was long and quiet.

Darius had found a small cache of blood in one of the chambers they'd passed through on their way to reach Emmy, but there were no uncontaminated humans here. The army must have taken them all on the expedition to the Blue.

At least the Invicti wouldn't be staying here.

The first of the blood went to Emmy, who was so emaciated that it was difficult to believe she was still walking, let alone powerful enough to take on the Red Shirts. In fact, most of her strength had left her shortly after they'd arrived in her cell, and despite having drunk three entire bottles she was now being supported through the tunnels by Viv.

She hadn't looked at Cam since she'd killed Charles.

The second ration of blood was wrapped up and given to Alistair, who went on ahead to take it to Lucas. With no uncontaminated humans left in the mountain, Cam's original plan would be enacted: they would send Lucas back to Lorelei with Cam's report on the army's deployment.

The boy had already left by the time they reached the new campfire, which was just as well given how blood-drenched they had become during the fighting. Cam didn't think Lucas was quite ready for that.

'How long do you think we have?' Viv asked Tommy as they approached the fire.

'A day probably, but we should leave tonight. We don't have blood to waste on repairing any extra injuries if the Red Shirts wake up early.'

There was still some blood left after Emmy and Lucas had taken their shares, but not an abundance. It would be enough to get the Invicti back up to strength, with a bit left over, but all of that would be needed by Emmy; she was going to require constant and consistent feeding if she was to make it back to the Blue in any kind of decent shape.

'Did Lucas get away alright?' Cam asked Alistair.

'He knows where he's going, and he knows to avoid the army. The blood he has should get him most of the way there.'

'That far?' Cam thought of the tens of bottles it had taken him to get back to the Blue the last time he'd made the journey from here. He'd been starved at the time, but still, Lucas was just a boy.

'The blood was fresh, and he's quick as a whip. You shouldn't underestimate him. How is she?' Alistair nodded towards Emmy.

Viv had settled her beside the fire wrapped in layer after layer of blankets, but she was still shaking. Her cheeks were sunken, her hair straggled in greasy strips, and her eyes still had a glazed look about them.

'Better than she looks, I hope,' said Cam.

'Did she say what Charles was after?'

'She hasn't said much of anything yet.'

Adewale called Alistair away then to help with the horses. In fact, most of the Invicti seemed to have found tasks to keep them away from the fire. Many of them were washing the blood from their clothes in the stream, but those who were already clean were busy too.

No one wanted to be around their queen, and Cam couldn't blame them. She looked feral. That ferocity might be why the other Invicti were keeping their distance, not because they feared it but because it inspired the kind of awe that had always attached itself to her and Sol.

Cam's reasons for staying away were quite different.

He remembered the weeks he'd spent travelling with Felix whilst he agonised over Peterke's death. He remembered the crunch of the bones in his hand, and how that had haunted him. He remembered worrying that Emmy would be disappointed in him, that she might think that it had been deliberate rather than a terrible accident.

But there had been nothing accidental about the way she had ripped out Charles's throat.

When Cam looked back at the fire, Emmy was watching him with a steady gaze. There was no regret in her eyes, only a determination that looked a lot like victory.

11

Julia was feeling defeated.

It was getting late, and she was starting to feel as though she were walking in circles through the trees. She hadn't seen another person since she'd left Tatiana at the fence, and there had been no other signs of habitation for the rest of the afternoon.

She'd kept the sun to her back, heading eastwards and away from the city, but she still wasn't entirely convinced that her course was straight. Everything looked the same in this place: green and brown and crackling dry in the summer heat. It smelled of once-damp things rotting hot in the sun, and of dead creatures baking in the dried river beds. The bugs congregated there in clouds that Julia's waving hand seemed only to drive into her nostrils. She'd stuffed her short cloak into her bag as a concession to the temperature, but she regretted that decision as the flies crawled over the skin revealed by her sleeveless shirt, sticking to her sweat.

She'd expected the insects. There were bugs in the Blue just like these, and they were no cause for alarm; they couldn't carry the contamination. What she hadn't expected were the birds that multiplied as she left the city farther behind until they flocked darkly in the trees above her. They were sinister shadows that blocked out the sun between the boughs. She tried to skirt them at first, but they formed a dense belt of cawing that orbited the Blue. There was no avoiding them.

In the end, it was the rushing noise of water that drew her through them. She'd already emptied one flask, and she could do with refilling it before she continued her journey. Not knowing the geography of this place had filled her with a sense of insecurity, so she would take any opportunity to replenish her supplies.

When the trees finally separated, she found herself on pebbled shingle that stretched as far as she could see in each direction along a wide shore. There were more trees on the other side of the water, but it looked to be miles away, with no way across.

Julia had never learned to swim properly, lacking both the facilities and the leisure time. It was a hobby reserved to Nobles, and now she could see why. If she couldn't get across the water, she could never escape.

The birds were thicker on the tideline, picking through the vegetal detritus that had accumulated there. It was as though the drought had lowered the water level as it had in the lakes and streams she'd passed on her way, yet the smell here was different. The air had a different tang: fishy and sharp rather than the thick, green odour of the stagnant ponds in the forest.

It didn't smell healthy.

Her boots crunched over the pebbles that were closest to the water, not just because they ground against each other but because they were covered with a white crust that crackled apart under her heels. One scoop of water to her lips confirmed her suspicions: the liquid was so salty that it parched her tongue. She wouldn't be able to refill her flask here.

She'd heard of the sea. Lucas had read her the stories of mermaids and princes, of lost islands and sunken treasures, but she'd never thought it would be like this. It might have seemed wide from her place on the shore, but this sea was so narrow that she could see from one side of it to the other. Julia had imagined it being larger, because how could boats ever get lost in it – like they did in the stories – when they could still see the shore?

A boat, though.

That was what she needed.

Lucas's fairytales had told her what she could use to build a raft: logs bound together with vegetation used as twine. She could do that. She could make a boat to get her to the other side of the sea.

Tomorrow, though. The sun was already low in the sky, and she didn't want to be standing on the shore when the night rolled in. She didn't know what lived in this place and she wasn't willing to risk encountering any creatures that haunted the beach. She needed to get back into the trees and find somewhere she could tuck herself away in the dark.

But it was difficult to shake a lifetime of being told that the ground in the Red would kill you. Julia still struggled a little with every footfall, thanking the guards for the boots she had stolen from them, but the thought of lying down to sleep with her cheek on the earth dragged spirals of fear through her chest. It sounded like insanity, to surrender herself to the contamination of the soil of the Red, and yet the alternatives were unappealing.

One, she could forgo sleep altogether. After a day of walking in this heat with her bag dragging her down, and exhausted as she was from her recent recovery and the fear-filled rush of her escape, that didn't seem like a realistic option. She could *try*, but she was already struggling to keep her eyes open. She would fail.

Two, climb up into a tree and sleep there. That would keep her away from the ground, and from any land animals that might exist in the Red, but it seemed likely that she would fall in her sleep. Dropping into the ground from a height was an even less appealing prospect than just lying down there in the first place.

Three, try to build a shelter that would suspend her from the ground. She had no blanket for a hammock, and her crafting skills weren't up to building a platform. All she could do was try to find a an existing shelter that would do the job.

The last was Julia's only real option, so she tracked along the shore, just within the curtain of the trees. She wasn't hopeful, but she found what she was looking for only a few hundred yards from her starting point: a large fallen tree that had tumbled back into the forest. It was wide and flat enough for Julia to lie comfortably along it without rolling off, even if she did move a little in her sleep, and that was the best she could hope for with dusk falling quickly over the water.

It wasn't ideal, though. Animals would still be able to climb the tree, and even amongst the dried branches Julia would be visible to anyone who looked for her.

But who would be looking out here? She couldn't imagine that Rufus cared enough to come after her, not in his position. He'd be able to summon up another Attendant with a snap of his fingers, despite their recent scarcity. Julia only hoped that he didn't have the power to bring Claudia back from the palace, because she needed her friend to be safe. She needed to believe that they had both escaped Rufus in the end, albeit by different routes.

As she shrugged out of her pack and settled it into the crook of the fallen tree's branches, she imagined Claudia settling down in her own bed. She would have soft pillows and lush fabrics, and she'd have the company of her roommate. Julia would have rough bark softened by her folded cloak, but it could be worse; she could still be wrapped in bleached sheets that barely hid her blood.

And Claudia had sent Julia off with everything she needed to survive this place. She had knives, medicine, and food and drink, a small portion of which she consumed now while she tried not to think about the rich fare Claudia would be enjoying at the palace. Tired as she was, Julia was happy with her bread and cheese.

She should be, because it would run out soon and then she would have to provide for herself. That was the fear that clenched around her chest and stopped her from sleeping. It wasn't the wind in the trees, or the swish of the water, or the infrequent sounds of the nighttime birds; it was the knowledge that she was on her own, untested and lonely.

She was already missing the creature comforts of her former life. If only she could wash the salt from her skin before turning in, but with just salt water available it seemed like bathing in the sea would be a futile gesture. Wasting her drinking water was out of the question. She thought longingly of the bowl of clean water in the room Rufus had given her, but then her mind ran back to the pink liquid turning red with her blood as Marcella sewed her wounds closed.

The stitches still sat thickly in her neck, but they didn't hurt now when Julia pressed them lightly with her fingertips. They came away dry and clean, which was a small blessing, but would she be able to extract them on her own when the time came? Would she be able to build a fire, and kill her food, and if she could, *should* she? What would happen if she ate the meat?

As if on cue, a howl sounded across the water, snapping Julia's head up from her makeshift pillow. It seemed to have come from the other side of the sea, but one of her ears had been pressed against her cloak so she couldn't be sure. It might have come from along the coast, or from the city behind her, or from the fenced fields where she had left Tatiana.

There was something niggling at her about that place, but she couldn't put her finger on it. A thought hovered just at the edge of Julia's grasp, but then it drifted away.

Something about Tatiana.

Tatiana, with her wrists and ankles bound, locked away in one of the huts, so she wouldn't even be able to run if the monsters did come calling.

The memory of her bloody wounds steeled Julia's resolve.

Julia was free. She might not be entirely safe, and she knew that her life from this point onwards would be the most difficult it had ever been, but she was free and she would be strong. She had survived Rufus. She had survived the Contamination. She had survived losing Lucas.

She would survive this too, even if she needed to climb a tree in the pitch darkness to do it.

Julia's boat building was not a complete success.

Her palms had suffered from the trip across the fence the previous day and from the retreat she had made into the treetops during the night. She'd had to bind them up again that morning. The bandages impeded her dexterity, although if she was honest with herself the problem wasn't just her hands.

It didn't help that she was exhausted. Spending the night tied to a tree branch is not conducive to a good night's sleep, but building a raft when you're unwilling to sacrifice your tree-sleeping rope is practically impossible, particularly when there are no creepers to use as substitutes.

And that was the thing that frustrated Julia the most. She'd just assumed that there'd be appropriate foliage available for her to tie her boat together. In all the stories Lucas had read her, the shipwrecked princes always found creepers or vines to fashion rafts, so they could sail back across the sea to save their princesses from the pirates. *Always*. So why were there no creepers or vines to be found in the huge forest that bordered the shore?

Infuriating, that's what it was. She felt cheated.

Fairytales lied all the time, she knew that. She'd experienced it too, much to her regret. She knew that Nobles didn't fall in love with Servers, that mermaids didn't save drowning people from the sea, and that fairies themselves weren't real, but why did the stories have to lie about the useful things too? She could understand why the fantasies were just that – fantasy – but couldn't they at least tell the truth about the practicalities of boat building?

It seemed unfair.

The more she focussed on it, the more angry she became until she was throwing sticks across the beach and kicking at the pebbles, because it was easier for her to be angry with the fairytales than it was for her to admit that she was really just angry with Lucas for leaving her behind.

It was the fairytales' fault that she'd almost believed he would stay for her, and it was the fairytales' fault that her raft was a mess.

In the end, she'd ripped up her old dress to make strips of fabric she could use instead of rope. That had been the easy bit, because once she'd solved that problem she had to get down to the business of finding logs with which to build the raft itself. That was not going well. Cutting down trees was out of the question, because the closest thing she had to a saw was the breadknife Claudia had given her. She could use it to hack off smaller branches from larger ones, but it was hard, time-consuming work.

She'd managed to amass a small stack of puny trunks and was working on an oak windfall in the tree line when there was a noise from the depths of the forest. That in itself wasn't unusual, because this far from the Blue the trees were a noisy place, but what was unusual was the tone of the noise. It wasn't the muffled crunch of foliage underfoot, or the ruffling of feathers in the canopy above, but the bell-like tinkle of metal on metal.

Julia froze.

Now the forest did seem truly silent, as though it were holding its breath with Julia. The birds were still and there was nothing moving in the undergrowth.

She waited in an uncomfortable crouch for long seconds, which stretched into minutes, but there was nothing more to hear. Eventually, the forest started to relax around her. Whatever it was must have passed on by.

People were the only possible origin of that kind of noise out here. It couldn't have come from the contaminated that she'd heard howling the previous night, because they lumbered with fists and teeth, unencumbered with tools. That left just two possibilities: the Nobles, or the humans Livia had talked about.

Julia's fear of the former was more than enough to stop her chasing after the sound in search of the latter.

She finished collecting the rest of the wood as quickly as she could, but it still took all morning. The sun was high when she thought she might finally have enough, and her stomach was grumbling its discontent at being deprived breakfast.

She couldn't stop thinking about the biscuits in her pack. If they were anything like the ones Marcella had given her, they'd be buttery and crumbly and so sweet that even the thought of them was already making her mouth water.

But she wouldn't eat them. They'd last the longest of all the supplies she'd brought with her, so she needed to save them until she had nothing left. Instead she ate a hunk of bread, an apple, and the last of her cheese, which was just as well because it was already starting to hum in the heat. It drew the flies closer until she had to swat them away, but she didn't dare to move away from their swarms amongst the trees. She was huddled at the edge of the forest, behind the nascent shape of her boat, because standing out on the shore felt like suicide; she'd be visible from any point on either coast.

It wouldn't be long before she would have to risk it though. She couldn't build the raft up here then drag it down to the shore; she could barely move some of the logs on their own, let alone combined with others. There was no getting around the necessity of constructing the raft in the shallows, so she was delaying it instead. Every mouthful of her food was over-chewed. Her tongue was dry with fear, exertion and dehydration. There was only half a flask of water left now, and her shirt was drenched with sweat.

Then she heard the noise again, tinkling high and clear. She might almost have believed it was bird song had it not silenced every other creature in the forest. It seemed closer this time. It had separated into tones that sounded rhythmic in their variation, peeling back and forth, as though it swelled and fell with the lilt of someone's stride, swinging metal from their belt.

Julia hunkered down behind the pile of logs she'd accumulated and prayed for the birds to resume their singing. Her palms sweated into her bandages, making the grazes sting with salt.

This wasn't like spying on Rufus in the city, or like following the guards out to the fence with Claudia at her side. She was alone out here, and no one was expecting her to return. If she died on this beach, she wouldn't be missed by anyone at all.

There was a faint crunching sound beneath the metallic one now, like the crush of footfalls. It was close. So close that if she peered over the top of the logs, she'd probably be able to see whoever was making it between the trees.

Julia took one breath, then a second, then rolled over onto her stomach so she was facing the forest. The logs still blocked her view, but there were cracks between them, and in the gaps she could see movement. Dark legs in the distance, two people, maybe more.

Another breath and then she'd move up to her knees so she could see over the top. Just one more breath.

One more.

But then there were voices, faint but still occasionally audible. Syllables filtered across to the beach, then individual words – *here... away... understand it* – until finally they crystallised.

'–waste of time.'

'Well, he doesn't think so.'

'Yeah, but what do *you* think? And why the hell did you agree to this?'

Their increasing volume could only mean that they were close, and coming closer.

'What I want to know,' the same voice continued, 'is what's so special about this one. It's not as if he hasn't already had hundreds.'

'Did you want to ask him? Because if you're going to antagonise the Empress's son then you can leave me out of it.'

Rufus.

They were practically on the beach now, about twenty yards along the tree line from Julia's position, but she couldn't move. If they were sent here by Rufus, then they were Nobles, and they'd hear her shifting in the leaves.

'I don't understand why you pander to him, that's all.'

Footsteps crunched onto the pebbles as they moved onto the shore. Twenty yards, maybe thirty, and they'd be far enough out of the trees that when they turned to head back to the Blue, they would see her.

'I don't understand why you don't. You saw what happened to Victor.'

'Yeah, but Victor was a dick.'

'Maybe, but he didn't deserve that. All I'm saying is that Rufus getting what he wants keeps me from ending up the same way, and I'm okay with that.'

'Coward.'

'Speak for yourself.'

There was silence for a few seconds. It was the complete silence she'd heard earlier, the silence of the forest waiting for the predators to leave, so Julia knew they were still around.

She just didn't know where.

Why weren't they moving?

She turned her head, careful not to shift her weight on the leaves beneath her, so she could look over her shoulder to the beach behind her.

There were three of them, not two, and they were standing on the pebbles gazing out at the sea. She could see their outlines clearly enough, so if they turned, there was a good chance they'd spot her.

'Look, she's not out here,' said the third man, sulkily. 'I told you: she wouldn't have made it this far. There's no way she left the island. Frankly, I don't reckon she ever even left the city. She's somewhere back in the Blue, holed up in one of the buildings that came down in the Contamination.'

'Bet me a week with your Attendant?'

'Bet you two.'

They clasped hands, palm to pulse, then laughed. Julia wasn't close enough to see their expressions, so she couldn't tell whether their laughter was happy or mocking, but the noise was harsh against the gentle whisper of the waves.

'Well, I hope you're right,' said the one who had been accused of pandering to Rufus, 'because if she's out there then we're all going to be in trouble.'

There was a howl from across the water then, faint but still chilling, and Julia couldn't stop herself from jerking a glance towards the opposite coast. That must have been where it had come from the previous night.

'Well if I'm wrong,' the third man said, 'if she has made it across the sea, then the Weepers will get her instead and we'll have nothing to worry about.'

'Rufus will still be angry.'

'Maybe, but he'll never even know she ended up on the continent. There won't be anything left of her to find once the Weepers have got their claws in her.'

'Or they'll turn her.'

There was a beat of silence.

'They can do that?'

'Yes. Lori said so.'

Lorelei again.

'So the girl would be a Weeper?'

'Yes. I hope I don't have to explain to you why that would be a bad thing.'

Apparently he didn't, because a moment later the third man said, 'Well then, do you want to keep looking?'

'No, but you two can. One in each direction around the coast, and stop when you get back here. Put on a bit of speed and it shouldn't take you more than a day.'

'And while we do that, what are you going to do? Go back to the city and put your feet up?'

'No, I'm going to go and tell Rufus that we've found nothing. Did you want to swap jobs? Did you want to be the one to tell him the girl's gone?'

A significant pause followed.

'Fine, we'll search the shore. Give me your bottle, though.'

'Fine.'

With that, the third man stomped off along the shore, past Julia's hiding place without even looking her way. The other two moved off shortly afterwards, one heading north along the beach and the other back the way they had come.

None of them saw her, which was strange, because they had clearly been looking for her, although not very well.

She wondered at that.

She wondered if they'd trailed her here, then wondered at the fact that they hadn't picked up on her scent or the thump of her heartbeat, but if they weren't even bothering to use their eyes then why would they engage their other senses? The whole encounter reeked of performance, as though they weren't concerned with finding her so much as they were with demonstrating to Rufus that they had looked.

Still, they would be back. She had a day, and then she needed to be off this beach, so she had to reach the opposite shore by nightfall.

That gave her very little time. She would need every second of daylight.

The raft didn't float.

Well, it did, but it only had enough buoyancy to keep Julia's pack dry. As soon as she tried to sit on it herself, it tilted precariously as her weight pushed it under the water. In the end, she resorted to tying her belongings to its top and pushing it along as she kicked from behind.

She'd removed her boots before wading into the shallows to assemble the raft and they now sat beside her pack and cloak. At least some part of her clothing would be dry when she reached the opposite shore, because everything else was soaked. Her shirt and trousers dragged at her as she kicked, doing nothing to make the process any easier.

It had taken her ages to get the hang of propelling herself and the raft through the water, having only rarely observed the technique at the lake. By the time she had mastered it, she was so exhausted that she was starting to doubt she'd ever make it to the other side. The shore never seemed to get any closer, and every kick took a little more out of her. It didn't help that, despite the heat of the day, the water was cold. It stung her stitches and her hands.

The more tired she became, the more the chill crept into her muscles. She could feel herself slowing down, like a spinning top running out of spin, and she had to rest more and more often.

Just halfway now, or so it seemed. When she looked back at where she'd started, it appeared as far away as her destination. There would be no point in giving up now; she either make it to the continent – as the Nobles on the beach had called it – or she'd run out of energy here in the sea.

The Nobles had said that she was on an island, but Julia hadn't understood how small that island was until she was out here in the middle of the water. It resolved itself clearly as she looked back, because now she could see the edges curving around and away from her. She could also see the water reaching wide to the south beyond the end of the island, fanning out into a sheet that stretched to the horizon.

The sea was big after all, just like she'd been told, it was just that she was on the edge of it. Or she had been, before she'd thrown herself into the water with little more than blind optimism that she'd somehow reach the other side.

Even if she did manage to make landfall then she wouldn't be out of trouble, because there had been more howls through the afternoon. Her feet faltered each time she heard them. They sounded so much closer here, though whether that was because she was closer or because they were, these Weepers, she couldn't be sure.

Weepers, the Nobles had called them.

For the bloody tears that ran down their faces, she assumed. The same tears that had run down Marcus's face when he'd howled like that at her and Claudia on the night of the Contamination. It seemed an appropriate name.

They were waiting on that shore for her. Maybe there were none left on the island after the guards had cleansed the city. Maybe they were only on the continent now. Maybe that was where they had come from in the first place. Maybe there were thousands of them there, stalking unseen between the trees.

In the face of that, it was a challenge to keep moving towards the shore, but she couldn't go back, not now.

There was no going back.

She pushed her legs. The next time she rested she was further away from the island than she was from the continent. She'd crossed the middle line, and that was all that mattered, because she knew she was getting closer now. It was a threshold moment that gave her the strength to cover the remaining distance over the following hours, slowly but surely, and when her toes finally caught against pebbles there was not even the first hint of dusk in the sky.

Julia knew she should drag the raft up the shore and dismantle it to cover her tracks, but she barely had the energy to retrieve her belongings before the current took it and swept it back out into the water.

She let it go. Let the Nobles find it if they wanted, but with any luck the tide would take it out to sea.

Her first few steps out of the water were like trudging through mud. She was shaking with exhaustion and her feet seemed to stick to the ground, although she could feel with her bare toes that there was nothing but pebbles beneath her. Every footfall dragged, and she might have face-planted straight onto the beach had a soft noise from the trees not sent a sharp rush of adrenaline through her.

The shingle was narrower on this shore. Only thirty yards or so separated the water from the woods, which were dense and dark. There was no telling what might be lurking there without Julia going and seeing for herself, which was not her favourite plan.

Her first thought was Weepers. That was terrifying enough, but then a second possibility presented itself: perhaps Rufus's searchers had changed their course. They could have seen her crossing the sea and decided to cut her off when she reached the shore, knowing that she'd be exhausted from the effort. It was the kind of thing Rufus would do. He'd enjoy giving her a moment to hope that she might have escaped, before crushing it utterly.

Whatever was waiting for her, she had to be ready to run, so with her eyes fixed on the trees she pulled on socks and boots, stuffed her cloak into her bag again and slung it over her shoulders. She didn't have time to find her crossbow, which was tangled up with the rest of her supplies at the bottom of her pack, so instead she pulled a knife from the sheath she wore on her thigh. The menacing effect she was aiming for was slightly spoiled when the blade emerged with a wet sucking sound instead of a clean zing, but at least it was sharp.

She stood poised as she waited to hear the sound again, torn between the desire to get off the beach and the desire to stay away from the woods.

She waited.

Not in silence this time, because the forest here was alive with movement. The birds were still cawing as they circled the trees and landed on the pebbles to pick amongst the weed and rot, and squirrels clambered from tree to tree while Julia watched, and waited.

She waited while the bag tugged her bruised shoulders. She waited while the weight returned to her exhausted limbs. She waited until she felt like falling over again. Then she heard it.

Someone was singing.

Julia couldn't make out the tune, but it was familiar. Something about the crests and falls of the melody tugged at a visceral part of her memory. It wasn't that it recalled an event, or a place, but it recalled a feeling. It was childhood and safety and love. It was that feeling she'd had for the few short years before she'd realised her place in the world, the human place in the world. It was from a time when her biggest disappointment in life had been finding out that her favourite fruit wasn't available all year round.

It sounded like home, and it was a siren song from which Julia couldn't run.

The singing gradually gave way to footsteps on leaves, then pebbles, and finally the singer came into view.

She wasn't that much older than Julia. That was the surprising thing. She knew it was ridiculous, but Julia had half convinced herself that she was about to see her mother. The girl in front of her – with light hair, rich skin, and straggling clothing that looked even more ancient than Julia's – couldn't have been more than eighteen.

Assuming, of course, that she was human at all.

'You're Julia,' she said; a statement, not a question.

More surprises.

'Who are you?' Julia stuttered.

'We've been searching all along the shore.'

Julia was about to run when the girl added, 'Livia told us about you. We never thought you'd try to cross here, though. We saw the raft and they sent me to get you.'

'Humans?'

The girl laughed. 'Of course humans. Who else would be looking for you?'

'My Noble is.'

Then the girl smiled. 'Well, they don't own us out here, Julia. He's not your Noble anymore.'

12

Cam was starting to think that he didn't even know Emmy anymore. He'd worried so much about how he had changed that he'd never stopped to consider how hundreds of years of captivity might have affected her.

Thoughtless, that's what it was.

But still, there was a seed of familiarity between them. He could work with that, if only she'd talk to him.

She'd stayed by the fire while Viv had tried to get her to open up, unsuccessfully. She'd remained silent as they'd mounted up, Emmy on Lucas's horse, for their return to the Blue. Now she rode alone, covering her eyes with one hand as though the day were too bright for her.

Viv had done her best to look after her. They'd thrown away her clothes and a couple of the women had taken her to the stream to try to get her clean, but none of the replacement clothes they could loan her had fitted quite right. Naia's trousers were too big, so they had to be folded and belted at the waist, and the only shirt the women could offer was tight enough to gape between the buttons. In the end, Cam gave Emmy his spare.

She didn't seem grateful to be clean. In fact, she barely seemed to notice.

That disconnection became difficult to work with when they were on the move. The army had a couple of days' head start, but the entire squad was determined to ride hard enough to overtake them in the first half of their journey.

The entire squad except Emmy.

Her lack of impetus was reasonable in the circumstances, it was just that Cam wasn't sure how to explain it. It might have been that she was traumatised from her captivity, or that she had no reason to care about the Blue because she'd never been there, or simply that she was too unwell to travel quickly, but Cam suspected her reasons were different. He had known her well enough that he could still read her face, and her mind was now far from vacant behind her eyes.

She watched, noting and filing in her head as she collected information, but there was a frantic edge to her attention. She was jumpy, and anxious, but in a directed way. She was hiding something, and Cam meant to find out what that was.

After spending all afternoon with her, Viv might have some insight. Cam was about to ride up alongside her when he was joined by Felix, who put a hand around Hades's reins to keep him alongside.

'Not now,' Cam muttered.

'We need to talk.'

'About you and your Izcacus friends? I'd rather not, right now.'

'You don't believe me,' said Felix.

'No, not really. You're keeping things from me. Can you honestly say that you've told me the truth?'

'I'd never betray you.'

'Yes, you've said that already, but that's not what I'm asking. I'm asking you whether you've told me the truth.'

A moment passed in which all Cam could hear was the gentle plodding of hooves into grass.

'The truth would change things,' Felix said eventually.

'Then either let them change or leave. Your choice.'

The words were said in despair not anger, so Cam had to screw them out of his throat. There was no alternative though. He couldn't go on like this, paranoid about Felix and yet protective of him at the same time. It would tear him in two.

But Felix said nothing, and so the choice was left to Cam. He yanked the reins out of Felix's fingers and, though it pained him to do so, he rode away to join Viv.

She had been watching over her shoulder. Not consistently, not invasively, but she'd seen enough of the exchange to know that he and Felix were fighting. She'd guessed what it was about, too.

'There might be a reasonable explanation,' she said as Hades fell in step beside her mare.

'If there was, don't you think he would have told me it?'

'He took that Red Shirt down, Cam. You saw him. He warned us about the blood. Would he have done that if he was working with them?'

'Maybe, if he's working both sides.'

Viv's forehead creased with concern. 'You don't trust him.'

Their conversation was interrupted as Tommy pulled up next to them, dropping his horse into a walk for a few seconds to let them catch up.

'Should reach the pass by nightfall,' he said. 'I want to camp this side of it if you know a spot?'

Cam nodded. 'There's a place.'

Tommy looked between him and Viv, picking up on the mood. 'What's up with you two?'

'Cam's worried about Felix, after what happened back there.'

'With the Red Shirts? I can see that. Well, you brought him here. If you think we should kick him off the squad, that's your decision.'

Viv shook her head. 'I love you, darling, I really do, but you can be bloody blind sometimes. Do you really think Cam's just worried about the squad? I mean seriously, why did you think Felix was here?'

Tommy just looked confused. 'He's a scout, isn't he? I thought the point was that he knew the area.'

'Because Cam doesn't?'

'I thought you wanted his help,' Tommy said to Cam.

'Not so much his help as, well,' Cam smiled ruefully, 'his company, I guess.'

'Oh,' said Tommy, then after a moment he said it again. 'I didn't realise that you were together.'

'We're not, not really.'

'But you like him,' Viv said with a smile.

'I did. Now I'm not so sure.'

'Can we afford for you to be unsure about him?' said Tommy. 'If you don't trust him then maybe we shouldn't either.'

'You're not helping,' said Viv.

'No,' said Cam, 'he's right. If we can't trust him then we should send him away before we reach the army.'

'That leaves you a couple of weeks to decide.'

Cam looked over his shoulder. Felix was riding alone at the back of the line, forehead furrowed, eyes fixed on the pommel of his saddle.

'It'll be enough,' he said. 'One way or another, things are going to have to change.'

They reached the camp at dusk.

It was the same spot where Cam and Felix had stopped with Chloe, and the memories were unwelcome: the stream where Cam had washed the blood from Felix's body, the bank where he had tended his wounds, and the marks of the campfire where he had cradled Felix's head in his lap as he finally opened his eyes.

Felix's injuries had healed now, and the only mark he bore of the violence of Charlestown was his missing tooth. In light of his current suspicions, Cam couldn't help but wonder if that fight had even been real. But Felix had been so broken afterwards, and Richard was dead, wasn't he? Felix had killed him.

For Otho.

While Cam tried to avoid his ghosts, the camp fell into its familiar rhythm. Aaron chopped vegetables while Gul and Linh went foraging in the pines. Cam doubted they'd find much this high in the mountains, but they were bound to surprise him; they always did. Eveline was setting up a perimeter while Alistair and Adewale saw to the horses, and the rest of the squad were either helping the others or setting up their shelters for the night with Felix.

The only person sitting idle was Emmy. She had built the fire with consummate efficiency, but as soon as the flames caught she'd become transfixed. She sat there on the ground now, gazing into its depths just as she had been doing for the past hour. It was as though she'd never seen fire before.

Perhaps it had been a while.

When Cam approached he walked gently, taking care to step on as many twigs and dried leaves as he could, so she'd realise he was there. She still didn't look up from the flames.

'How are you doing?' he said as he lowered himself to the ground. It was still damp here from the previous night's showers, and Cam's heels left gouges in the earth as he stretched out his legs.

There was no response from Emmy, but he smiled at her anyway, because Viv had told him it might help if he put in some time. They'd been close once, him and the Queen. After Ed and Carrie had left, Emmy had been the best friend he'd had. He liked to think that she had felt the same way about him. If only he could remind her of the easiness they'd once shared.

'Do you remember that night in the bar back in London?' he said. 'You know, the one with Ed and Carrie, and all the vodka?'

Still no response.

'I think about that night a lot. Seems like whenever I sit down at a campfire, I either remember it or I remember Delphi.'

Emmy flinched a little at that, but she still said nothing.

'I've been searching, Ems. Every single day since then, I've been out here searching for you.'

'I've been right here,' she said.

'The whole time?'

'I don't know. I was out for a while. A long while, I guess. Viv told me how long it's been and that's…'

She combed her hair back from her temples then rested her elbows on her knees. It was a while before she moved again, as though someone had paused her there, head hanging and eyes unfocused. When she looked up, she looked straight at Cam.

'It's crazy,' she said. 'I don't recognise this world.'

'Neither do I, some days. A lot of things have changed, and I don't want to inundate you, but you must have questions. You can talk to me, Ems. You can ask me anything. You can tell me anything.'

She nodded to herself, but her attention had gone again, drifting away from the conversation to somewhere else. Cam wished he could see what she saw. He wished he knew what it was that made her close her eyes, crushing them shut as though she were blocking out the pain of her memories.

'Do you want to talk about it?' he asked.

'I want to go home, but I guess home isn't there anymore, right?'

Cam hesitated before answering, but he had to tell her the truth. She'd find out sooner or later anyway.

'No,' he said. 'It's gone. I'm sorry.'

'I just want to go home, Cam.'

Her face crumpled then as the tears came. Cam scooched closer and pulled her into his arms, but she felt like folded paper. She was angles and bones that felt lighter than they should, stiff with tension, and he didn't know how to hold her anymore. She didn't relax into his embrace.

'I want to go home to my family,' she said between breathless, silent sobs against his chest. 'I want to sit on my s-sofa, put on my pyjamas and drink a cup… of tea. That's the one thing… that's what got me through this, thinking of that… normality waiting at home. And now… it's gone. Cam, how do I…'

Her hands fisted in his shirt, and then she finally let her meagre weight fall into his arms, shaking as though the heat of the fire wasn't warming her limbs at all.

'I don't know, Ems,' he said. 'I can't tell you things will be okay, but I'll be here.'

'Twenty years,' she mumbled against his chest. 'That's how long Charles said.'

It had been more than twenty times that long since she'd been taken.

Initially, Cam had thought it was a blessing that she'd been mostly unconscious during that time, but it would bring problems of its own.

'I'm so sorry I didn't find you sooner.'

'No,' she said, sitting back and wiping the tears from her cheeks. They were still coming though, however much she tried to deny them. 'You found me. Thank you.'

'Emmy…' he said, moving to pull her back into his arms, but she waved him away as she smiled awkwardly through her tears.

'This isn't very queenly, is it?'

She had been working hard to make a good impression on the other Silver when she'd been taken. Apparently the instinct ran deep enough that it was still there, even after everything.

'Ems, you don't have to worry about that. Not with me, and not with them,' he said, tipping his head towards the shelters.

Only a few of the Invicti were still around, just Aaron and the ones who were building with Felix, but they were casting occasional glances towards where Emmy sat by the fire.

'Who is that?' she asked as she wiped her nose on her sleeve. Well, Cam's sleeve, because it was his shirt.

He turned to follow her line of sight, but he knew before he looked that she was talking about Felix. He was under the trees with Darius and Konrad, but Emmy knew both of the Silver well. She wouldn't have forgotten them.

'The man with the beard,' she prompted.

'Oh,' Cam said dismissively, 'he's been helping us with scouting the mountains. He lives around here.'

He didn't know why he'd trotted out the familiar lie. There had been a time when Emmy was the only person he would have wanted to talk to about Felix, but he judged that this wasn't the best moment to start complaining about his comparatively insignificant problems. That judgment was influenced by his argument with Felix that afternoon, and by the distance that still hung between him and Emmy, despite the minor breakthrough they'd just shared.

But there was something else making him cautious.

Emmy was speaking too carefully. She was still holding back, and her next words were spoken with strange calculation while she studied Cam's face for a reaction.

'Viv said Sol's waiting for us at Laila's city, the place we're heading to. Is that right?'

'Of course,' Cam said, trying to convince himself that it wasn't a lie. The King was waiting after all, he just hadn't exactly been alive when Cam had last seen him.

'And?' she said.

'And what?'

'And who else is waiting?' said Emmy, the lilt of her voice making it clear that she was angling for a particular answer.

She wasn't suspicious about Sol then, but who else would she want to know was waiting for her?

Oh.

There had only been one other.

'Ems, I'm sorry,' he said, taking her hand, 'but he's gone.' Emmy's forehead creased with pain, but Cam pressed on because she had a right to know. 'He was cured and then, well. I'm sorry, but Drew's gone.'

Her brows twitched for a tiny fraction of a second.

'Was that not who you were asking about?' Cam said, confused.

'No, I mean yes,' she said, wiping at her cheeks again, although they were now dry. 'It was. Thank you for telling me. And thank you for finding me. And I'm sorry, I'm just feeling a little overwhelmed right now.'

'You don't have to apologise.'

'I just… If you don't mind,' she said, her gaze swinging back over towards the shelters, 'I think I need a bit of time alone right now. Would that be alright?'

'Of course. I'll leave you to it. I'll see you at dinner?'

She nodded, but her eyes didn't move from the trees. She had gone again, her mind full while her empty body failed to warm by the fire.

Alistair went missing in the night. No one could say when or where he had gone because with a camp of sixteen no one kept track of other people's nighttime excursions unless the alarm was raised, and Alistair had been the one on watch. Cam found his tracks leading off to the northwest at dawn, in the direction of Charlestown, and roused the others. All except Felix, whom he didn't care to see, and Emmy, who could use the extra sleep.

'His horse is gone,' said Adewale, rushing back towards the fire. 'He's taken his kit too, and his weapons.'

'Bastard's been in my supplies,' said Aaron, rifling through the bags in which he kept their food. 'Potatoes, and those biscuits we picked up from the last caravan. Other bits and pieces too, I'm sure.'

'He wasn't taken then,' said Tommy. 'He left.'

'Towards Charlestown,' said Cam, 'where Laila's allies are. The trail went that way. It was a good few hours ago, I'd guess. If he was riding hard then he'll be there by now.'

Adewale had looked relieved to discover that his friend hadn't been kidnapped, but now a darker kind of grief had settled over his expression.

'Adewale?' said Tommy. 'Did you know anything about this?'

He shook his head.

'He promised me,' he said. 'He promised me that he had no part of Laila's plans. He *promised* me. After all the centuries of our friendship…'

Adewale hesitated for a moment, opening then closing his mouth as though he was uncertain whether or not to divulge what he knew.

'He would leave sometimes,' he went on eventually, 'for a day or so, before the Contamination. He liked to travel, he said, to see the places he had been before. He said it gave him the push he needed to carry on. Even when I asked him about it again after Laila's deceit was discovered, he swore to me he had no part of it.'

'And you think he lied?'

Adewale nodded sadly. 'He came back smelling of blood, though he took none with him.'

'Shit,' said Cam. 'He must have been using the caravans to travel up to Charlestown.'

'Spying for Laila,' said Adewale, looking very small for a man who was over six feet tall.

'He'll tell them we've found Emmy,' Cam said to Tommy. 'He'll tell them about the attack on the mountain, and about Lucas, and the army–'

'Oh god,' Viv said as she covered her mouth with her steepled fingers. 'My notebook. I copied Cam's report about the army into it, so we'd have a note of it for ourselves. Alistair asked if he could borrow it last night. To plan, he said. Oh god, I didn't realise…'

'But why would he want to know about the army?' said Darius. 'Unless Charlestown is planning to attack it, which would actually help us–'

'Why don't you tell us?' Cam said, his tone accusatory enough to raise eyebrows as the other Invicti turned to look at him. 'And while you're at it, why don't you tell us all why you were in Charlestown six years ago?'

'What? I wasn't.'

Darius seemed genuinely surprised, but Cam wasn't about to be taken in by that. He'd had enough of everyone's secrets, and he was going to get this one sorted out right here and now.

'Don't lie to me, Darius. Chloe told me.'

Gazes flicked between the two of them as the Invicti tried to gauge the significance of those last words, but Cam's eyes remained locked on Darius's. Still, Darius didn't flinch under the scrutiny.

'I'm not lying to you,' he said. 'I've never been to Charlestown, not since it became whatever it is now. This is the closest I've come since we last searched the coast for Emmy.'

'Then how do you explain Alex?'

He probably shouldn't have brought the boy into it, but Cam had almost forgotten that the others were there, watching the whole exchange. It had always been impossible for the Invicti to resist the call of drama, particularly when it involved their own, so he had expected some kind of reaction from them.

Just not the one he got.

'He's yours?' said Zita, and a flicker of disappointment crossed her face before she hid it away.

Darius looked at her briefly, then dropped his gaze as she met his eyes. There was shame in his expression as he wiped a hand down his face.

'I don't want to do this here,' he said.

'I think you'd better,' said Tommy. 'After last night, I'm not having any more surprises. Tell us what's going on.'

'Fine,' he said on a heavy exhalation. 'If you all really have to know. I came up this way a while ago, because I'd heard there were people living up in the mountains. And before you tell me off, Cam, you were away and weren't expected back for weeks, so I decided to check it out myself. Quietly, so if I did find something, you'd be the first person I told.'

'And?' said Tommy.

'And I found a little settlement, just a few dozen people living in the Czech hills, but no sign of Emmy. They did have one Silver with them, though.'

'Chloe,' Cam said, and Darius nodded.

'We'd been friends before the Fall and we sort of... reconnected.'

Naia's lip curled up in disgust. 'Jesus, Darius. After what she did to the Queen?'

Bartek looked between the two of them.

'What did she do?' he asked, because he hadn't been in London for the Fall. He hadn't lived through those first days like most of the others had.

'She betrayed Emmy,' Cam said, still staring at Darius. 'She was working with Benedict to kill her, and to kill the King.'

'Don't look at me like that,' Darius said. 'You're the one who saved her from Charlestown. She's changed, you saw that for yourself. It was a mistake. She's trying to make up for it.'

'As though you can ever make up for something like that,' said Naia.

'In our long lifetimes?' Darius shrugged. 'Why not?'

Naia took a breath to reply, and Cam could guess there would have been some choice words exchanged had they not been interrupted at that moment by Emmy.

'What's going on?' she said.

'Everyone back to work,' Tommy said to the Invicti. 'Pack it up, and get ready to move out fast. No time to lose. Cam, we'll talk later.'

They all dispersed then, leaving Cam and Emmy alone by the remains of the fire.

'Just a slight problem,' Cam said. 'One of the Invicti has deserted.'

The old Emmy would have been burning with curiosity. She would have insisted on being told every detail, then would have tried to solve the problem herself in a reckless scheme that would have saved the day, against all odds. The old Emmy would have wanted to storm into Charlestown and drag Alistair out by his hair.

But this wasn't the old Emmy. This Emmy just nodded vaguely and said, 'So we're going?'

'Yes. Do you need a hand with…'

But she was already walking away back to her shelter. Cam wasn't sure what he would have offered to help with anyway, because it wasn't as though she had anything to pack. He had just wanted to find an excuse to speak with her again.

They still didn't know what had happened in that place. They didn't know what Charles had done to her, and she wasn't saying.

All they knew was what Chloe had told Cam: the legend of the sleeping queen, and the awful suspicion that Charles might finally have taken what he wanted from her.

They followed the army's tracks for two days, but on the third there was something else in the air too. Adewale tracked it for a few hours until it led them to a different path, away from the streams that watered their horses, where a small pile of empty bottles was stacked in the hollow of a tree. Each of them was stained with blood.

'It's him,' Adewale pronounced after a couple of seconds.

'Then he's overtaken us,' said Tommy.

'How long ago?' Cam asked.

Adewale picked one of the bottles out of the hiding place, turning it back and forth, then sniffed the rim.

'A day at least,' he said.

'Then he'll be in the Blue by now,' said Cam. 'Shit. He'll be back with Laila.'

'Then we need to send a messenger back ourselves,' said Eveline. 'We can't just let him take that information back to her.'

'We've talked about this,' said Tommy.

They had, at some length. Viv had walked them through her notebook page by page as they tried to understand why it would be important enough for Alistair to steal. They already knew it contained the army formation, but that was of more use to the Invicti than it was to Laila's people. Konrad had suggested that might be the very reason why Alistair had taken it – to deprive the Invicti of it – but Lucas was already on the way to Lorelei with the original, so the gesture would have been pointless.

And anyway, why would Laila want to hamper the Invicti in their attempts to defend the Blue? She'd be shooting herself in the foot, particularly now that she'd been cured. She needed all the Silver she could find to fight for the preservation of her city.

Other information in the notebook was valuable too – Invicti names and ranks, with training notes and key dates – but it would have little meaning for anyone outside of their group, and it would give their enemies no advantage over them.

The most convincing argument so far was Naia's. She thought that Alistair had just been nosy, and had then forgotten to return the book before he left. It certainly made more sense to assume that it was Emmy's liberation rather than the liberation of Viv's notebook that had prompted Alistair's desertion.

After all, Emmy coming back was the last thing Laila wanted. She'd told Cam that herself. It would mean Sol waking up, which would ultimately mean a change in leadership for the Blue. Laila would want to know when that change was coming, so that she could prepare to defend her throne.

Cam could well believe that Alistair had gone ahead to warn Laila about Emmy, but it was too late to stop him now.

'Anyway,' Tommy went on, 'the point's moot because we don't have enough blood for a trip back to the Blue. So we do as we planned, and try to overtake the army within the next couple of weeks.'

When they mounted up again Viv rode ahead with Emmy, so Cam found himself at the back of the column with Felix. He shifted awkwardly in his saddle, because this was not where he wanted to be.

Sandor and Hades seemed delighted to be walking side by side again. If only things were as simple for Cam and Felix.

They still hadn't talked things out. Cam wasn't sure he wanted to hear Felix's explanation, because he suspected it would be the end of whatever they had shared. He had been using the excuse of Emmy's rehabilitation to avoid Felix. In truth, he was doing little more than just sitting with Emmy by the fire while the others bustled around them, but he hoped that eventually she might confide in him, and then it would all be worth it. In the meantime, at least it had encouraged Felix to keep his distance.

Until now, apparently.

'I'd like to talk,' said Felix. They were strong words coming from him, the master of one-word responses.

'I haven't changed my mind.'

'I know.'

Cam looked at Felix, waiting for him to speak, but nothing further appeared to be forthcoming. That left Cam struggling to grasp the purpose of the conversation.

'What are you expecting me to say? If you still won't tell me what's going on then I can't trust you, and if I can't trust you then the others can't trust you either, and you need to leave.'

Felix looked pained as he said, 'You want me to go?' and despite himself Cam wanted to take his words back.

He knew he was being manipulated, that was the worst thing. He could feel Felix pressing his buttons, but it didn't stop him from feeling exactly what Felix was trying to make him feel. He didn't have the defences to deal with it, not on top of Emmy and the army and everything else.

But he was lying to himself if he thought he wouldn't have rolled over for Felix anyway, like the faithful puppy everyone had always said he was. He was too far gone to stop himself from falling for the woodsman, however deceitful he was being right now.

Cam reined Hades in, pulling him to a halt. Felix stopped Sandor beside him, and Cam waited for the others to ride on. This was a conversation he'd prefer they didn't hear.

'Of course I don't bloody want you to go,' he said when the others were out of earshot. 'What I want is for you to tell me the truth. Why are you fighting this so hard? Why are you trying to play me instead of just talking to me?'

Felix reached out for Cam, taking his wrist in his hand to signal that old bond between them, but Cam shook him off.

'No,' he said, gritting the word out through a clenched jaw. 'Stop it. Stop trying to get around me and just talk to me, Felix. How hard is it to tell me what's going on?'

Felix let his hand drop to his side, and Cam saw uncertainty in his expression for the first time.

'I don't know what to do,' he whispered, and there was truth in the desperation pinching his eyes.

'About what?'

'There are things I should tell you, but it's not safe, and I don't want to lose you because of them.'

Cam shook his head and smiled sadly. 'You never had me.'

Then Felix's hand was reaching out for his again, and this time Cam let him take it, because he wanted to feel the roughness of his touch. He wanted Felix to stroke his fingers down his cheek again, like he had that night in the hut at the mountain lake, where everything had seemed bewilderingly perfect for just one night.

He didn't know how to get back to that place, not with so much left unresolved between them. It was as though he were grasping at thistledown floating in the air, trying to catch it so he could make a wish, but ending up with only a handful of nothing.

'This is just a beginning,' Felix said. 'It can't be the end.'

'It doesn't have to be.'

Felix nodded, resigned, but then they were interrupted by Eveline riding the rearguard. Cam never found out whether that nod had meant yes or no.

13

Julia was bringing up the rear for the hundredth time. She and the girl had been walking for days now, and she just seemed to fall farther and farther behind.

When Galatea – that was her name – had told Julia that she'd been sent to fetch her, Julia had thought that meant that they were only a little way from their destination, requiring perhaps a stroll through the woods, or a short trek up the hill from the water.

She'd been wrong. If humans were going to live out in the Red, they'd hardly do it right on the doorstep of the island where their former captors lived. That was obvious, in retrospect.

But she hadn't been prepared for this. They'd stopped only to sleep and eat, and the path seemed to get more steep and more treacherous with every step. Julia was working so hard to focus on her feet that she'd had very little attention to devote to worrying about where they were going or why.

Galatea was irritatingly close-lipped about their destination. She told Julia how far it was, but would say nothing about its nature or population, or anything about her own life. Questions about Livia and the Blue were met with silence, so Julia had stopped asking them. Instead, Galatea passed the time pointing out useful plants and singing songs that Julia only half recognised.

'Won't be long now,' Galatea said as the afternoon drew on. Her breathing was still completely steady, despite the gradient. 'Another few hours, I reckon, and we'll be there.'

The girl had barely broken a sweat, while Julia was drenched and panting. She still hadn't recovered fully from her injuries, and the exertion of her flight was taking its toll.

'Do you need to rest?' Galatea asked her.

'I need more water,' she said. She'd been able to refill her canteens a couple of times on the journey, but it had been early yesterday since they'd passed a stream and she was on her last few sips.

'Have mine,' Galatea said, passing her a bottle. 'We can't stop now until we get to the camp.'

'Why not?'

'It's not safe. The Were-People, you know.' It was a moniker she'd used before to describe the Weepers, an abbreviation of *Creatures Who Were People*, she'd explained. 'There are lots around the camp, so we stick to the trail until we're inside.'

'You mean they're out here now?'

They'd heard a few howls on their trip, but they'd not yet encountered any visible trace of them. The Weepers mostly howled at night, and Julia and Galatea were safely tied up in the trees by then. If the Weepers had been walking through the forest below them while they slept, they might not even have noticed.

'They'll be close,' said Galatea. 'They never go far from the camp.'

'So what do you do?'

Galatea sighed, as though this were a long-running argument. 'I take down the ones I can. Not everyone likes that, though, because some of the Were-People were *our* people, you know. Mostly, we just ignore them.'

'What? How can you ignore them when they're attacking you?'

'We're immune. You're not, though, so we'll have to be careful.'

Julia wiped her hair away from her forehead, where the sweat had stuck it.

'Immune?' she said.

'Yeah, they can't hurt us. Our blood hurts them, though. Kills them, actually. You'll be the same if you live out here long enough. Now come on, cause I'm not spending another night in a blood-sucking tree, and you look like you're ready to drop.'

She was indeed. The further Julia got from the Blue, the more she found herself thinking about the comfortable bed she'd left behind. It might have been soaked in blood, but at least she'd been able to get more than a couple of hours' rest a night in it.

Her mind went on an unwelcome journey after that, reminding her of all the things she would never have again, all the places she would never go again, and all the people she would never see again. It passed the time more quickly than she realised. Although she couldn't say her thoughts had been comforting, the emotional pain was at least a distraction from the physical pain in every part of her body.

When Galatea finally stopped walking, they were at the top of a hill. Julia had noticed the rise as they'd been trekking, because it was impossible to miss, but it had been difficult to judge its steepness under the cover of the trees. Now that she could look out and down from the hill's peak, Julia could see that it was more like a crag.

'Good, right?' said Galatea. 'We can see for miles from here. As far as the water on a clear day, with the glasses.'

Two more twists in the path took them to a plateau that was filled with trees and fenced around with wicked-looking spikes.

'Gala!' someone called from beyond the boundary. 'You're back. Is this her?'

'Who else would it be?' Galatea replied as she opened a gate in the fence that Julia hadn't noticed. 'Julia, this is Sabina. She likes to think she's in charge here.'

Sabina clipped Galatea around the ear in an affectionate way that reminded Julia of Livia. Sabina was younger, thirty at most, but she gave off that same air of authority. Julia suspected that liberties would only be tolerated when taken by Sabina's favourites.

'Come in, come in,' she said, ushering Julia inside. 'You poor thing. You look as though you could sleep for a week.'

Julia wondered at the hive of industry the open gate revealed. There were pots bubbling over fires, skins stretched out to tan in the sun, fruit growing up against the inside of the fences, and in amongst the bustle small children and goats chased between busy legs.

'What is this place?' she said.

'I like to think of it as a refuge,' Sabina said. 'We were forty-three here at last count, forty-four if you decide to stay. We're mostly women, and mostly runaways from the Blue like you, *puişor*, but there are some like Galatea here who were born and raised on this hill.'

'*Puişor*?' Julia whispered to Galatea as Sabina led them further into the refuge.

'It means *little cub*,' Galatea whispered back, 'but don't worry; she calls everyone that. You'll get used to being mothered after a while. You might never like it, but you'll get used to it.'

'This is where you'll be staying,' Sabina said as she stopped at the bottom of a tree. There was a small platform built into its branches about fifteen feet up, accessed by means of a rope ladder that hung from its edge.

Julia's heart sank. Seeing all the huts that crowded on the hill, she'd really been looking forward to sleeping on solid ground for once. Another night in the trees was the last thing she wanted.

'Don't panic,' said Galatea. 'I'll get you a hammock, and I promise you'll sleep like the dead.'

'I know it doesn't look like much,' said Sabina, 'but Gala's right, and you'll be safe up there. We can't have new arrivals like you sleeping on the ground, can we? Not until you're immune, if you decide that's what you want.'

'Of course she does,' said Galatea.

'And you're going to make everyone's decisions for them, now, are you? Go on and fetch her a hammock and some food. The girl must be exhausted.'

'What about me? I've been halfway across the damned continent to fetch her.'

'You're family. Guests come first. Now go on.' Sabina turned back to Julia with a smile and said, 'Right. Let's get you washed up.'

There was a spring a little way down the other side of the hill. Sabina helped Julia wash in the pool that had collected beneath it, using vinegar to strip the dirt and grease from her hair for the first time in weeks. She took out Julia's stitches too.

'This is why you left?' she said as she teased the threads from Julia's healing skin with nimble fingers.

'Part of why,' said Julia. 'I'd always wanted to leave, though. My parents left when I was a baby, so I had some idea that I might find them. But they're not here, are they?'

Sabina's sympathetic look finally extinguished Julia's hopes.

'I'm not sure why I thought that would be the easy bit,' she said.

'They left you behind? Their baby?'

'Yes.'

Sabina was silent for too long. Julia could hear nothing but the gentle splash of the spring and the scratching of the blade as it picked through the thread in her neck. It felt like an accusation, that silence, and Julia had the urge to rush to her parents' defence, as she always had.

Instead, she just said, 'I know.'

'I'm sorry, *puişor*. I just can't imagine it. No one here would do such a thing. If I were ever lucky enough to have a child, nothing would make me leave her behind in that place.'

'You were born there?'

'I was. I was a Candidate, but then I found out what that really meant, to be bound to one Noble for the rest of your life, and I ran.'

'He didn't try to fetch you back?' Julia said.

'He did. He must have cared for me a little, though, because when I explained how I felt he let me be. Told everyone I'd died, I think. For the best, probably. There,' she said, pulling out the last thread with a flourish. 'All done. Get yourself dried and into some clean clothes, and I'll see these ones washed for you. Gala should have made up your hammock by now, so you trot on ahead and I'll see you in the morning.'

'Thank you,' Julia said as she slipped into some fresh clothes from her pack. 'You've been very kind.'

Sabina smiled. 'Go on now. Food, sleep and you'll feel like a new woman tomorrow. You'll see.'

Sabina had been right, as Julia suspected she often was.

The hammock was bliss. It was a tough rope and canvas construction strung between two branches that protruded from the trunk of her tree at similar levels, but at right angles to one another. She'd had a moment of bottomless horror as she'd shifted from the canopy into the fabric, sure that it would tip or tear with her weight, but as soon as she was tied into it she'd felt instantly secure.

She'd been asleep in seconds, and when she woke Galatea was waiting at the bottom of the tree with her breakfast and her crossbow.

'So,' Galatea said abruptly, 'are you going to stay?'

'I don't know,' said Julia as she took the proffered bowl of grains from Galatea's hands, ignoring the crossbow. 'I haven't really had time to think about it.'

'Well, can we go shoot some things while you decide? I've been dying to have a go with this thing ever since we left the coast.'

'If you like.'

So that was how they spent the next few days. Galatea would meet Julia in the mornings, then they'd go and shoot at tree trunks just outside the camp. Julia was getting good at it by the third day, so good that between the two of them they managed to take down a couple of rabbits and a fat pheasant.

In the afternoons they'd go foraging in the woods – which seemed to be Galatea's job in the refuge – then bring their spoils home to be cooked up and shared out for dinner. Julia watched and listened as Galatea chatted happily about the types of plants and herbs they found, trying to learn all she could in preparation for the day she would leave this place.

Because she would be leaving. She knew that now, although she hadn't yet told Galatea or Sabina.

It wasn't that she wanted to go. The camp was a kind of paradise, leafier and messier than Lucas's rooftop, but still productive in the same way. It felt like a community that Julia could have been a part of, but there was somewhere else she needed to go first.

She'd overheard one of the older women talking about it, another settlement about three days' journey north, up in the mountains. They traded with Sabina's camp, and from what Julia could make out it sounded like the place was filled with humans from the Red and the Blue.

She had to go, just so she could be sure, just in case her parents had somehow ended up there. She had to leave, even if she ended up coming right back here.

There were things she needed to know first, though, things about the Weepers, and about the Contamination. She'd been thinking about it more and more over the past few days, because after a decent rest the connections that had eluded her in the heat and fury of her escape were starting to come into focus.

Contamination wasn't binary. It couldn't be, because there were the Weepers, who walked the contamination into the Blue, and the contaminated, in their fenced fields out in the Red, locked away from everyone they knew.

Julia had known one of each: Marcus and Tatiana. Two people both apparently carrying contaminated blood, but with very different results. Tatiana looked just like she always had done, whereas Marcus had been completely changed.

How was that possible? Did the contamination take time to develop into what Marcus had become? Or did it affect different people in different ways? Or perhaps there were two different types of contamination. That could explain it.

Their bloodied wrists were bothering Julia too, but they made a kind of sense if contamination developed over time. She could imagine the Nobles tying up the contaminated for their own protection, just in case they went the way of the Weepers. Maybe they'd start by binding them only at night, when the contaminated were asleep in their huts. Then maybe they woke up one day and just weren't themselves. Maybe they'd twist and turn in their restraints, maddened by the disease, heedless of the damage they caused themselves as the rope rubbed through the skin.

Maybe that's how the Weepers were made.

'How do you become immune to the Were-People?' Julia asked Galatea.

They were collecting mushrooms in the forest to go with the game they'd shot that morning, but Galatea had been quiet all afternoon. She wasn't singing or chatting about their task like she normally did, as though she had something on her mind.

'You're leaving, aren't you?' she said.

Julia stood up from her crouch so she could face Galatea.

'For the moment,' she said.

'You don't like it here?'

'No, it's not that. I like it a lot, enough that I'm planning on coming back. It's just that I heard about a place where my parents could have gone, and I need to see if I can find them.'

'Why? They abandoned you.'

This conversation was starting to sound horribly familiar. Julia had to shut it down before she remembered all the times Claudia had said the same thing to her.

'Look,' she said, 'I know it doesn't make sense, but it's something I have to do. I can't explain it. I just have to know. If you can tell me anything else about how I become immune, then that would help.'

Galatea stood for a moment, hands on hips as she considered, then she said, 'Give me your hand.'

Julia wiped it on her trousers to rub off the dirt, then held it out. Taking Julia's hand in her own, Galatea pricked both their index fingers with her paring knife then pressed them together quickly, transferring the blood between them.

'There,' she said. 'Now you're immune.'

Julia stared at her bleeding finger. 'That's it?'

'That's it.'

'Then why didn't you just do that in the first place?'

'Because Sabina's going to kill me for it,' said Galatea with a grin. 'You wait and see.'

She was right: Sabina was furious when they told her the next morning.

'Of all the high-handed—'

'Well, what would you have done?' said Galatea. 'Let her just go out there with the Were-People, so she'd turn into one of them? It's not like it matters. It's not like she's ever going back to the island.'

Sabina pointed a finger at Galatea, saying, 'I'll deal with you later,' then she turned to Julia. 'You know you can't go back there now? If you do, then they'll find out about it, and they'll kill you for it, *puişor*.'

Julia was confused.

'For being immune to the Were-People?'

Sabina cut her eyes sideways to Galatea, her cheeks pinking with rage. 'You didn't tell her, did you?'

Galatea shrugged. 'It didn't matter.'

'This is why it should have been her decision, Gala, not yours. You weren't raised there. It'll matter to her.'

'What will?' Julia asked. She knew she wasn't going to like the answer when Sabina took her hands and cradled them in her own.

'*Puişor*, you're contaminated now. That's what it means to be immune.'

Julia felt like her legs were going to collapse out from under her.

'You mean I'm going to turn into one of them?' she whispered, looking at Galatea in disbelief. 'You mean I'm going to become a... a Were-Person?'

'No!' Galatea said, apparently horrified at the suggestion. 'Of course not!'

'It just means that you can't go back to the Nobles,' said Sabina. 'You're safe from the Were-People, and you can never turn into one of them now, but you'll never go back to the Blue either. They won't drink the blood of the immune, the contaminated.'

Julia nodded, thinking fast.

'That's fine,' she said. 'It's for the best.'

And she knew that it was. She knew that she wasn't going back to the Blue. She knew that being immune to the Weepers was worth giving up her life with the Nobles, but her heart didn't know it. It constricted in her chest as she thought of what it had felt like to have Lucas's mouth on her skin, pulling the blood from her veins.

She'd never feel that again. She'd probably never even see him again. She'd resigned herself to that, but it didn't mean that she'd been ready to lose all hope of ever feeling that pull of desperate connection again.

'Are you alright?' Sabina asked.

'Yes,' Julia said, faking a smile. 'I'm fine. I'm just thinking about the journey. I need to get started, really.'

'If you're sure you want to go.'

'I do.'

'Well, then. We can give you some supplies to help you on your way: food, water, and a hammock if you'd like one.'

'Yes, please,' Julia said, answering without thinking.

'Well, then,' Sabina sighed. 'Let's get you packed up and ready, and then maybe you'll come back to us in a week or so?'

Julia nodded, her counterfeit smile still in place. Sabina didn't seem to notice, but Galatea had spent enough time with Julia to know that the expression was odd.

'Is something wrong?' she whispered. 'Did I do the wrong thing?'

'No, it's fine. Really. I just hadn't realised my blood would be contaminated, that's all.'

'But that's a good thing, yes?' Galatea said, her eyes on the scar at Julia's throat. 'Now that your blood's contaminated, none of the

Nobles'll want to feed from you. You're safe from them and from the Were-People, so it's win-win. Unless, I mean, you weren't intending to go back there, were you?'

'Don't worry,' Julia said. 'I've said my goodbyes.'

But of course she hadn't. Lucas had never given her the chance.

Julia was only two days out of the camp when he found her.

It was getting towards dusk, and she had just stopped to search the treetops for an appropriate place to spend the night when she heard a noise from the other side of the copse. At first she thought Galatea had followed her, because the noise sounded like singing, but the tone was too low for her new friend.

It was a man's voice, rich and silky, soft and warm, and close now as it passed behind the trees.

'*My love she told me she was true, she'd always love me through and through,*' it sang. '*And when we died and we were damned, we'd fall together hand in hand. Now to have and ever hold, bound in silver, sealed in gold.*'

She'd heard the song before, back in the Blue. She knew the words too, because they were part of a fairytale Lucas had once told her. He'd sung them to her on the rooftop while they'd worked together, chopping vegetables side by side.

She knew that song.

She knew that voice.

She pulled her pack tight over her shoulders and ran, the wind catching her short cloak as she chased the song through the trees, pushing through undergrowth while brambles dragged at her boots and trousers until finally she could see the figure weaving along the path away from her.

She should have been more cautious. It was dark in the shade of the woods, and the strange acoustics of the trees distorted sound, rendering voices unrecognisable. She knew all of this, just as she knew that she couldn't be sure that it was him, and yet she was. She was already tasting sugar and mint on her tongue while he was nothing more than a darker shadow in the fast-approaching night.

'Lucas!' she called.

The figure turned, and for a long moment Julia thought she had made a terrible mistake. She stopped where she stood, her hand on the hilt of her knife, because now that she could see him from the front the figure's shoulders were wider than she remembered

Lucas's being, and his stance was different. There was muscle there that Lucas had never had, and the figure looked more poised. In fact, he looked downright dangerous.

This wasn't a boy of twenty. The figure she was looking at was a full-grown man.

She was already turning to run back the way she had come when he called out to her.

'Julia?'

She stopped. Everything stopped as the figure pulled his hood down to reveal the face that Julia knew so well. His skin was darker, and his arms were thicker, but the dark eyes and darker looks still belonged to the Lucas she'd known.

'It is you,' she said, smiling as she pulled her own hood away from her messy braids.

She'd hoped that he might have been pleased to see her too, but in that moment he just looked horrified. His eyes narrowed as he started striding towards her, and it took her a second to realise that his anger wasn't directed at her exactly, but instead at the marks that now decorated her cheek and neck.

'What happened?' he asked, stroking his fingers across the scar from which Sabina had removed her stitches, but his eyes had found the writing on her cheek before she could answer him.

The anger in his expression turned to fury.

'Why is Rufus's name painted on your cheek?' He bit the words out as though they burned his tongue.

His accusatory look set off the resentment that Julia had nursed throughout her flight. She couldn't have held her next words back even if she had wanted to.

'Because you left,' she said, punching him in the chest. 'Because you left me behind in a city of fighting Nobles, and when the dust settled Rufus made sure I was allocated to him. He bled me out, Lucas. I nearly *died*, because Rufus wanted you to react exactly how you're reacting now. You left me behind and so he took me, because there was no one there to stop him.'

Lucas looked more than a little taken aback. He probably hadn't expected such a barrage from his former Attendant, but a lot had changed since he'd left the Blue. Julia was no longer the semi-deferential girl she'd once been.

In the Red, no one was her master.

To Lucas's credit, he recovered quickly.

'I'm sorry,' he said. 'I didn't want to leave, and I was going to tell them no, but I wasn't given a choice. By the time I found out that it had been Lorelei who had wanted me to leave, not the rest of the Invicti, I was already on the other side of the continent. After that, I did everything I could to come back to you as quickly as possible. I was stupid, and I'm so sorry. Please forgive me.'

Julia was still angry, but she nodded her grudging forgiveness anyway, because what more could she really ask for in an apology?

'You're still wearing my silver,' he said with a smile, reaching out to stroke her skin. He must have found the scars in her earlobe then, because his mouth turned down into a frown.

'Rufus liked your silver in my ear about as much as you like his name on my cheek,' she said. 'He ripped it out. Claudia sewed it back in.'

'I'll kill him,' Lucas said. 'I'll kill him for all of this. He shouldn't have touched you anyway when you were wearing my silver, but to take you as his Attendant? To hurt you? I'll kill the bastard.'

'No, you won't,' said Julia, suddenly feeling very tired, because this was why she'd left the city in the first place. 'He's the Empress's son, and the Blue has changed while you've been away.'

'Not as much as it's about to change,' said Lucas, his face lighting unexpectedly with the excitement of sharing a secret. 'It's all true, you know, everything I told you about the King. We found the Queen, and when the Invicti bring her back to the Blue in a few weeks' time the King will wake up. Then things in the Blue will *really* change.'

'He's already awake,' she said.

Lucas's face fell. 'What?'

'He's the one who saved me when the Nobles fought after the Contamination. He helped me escape too, so I could get away into the Red. I'll tell you all about it if you like, but look,' she said, conscious of the encroaching dark, 'I was about to find a comfortable tree to sleep in for the night. Shall we try this one?'

Lucas seemed to see her for the first time then. He took in her outfit, the knives strapped to her thigh and the crossbow hanging from the belt that held her short cloak closed around her waist. He looked confused, as though he were looking at a stranger.

Julia sympathised.

Lucas seemed ten years older to her, and it had barely been a month. So much had changed that she didn't know how they fit together anymore. She'd been so sure of him back in the Blue, back when he'd been the Noble who'd escaped into his garden and she'd been his reluctant Attendant, but out here in the Red they were different people.

Julia had imagined that when they saw each other again there might be kisses. She'd thought that they would at least want to hold each other, but they and their relationship were now made from different shapes. She could see it in the way they kept the air between them. With the exception of when Lucas had examined her wounds, they hadn't yet touched at all.

Maybe that was for the best, given that her blood would now be distasteful to him.

They needed to get to know one another again, she supposed.

'A lot's changed, hasn't it?' he said.

She smiled as she hauled herself up into the nearest tree and said, 'Mostly for the better, I think.'

He followed her up into the branches, and it only took ten minutes or so for them to secure Julia's borrowed hammock in the canopy. They would have to curl up to fit in it together, but once Lucas had hung up his cloak and pack in the tree next to Julia's, that started to seem like a more attractive proposition. Without his cloak, he was magnificent.

She let him climb in first, then shuffled herself over from the branch into the canvas, rolling into his side with a soft thud.

Everything about him was familiar in the darkness. His shape might have changed, but he still smelled the same, his skin felt the same, and the rhythm of his breathing seemed to regulate her own.

'Great view,' he said.

'It's better than sleeping on the ground.'

'Do you remember that night on the roof?'

'Which one?' she said. 'There were a lot.'

But she knew which night he meant: the night of the Nomination, when they'd watched the stars together with easy intimacy and easy kisses. Maybe he had only mentioned it to remind her of what they'd had then, and what they could have now, but she needed to tell him about the contamination before she would let him hold her like that again.

Instead, she remembered the conversation they'd shared later that same night, when they'd wondered aloud whether they'd been deceived about the Red.

'There are other humans who live out here,' she said. 'Did you know?'

'I know.'

'So we were right, after all. The contamination isn't what we think it is. Humans are perfectly safe out here, as long as they avoid the Weepers.'

'That's what I've heard,' Lucas said, though his words sounded uncertain.

'So there's no reason for us ever to go back to the Blue.'

Lucas turned his head towards Julia, though she couldn't see his expression in the darkness.

'No,' he said, 'we're going back.'

'To Rufus? Please tell me you're joking.'

'I'm serious, Julia. We have to go back. There's going to be a battle, and I need to be there.'

'You may need to be, but I don't.'

'Then what about Claudia and the others? Aren't you going to go back for them?'

Claudia.

Julia knew that if her friend was in danger she would force her way back to the city without a second thought, but she couldn't even consider it right now. She'd escaped the Blue, crossed the sea and trekked through miles and miles of forest, only to have the incredible good fortune to run into Lucas. The last thing she wanted was for him drag her right back to where she'd started.

The monsters were waiting for her there.

But she didn't want to sour their reunion with those thoughts, so instead of replying to Lucas she just changed the subject.

She would enjoy tonight, so close to his arms without committing to them, then she'd think about everything else in the morning. Tonight, she could pretend she was staying in the trees forever.

14

Alistair's desertion had soured the mood in the camp.

Aaron was even grouchier than usual, Bartek had altogether given up on words of more than one syllable, and Konrad hadn't teased Darius about Chloe for days in a row.

Zita probably had something to do with that last one. Everyone had been caught off guard by her secret relationship with Darius, but no one was asking questions. Instead, they were treading on eggshells around her, because she had a tendency to lash out when she was unhappy. No one wanted a broken nose when they had no blood available to help them heal up afterwards.

But the revelations of the previous week had hit Adewale the hardest. His jovial nature had disappeared beneath a fog of grief. Eyes that normally twinkled with playful mischief now twinkled with unshed tears instead, and he rose from the campfire most mornings looking as though he hadn't slept a wink.

Cam found himself similarly afflicted.

He still didn't know what to do about Felix. He lay awake staring at the stars through the leaves, trying to push away the memories of Felix's hand in his own, and of the joyful kick in his stomach as their lips had met.

The worst thing was that Cam could go to him if he wanted. Felix still slept closer to him than he did to anyone else, although he moved his blanket away from the fire these days, but it would only take a couple of crawled steps to put their hands together, palm to pulse. Three seconds, or maybe as little as two, and Cam could have been wrapped in the green nutmeg scent of him, nuzzling into his throat.

That proximity was what tormented him, because he couldn't forget the reasons why he shouldn't take Felix in his arms. He couldn't stop himself from remembering why he should be sending the woodsman away.

Because in all those long days, Felix had said nothing that Cam hadn't heard already.

He would have to send him away.

Tomorrow, though. He'd do it tomorrow.

In the meantime, Cam tried to focus on his main problem: Emmy. They were already well into Slovakia, and she still hadn't said a word about what had happened inside the mountain. He was so anxious about her that he kept catching himself grinding his teeth.

She wouldn't open up to him. He didn't know how to make her, or even if he should, but he was desperate to do something.

They needed her to be more than the broken thing she was now.

After so many centuries without Sol, the Silver needed him back, and they couldn't wake him up without Emmy.

Well, that was why the Invicti needed her, but Cam's own reason was a little different.

He had spent centuries searching for her. He'd spent half a millennium looking for Emmy while the world changed around him, fixating on the past while the future became the present. That had to have been worth something. This heartbreak he was feeling now had to be worth something, because otherwise he wasn't sure how he would go on.

After waking at dawn from yet another night of poor sleep, Cam's patience was paper thin. When he and Emmy were left at the fire together after breakfast, she evaded yet another question, and Cam snapped. Between her and Felix, he'd had enough of circumlocution.

'I wish you'd talk to me,' he said, running his fingers back through his hair. 'It's impossible to navigate this situation without knowing what I'm dealing with. I don't know how to do this, Ems. I don't know what to say to you. I don't know how to show you that you can trust me, just like you always could.'

Emmy smiled at him with tired eyes.

'Do you remember the first time we met?' she said.

It had been during the Revelation in London, when the Silver had been trying to gather everyone into safe houses away from the Weepers. But Emmy had never been very good at doing what she was told, and she hadn't been willing to trust the Silver, so she'd tried to evade them and go it alone. They'd tracked her down, though, Cam and Drew. Cam had hidden the Silver in his eyes, passing himself off for human, and had delivered her straight to Drew.

Gods, but she'd been angry at that, kicking and screaming and fighting every step of the way until Drew had to knock her out just to stop her from committing suicide by Weeper rather than letting him save her.

Cam smiled at the memory. She had always been so stubborn.

'You never let me forget that,' he said. 'You never let me lie to you again either.'

'You promised you wouldn't.'

'And I haven't, Ems.'

She picked at the crackers that were the remains of her breakfast. Cam had already demolished his, and he was still hungry. Emmy saw him watching her play with the water biscuits and offered him one, but he waved it away.

'You need them,' he said. 'We're not going until you've finished them all, so eat up.'

'Fine,' she said as she started to nibble at them unenthusiastically. 'The point is that when we met, you weren't who I thought you were.'

'I know.'

She looked over towards the rest of the squad. They'd been camping in the shell of an old concrete building, which was convenient for sheltering from the drizzle, but it was half an hour's walk back to the last water source. Most of the squad had taken the horses and the canteens back in that direction, leaving just a few behind to scout, guard and clear away the remnants of their camp. The only people still in the vicinity were Aaron, who was cleaning his pots, Gul and Linh, who were picking through the spoils of their latest foraging excursion, and Felix, who was sitting on a tree stump at the edge of the camp while he whittled away at something with his knife.

'Sometimes you don't know people,' she said as her eyes alighted on Felix.

Cam followed her gaze.

'What are you saying?'

She tucked her hair behind her ear and gave Cam that look again, the one that told him she was scrutinising his expression in case he gave something away.

'I've got nothing to hide from you, Ems,' he said. 'Whatever it is you're trying to get out of me, just ask and I'll tell you.'

'Alright. How well do you know him?'

'You mean Felix?'

'There's something up with you two.'

Cam shifted his legs around. This conversation wasn't going the way he had expected it would.

'We met a couple of months ago,' he said.

'And?'

'And I thought something was going to happen between us. It looks like maybe it's not anymore.'

'Because…' Emmy prompted.

Cam looked over at Felix, who was still engrossed in his work.

'I like him,' he said. 'I really do, but he's keeping things from me. I just don't think it's going to work.'

Emmy nodded to herself as she chewed on the last of her crackers.

'I think that's for the best,' she said.

'Oh?'

'Thing is, I recognise him, Cam. I've seen him inside the complex.'

'Well, yeah, he was there when we got you out.'

'No. Before that. Way before that. Decades before that, if what everyone's been telling me is true.'

She'd told Viv that she'd woken up briefly when they'd moved her from Charlestown to the mountain, and according to Chloe's information that had indeed been decades ago.

But Felix was only twenty.

'That's not possible,' said Cam, shaking his head to dismiss the doubt. 'He's human.'

'Yes, but has he always been?'

Cam looked back over to where Felix sat, just off the path, as though he were keeping watch. His eyes weren't on the forest anymore though; they locked with Cam's at the moment when his thoughts finally started to crystallise.

Felix always had seemed older than his years. Then there were all the other clues Cam had missed: Silver oaths they had sworn to each other, Felix's implicit understanding of Silver culture, his knowledge of the cure, his acquaintance with Richard and the Red Shirt at the mountain.

There was a reason that Felix understood what it was to be Silver, and it had been glaring Cam in the face this whole time.

He knew the Silver because he had been one of them.

And he'd been working with Charles.

Cam told Tommy first. He and Viv agreed – despite Cam's protests – that they couldn't send Felix away now, not with all he knew about the Invicti. They also agreed that Cam shouldn't be the one to question him, but that was the one point on which Cam wouldn't be challenged.

He had earned the truth, and he wanted to hear it straight from Felix's lips.

Cam walked with purpose as he approached the stump where the woodsman still sat. He had expected denials, but Felix had already put down his whittling and set his knife on the ground, just far enough away that it was out of his reach. He didn't move when Cam stooped to retrieve it from amongst the leaves.

'She remembers me, doesn't she?' Felix said. 'I thought she'd recognised me that first day.'

'She had.'

Cam leaned against the tree trunk opposite and crossed his arms over his chest. He'd been angry when he'd walked over here, but Felix's opener had defused him so all he could feel now was the hurt.

First Carmen, then Alistair, and now Felix. He wasn't sure how much more betrayal he could take.

'If you knew we were going to find out,' he said, 'then why didn't you just run while you had the chance?'

'Where to? There's nowhere else.'

Felix shrugged, and the familiar gesture pulled at Cam's memories. He closed his eyes against it, trying to control his pain, but the words that were burning in his stomach still found their way out.

'You said you'd never betray me.'

'And I never would,' Felix said, leaning towards Cam.

'But you have. You were Silver, and you never told me. You were working with Charles, and you never told me. You're working with the very people who captured and kept my friend and queen from me, for centuries, and you never bloody told me, Felix. How is that not a betrayal?'

'Because I didn't know what she was to you. I didn't even know you, Cam. I was just trying to save Otho, and they told me they could get him out of Charlestown if I spied for them.'

'On me? You were spying on me? All that time we spent together–'

'Not on you,' Felix interrupted. 'On the caravans to start with, so they'd know where to find them, then after I met you they told me to keep you away from the mountains, but by then we'd found Otho and then things between us… Well, things had changed.'

Cam wanted to cry. He could feel the tightness in the back of his throat as he tried to keep a lid on his emotions, but his next words came out more ragged than he would have liked.

'You were trying to keep me away from Emmy?' he said.

'No, that was just what they wanted me to do,' Felix said, but Cam barely heard the words. Then Felix was standing in front of him, demanding his attention.

'Cam, I'm begging you: think back. Did I ever do anything except help you? I didn't know the mountains well enough to find the place again as a human, but I went with you when we found the stone door. I helped you get back to your island, and everything I've done since then has been to keep you safe and slow the army down. I swear to you, I'm not working with them. I made an oath to you, and I took it seriously.'

'You've lied to me.'

'Because I didn't know that I could trust you at the start, any more than you could trust me, and then it was too late to change my story.'

'But I still can't trust you now. We can't let you leave, knowing what you do about us.'

Felix crossed his arms, mirroring Cam's stance.

'Good,' he said, 'because I don't want to go.'

'I can't let you out of my sight.'

'Then don't,' Felix said, taking a step closer. 'I won't fight you.'

The words were laden with a promise that was completely inappropriate in the circumstances, and yet so appealing that Cam could feel his body responding despite himself. His arms uncrossed themselves and were on the verge of reaching out for Felix when he managed to catch them back.

'Gah,' Cam said, clutching at his hair. 'Why are you doing this? Why are you still trying to manipulate me? Do you really think that it's going to work, that you can somehow distract me with your… your manly wiles?'

'Manly wiles?' Felix said as his mouth quirked up into a tiny smile. He was laughing at Cam, again. Now. At a time like this.

'What do you want from me?' Cam said, dropping his hands in exasperation.

Felix picked them up in his own. He was close enough that Cam was already drowning in the cut-grass spice of his scent. After so long without it, he could barely suppress his groan.

'Why are you doing this?' he said again, slumping back against the tree.

'I'm not trying to manipulate you,' Felix said, squeezing Cam's hands. 'This is just about you and me. I'm sorry I lied, and I'm sorry I didn't switch sides sooner, but I've been on your side for weeks, and that isn't going to change.'

'Since when?' Cam asked. 'When did you switch?'

Because he had to know.

'Step by step,' Felix said, stepping closer as he spoke. 'The oath, the hot springs, the shore by your island, then the mountain lake. By then, I think.'

He was so close now that Cam would only have needed to tilt his forehead down to meet Felix's, but he didn't, because Felix was already leaning in, his cheek against Cam's, his lips at his ear.

'*Ich liebe dich*,' he whispered.

The bottom dropped out of Cam's world. He pulled away as far as the tree at his back would allow.

'What did you say?'

Felix looked down at their hands for a moment before he met Cam's eyes again, shyly this time.

'I love you,' he said. 'Why, what did you think this was about?'

'You don't mean that,' Cam said, because it had been so long since anyone had said those words to him and meant them in *that* way, and because he'd never expected to hear them now, when he was supposed to be questioning a traitor.

But Felix wasn't done yet.

'I'm not as young as I look, Cam. I've lived enough to know that if I were still an Izcacus, as you say, then I'd have silvered for you weeks ago.'

The concept was too big for Cam to handle.

'You can't know that,' he said.

'I can. I do.'

'Felix, if you're playing me–'

'I'm not,' he said. 'I love you. How could I be on any other side?'

Cam stared into the ice blue of Felix's eyes, trying to pick out the lie, but there was nothing. His eye contact was steady and his body language was open. His heart was racing, but then so was Cam's. That's what being close to Felix did to him.

But Cam still couldn't let himself believe it.

He said, 'But we haven't even…' then trailed off as he grasped for a delicate way to phrase it.

Felix grinned.

'Not yet,' he said, then he was leaning in while his fingers tangled in Cam's hair.

Cam gave up the struggle, because his heart wasn't in it. His heart was with Felix, and it wanted to stay there. He closed the last few inches between them and caught Felix's lips with his own, sliding his palms around Felix's hips to draw him close. Felix's other hand was already on Cam's chest, pushing him back against the tree trunk until he was trapped there between the woodsman and the woods.

'Shit,' he breathed. 'You do know that I'm supposed to be interrogating you?'

'I'll say anything you want,' Felix murmured against his mouth.

Cam moaned quietly. 'Gods, *Ich will dich.*'

'*Dann küss mich, du Narr.*'

Felix dragged Cam's lips back down to his own, and then the next few minutes were something of a blur. Cam was lost in nutmeg and warmth and the press of Felix's body and his mouth and the overwhelming sensation that this was *right*, so right that he didn't ever want it to stop, because then he'd have to think about what had led them to this point and it might all fall apart. He might never have relinquished Felix's kisses had they not been interrupted by a throat clearing from worryingly close by.

'When you said you were going to force the truth out of him,' said Viv, 'I didn't realise this was what you had in mind.'

'Shit,' Cam muttered, pushing away from Felix as he tried in vain to straighten his clothes.

Felix was trying not to smile, but as soon as he caught Cam's eye the corner of his mouth started twitching up, and Cam found himself mirroring his expression.

'Jesus Christ,' Viv laughed, 'you two are like naughty schoolboys. Go on, Cam, bugger off. I'll talk to Felix.'

Accepting that he'd clearly lost all objectivity, Cam handed his prisoner over to Viv and slunk away to the fire. When he looked back, Felix was grinning after him.

'He was sending carrier pigeons, if you can believe that,' said Viv as she joined Cam and Tommy by the edge of the tumbledown building that housed their camp. 'He said the army had wanted to cross paths with us, and he'd lied about our position to keep them waiting at the mountains for as long as he could. Apparently they offered him a way to turn Silver again using Emmy's blood, but since Charles was still human himself I don't think they ever found one.'

They looked back at Felix, still in the same place Cam had left him that morning. Viv had been questioning him for a while now, but he hadn't once tried to run.

'You believe him?' Tommy asked.

'I don't know when he switched sides,' Viv said, her eyes on Cam's, 'but I do believe he's with us now, and I believe we have him to thank for delaying the army.'

Cam shook his head. It wasn't that he didn't trust Viv's assessment, it was just that he didn't know what to believe anymore. He'd been picking over every interaction he'd ever had with Felix, trying to fit the pieces into this new knowledge. So many things made more sense now, and so many things still bewildered him.

Like Felix's feelings for him, enthusiastically declared that morning. He found himself shivering pleasantly at the memory and had to crush it into the back of his mind to drag himself into the present.

Viv reached over and took his hand.

'You remember in the mountain complex when we went in to get Emmy?' she said, her voice pitched soft. 'He walked out to those Red Shirts, playing nice to get close, then he took them down. He betrayed them, Cam, not you.'

'And do you remember how they were waiting for us,' said Cam, 'right inside the cave entrance, as though someone had tipped them off? I found Felix in the woods that morning talking to one of them.'

He had expected surprise, but Viv was nodding along.

'He told me that, but he told me something else too, another reason why he's been keeping us in the dark. It also might explain why Eveline left to go scouting this morning, and why she still isn't back.'

There was a beat of silence while Viv waited for them to connect the dots.

'Oh gods,' Cam said, dropping his face into his hands, 'not another one.'

'Bloody hell,' said Tommy. His cheeks were white with the shock of it.

Viv nodded.

'She's been using her position as rearguard to relay messages back to her allies, who've been trailing us since we left the city. He thinks we're probably catching up with the army, which would explain why Eveline has left now.'

'Then that's some good news, at least,' said Tommy.

Viv grimaced. 'It gets worse, I'm afraid. Eveline's not alone. She's been working with Lorelei.'

'Lorelei?' Cam whispered as he watched the blood rushing back into Tommy's face.

'What?!' the Secundus yelled.

His roar was loud enough to attract the attention of the other Invicti by the fire, who came running out to see what the fuss was about. Viv told them, and Cam watched their faces change one by one: anger, confusion, and a decent dose of panic.

Lorelei was the Tertius, Tommy's second-in-command, and they'd left her in charge of defending the Blue. If she was a traitor, then this was the end of the city. They would have lost before they'd even reached the island, because the army wouldn't need their siege weapons. Lorelei would just open the gates and let them in.

If there had ever been a time when they needed the King, that time was now.

'Right,' Tommy said. 'From now on, no one goes anywhere alone, and I mean anywhere. Watches are in pairs, riders go in pairs, everything happens in pairs. Aaron and Bartek, Darius and Linh, Zita and Konrad, Naia and Gul, me with Adewale, Viv with the Queen, and Cam with Felix. No one lets their buddy out of their sight, even for a second. Tie your hands together while you sleep if you have to, but I'm not having this happen again. No one else leaves. Are we clear?'

A round of obedient noises followed, but Cam couldn't stop his eyes from meandering back to where Felix sat beneath the tree.

It made sense for Cam to be the one to keep an eye on him, but it was a kind of cruel torture when his body kept betraying him and his mind still wasn't sure what to believe.

Cam sat with Emmy by the fire that night, partly because it had become their routine, and partly because Viv was the only one who would swap pairs with him for a short while. He hadn't been able to face Felix yet, not after what had happened that afternoon, so Viv had taken him scouting to look for the army. It had been hours now, and Cam was starting to get worried.

Not yet worried enough to go looking, but worried enough that as Emmy finally opened up to him, his eyes were roaming between the darkening shadows beneath the trees, looking for their return.

'He wanted my blood,' she was saying. 'They did tests, then took more, then did it again, over and over. After a while, they just stopped replacing the blood, and I went to sleep. That was about twenty years ago, as far as I can work out.'

'Testing for what?'

'Trying to find a way to create immunity to the cure.'

Cam remembered what Laila had told him that night in the palace, about how Emmy had gone into the water at Piraeus with contaminated blood in her eyes and her mouth, but that she'd come out still Silver.

'It's true then?' he said. 'You really are immune?'

'That's what Charles told me. The tests all said the same, but he couldn't figure out how to pass my immunity on to other people. That's what he wanted, so he could be Silver again.'

'So that's what this was all about?'

'Well, not to start with,' she said, staring into the flames. 'In the beginning, I think he just wanted what he'd always wanted: power, control, influence. I don't know what he was planning to do with me back then, whether he wanted to ransom me, or use me to kill Sol, or what, but he put me under almost the moment he took me.'

Cam had his suspicions. If he were Charles and he'd wanted to take Sol out of the picture without being cast as the villain, then using Emmy to send the King to sleep seemed like a good solution. But what then? Had Laila acted before Charles could make his move?

'I think that was the longest time,' she went on. 'I think that was where the centuries went.'

She threw a twig into the fire and watched it catch.

'Centuries,' she said. 'Jesus.'

'What happened after that?' Cam asked, keen to keep her talking.

'He woke me up and I was somewhere new. Not the mountain yet, somewhere else. He was angry about it, too, and he was human. Something had happened, I don't know what. He didn't say. Then the tests started, and then… Shit,' she said, blinking back tears. 'Things got complicated then.'

'How?'

Emmy just shook her head and said, 'Not yet. I can't talk about that yet.'

'Ems, did he… do something to you?'

She was still shaking her head, but not to deny it.

'I can't tell you, Cam. It's not that I don't trust *you*, it's just that I can't talk about it, and with everything that's happened over the past few days–'

'It's fine, Ems. You don't have to tell me. You can talk to me about it when you're ready.'

She wiped her cheeks then looked up at him. He'd expected to see pain in her eyes, but the only thing they held in that moment was pure vitriol.

'I saw the way you looked at me when I killed him,' she said, 'but he deserved it, Cam. He deserved every single bit of pain. If I could kill him a hundred more times then I would, and I still wouldn't have hurt him like he hurt me.'

The ferocity in her expression unnerved him.

'Ems…' he said, but she wasn't done yet.

'He doesn't deserve pity. You don't know what he did to me. He took everything away from me. *Everything.* You know what makes me smile these days, Cam? I remember my fingers closing over his windpipe, pinching it shut then ripping it open. My fist in his flesh is what brings me joy, and isn't that sick? That's what he's done to me. He made me into that, because he left me with nothing but the fantasy of wrapping my hands around his throat and squeezing.'

There was a terrifying moment in which everything seemed to stop. All Cam could see was his friend in front of him, but something else was living in her, something feral.

Then just as suddenly she was crying again, with so much anguish that Cam could feel her keening scraping at his insides. He had to pull her into his arms so she could muffle her sobs against his shoulder.

She clung on so tight.

'I feel like a monster,' she whispered.

'But you're not. You know you're not, and so do I.'

'I feel like I'm losing my mind.'

'Then we'll find it together. I've got you, Ems,' he said, rubbing her back. 'I've always got you.'

'I missed you so much.'

He scooped her into his lap then and wrapped her in his arms, kissing her cheek, stroking her hair and rocking her back and forth as she wept against his shirt.

That was how Viv and Felix found them when they returned to the camp about half an hour later.

'Everything okay?' Viv mouthed to Cam.

He nodded and whispered, 'I think she's asleep now.'

'Did she say anything?'

'Yeah,' Cam replied, but he didn't elaborate because Felix was listening in from the other side of the fire. It wasn't his fault, because of course he wasn't allowed out of their sight, but what Cam had to tell Viv about Emmy wasn't for his ears.

Immune, he thought.

The vaccine wouldn't wipe out the Silver after all.

Not everyone, anyway.

Cam tried not to be disappointed about that, but it felt like the demise of nature's elegant plan to eradicate them. It had been such an apt design: using contaminated blood to render them as human as their prey.

It would have been so neat, but life was never like that, was it? Life was always messy.

15

Julia panicked when she woke the next morning.

They'd moved in their sleep, and somehow she was right back where she always seemed to end up: in Lucas's arms. Her head was on his shoulder and her wrist was resting against his neck, pulse to pulse, contaminated blood against Noble.

She tried to extricate herself without waking him, but she'd never had a chance of making that work in the hammock, even if he hadn't had the enhanced senses of a Noble.

'Julia,' he murmured, pulling her back into his arms as she tried to shrug out of them. 'Don't go yet.'

'I have to,' she said. 'I'm thirsty.'

Lucas's gaze drifted down to her throat as though he were having the same thought, but then he caught sight of her scarred skin and his arms fell away.

'I'm sorry about yesterday,' he said. 'It's been a long time since I rested, and I wasn't thinking.'

'Sorry about what?'

Julia scooched into the tree's branches and stood amongst them slowly, using their density to support her until her legs had woken up properly. She'd learned quickly that it was a bad idea to start trying to climb down from her bedtime trees before the fog of sleep had cleared.

'Sorry about saying what I did,' he said. 'You don't have to come back to the Blue if you don't want to. It can't have been easy to leave.'

She grabbed her canteen, draining the last mouthfuls before she'd thought to offer any to Lucas.

She was too used to being on her own.

'You're going back though?' she said, returning her canteen to her pack before carefully slinging the bag over her shoulders.

Lucas nodded, and Julia found herself mimicking the gesture.

'What?' he said.

'Nothing, really. It just seems like we always want to be in separate places, doesn't it?'

Lucas moved from the hammock into the branches beside her. Apparently he didn't need to wait for his legs to wake up.

'Not always,' he said. 'We're both here now.'

'And I was going to head north today. You'll be going south, I guess.'

'Eventually.'

Julia took a moment to let that sink in before she replied. Did that mean he was staying here for the time being, with her?

'When's *eventually*?' she said.

Lucas rubbed his face.

'Truth be told, I'm not sure exactly what I'm doing. Something happened on the way, and I don't know who I can trust anymore.' He smiled at her. 'Except maybe you.'

But his smile was nervous rather than confident, and the tension between them felt uneasy. The changes in Lucas were even more obvious now, in the light of the dawn, and part of Julia wished she had never left the hammock. Maybe it would have been easier to get used to him again without the awkward distance that was now between them.

There was nothing to do but brazen through. It would help if they could get out of the bloody tree, though.

'Let's get the hammock down,' Julia said. 'Then we'll talk.'

It didn't take long. Ten minutes later they were on the ground, Julia making a fire while Lucas fished around in his pack for food.

The day was bright, but not yet hot enough that the fire was unwelcome.

Julia was beginning to love it out here in the trees. She could understand why some people might find it creepy, particularly when they'd grown up on the fairytales of the Red as she had, but there was beauty in it too. She'd often looked out from the boundary fence and wondered what it would be like to be beneath the reaching limbs of the forest, because that was how they had been taught to see them.

In reality, their shade was an embrace of rustling verdancy. The solitude here was peaceful in a way she had never experienced before. Part of her would have preferred not to share it.

'It happened when I was about halfway back,' Lucas was saying.

He had already shared his story of the journey up to the mountains in the north, rushing through it as though it weren't the important part. Julia had wanted to interrupt him, to ask about the Invicti and the Queen and the places he'd seen on the way, but she'd held back.

She knew how to wait.

'Do you remember you told me about that day at the temple?' he went on. 'About how Rufus had been expecting the attack, and how Lorelei had something to do with it?'

'Yes,' Julia replied.

'I think you were right. She was the one who sent me into the Red after the Invicti, telling me I had to go, even though I found out later that Cameron and the Secundus hadn't asked for me. Then when I passed the army on my way here, I thought I saw her with them.'

'I wouldn't be surprised by anything she did at this point.'

It had shaken Julia the first time he'd mentioned the army.

The idea of so many fighters descending on the Blue... That was what had made up her mind.

She needed to go back to the Blue, and she needed to go now.

Yes, she was desperate to investigate the mountain lake, particularly after what Lucas had told her about it, but she'd been missing her parents her entire life. A little longer wouldn't hurt.

Waiting to return to the Blue would, though. She needed to get Claudia and Marcella out of there before the army arrived at their door.

'There's something else, too,' Julia said. 'Something I didn't have a chance to tell you before you left.'

Lucas was sitting opposite her now, raking out some of the embers so he could put a pan over them. He looked at her properly for the first time that day.

Julia had forgotten how deep the brown of his eyes was.

'It was on the night of the Contamination,' she went on, looking away. 'I saw Rufus meeting with someone. Rufus gave him some little bottles full of liquid. I think they might have been full of contaminated blood.'

Julia had been thinking about that over the past couple of days, ever since she'd found out about the immunity. As an explanation, it made sense.

'The man told Rufus he should save some to give to Claudia,' Julia went on, 'but only if he wasn't going to drink from her afterwards.'

There was a beat of silence before Lucas replied.

'You know about the contamination, then?'

'Yes,' Julia said. 'It makes humans immune to the Weepers, right?'

Lucas held her gaze as he replied. 'Right.'

'So Rufus must have known the Contamination was going to happen. They were trying to make their favourite humans immune.'

Which didn't include Claudia, apparently. Yet another black mark against Rufus's name.

Lucas was quiet for a while, chopping things up to heat in his pan. They could almost have been back on his rooftop in the Blue, except he wasn't the one who owned this space. It was Julia's as much as it was his.

'And you think Lorelei had something to do with it?' he said eventually.

'I think she made it happen. All those meetings with Rufus... I'm sure she was in charge. They were waiting for the right time to do something. I think that thing was the Contamination.'

Lucas stirred his pot, looking down into the steam as it bubbled free.

'I've been thinking the same thing,' he said. 'You said it was Marcus you saw that night?'

'Yes, and I know: she's the one who had him banished.'

'Right. She's the one who had him banished,' Lucas repeated, looking at Julia for a moment before turning back to his cooking.

It all fitted together. Lorelei had Marcus banished specifically so she could send him back into the Blue when she was ready, so he would decimate the human population as a Weeper. How she'd managed to turn him into a Weeper was anyone's guess, but the message against the Empress was clear: stop making more Silver – just as the blood daubed on the temple had demanded – or we'll attack your blood supply so there isn't enough left to support any more.

'There are two things I don't understand, though,' Julia said. 'Firstly, why would she want to kill so many people when she needs their blood as much as any of you, and secondly, why did she save us that night on the rooftop?'

Lucas shrugged as he pulled the pot from the fire.

'I don't know why she saved us,' he said. 'Maybe she didn't have a choice. Cameron was there that night too, you know. He was the one in the square, the one who stopped them all. Maybe she knew he was watching, and she couldn't give herself away.'

'Maybe.'

'I do know why she doesn't care about the blood though.'

'Oh?' Julia said, meeting his eyes over the fire.

'She's got more. Lots more, marching this way with the army. After all, there wouldn't be any Weepers out here if there weren't uncontaminated humans too.'

'Because they're the only ones who aren't immune,' Julia said, catching on. 'And because there have to be uncontaminated humans out here if there are Nobles invading us from the Red, because otherwise they'd have no blood. And if they're working with Lorelei, she can share it. She doesn't need any of the humans in the Blue.'

Lucas nodded.

'To her, they're disposable,' he said. 'All of them.'

Julia wanted to head straight back to the Blue after they'd eaten, but Lucas wouldn't be moved.

'What would we do when we got there?' he'd said, in a tone so reasonable that it made Julia want to scream. 'The best thing we can do is wait for the rest of the Invicti, so we can warn them before they get back to the city. We can go in together, then. It's the most sensible plan.'

And it did make sense, of course it did. When the only Nobles Lucas could trust were the allies he'd just left in the north, it would be suicide to go charging into the Blue without them, straight into Lorelei's hands.

But that didn't stop Julia from chafing under the necessity of the wait. All she wanted to do was turn and rush back to the Blue, to get Claudia out before it was too late.

Lucas told her they had time, that they were well ahead of the army, but all she could think about was the breadth of forest between her and her best friend.

At least they were moving, though. They'd set off later that afternoon, moving westwards on a course that Lucas thought would intersect with the Invicti's route. Julia was still arguing about their direction, though, trying to find some sensible strategy that would require a quicker return to the city.

'It was Lorelei's own squad that stayed behind with her, Julia,' he said as they made their way down to the river to fill their canteens. 'I think every guard left in that city is probably with her.'

'Empress,' Julia muttered.

'I don't think she can help you now either.'

Julia shook her head. 'It wasn't a suggestion. It's just habit.'

'It might not be for long. Lorelei will want to change things up.'

'The King?'

'No. I don't think so. I don't think she'll have anticipated that, so at least we have that on our side, but I don't think we can assume he'll be with us either. I don't think we can assume much of anything.'

'But your friends have the Queen, don't they? And aren't they his soldiers? I thought that was the point.'

Lucas looked up at her from his crouch by the water.

'A lot can change in half a millennium,' he said. 'I don't think we can trust that the past will mean anything to the King at all.'

But Julia remembered how he'd spoken to her on that morning when he'd helped her escape, about reciprocity and corruption. She hadn't understood what he'd said, not entirely, but she didn't think the King would be on Lorelei's side either.

He'd been on Julia's side when she'd needed him.

She'd told Lucas what had happened that day, but she'd kept the King's words to herself. She didn't reveal them now. She probably would have remembered them wrong anyway.

Instead, she just said, 'We'll see,' as she joined Lucas at the water's edge.

'You've changed,' he said with a smile that hit his eyes.

'You have too,' Julia replied, a touch defensively, then berated herself for it. She always seemed to be poised for attack these days, one way or another.

But Lucas didn't seem perturbed by her reaction.

'Do you know what I thought when I first saw you,' he said, 'that night in the square?'

Julia said nothing, concentrating her attention on filling her water skins. The water was only four feet wide here, but a good three feet deep. In the winter it would be an impassable torrent, but in this dry summer it was idyllic clear water that reflected the sky.

'I thought, *She's made of iron beneath the skin*, you know?' he went on. 'As though you'd never give an inch. I remember thinking you weren't meant to be a Server.'

'None of us are meant to be Servers, Lucas,' she said, tying the skins shut with sharp, jerky motions. 'If you can't see that by now, then you must have been walking through the Red with your eyes closed.'

'That's not what I meant.'

She turned to face him, filled with indignation.

'Then what did you mean? You talk about blood supply and the way we humans are treated by your kind as though it's only me who doesn't deserve it. What about the rest of them? Do you think Claudia deserves it? Do you think your Baba does?'

Lucas reached out towards her but she knocked his hand away, stuffing her canteens into her bag as she walked back up the bank.

'You know that's not how I feel,' he said as he scrambled to follow. 'Why do you think I'm trying to get back to the city so badly? What have I got to save except its people?'

'Its Nobles.'

Julia had known the comment was unfair before she'd said it, and Lucas's reaction was just as strong as she'd expected it would be.

'The same Nobles who've ostracised me my entire life?' He said, his voice rising. 'I'm going back for *you*, Julia. To get the humans out because I promised you I would if it was possible, but also because I can't *not* do it, because I'm not like them. I'm like you. Don't you know that by now?'

'You're not like me,' she said, her pack tugging her sideways as she whirled around to face him, furiously struggling to retain the moral high ground.

'You've never had to work in your entire life,' she went on. 'You had a garden full of luxuries that someone would have brought you if you hadn't grown them for yourself. You had a person allocated to feed you blood whenever you wanted it. Me.' She pointed at her chest. 'My blood. You had the best view in the city, and a roof over your head, and you knew that whatever happened you'd never end up mauled to death by fighting Nobles who were after your blood. You wanted to leave the Blue because you were searching for adventure. If I hadn't left then Rufus would have drained me dry. So no, we're nothing alike, Lucas, because you've always had choice, and I've only ever had necessity.'

'Julia–' he said, but she wasn't done yet.

'I need to do something to help Claudia and, as usual, there's *nothing* I can do. I have nothing. I have no power, and you have no idea how that feels. You don't know what it's like to know that your best friend, the person you care most about in the whole world, is stuck in there with them.'

'No,' he said quietly. 'I don't know what that feels like, because other than Baba, I don't think I ever had a friend until I met you. I only know what it felt like to have to leave you behind with them when Lorelei sent me away.'

'Lucas...'

There was a long, empty moment in which the only sound was Lucas's pack dropping to the ground. Julia took a breath, but before she could carry on, Lucas was speaking.

'Why are you even still wearing my silver if this is how you feel? If you think I'm just like them, that there's no difference between me and Rufus, then you could have taken that out of your ear at any time.'

He was walking towards her now, and Julia was more aware than ever of how his posture had changed. He moved like a cat, all slink and slow stalk.

'I don't think you're like them,' she said. 'I just don't think you're like me, either.'

'Maybe not,' he said, so close now, 'but you're wrong about one thing: you do have power. Can't you feel it? It's not the blood in your veins,' he said, taking her hand so he could trace the blue under the skin of her wrist. 'It's always been there, but it's running off you in waves now you're out here. You're strong.'

'I know,' she said irritably. 'I don't need you to tell me that.'

'Then what do you need from me?' he said as an edge of desperation crept into his tone. 'Why are you wearing my silver?'

It was a good question. She'd kept it without really thinking. When Claudia had offered to put the stud back, she'd accepted because there had been no time to contemplate the decision.

But she'd wanted it. Every time she'd fiddled with it, or caught sight of it in Rufus's mirrors, it had made her a tiny bit happier. When she'd thought Rufus was going to take it from her she'd honestly had more concern for losing the trinket than she'd had for losing her earlobe.

'I think what I need,' she said slowly, planting her words with thought, 'is to know that, one day, there could be another rooftop.'

He blinked.

'You want a garden?' he asked.

'No, I want a sanctuary. Nowhere's safe here, not the Blue, not the Red when it's filled with Lorelei's soldiers and the Weepers, but maybe one day there'll be somewhere. Maybe one day, when this is all over, there could be another little paradise, because I thought it existed once before.'

Lucas didn't reply right away. He was so close that the familiar minty scent of him was sharp in Julia's nostrils, but she didn't pull him closer, and he didn't close the gap himself.

'Would there be a place for me in it?' he asked.

He wanted a promise she couldn't give. The truth was that she'd been thinking of Galatea and Sabina when she'd spoken of paradise, not of him.

'I don't know,' she said.

He let her hand drop to her side and took a step away.

'Well, I'll be waiting when you do.'

Lucas slept in the branches for the next few nights, leaving Julia to occupy the hammock alone. She couldn't decide whether or not she was happy about that. Some days she wanted nothing more than to tell him to join her, but then she remembered her contaminated blood and thought it was probably for the best.

She still hadn't told him. That was the problem: she knew and he didn't. It was nothing to do with how alike or not they were, or how much more one of them had suffered than the other, which was a stupid thing to compete over anyway.

They'd had something, the two of them, but they'd lost something too.

Julia knew they'd never again be as close as they had been in the Blue, because Lucas would never feed from her again. They'd never have that intimacy again, and she'd never again have the darkly addictive power that it gave her over him. It shouldn't have mattered in the scheme of things, but in her anxious state everything felt colossal.

What made it worse was that she was mourning the loss of something he didn't even realise had been taken away.

No wonder he was confused.

She'd have to tell him.

They travelled together quickly, but by no means silently. Julia had the impression that Lucas was trying to rekindle the romance, because he entertained her by retelling the fairytales he'd read to her on the rooftop in the Blue.

But that book was gone now, burned away in the cleansing after the Contamination, so all Lucas had left were the memories of the stories. Still, Julia had to give him credit for his efforts. He even remembered most of the songs, and sung them exuberantly, which was why they didn't notice their stalker until it was too late.

They were climbing a rise out of a tree-filled valley when he made his move. The dirt was dry and unstable underfoot, so there was nothing for it but to clamber up on all fours, blinkering their vision as they concentrated on the ground in front of them.

He hit Julia first. One strike to the shoulder sent her rolling fifty feet down the slope and into the stream at the bottom. That got her out of his way, so he could concentrate on Lucas.

Julia could do nothing but watch as Lucas tried to fend off the attack, but his assailant was moving at speed, and Lucas was not. He hadn't fed in the whole time he'd been with Julia. It had been a relief at the time, not having to explain about the contamination in her blood, but as she saw his feet sliding in the dirt she wished that she'd refused Galatea's offer back in the refuge, so she could have given him a fighting chance now.

He fell seconds after she did, gouging dark lines in the slope as he tumbled back into the water and landed next to her in the stream.

The attacker didn't give him a moment to rest. By the time Julia had wrangled one of her knives out of its sheath, Lucas had already been dragged backwards thirty feet into the trees. He was being slammed into the trunks so hard that Julia could hear something breaking. She prayed it was wood rather than bones and, stumbling to her feet, ran after them into the undergrowth.

'Lucas!' she yelled, trying to keep up as the fighters moved through the forest faster than she could track them.

'Run!' he yelled back, somewhere over to her left.

She obeyed, in a fashion. He probably meant for her to run away from the fight rather than towards it, but she wasn't ready to let him go.

Not yet.

She needed him to help her save Claudia.

Julia was pleasantly surprised to see that Lucas had the upper hand when she finally found them in a small clearing beyond the stream. He'd managed to impale his attacker on a broken branch, which now protruded sickeningly from the man's stomach.

Julia covered her mouth with her hand, but managed to keep her breakfast down.

'He won't stay like that for more than a few minutes,' Lucas said, rushing towards her.

'What? With that sticking out of him?'

'You'd be surprised, and he's been well fed. Julia, I hate to ask…'

He left the rest of his request unspoken.

He wanted her blood.

'I can't,' she said, glancing frantically between him and their assailant, whose fingers were just starting to move.

Lucas looked confused, then offended.

'I know things aren't the same as they were,' he said, already reaching for her wrist, 'but can we argue about it after I've got us out of here? Please?'

She snatched her hand away.

'No, you don't understand. I mean I would, but it won't do any good, or that's what they told me, anyway. Lucas, I…' She took a deep breath. 'My blood's contaminated.'

The silence that followed was broken by the rustling of the leaf litter as their attacker struggled into a sitting position. His hands were wrapped around the branch. Julia had to look away when he pulled it out with an unpleasant grating noise as it scraped against his bones.

'You're contaminated?' Lucas said.

'At the refuge I told you about. One of the girls did it to keep me safe from the Weepers.'

'Shit,' he said. 'Well, no, it's good. It's what I would have done. It's just that it'll kill me, and right now–'

Right now, their attacker was already speeding towards them. He was moving a little more slowly from the power it had taken to mend his still-healing wounds, but still faster than any human would manage.

'Run,' Lucas said again, but Julia had a blade in each hand now, and she wasn't backing down.

Their attacker couldn't fight both of them at once.

He landed a punch on Lucas's chin, which Lucas dodged only enough to make it a glancing blow rather than a jaw-breaking one. While their assailant was twisted away from Julia with the force of his swing, she pressed her advantage.

She didn't hold back. She struck with both blades, forcing them into his side with all her strength. One hit bone and was jarred out of her hand, but the other sank hilt-deep into his chest.

There was no sound, that was the eerie thing about it. The pain must have been excruciating, Noble or not, but all Julia heard was a faint grunt as she drove the knife home, and the sucking noise of the flesh as she pulled it back out.

It was only when the attacker turned to level a punch at her head that she saw the stitches, lined neatly across his lips in pink thread that matched the colour of his skin.

His mouth had been sewn shut.

While Julia stared, Lucas threw himself at the man and knocked him aside just before he landed his hit. Lucas was on top of him then, straddling his body as he threw punch after punch at the man's head, but each one was blocked by the man's palms. It wasn't long before he'd brushed Lucas off him like a bug and rolled up to his feet for another round.

Julia wasn't the only one with knives, either. The man pulled two stubby blades from his belt and he was now swiping at Lucas as he walked forwards, pushing him back towards Julia.

'Will you run now?' he yelled as he ducked and swerved.

Julia responded by stepping forwards to hand him her remaining two knives, which he grabbed before taking a second to push her away.

That second cost him.

The sewn man swung his blades low and buried them in Lucas's stomach, bending him forwards over the wound so he could bring his knee up into Lucas's nose as he pulled the weapons free.

It toppled Lucas.

He dropped onto one knee, letting one of his own knives go as he flattened his palm into the earth to hold himself up. He still had the other, but the attacker was already leaning in for another swing, and Lucas's swipes were wide and unsteady.

He was in trouble. He was going down, and after he'd fallen, Julia would follow him.

She grabbed at her belt, her hands searching desperately for the weapons that her mind was too panicked to catalogue, and then her fingers closed around the prize.

The trigger was smooth, the action practised from recent days spent hunting rabbits with Galatea, and the crossbow felt as familiar to her hand as Lucas's whispered voice did to her ears.

When Julia aimed at the tight-sewn lips, her bolt didn't miss.

16

Viv and Cam had swapped pairs permanently in the end, because Emmy wouldn't let Cam leave her.

He was heartened by that initially, because she'd said she wasn't prepared to confide in anyone else. That had led him to expect confidences, but still her lips remained sealed on the subject of Charles's abuses. Cam was starting to worry that they might have been even worse than he'd imagined. That possibility plagued him as they journeyed southeast chasing the army.

They just needed to get back to the Blue. As soon as they were home, Sol would wake up, and he'd know what to do. He'd know how to soothe Emmy's anguish, or how to help her give it voice. He had always known what was going on in her head.

'They're setting up camp for the night, about five miles ahead of us,' Naia reported as she rode back to the squad with Gul in tow.

'We'll overtake the army tomorrow,' he said, but Tommy was shaking his head.

'No. We'll do it tonight. We can't set our camp this close to theirs, not when they have blood and scouts. It's too dangerous.'

'You want us to ride through the night?' said Cam.

'Come on, Cam. It's not like you haven't done it before.'

Cam rolled his eyes, then cut them left to where Emmy sat listlessly on her mare. He hoped Tommy would get the hint. Emmy was still recovering from her ordeals, physically as well as mentally, and Cam was far from confident that she could manage thirty-two straight hours in the saddle. The others would brazen through it with a bit of moaning, which had in fact already started up behind him, but Emmy just looked exhausted.

They'd run out of blood days ago, and without it she was fading fast.

'I know,' Tommy said, leaning close to Cam. 'But I don't think there's another option. We've got to push on.'

Cam nodded reluctantly, because he couldn't come up with a better plan. They'd have to take more regular breaks for the horses, but they'd still get further by travelling through the night.

He would just have to keep an eye on Emmy, and hope she was strong enough to hold on.

Meanwhile, Felix was keeping an eye on him.

Naia and Gul rode vanguard while Zita and Konrad rode rearguard, leaving ten of them in the main squad. As it became darker, Tommy sent Aaron and Bartek out to the left, and Darius and Linh out to the right, so there were just six of them left in the centre.

Cam could practically feel Felix's gaze then.

They'd not had any time alone since the day Cam had "interrogated" him, and honestly he was sick of it. There'd been one thing or another keeping them apart since the day they'd left the Blue, and he'd run out of patience for it.

He believed Felix. Viv believed Felix. Hell, even Tommy believed that he was on the side of the Invicti.

And Cam had believed him when he'd said he loved him. Even if Cam didn't know whether he felt the same, he did know that he wanted to see if he could.

But he had Emmy to worry about now. She had to be his first concern at the moment, so he packed his feelings away as he had done every day for hundreds of years, and he focussed on his mission.

There was a whistle up ahead. The remaining squad jerked their heads up to follow the sound. All except Emmy, that is. Her eyes were drooping closed as her chin dipped down to her chest.

Another whistle.

'Contact?' Cam whispered.

Tommy nodded and motioned for the squad to halt as he slid from the saddle. They'd taken a wide route around the army's camp, hoping to avoid the scouts, but it sounded like they may have been unlucky.

Cam handed his reins to Felix, trying to ignore the lingering touch of his fingertips, then joined Tommy as he slunk into the undergrowth on foot. The whistle sounded a third time as they approached through the trees, lower in pitch this time, but no less incongruous in the silence of the nighttime forest.

It wasn't usually this quiet, even in the darkness.

Tommy must have picked up on the strangeness of it too, because they both began to run at the same moment, feet crunching on desiccated leaves as they flew through the parched foliage.

When the whistle sounded again it was off to the left, and then Cam knew they were under attack. The vanguard had no blood, and the only way they could have moved that far that quickly was if someone had carried them there at Silver speed.

'Shit,' Tommy muttered under his breath.

'Naia and Gul can take down a Red Shirt on their own, no problems,' said Cam.

'And if there are two of them?'

After twenty hours of riding, and no blood, the odds might not be quite so much in their favour. Cam wasn't going to say that out loud though. He didn't need to because they could already hear the crashing now as bodies slammed against trees and ground and stone. One more corner took them into view of the fighting, where Naia and Gul were facing off against a single scout.

He wasn't a Red Shirt, though.

'Jesus,' said Tommy. 'Is that a Tacitum?'

The woman was poised over Gul, swiping at his neck while Naia barrelled towards her from the side. In the moment before they both hit the ground the woman turned towards Tommy and Cam, and they had a clear look at her mouth.

Tacitum.

It had been hundreds of years since Cam had last seen one of the mutilated scouts, long enough to hope that everyone had forgotten how to make them. But apparently memory of that particular talent was long-lived in the Silver.

The woman's lips had been cut open then sewn back together, so the flesh had knitted her mouth shut as it healed. Her tongue had probably been mutilated too, healed to the base of her mouth so she would be unable to speak even if her lips were cut apart. The practice had been common once amongst the more barbaric factions of the Silver, particularly during the Revelation and the

Fall, because it left scouts unable to divulge information in the event that they were captured. It would take days of healing to reverse the mutilations, and enemies often had neither the time nor the blood to spare for those purposes.

The Invicti were certainly short of both.

Naia and Gul had managed to pin the Tacitum to the ground, but Tommy didn't even consider the option of interrogating her. He just slammed his fist into her skull while the others held her still.

The result was a gruesome detonation.

'Fuck's sake,' Naia said as she spat and wiped the gore from her cheeks. 'Could you warn me next time? I had my bloody mouth open.'

Tommy threw her a rag from his pocket, which she caught as it hit her in the face.

'What did you think I was going to do?' he said. 'Talk to her?'

'Well, what *are* we going to do with her?' asked Cam. 'Was she the only one, or did you see more?'

'Just her,' said Naia, rubbing the rag across her face. 'She didn't run either, so she wasn't on identify and report. She came right at us, as soon as she saw us. I get the feeling that if there had been any others around here, they would have just come and joined in the fight.'

Gul nodded along beside her as she spoke.

'Agreed,' he said.

'Then we're on the edge of their patrol area, but not out of it,' Tommy said. 'We need to push the horses for a while, put a day's distance between us. They'll be moving slower on foot anyway, so we can rest in the afternoon.'

'And her?' Cam said, gesturing at the body.

Tommy shrugged. 'Leave her there. Let the army collect her on their way through.'

That felt like the wrong answer to Cam, but without any blood there was no way to revive her anyway. Better to let the army take care of its own, so the Invicti could take care of theirs.

The sun was high and hot through the trees when Tommy finally called a halt. It was a miracle that they hadn't lamed any of the horses, but that wasn't to say there had been no casualties at all.

Naia and Gul were both nursing knife wounds from their fight, and Emmy had fallen out of her saddle not long after they'd killed the Tacitum. She'd been riding with Cam on Hades ever since, but he felt like a useless nurse to her because what she really needed was blood, and there were no caravans to be found. They'd followed the traces of them here and there, and there was enough evidence of fighting to suggest that perhaps the army had been assimilating them as they marched, but there wasn't a single uncontaminated human left behind.

This far south, he was no longer expecting to find any.

They were only a week or so out from the Blue, but that was another unnourished week that the Invicti's strength could ill-afford. They were all going without, which could perhaps explain Cam's current failure to put two and two together, though it didn't excuse it.

He'd been so fixated on finding uncontaminated humans that he'd missed the obvious point: Emmy was immune. She didn't need uncontaminated blood. Any blood would do.

As they approached the hilltop the vanguard had earmarked for their camp, it finally occurred to him that they already had what Emmy needed, right in the middle of the squad, riding only a few feet away.

Felix.

She could feed from Felix.

That was an uncomfortable thought: Emmy's teeth in Felix's neck.

Even if they got through this, then Cam would never get to share that experience with him. Emmy could though, right now, and that seemed painfully unfair. Cam's reluctance was selfish, he knew that, but it didn't stop the jealousy from burning in his stomach.

It wouldn't stop him from making it happen, either.

'Hey, Tommy,' he said as he handed Emmy down to Viv. 'Can I have a word?'

'Sure, when we're settled.'

Cam looked at the Queen. She was pale and sickly, curled so lightly in Viv's arms that Viv probably would have been able to carry her just as easily without her Silver strength.

'It won't wait,' he said as he dismounted.

Viv raised her eyebrows at him and, sensitive to the mood as always, handed Emmy off to Bartek so she could follow Tommy and Cam down the slope a little way.

Cam told them about Emmy's immunity then, confirming that Chloe's fairytale really had been true. He broke the confidence because he had to, but then wished he hadn't. They were too excited, as though his words heralded the saving grace for the Silver, the magic bullet that they'd been searching for.

That wasn't what Cam wanted. It was what Charles had wanted.

In the moments after he'd told them the news, Cam had struggled to tell the difference between his dead enemy's avarice and that of his friends. Viv's hand resting on her newly-visible bump was one difference, but was that enough? Could coveting their queen's blood be excused if they were doing it for the sake of their child rather than for themselves? Would Laila be excused for coveting it for herself, for the sake of their entire city?

That was when the doubts started creeping in. They were getting closer to the Blue every day, and there was no telling what they might face when they arrived. Lorelei could have taken over the city, or let the Silver tear it to the ground with their fighting. If the bond between Emmy and Sol didn't trigger the King's awakening as Cam hoped it should, then what would happen to Emmy?

If they weren't careful, she might just become a test subject all over again, and Cam couldn't let that happen. For the first time, he wondered whether he should just take Emmy and run.

'Are you going to talk to Felix, then?' Tommy asked.

'It should be me,' said Cam. 'I'm not going to make him do it, though.'

'But he will,' Viv said. 'He'll do it if you ask.'

'You're not making me feel any better about it.'

Viv smiled at Cam and took his hand, stroking the backs of his fingers with her thumb.

'Look,' Tommy cut in, 'Emmy needs it. End of discussion. Sort it out, Cam.'

Cam was going to respond with pithy sarcasm, but Viv punched Tommy in the arm before he could get a word out. Or even put the words together, truth be told.

'Quiet, you,' she said to Tommy. 'You're not helping, as usual.'

'Why? What did I do?'

With a sympathetic look at Cam, she dragged Tommy back towards the camp. Cam fell in step behind them, because there was no avoiding it now.

He was going to have to ask Felix for his blood.

* * *

Cam found him by the fire, which was strange because Felix usually kept his distance from the other Invicti when Cam wasn't around. They still weren't entirely comfortable sharing their space with a contaminated human, particularly one whose allegiance had been called into question. They tolerated him, but not enough to encourage friendliness.

They seemed to be managing it now, though.

Gul and Linh were by the fire with Aaron, handing him ingredients for his pot, while Bartek and Adewale stoked the fire. Felix wasn't more than six feet away, Emmy curled up at his side, sitting with his back to their approach.

Then Cam saw what he was doing.

He had a bottle propped up between his feet while a shard of metal nestled in his hand dripped blood into the glass.

'Felix,' Cam said.

Felix looked up at him with a little smile.

'They overheard you.' He nodded at the Invicti. 'I thought I'd save you having to ask.'

Cam sat down at his side, close enough that if he'd leaned slightly to the side then their shoulders would have rubbed together. He didn't lean, though, he just sat and watched the drops falling.

'Thank you,' he said.

'She was right,' said Felix.

'Who?'

'Viv. There are a lot of things I'd do just because you asked.'

Cam could feel the blush heating his cheeks at the same moment that the rest of Invicti realised they had something urgent to do on the other side of the camp.

'They can hear you quite well, you know,' said Cam, rubbing at the back of his neck, cheeks still blazing.

'I know,' Felix grinned. 'I used to be one of you, remember?'

'I remember,' Cam murmured, but it was something he kept forgetting. 'How old are you, really?'

'Younger than you.'

'Felix...'

'Alright,' he said, moving the bottle between his knees so he could lean back against his pack and still keep the blood flowing into the glass. 'I'm a few hundred years old.'

'Older than Charlestown?'

'Not quite. I was born there in the beginning, before it had that name. Were you born on your island?'

'No,' said Cam. 'You know that, though. I told you I remembered the Fall. You really didn't know about the Weepers, though?'

Felix smiled ruefully.

'That happened after I was banished,' he said. 'Or before, but secretly. Richard was always one for his secrets.'

Felix's smile soured, his fist clenching around the blade as he spoke of the Silver whom Emmy had called Lestat.

Felix had a list of grievances against the dead man that was a mile long. He told Cam about the hierarchy, the tributes paid, and the tasks that had sent Felix away into the Red to hunt for uncontaminated humans. Richard had liked to send Felix away, because then he could do as he liked in Charlestown, every vice unchecked.

'So we travelled,' Felix said. 'When Otho was assigned to me, we could.'

'He was your Attendant then?'

Felix shrugged. 'He fed me. If that's what you call it, then yes. But then Richard took Otho from me, and gave me someone tainted instead.'

'You didn't realise?'

Felix shrugged again. 'I wasn't looking for a trick. I wasn't suspicious enough.'

'Neither was I, I guess,' Cam said. 'Suspicious enough. Of you, I mean.'

'You don't need to be.'

'But I should have been.'

Cam was remembering Charlestown now, with the two bottles of blood in the cellar – one contaminated, one not – and that train of thought led him onto why he had been there in the first place. It had been his last attempt to find Emmy, in a place that had turned out to be miles away from the mountains where Charles had been keeping her.

'You knew Emmy wasn't there,' he said to Felix. 'You'd seen her in the mountains, but you still let me go to Charlestown looking for her so you could get your revenge on Richard.'

'We made an oath, Cam. We each did our part.'

'You tricked me.'

'And we both got what we wanted,' Felix said as he set the bottle aside and rubbed his blade clean in the grass. 'Do you really want to fight over the details?'

His hand was still bleeding. It was slow, already clotting now that the metal was out of the vein, but still bleeding. It dripped down Felix's wrist as he shoved a cork into the bottle's mouth.

Cam knew it was contaminated. He could smell the flatness in the odour, just slightly less salted and spicy than fresh blood should be, but it had been weeks. He hadn't drunk anything but water since they'd rescued Emmy from the mountain. Even if the odour had been just a shadow of the scent of uncontaminated blood, he would still have been salivating, and that was before he'd attached the scent to Felix.

Felix, with his nutmeg spice and earth green, with eyes like the dawn sky and lips that twitched with mischief.

Gods.

Cam pulled a strip of fabric out of his pack and handed it to Felix, unable to look at him until the wound was safely tied away.

'Too much for you?' Felix said.

'Far too much. You're far too much.' Cam pushed his hair back from his face with both hands. 'I don't know what to do with you.'

The smile was back again. 'Yes, you do.'

'That isn't helpful.'

'You're still worrying,' Felix said as he reached over to rest his hand on Cam's thigh. The gesture was comforting rather than demanding. 'You have your friend,' he said, tipping his head towards the still-slumbering Emmy. 'You have my blood to get her back to strength. You've overtaken the army. You'll have your victory over this enemy. In the meantime, you have me.'

Cam blew out a heavy breath.

'You want me to relax?' he asked. 'When we're a week away from fighting for the Blue?'

'Yes. It's a week away.'

'I haven't relaxed for half a millennium,' Cam said, with a laugh that was meant to sound dismissive but ended up being bleak and empty. 'I think I might have forgotten how. I think I've forgotten how to be myself, if I'm honest.'

Felix raised his hand to Cam's cheek.

'I suppose you're going to remind me,' Cam said.

'Nothing so trite.'

The kiss was soft this time.

There was longing in it, as there always was when their lips met, but it hadn't been intended to fan that emotion. Instead, and for the first time, Cam found something else there too, something like solace.

It settled him.

The smell of Felix's skin, his breath... They grabbed hold of Cam's racing heart and, instead of racing it further, stroked it into a rhythm that felt manageable.

He hadn't realised how fiercely his anxiety had bubbled beneath his skin until it had retreated back into his bones.

'You're still worried,' Felix said with a smile, brushing the hair from Cam's forehead.

Cam smiled back, then lowered himself down so his head rested on Felix's shoulder. The afternoon was wearing on, but it would be a while yet before the sky was pale enough to match Felix's eyes.

'I wish I could stop fixating on the future,' Cam said. 'The problem is that I don't know what's going to happen when we get there, back to the city. If the King doesn't wake up, and if they start looking to Emmy for a solution to the contamination... Her immunity, you know.'

'Then what?' Felix nudged when Cam didn't continue.

'I'm running. I'm taking her out of there, and I'm running. There must be somewhere. I don't know, Japan? Hawaii?'

Felix looked puzzled. 'Where?'

'Islands,' Cam said. 'Places people don't go anymore. They were beautiful once, before the world broke.'

Felix curled his arm around Cam's side, pulling him closer.

'Why would you run?'

'Are you kidding?' Cam said, half sitting up. Felix coaxed him back down. 'She was a test subject for decades, Felix. Centuries. Charles bled her dry. You don't know what he did to her. Hell, I don't know what he did to her. I'm not letting that happen again, not to Emmy.'

'You think her friends would treat her the same way Charles did?'

'I'd bloody well hope not. I don't know, though. I don't know what any of them would give up to make sure the contamination didn't affect them anymore.'

'But you'd take her away from them again to make sure it still did?'

Cam was silent for a moment as he puzzled out the implication behind the words, then he groaned.

'I'm not like Charles, Felix.'

'But it's not your choice. You found her, and she's awake.' Felix looked down at Emmy's sleeping figure at his side. 'Or she will be later. It's her choice to stay or go.'

'I can offer,' Cam protested.

'But you can't force. So stop worrying about it, because it's not your choice anymore.'

That should have felt liberating. Cam hoped that it would, in time. It wasn't his responsibility anymore. He could leave the decisions to someone else, just as he always had before the Fall.

He curled closer against Felix, his eyelids dropping shut as he was warmed by the afternoon sun and the heat of the woodsman's chest beneath his cheek.

He'd forgotten what it was like to relinquish control. Maybe it was time for him to remember.

Emmy was finally on the mend.

The freshness of the blood must have helped, because her cheeks were starting to pink, and it wasn't many more days before she was tearing into her food with as much enthusiasm as the Invicti. More, probably.

After all, she had some catching up to do.

When they finally reached the Carpathians, they skirted the south edge of the mountains to avoid Ana's lakeside community. Chloe and Alex would have arrived by now, and the last thing the Invicti needed on this trip was more drama from Darius. Tommy just wanted to get back to the Blue without any further interruptions.

It had been wishful thinking on the Secundus's part, Cam thought. Probably the hope alone had jinxed it.

They smelled the blood first. It led them into a valley floored by a rambling stream that was currently more pebbles than it was water.

Cam left the others there with the horses and followed the tracks across it into the trees, where spatters and sprays surrounded a larger area where blood had pooled in the ground. The scent led off in different directions from there, in a deliberate starburst that raised the hairs on the back of Cam's neck.

This had been designed to distract.

'Tommy,' he called over his shoulder. 'You're going to want to see this.'

When he arrived, they stood side-by-side for a moment as they studied the ground.

'You've picked up the scent?' said Cam.

'Yeah, going in all different directions. That's not an accident. Someone didn't want us to find them.'

Cam shook his head. 'Not what I meant. I meant, have you picked up the *personal* scent? It's a few days old, but it's there, underneath the blood.'

There was more silence as Tommy stood still in the clearing, letting his eyes close while he inhaled the air.

'Shit,' he said eventually.

'Yeah,' Cam agreed. 'We fucked up.'

'Jesus. Do you think he's alright?'

'If he is, it'll be no thanks to us. We set the boy training with Alistair, and then the old bastard betrayed us to Laila. Then we sent the boy back to tell Lorelei about the army, and we found out she's a fucking traitor too. Any one of them could have done this.'

'But no bodies.'

'No,' Cam said as he crouched in the undergrowth. 'No bodies. The blood's dried, too.'

'But why?' said Tommy, poking amongst the leaves. 'Why would anyone want to kill him? It can't be about the message, because Lorelei would already know what to expect from the army, and I can't imagine that Alistair won't have told Laila the same by now.'

'Maybe they just wanted it to slow us down.'

'So we don't let it.'

Cam turned to look up at Tommy, horrified at the suggestion.

'We can't just ignore this and carry on,' he said.

'No, but we don't have to follow all the trails. We only have to follow one. Can you track his scent from here, just his?'

'I don't know,' Cam said. 'I think I only picked it up in the first place because a lot of this blood is his.'

'Not most of it, though?' Tommy looked pointedly towards the large area of maroon crusting that stained the greenery of the glade.

'No,' Cam agreed. 'Here is him,' he said, pointing to a smaller patch, 'and here, but not that.'

'So?'

'Alright, alright. Give me a minute.'

Cam stood and walked to the centre of the space, putting his back to the bigger stain. It was irrelevant. After a second, he saw the marks that were a better trail than his nose could ever have found after so many days.

'Look,' he said, pointing them out to Tommy. 'Tracks going south.'

'His?'

Cam leaned closer to examine the dirt.

'It's his blood,' he said. 'Must be someone else with him, though. You can see the trail as well as I can.'

That brought neither of them any joy though, because Lucas clearly hadn't walked out of this place. He'd been bleeding, and the marks in the earth were furrows left behind by his dragging heels.

'Come on, then,' Tommy said.

They ran. The tracks weren't difficult to follow from the edge of the clearing, because once they were clear of the scent of the other person's blood, Lucas's sang out to them.

'Can you make out the other scent?' Tommy asked as they forded a tributary of the valley's stream.

'No. I don't think it's any of the guards, but it's old. Can't be sure.'

But that changed as Cam approached his target. It was definitely a scent he didn't know, and it was layered with oil and acid, like lemon juice and lanolin mixed together to make an aroma that was strangely appealing.

'This is it,' Cam whispered as they approached a dense copse. 'They're here.'

'Just two?'

'I think so.'

'Alright, then,' said Tommy, leading the way through the low branches. 'Let's find out who's taken our boy.'

17

Lucas had been unconscious for so many days that Julia was starting to worry he would never wake up.

Their attacker's last strike had gone into his eye. The two had fallen at the same time, but Julia was sure they would both live. She'd heard the stories and she knew the folktales that Livia had handed around the hearth at night.

Lucas would come back. She was sure he'd be fine.

Their attacker would too, but Julia had made sure he wouldn't do so any time soon. That had required her to engage in some creative butchery that she'd rather not recall, but at least it had bought her the time she'd needed to drag Lucas away to somewhere safe. They'd be alright until someone found the pieces of their attacker and put them back together, but hopefully Lucas would be on his feet by then.

She was sure he would, because he had to wake up soon.

If only he would wake up soon.

But she knew what the problem was, and she could do nothing about it. He needed blood, but she couldn't give it to him.

She was contaminated.

Her blood would kill him.

It had taken her a long time to work through that, but then she'd had plenty of that in the silent days that followed the fight.

They'd never known how the contamination really worked, not the Servers at least. She hadn't heard even a whisper of that truth, not in the fairytales Lucas had told her, and not in the stories at Livia's hearth.

Unless you assumed that all the stories were written about Nobles instead of humans. If the girl who ate the poisoned apple was a Noble, if the boy who slew the beast and died from its contaminated blood was a Noble, then it all made perfect sense. They were cautionary tales for Noble children, not human ones, and she could only assume that the more aspiring of her Server ancestors had adopted the stories as their own.

And why would the Nobles correct them?

Of course they wouldn't tell their Servers about the contamination. If the humans had known that it wasn't dangerous to them, only to the Nobles, then they would all have just walked out into the Red and contaminated themselves.

Then the Nobles would have died.

It occurred to Julia that her blood would have provided an easier way to deal with their attacker. She could have simply bled on him, and he would never have got up again.

She wasn't sure whether or not she regretted the fact that the realisation had come too late to be of any use. She could only hope that their attacker remained as still as Lucas was now, his wounds clotted but not healing.

Julia had tried everything she could think of to wake him. Now she was out of ideas.

Her first stop had been the river, so she could wash the blood from his face and stomach. It would make it harder for them to be tracked, she'd guessed, but she also just couldn't stand to see him coated in it. Still, he'd stayed unconscious as she'd dragged him for hours through the forest, soaking her shirt with sweat as she hauled both of their packs along with him.

The spot she'd eventually chosen for their den was deeply overgrown, but with a small circle of clear ground in its centre that was large enough for a fire. She kept him by it night and day, heedless of the smoke signals she was sending up as she desperately tried to warm his freezing limbs. She could only hope that the foliage would obscure them, particularly since the fire was small and the branches she'd chosen were dry as a bone from the hot summer.

Still, days later, he stayed cold. He looked and felt so much like a corpse that she was starting to believe that he might really be dead.

'Please,' she begged him. 'Please wake up.'

He remained resolutely still.

'How dare you?' she said, her voice rasping at the back of her throat. 'How dare you do this to me? You can't just die on me when we're in an argument. That's not how it works. You have to give me time to realise how unreasonable I've been so I can apologise. You didn't give me enough time.'

She clasped her fingers around his wrist for the fiftieth time that day, searching for a pulse that was never there. She tried to ignore the threatening tears that tickled her sinuses and made her eyes burn, constant and persistent, like the worst kind of allergy.

'You're not going to wake up, are you?' she said, lying down beside him.

She propped her chin up on her hand so she could watch his face, and in the flickering firelight she could almost make herself believe he had moved. Almost, because his pulse was still missing, and his skin was as cold as it had always been since the attack.

She was probably only alive because he'd pushed her out of the way.

The idiot had pushed her out of the way, and if he hadn't done that then he'd still be awake. He'd still be alive.

He hadn't trusted her to be able to handle herself in a fight, which had been his mistake. She'd been too eager to throw herself into the fray against a Noble, which had been hers. She should have stayed at a distance and used her crossbow, just as she had trained herself to do.

She'd never have the chance to apologise for that if he was dead. He had to wake up so she could say she was sorry.

She laid her head on her pack, turning so she could still see his face. She wouldn't have lain so close to him if he had just been sleeping, but if she had put herself any farther away then she wouldn't have been able to listen for his breath.

When her eyes started to close she let them, because she heard better that way. When she felt sleep pulling her down she let that take her too, because there was nothing else to do, and because she wouldn't sleep that night. She liked to stay awake in the darkness just in case the Weepers found them. There was no way she would have been able to haul Lucas up into a tree, but she wasn't prepared to leave his side either.

Some part of her must still have been listening as she dozed, because it was a noise that woke her, although she couldn't identify it at first. She heard it again as she opened her eyes, almost like the rustling of leaves, but with a base rasp underneath.

Then Lucas moved.

It wasn't the twitch of a finger or the flicker of an eyelid that Julia had been expecting. Instead, he launched himself at her, closing the distance in a heartbeat. His mouth fastened onto her neck before she realised what he intended to do, and then it was too late to stop him.

She wouldn't have had a chance anyway, because even with all his injuries he was still so much stronger than her that every ounce of force in her body couldn't budge him an inch.

His teeth were already in her neck and there was nothing she could do about it. Her blood would already be in his mouth, and then he'd die. He'd be dead, really dead, not just fake dead like he had been for the past few days.

But it felt so good. This wasn't Rufus, it was Lucas, and her body knew the difference. He wasn't teeth and agony; he was caresses and shivers despite the violence of the act.

'Lucas,' she said, trying to protest against her body's wishes. 'Lucas, stop. You can't drink it.'

But his hands were in her hair now, tugging it loose from its braid, and hers had wrapped around his back without her giving a conscious thought to it. It was more intimate than a kiss, more heady than Livia's home-brew, and the tugging through her body was so hypnotic that she felt herself starting to drift away.

That was the moment when Cam and Tommy burst through the trees, just a few seconds too late. Julia could already feel her consciousness slipping away from her, and by the time they'd pulled Lucas off her she was already out.

She woke up to pain. There had been none on the way down, but there was a hell of a lot of it on the way back up. She must have moaned or moved with it, because a hand was wrapped around her own before she'd even tried to open her eyes.

'There,' a female voice said. 'Didn't I tell you? Give her a few days and she'll be good as new.'

'Stop torturing yourself over it,' said another voice. Male, but not Lucas. 'It happens. You weren't in control.'

'That doesn't make it okay.' That one did sound like Lucas.

'No, it doesn't,' the woman said.

'Viv–'

'She might still forgive you, though,' she went on. 'When she's recovered.'

Julia's eyes wouldn't open. She should tell them she was awake. She didn't want to listen in like this, not because of any moral imperative against eavesdropping – after all, she'd done enough of that in her time – but because she was afraid of what she might hear.

She managed to move her hand, and to flicker her eyelids open enough that she was blinded by a single flash of light before they closed again, but that was all that seemed to be in her power.

Had she been drugged? She knew what it was like to wake up from being drained, because it had last happened only a few weeks ago, and she shouldn't have been this lucid. For her body to be frozen but her mind to be clear… It was strange.

'She's coming round,' Lucas said.

'It'll take her a while to come out of it. The stuff Aaron gave her would knock out even Cam's horse.'

Ah. Drugs, then.

'She said she was contaminated,' said Lucas.

'Well, lucky for you she was wrong about that,' said the man.

'Or she lied about it,' the woman added.

'Why would she do that?'

Something tickled across Julia's neck, featherlight against the skin that Rufus had scarred. At least Lucas had gone for the other side, so she'd be balanced out now.

'Oh,' Lucas said.

They left then, and Julia was on her own.

Things were quiet for a while after that, enough to let her get a feel for her surroundings. It was warm, but not yet hot, so it was either early morning or late evening. Footsteps crunched around her, so she must have been lying on the ground. She could smell smoke.

A camp, then.

The woman came back a little later and took Julia's hand again.

'Don't worry,' she whispered. 'You're safe, and we're on our way back to the Blue. Lucas thought you'd want to know that.'

Julia finally managed to open her eyes this time.

The woman looked like a faerie. Her hair moved like waterweed in the breeze, haloing her face. Julia didn't recognise her, but she knew from the gold filaments in her eyes that she was a Noble, and a Noble in love.

The stories Lucas had told her about silvering eyes and sealing gold must be true after all, because there was the evidence, looking down at her from close enough that she couldn't be mistaken.

'Ah,' the woman said with a smile. 'You are awake, then. I'm Viv.'

Julia tried to reply, but had to stop to clear her throat. The vibration pulled at the broken skin on her neck, sending tendrils of pain reaching down into her body. She grimaced and reached up towards the wound without thinking.

'Ah-ah,' said Viv, catching her hand before she could touch it. 'It's clean and stitched, but I haven't covered it yet, so don't go putting dirt in it.'

'Thanks,' Julia said.

'It wasn't me. It was Lucas. He insisted, but don't worry, he did a good job. Penance, you know. He's trying to make it up to you, if he can.'

Julia didn't reply to that, because it didn't seem right to talk to a stranger about it when she hadn't yet spoken to Lucas.

'He said you told him you were contaminated,' she went on.

'Yes,' Julia croaked.

Viv tucked her hair behind her ears and leaned forward over her crossed legs, then she propped Julia's head up and held a canteen to her lips. The contents were lukewarm and tasted of pond water, but the liquid was so welcome that Julia could have cried with relief if she hadn't been so dehydrated.

'Better?' Viv asked as she helped Julia up into a sitting position and dragged a pack against her back to keep her there.

'Much, thank you.'

Julia could see the camp now. They were in a patch of scrabbly yellow grass between the trees, and it had to be evening because people were setting out their bed rolls around the fire rather than packing them away. There were fewer than Julia had expected for the defensive force that was supposed to be saving the Blue, maybe only ten or fifteen. She couldn't see how they were going to stand against an entire army.

'You're safe,' Viv said again, misreading Julia's concern for fear. 'They're a good bunch, and they're not going to hurt you, or try to bleed you, even if you are uncontaminated. I understand why you might not trust us…'

Julia expected her to continue, but instead her pretty brow creased and she looked away as though she were being chased by a memory.

'I didn't lie about it,' Julia said. 'I did think I was contaminated. A girl in the forest gave me her blood.'

Julia had just assumed that Galatea was contaminated, though. The girl certainly seemed to believe she was, as did Sabina, but maybe they were wrong. Or maybe the transfer had gone wrong, and whatever had been supposed to pass from Galatea's blood to Julia's had been blocked somehow.

'Well,' Viv said, 'for what it's worth I'm glad you were wrong. Lucas is a good kid. Or he tries to be, anyway.'

'He really would have died?' Julia asked.

'Sort of. It's not quite that straightforward, but near enough.'

'And I'm not immune to the Weepers?'

'No.'

'I didn't know,' said Julia, thinking about all the days she'd spent wandering through the trees alone, and the days she'd camped with Lucas on the ground while she'd been waiting for him to recover.

On the *ground*.

She'd thought that if she had come across a Weeper then it would have died as soon as its teeth had broken her skin. That's what Galatea had told her. It had made her feel invincible. It had made her feel like she was magic.

That knowledge had given her power in the Red, but it had all been in her head. It had let her roam the forests as she'd learned to look after herself in the wild. It had even let her take on a Noble when it was the last thing she should have been doing. If the attacker had taken her blood…

'Better to find out this way than by Weeper bite, right?' Viv said. 'At least there was no harm done.'

'Right.'

Except the fear was now creeping up Julia's spine. There had been a couple of howls already this evening, even though it wasn't yet dusk. Julia wondered if they were close to Sabina's camp, where the Weepers congregated. Maybe she could run back there to find Galatea, so they could try again.

But that was just the desperation talking. She'd managed to navigate the Red perfectly well when she'd still been on the island, before she'd even known about the immunity. She could do it again now.

She needed to focus on getting back to the Blue, so she could get Claudia out.

'You don't have to worry about the Weepers while you're with us,' Viv said. 'We'll keep you safe. In fact, I'm not sure Lucas is ever going to let you out of his sight again.'

Julia followed Viv's glance and saw that he was watching them from the other side of the fire. His eyes didn't leave Julia as he accepted a bowl from a large man who was spooning out food from a pot.

'I can have a word with him about that, if you like,' Viv added.

'What? No, it's fine. I'll talk to him.'

'He's just anxious.'

'I know.'

'And I know that doesn't make it okay. He cares a little too much, I think, and he doesn't know how to control that.' Viv smiled. 'He's young.'

'He'd hate to hear you say that.'

Viv laughed, and the tone was sweet and melodic. Faerie-like indeed.

'I'll keep it to myself, then,' she said as she reached over to wrap a dressing around Julia's throat, like a styleless necklace. Or a noose.

'Before you speak to him, though,' she went on, 'there are some things I need to ask you.'

'Alright.'

'About the King.'

Julia should have guessed that would've been what Viv wanted to talk about. After all, Lucas had told her they'd found the Queen. Julia had never seen anyone who suited the role more. It would be just like a true queen to introduce herself by her name, instead of by her title.

Empress, she was beautiful. Or Queen, rather. Maybe Julia should start swearing by her now instead.

'Lucas said you'd seen him?' Viv prompted.

Julia cleared her throat, and more water was proffered immediately. She could manage it herself this time.

'Three times,' she said. 'Things were bad after Lucas left. There was fighting, and I got stuck in the middle of it. He saved me.'

'I bet he had fun doing it, too,' Viv chuckled. 'After that long asleep, he must have been dying to blow off some steam.'

'He was…' Julia paused, choosing her description carefully. 'Angry.'

'He does that well,' she smiled. 'And after that?'

'Once in the square. He was there with the Empress, announcing the Attendant reallocations. The last time was when I left the city. He helped me to escape by getting the guards out of my way.'

'He's not playing along, then,' Viv said.

Julia didn't know how to respond to that, so she took another drink so she wouldn't have to.

'How did he seem when you left?'

Julia thought back again to that morning in the kitchen, and remembered what Claudia had said about finding him in the kitchen late at night, staring into the fire.

'He looked tired,' she said eventually, 'and a little sad. He was talking about how corrupted the city was, and how things weren't the way he would have made them.'

'No,' Viv said with a faraway look in her eyes. 'They wouldn't have been too different, though. Don't make the mistake of thinking that our king would be your saviour.'

'But he was. Twice.'

'When it was easy. He always had that way about him. He'd convince you his way was the only way, and before you knew it you'd do anything he said without thinking, just because he was the one saying it.'

Julia was confused at the turn the conversation had taken. Wasn't Viv supposed to love him?

'I thought he was a good king?' she said.

'For us, yes. He'd be worlds better than Laila anyway, but I wouldn't say that he was a good man. In a crisis he's probably the best person to be in charge, because he deals in numbers: sacrificing three to save fifty, rationing the blood we have so everyone can be fed… But survival isn't always the only thing at stake.'

She looked troubled at that, but Julia couldn't follow her thoughts.

'Just don't forget that he's our king, not yours,' she added. 'The distinction matters.'

Julia nodded, wondering why Viv had felt the need to impress that upon her. It wasn't as though the humans of the Blue would ever be able to change its leadership. The Nobles had always been in charge and they always would be, so for all intents and purposes their king was the humans' king too.

For better or for worse, they were in this together.

As soon as Viv had left Julia's side, Lucas arrived bearing a bowl of food for her. She was a little disappointed by that, because she was curious about the other Invicti who were sitting by the fire. She would have liked to go over and meet them for herself.

'I'm not an invalid,' she said.

'Yes you are.'

'No, I'm not. Look,' she said, putting the bowl aside so she could get to her feet. 'I can stand, I can walk, and I'm fairly sure that I could climb that tree if I needed to.'

'Julia,' Lucas said, tugging her hand gently to encourage her back to the ground.

She gave in and took a seat beside him. It was no hardship. Truthfully, she was a lot more tired than she was letting on.

'I nearly killed you,' he said.

'Now you're just being dramatic. I passed out, that's all. Viv said I'll be fine tomorrow. It was nothing. I mean, I was only out an hour or so. You were mostly dead for three days.'

She smiled, but Lucas didn't smile back.

'I'm so sorry,' he said.

'Look, it's fine. It's done, and I don't want to talk about it anymore.'

She had to shut down this conversation, not because his bite had hurt, as Lucas seemed to fear, but because it had been a reminder of exactly what she'd thought they'd lost.

She could have it back again, that frisson of the feed. Julia had no reason to push him away anymore. But still she pushed, because it didn't feel right to reach out to him.

'Tell me about the rest of them,' she said, partly to distract him and partly because her curiosity was killing her. 'You mentioned Cameron, but I was too far away to see him properly that night in the square. Which one is he?'

The Invicti were all bundled around the fire now. It was only Julia and Lucas who sat off to one side, close to the trees where it was quieter and cooler.

'He's the one sitting there,' Lucas pointed. 'The blond, next to the man with the beard.'

Cameron was laughing while the other man smiled at him. Their hands rested close together on the ground, almost touching, but not quite.

'You're not the only human here, either,' Lucas said. 'The one with the beard – Felix – he's human too.'

'Oh.'

She knew they would have to be getting blood from somewhere, but the idea of taking an Attendant out into the Red didn't sit well with Julia. It felt wrong for the interaction she was watching, too. Felix was perhaps a little on the outside of the group, because he and Cam were sitting at the edge of the circle, but Julia hadn't missed the way their fingers brushed together every so often, as though they were reassuring themselves that the other one was still there. Those smiles looked genuine as well. They were the kind of smiles that she'd shared with Lucas in their better moments, the smiles of two people who had nowhere else they'd rather be.

The thought of him being Attendant to the whole squad... That couldn't be what this was.

'And he just serves Cameron?' she asked.

'No, not Cameron. He's contaminated.'

'Recently?' Julia asked, because it would make sense if he had been brought for the purpose.

'I don't think so. I think he was born in the Red.'

'Then why's he here?'

Lucas smiled wryly and said, 'You sound like you can't imagine any reason for him to be here other than for his blood. What was it you said to me at the river the other day?'

Julia raised an eyebrow at him, unimpressed.

'I know very well that we have value beyond our blood,' she said. 'What surprises me is the suggestion that a Noble would agree with that.'

'You know I do, don't you? Please tell me you know that.'

Julia shrugged. 'I was your Attendant. That was my job.'

'And I didn't take anything from you until I had no other choice.' Lucas shook his head. 'You really think your blood's all I cared about? I couldn't care less if you're contaminated or not. Empress, I'd rather you were, because at least then I'd know you were safe from the Weepers, and from Rufus, and from any other Noble who decided my silver didn't matter anymore. Let's get Felix over here right now if it's what you want.'

It wasn't a flippant offer. Julia could see he was serious from the intensity in his eyes. He was genuine, even excited about it.

'I mean it,' he said when Julia didn't reply.

'I know.'

'And?'

'I'm thinking.'

He was too enthusiastic, that was the thing. She could understand that he wanted to prove himself, and she could understand that he'd feel better if she were safe from the Weepers, but she'd be staying with the Invicti all the way back to the Blue, so the Weepers were irrelevant. Once they arrived, Rufus probably would be a threat, but her being contaminated wouldn't stop him from breaking her neck.

There was only one reason why Lucas might want her to be contaminated right now, before they arrived back at the island.

'I can't go back into the Blue if I'm contaminated, can I?' she said. 'You're trying to stop me from coming back with you.'

Lucas picked up her bowl from where she'd discarded it earlier and rested it in her lap.

'Eat,' he said.

'Lucas.'

He ran his fingers back through his hair, dragging the dark strands away from his forehead.

'Yes,' he said eventually. 'I'd rather you weren't in the middle of that fight. I want you somewhere safe.'

'The Red? Safe?'

'If you're contaminated, so you have immunity from the Weepers? Yes, safe enough. Safer than you'd be in the Blue, anyway.'

'Why the sudden reluctance? You were the one trying to persuade me back to the city a few days ago.'

Lucas didn't reply to that, probably because they both knew the answer to her question. He was feeling guilty about biting her, and his protective instincts were acting up.

'Does Felix have to stay behind too?' she asked pointedly.

'I don't know,' Lucas said, as though it had been a real question. 'He's Cam's friend, so I suppose that'll be his decision. But Felix feeds the Queen. They might want to take him with them.'

Julia ignored the casual assumption that the Nobles got to decide what happened to their humans – for now – because something else in that comment had caught her attention.

'Wait,' she said. 'You told me Felix was contaminated.'

'Right,' Lucas said with a sly smile. 'But she's immune.'

The drugs must still have been clouding Julia's head, because she couldn't put that together.

'Immune to the Weepers?' she said. 'Aren't you all?'

'Yes. And no, not the Weepers. She's immune to the contamination. You know I said your blood would kill me?'

Julia nodded as she swallowed a spoonful of stew, thinking about how close they had come to that end. It was only pure luck that had saved him, and her.

'Well,' he said, 'it's a bit more complicated than that.'

'So I've heard.'

'You too, huh?' Lucas smiled. 'It was all they'd tell me to start with too, but it really is complicated. The Weepers are made by one kind of contamination, and they're only really dangerous to uncontaminated humans. The other kind of contamination – the thing that makes humans immune to the Weepers – also makes Nobles human.'

Julia dropped her spoon back into her bowl.

'No,' she said.

'Yes. If I drank contaminated blood, I'd be as human as you are.'

Julia wondered for a moment if that would be such a bad thing. Having feelings for a human version of Lucas would be so much easier. It would make sense. It would feel like they could belong together then.

'But not the Queen,' Lucas went on, 'or the King apparently. Something about their blood makes them immune.'

It was a lot to digest. Thankfully, Julia had the excuse of shovelling stew into her mouth to give her time to think it through. For something cooked on a campfire in the middle of nowhere, she had to admit that it was delicious.

'What does all of this mean for her?' Julia said with cheeks full of stew as she nodded towards Viv.

'Viv?'

'Does she even know what she's walking into? If she's been asleep so long, has she ever even been to the city?'

Lucas's brow creased for a moment before understanding dawned.

'Viv's not the Queen,' he said. 'She's one of the Invicti, and she's with the Secundus. The leader, Tommy, over there next to her. The one with the grumpy face on.'

She saw the gold in the leader's eyes across the fire, and the looks that passed between him and the queen of the faeries, as Julia had come to imagine her. Not the queen of the Nobles though, as it turned out.

'Then where's the Queen?'

'The brunette curled up next to Cameron and Felix.'

Julia hadn't even noticed her. She'd been sitting here for ages, watching the figures around the fire as first Viv and then Lucas came to speak with her, and she hadn't once realised that the pile of material next to Cameron was a person.

'She's been through it,' Lucas said. 'They hadn't been feeding her. She mostly sleeps at the moment, but Adewale told me she broke free and took down twenty of the Red Shirts on her own back in the mountains.'

'She's tiny,' Julia said.

'When she's folded up like that. But they're all terrified of her.'

'The Red Shirts?'

Lucas shook his head. 'The Invicti. All of them except Cameron and Viv. If she can take out so many Red Shirts when she's in that state, imagine what she can do in a couple of days when we get back to the Blue.'

'I won't have to imagine it, because I'm going to be there,' Julia said, making her decision.

Lucas wasn't happy about that.

'But if you just–'

'No,' she said. 'You're not leaving me behind, Lucas. Not this time. I might be human, and I might not be as strong as you are, but I'm coming with you to get Claudia out.'

'But you're still recovering–'

'I'm fine, and I'm coming with you.'

He reached out to take her hand, and she knew from the way he looked at her that there was some persuasive entreaty on his lips.

She couldn't listen to it though, because she needed her resolve for what she had to do next.

'Please don't argue,' she said, 'not about this.'

Lucas didn't reply. He looked crushed, but instead of trying to change her mind he just nodded and left her under the trees while he went to tell the others her decision.

18

The girl was fine, thanks to Viv and Aaron, but the Invicti were arguing about what to do with her. It was already pitch dark, and there was no sign that they were going to be turning in any time soon.

Cam's head was starting to nod. He wished they'd hurry up about it so he could get back to Felix and get some sleep. How long did it take to figure out a simple deployment anyway? And did this discussion really need *all* of them?

'I don't care either way,' Tommy said. 'We already have one human. Another's not going to be a problem. She can ride with you, Lucas.'

'But it's dangerous,' he said.

Tommy raised an eyebrow. 'I thought you said she wanted to come with us?'

'She does,' Viv said with a smile at Lucas. 'He'd rather she didn't, though. Right?'

Lucas looked at his feet, a childish gesture that sat strangely on him now that he looked like a soldier.

'She'd hate that, you know,' Viv added. 'She knows her own mind, and she doesn't need you to make it up for her.'

'I don't want her to get hurt,' he said.

'I know, but this is her fight too.'

Viv gave Lucas a pointed look, but rubbed his arm sympathetically as she did so. Always the mother, always the teacher.

'Well then,' Cam said, clapping his hands together. 'Is that settled? Tommy doesn't care, I don't care, and I imagine none of the rest of you care as long as the girl isn't sharing your horse. Can we please get some shut-eye now?'

'Why are you in such a rush, Cam?' Naia said. 'Could it have something to do with the lumberjack in your bed, perchance?'

'*Perchance*,' Zita snickered, and she wasn't the only one. Even Adewale cracked a grin, and Cam hadn't seen him smile since the day they'd lost Alistair.

'Yes, yes,' Viv interrupted. 'Very funny. Leave him alone. We all need some sleep if we're going to make the run to the Blue tomorrow.'

'If I had him in my bed, I definitely wouldn't be sleeping,' said Naia.

'It's two days to the island,' Tommy said, ignoring her, 'but I think we can make it in one.'

Cam tuned out as the Secundus went on to describe the route, and the regularity of the stops they'd make along the way, and how they'd cross quickly when they arrived, and every sickening detail that frankly Cam didn't give a toss about because Felix was looking at him from the trees beyond the fire where he sat with Emmy and Julia.

He just wanted to lie down and let Felix hold him until the world felt right again. It was the only time he could believe they might actually win this fight, because in the light of day the odds felt insurmountable.

The news that Sol was already awake had been encouraging at first, but the more Cam thought about it, the more it worried him.

Why hadn't he come looking for Emmy? What was going on in the Blue to keep him there, when he must have known that his queen was out on the continent? Cam wouldn't have thought that anyone could keep Sol somewhere he didn't want to stay, but Laila and Lorelei had enough deviousness between them to be capable of anything.

'Cam?' Tommy was saying.

'Sorry, what?'

'Daydreaming, lover boy?' said Naia.

Zita sniggered again.

'Oh, forget it,' Tommy said. 'Everyone bugger off and get some sleep. Up with the dawn, and we'll push to the ferry.'

* * *

The next day went almost exactly as planned. They rode the horses hard and reached the ferry crossing by nightfall. All that was left between them and the Blue now was the lake and the stretch of the Red that surrounded the city on the island. Another fast riding day should see off the latter, but the former was going to be a problem.

'It won't work,' Cam said to Tommy as they sat by the fire that night. 'There are sixteen of us, and fourteen horses. It's going to take hours to get across using the ferry. Our only chance is to swim the horses across.'

'Or we take two days to do the journey,' Viv suggested, but Tommy was already shaking his head.

'No time.'

'So the horses will be exhausted before we even hit the opposite shore for the long ride?' she said.

'Or…' said Cam.

Viv and Tommy waited for him to continue.

'We could get a couple of hours' sleep then make the crossing tonight.'

'In the dark?' said Tommy. 'You want to take that rabid creature of yours across the salt lake in the dark, when three months ago he'd never seen a body of water bigger than a puddle?'

'Of course I don't *want* to, but I'll do it if I have to. Hades will too, as long as he has Sandor beside him.'

'So cute,' Naia chimed in. 'Even your horses fancy each other.'

Cam ignored her, as usual.

'The point is,' he said, 'that they might not be able to manage a full day's riding and a swim in one day, but if we rest them on either side of the crossing then they should be fine. If the worst comes to the worst, we can carry them to the shore.'

Not a prospect Cam was relishing. Hades was still voracious in his pursuit of Cam's toes, and he couldn't imagine what mischief the horse would get up to if he had to drag the creature out of the water.

Tommy sank into his thoughts for a minute or so before he spoke again. The other Invicti watched him, waiting for his verdict.

'Does anyone else have a better plan?' he asked.

Seconds passed in sullen silence.

'Then we go with Cam's. Three hours' sleep, then we cross and sleep again until dawn on the opposite beach. Darius and Linh on first watch.'

Cam found Felix sitting a little way up the slope with his usual crowd: Julia, Lucas and Emmy. Tommy hadn't officially reassigned their pairs since Eveline's departure, but the Invicti had so many conversations without the others that it made sense for Felix and Emmy to buddy up. It didn't matter that they had nothing in common except Cam, because Emmy wasn't a demanding companion. Every second that she wasn't in the saddle she was either eating or sleeping, and that seemed to be just fine with Felix.

He'd never had much use for casual chit-chat. It was stemming his conversation on deep and meaningful subjects that Cam found challenging.

'Did I hear something about crossing tonight?' Lucas asked as Cam approached.

'It's the only way,' Cam said. 'A few hours' sleep now, then we'll cross and rest till dawn on the other side.'

Felix stood and took Cam's hand, leading him and Emmy over to the patch by the fire where their blankets were already laid out. Emmy went straight back to sleep as soon as Cam had settled her next to him, like a hedgehog waking briefly and resentfully from its hibernation.

Maybe hibernation was exactly what this was, because Cam had never known anything like it. It was as though Emmy were storing her energy until she needed it, coiling it tight within herself for the moment she needed it to explode. At least, Cam hoped that was what she was doing. If she was simply too damaged from her captivity to function, then they would be in trouble when the army arrived.

Julia and Lucas followed the three of them to their beds shortly afterwards, and it didn't take long for the camp to fall silent but for the distant howling of Weepers and the hooting of owls.

It didn't last.

Cam was jerked from sleep by something in the air.

It couldn't have been time for the crossing yet, because the watch hadn't woken them. When he turned to check for Darius and Linh, they were exactly where he had expected them to be: one watching the water and the other facing back up the slope towards the continent.

'Did you hear something?' he whispered to Darius, who was closest, sitting on his perch a little farther back from the water.

His expression was one of surprise when he looked over his shoulder at Cam.

'Not a thing,' he said. 'Did you?'

'I don't know.'

The others were still flat out around him: Emmy and Felix to either side of him, with Julia and Lucas a touch closer to the fire. The boy had the Attendant wrapped in his arms, which explained why he was happier sleeping alongside Felix and Cam than he was with the rest of the squad.

All of whom were fast asleep around the fire.

Then Cam could smell it: a faint wisp of something familiar. It made him anxious, sending his heart racing, but he couldn't put his finger on why. Still, he'd spent enough time in the forests of the Red that he knew to trust his instincts.

'Everyone up!' he yelled, just seconds before the first of the scouts poured down the slope towards them. 'Tacitum!'

Hands were on weapons while the word was still leaving Cam's mouth, but that wasn't quickly enough to counter their attackers. They were moving at Silver speed, tens of them, and the Invicti were starved of blood, under-slept and lethargic from their rude awakening.

Darius was the first to fall, because he found himself in the defensive front line. He went down hard, his head slamming into a nearby tree while Cam was still struggling to get out of his blankets.

They reached Cam next, crowding around him until all he could do was keep trying to push them away. There was no time to grab a weapon and no time to call for help, because within split-seconds all he could see were sewn lips and grasping hands, reaching down towards Emmy as they crushed in on him.

He heard someone shout, 'They're after the Queen!'

She was curled between Cam's legs like a frightened puppy, covering her face with her arms. Apparently she wasn't coming out of hibernation any time soon. Felix was crouching right next to her, trying to stand and failing because of the sheer weight of the bodies that were bearing down on them.

Then Cam saw the vials of blood hanging from the attackers' belts, just like the bottles they'd snatched while fighting the Red Shirts in the mountain. Most of them were empty, but a few still glinted darkly in the moonlight.

Barely seconds after the fight had started, Cam had stolen one of the vials and downed it.

That would level the odds.

He could feel the energy coursing back into his muscles, but he didn't wait for it to settle; he just moved, spinning as he pushed the bodies of the Tacitum tens of feet away, where they stumbled to the ground. They might have had numbers on their side, but once he'd removed their blood advantage he was more than a match for them all.

The rest of the Invicti had already descended on the fallen targets, dragging them back by ankles and throats as they tried to speed towards Cam and Emmy.

'You okay, Lucas?' Tommy yelled.

Cam followed his line of sight to see the boy wrestling a single Tacitum away from Julia. He'd wrapped himself around it from behind, making its Silver speed useless, and he was punching at its head while it tried to shake him loose. Suddenly the creature fell still, then it dropped to the ground with Lucas still clinging to its back, revealing Julia behind them. She was holding a small crossbow that looked familiar. The bolt was sticking out of the Tacitum's forehead.

'Fine,' Lucas shouted back to Tommy.

While he and Julia joined the other Invicti, a hand wrapped around Cam's calf. He looked down to see Emmy looking back up at him from her place amongst the leaves.

'They took him,' she whispered.

'Who?'

But Cam hadn't really needed to ask, because the dread tugging at his stomach answered for him. He could see the place where Felix had been fighting just seconds beforehand, now empty but for a few spots of blood. A quick tally of the Tacitum who were either down or pinned suggested at least a few of them were missing.

'Shit,' he muttered, then yelled, 'Tommy, they've got Felix! I'm going after them.'

He waited only until Viv had retrieved Emmy before sprinting off into the trees, using his Silver speed to trail the path of the captors.

He would never have had a chance of catching up if Felix hadn't been such a disagreeable hostage.

When Cam tracked them down a few miles from the coast, Felix had already unleashed his greatest weapon: his blood. His hands were covered in it. Two of the Tacitum were down, but there were still three left, and one of them was doing his damnedest to carry Felix away. Cam aimed for the other two, because Felix was already jabbing a bloodied finger into the eye of the one who held him in his arms.

The Tacitum dropped Felix in an attempt to avoid the contamination, but it was too late. The blood had done its work. He buckled over as the wounds that hadn't hurt him when he was Silver started to cripple his newly-human body. He didn't look to be fatally injured, but he was definitely out of this fight.

'Everything under control here, then?' Cam said as he sliced the throat of one of the others, taking him to the ground.

The last of them ran then, leaving his fallen companions behind.

Felix brushed the blood and dirt from his hands.

'I could do with a lift back,' he said.

'Alright, but only if you keep your fingers out of my face, otherwise we'll both be walking to the shore.'

'I'll behave.' Felix grinned. 'For now.'

The Invicti had put down the rest of the Tacitum by the time Cam and Felix made it back to camp, but the night was far from casualty-free. Darius had taken a bad injury to the head that was taking its sweet time to heal up, Felix had been bashed up in the course of his kidnapping and Julia had a new gash running up the length of her lower arm. It would be fine with a few stitches and the girl was bearing the pain with her customary resilience, but between that and the bite at her neck she was starting to look like a patchwork girl.

'This wasn't an accident,' Tommy said as he wiped the blood from his mouth. 'They attacked us in the dark while we had our backs to the water. They knew we were coming this way, so they waited until we'd be vulnerable.'

'They wanted to take us out of the picture before we reached the island,' said Darius, prodding gingerly at his wounds.

'They wanted Emmy and Felix,' said Cam.

Curious eyes turned towards Felix, but Cam was sure that those who were still suspicious had no right to be. They hadn't seen how Felix had fought with the Tacitum who'd tried to take him.

'Emmy I understand,' said Naia. 'They want her back, and I get that. What I don't get is why they're after the lumberjack.'

'Information?' Viv suggested.

'No,' said Felix. 'Revenge.'

'Against you?' Cam asked.

'And you. It's not enough to win; she wants to make you suffer too.'

Eveline would have known what Felix had become to Cam by the time she'd deserted. She also would have known that he'd swapped sides, and everything she'd known would have been reported back to the person in charge.

'Well, I think we all know who's behind this,' Tommy said.

Lorelei.

She'd always been the sort to put her pieces in place in advance, then wait for the perfect moment to strike.

'Found these,' Bartek said, handing two small bottles to Tommy.

'The others had already drunk theirs,' Aaron added as he turned over the last of the bodies to reveal a mess of broken glass. 'Or dropped them. Bloody idiots.'

'Well it's something,' Tommy said, then he turned to Cam. 'Fourteen horses and sixteen of us, right?'

'Right.'

'Okay then,' he said as he tipped the bottles so their contents shone in the moonlight. 'Which two of you want to go scouting?'

They sent Konrad and Naia in the end, because they always had been the sneakiest of the bunch.

In the meantime, Cam used the ferry to take all the supplies across the water, then led the others into the lake on horseback.

Their night-swimming adventure was as much of a success as they could have expected, particularly given that all of the riders were needed, but not all of them knew what they were doing. Emmy had reverted to her state of catatonia and Julia was a complete novice who barely knew how to swim. They were each bracketed between other riders, but it was a nerve-wracking experience nonetheless.

By the time they reached the beach on the other side, some so gratefully that they looked as though they were ready to start kissing the pebbles, Konrad and Naia had returned. Still running on Silver speed, it only took seconds for them to nip across the lake on the ferry to join the others on the island.

'Lucky bastards,' Aaron muttered.

It had been a very long time since the rest of them had last had any blood, and it was starting to wear on everyone. Cam almost felt guilty for the vial he'd snatched earlier, because there hadn't been enough to share. That was bound to sour the mood.

It didn't help that they were all now soaking wet and sticky from the salt water in the lake. Weeks of blazing sunshine had concentrated it so much that Cam could feel it crusting on his skin and scratching where the fabric caught between his underarms and legs. The material was going to set solid with the salt, then start rubbing holes in his skin when they set out again at dawn.

No wonder everyone was so grouchy.

Unfortunately, the news from the scouts wasn't good either.

'They're about fifty miles back,' Konrad said.

'Okay, well it'll take them another two or three days to get this far then,' said Tommy.

Naia's face screwed into a grimace. 'Yeah, actually, not so much. They were lining up the uncontaminated humans, getting them ready for tomorrow. We think they're going to load up on blood then just blaze straight through.'

Tommy and Viv exchanged a look.

'They're going to use the blood to get past us?' he said.

'Looks like it.'

'But then they'll have less for the fighting.'

'I don't think they'll care,' said Konrad. 'It'll be more important to them that they get there before us than that they have stamina in the fight. Think about it: the only guards left in the Blue are Lorelei's, and we can assume they're with the army. If the army can get to the city before us, then all their soldiers would be in one place and they could work together to keep us out.'

'Shit,' Tommy said.

'Shit indeed.'

'Then we don't have time to stop. We need to keep riding.'

A collective groan rose from the surrounding Invicti, but off to one side Julia and Lucas were in the middle of a whispered argument. When Lucas saw Cam's attention on him, he turned to Tommy.

'Can I make a suggestion?' he said.

'At this stage, I'd say any and all suggestions are welcome,' the Secundus replied.

'Then one of us needs to go on ahead to see if we can get a message to the King. Julia and I can go together.'

Viv scowled. 'You're not really going to take more of her blood, are you?'

'It's fine,' the girl said. Cam got the distinct impression that this was her idea.

'I won't need much,' Lucas said.

'If she can spare the blood then it should be one of us who goes,' said Darius. 'We're the ones who know him, for fuck's sake. And how's Lucas going to stand up to Lorelei if it comes down to a fight? He's just a boy.'

Cam could see the clenching in Lucas's jaw.

'I really think it has to be me,' he said.

'Watch out,' said Naia, mock fear playing over her face. 'Don't push him, Darius. He's a boy on the edge.'

'I'm not a *boy*.'

Tommy held the sides of his head and groaned.

'Will the lot of you please shut the hell up?' he said. 'Haven't we got enough ·to deal with without you arguing all the time as well? Lucas, take Julia and go. You're the fastest runner we have,' he looked pointedly at Darius and Naia, 'and we need to give Sol all the warning we can. The rest of you, mount up. We're pushing on.'

The Invicti weren't happy, but Tommy was having none of it.

'What is this?' he said, looking around at their moping faces. 'Where's this morale problem coming from?'

'Where isn't it?' said Aaron. 'Half the Invicti betrayed us to Laila back in the Blue, then Alistair betrayed us, Eveline betrayed us, Lorelei betrayed us, we've just got out of a fight and now you want us to ride through the night into a battle with every other Silver in the world, without blood. And you ask what our problem is with morale. You're having a giraffe, aren't you?'

There were several murmurs of agreement.

'But we've found the Queen,' said Cam, 'and the King's awake. Isn't that enough?'

The Invicti looked over at Emmy. She was lying on the pebbles like a dark puddle of material, sifting the stones through her fingers as though they were utterly fascinating. Cam was willing to bet she'd be asleep again within the next five minutes. She wasn't paying the slightest bit of attention to the discussion happening at her back.

'Who says the King's even in the city?' said Adewale. 'It's been weeks since the girl left.'

'And the Queen doesn't care,' Linh said softly. 'We're fighting for her, and she doesn't care.'

'She's not well,' said Viv.

'I care,' Cam said. 'I've been searching for her for centuries. You all know that. I've finally found her, and we're less than a day away from bringing her home, and you're all just going to give up now? Is that really what you're saying? You're going to let Lorelei – *Lorelei* – scare you away from this fight by throwing a bunch of paper-thin Tacitum in your way?'

Cam looked around at their faces, but none of them responded. Tommy and Viv were the only ones who would even meet his eye.

'You're the Invicti, for fuck's sake!' he said. 'Have you forgotten what that means?'

'They're tired, Cam,' said Viv.

'So am I, but it doesn't mean I'm going to forget my oath. This is our purpose. It's what the Invicti are for: we serve the King. Yes, some of our comrades turned out to be traitorous little shits. And yes, it's been a hard road, and we have no guarantee of victory at the end, but when is victory *ever* guaranteed? Have you got so used to living in Laila's little fish tank that you can't remember what real danger feels like?'

'And think of the victory,' said Tommy. 'Think about what would happen if we pull this off. Twelve Invicti – hell, thirteen, because the boy counts by now – bringing the Queen home so the King can take back his throne. Can you imagine how much our world is going to change?'

'How much it needs to change,' Viv said.

'But if you want to be like Lorelei,' said Cam, 'then go ahead and make yourselves into oath-breakers too.'

He looked at each of them as he spoke, and this time they were looking right back at him.

'Well,' Naia said after a moment, 'I can't pretend that I haven't been bored as all hell for the past five hundred years.'

Zita groaned and said, 'So bored.'

'And fighting together again has been a good thing,' said Bartek.

'Even when I'm the one taking down all your attackers,' Zita said.

Cam let go of the tension in his chest as the Invicti degenerated into their usual bickering, because then he knew the crisis was over.

Felix took his hand and threaded his fingers through Cam's.

'Well played,' he whispered.

Cam smiled, but darkly, because they both knew that this wasn't a game they could afford to lose.

Lucas and Julia left while the Invicti were getting ready to move out. Cam watched them go and hoped against hope that they would find Sol strong and well in the Blue, though he was starting to expect the worst.

The King would have been here by now if he had been able to leave the city.

Cam kept those doubts to himself though, because for the moment they had enough problems to worry about out here in the Red, first of which was that they didn't have enough horses. They were barely halfway through the forest when the first of them stopped by a stream and refused to go any further. That meant that Darius had to run alongside the others on foot. He wasn't happy about it, but the remaining horses were too spent to carry any extra weight. It wasn't long before he was joined by Gul and Bartek too, but neither of them complained.

They were sold on Cam's speech. Most of the Invicti seemed to be, because they still had their heads down and eyes focussed forwards as the morning grew late.

It was a responsibility Cam bore poorly, because he'd already resolved to step back and let Tommy make all the speeches and decisions from here on out, but this was too important for him to ignore it. This was everything he'd waited for, but more importantly, Felix was at stake. Even though he hadn't silvered for the human, Cam knew their lives had become too intertwined to be separated now.

He was musing on this when the first strike hit. They didn't come from behind, as Cam had expected, but from the side.

'Left!' Tommy yelled as a Red Shirt barrelled into Viv's horse. She was thrown up into the air, but miraculously Tommy was there to catch her before she hit the ground.

'Run,' Cam said to her as he joined Tommy. 'The baby.'

She didn't hesitate. By the time the rest of the attackers reached them, she was already out of sight.

'Ride on!' Cam yelled as the Invicti started to slow their horses to meet the army, but it was pointless anyway. The Red Shirts were full of blood, so the whole squad had been pulled from their mounts before Cam had even finished speaking.

They meant to finish it, then.

Konrad had been right: Lorelei wasn't going to let the Invicti reach the city first.

19

In the Blue, Julia had started running the moment she and Lucas had reached the city.

'Come on!' she shouted as they raced up the palace steps in the darkness.

'I'm going faster than you are,' Lucas replied.

'I wasn't talking to you! I was talking to my feet.'

Speed was pointless though, because nothing was getting them past the guard at the palace door.

'Please,' Julia begged. 'My friend Claudia works here as an Attendant. I know the King. We have to get in.'

'Yeah, right,' the man scoffed. 'Everyone knows the King. I personally had lunch with him only yesterday, out on his yacht in the Maldives.'

Julia blinked.

'What are you talking about?' said Lucas.

'Just bugger off, will you?' the guard said.

'You don't understand. There's an army on its way here. We have to warn him.'

'You can make up whatever stories you want, mate, but it's the middle of the night. Don't make me call the others over to throw you out of here. Come back in the morning.'

Lucas and Julia exchanged a desperate look, then Lucas went still. A few seconds later he shook his head, then took Julia's hand and led her back down the steps.

'There are more of them inside,' he whispered when their feet hit the paving slabs of the square. 'A lot of them. Too many.'

'I've got my crossbow.'

'Still too many. They'll be positioned all through the palace, anyway. It's shut up tight.'

Julia propped her hands on her hips, wondering for the first time why the guard hadn't reacted to her outfit. He should have commented on it, at least. He would know that she wasn't a Noble, and a Server had no business wandering around in trousers with a crossbow belted to her waist.

They'd been stupid. She'd been in such a rush to get here and get Claudia out that she'd forgotten how different things were in this city.

But the guard wouldn't have. He would have seen the incongruity the moment they walked up to him, and he should have challenged her on it.

Damn.

'They're working for Lorelei, aren't they?' she said.

'Probably.'

'And we've just told them we're here.'

'Yes,' Lucas said, his face darkening. 'Maybe that wasn't our best idea.'

They looked back up at the guard to see him watching them. He wasn't the only one there anymore; there was a second guard by the now-open door, and they were deep in conversation.

'Empress,' Julia said. 'We can't come back in the morning now, even if we did have the time to waste. We've got to get out of here. Come on.'

She'd had an idea.

Lucas didn't ask questions, he just followed her as she crept quickly around the side of the palace. She had goose pimples before they'd even come into view of Rufus's house, but she'd have to get over that, because there was only one way they were going to get into the palace.

'How's your jumping?' she whispered to Lucas.

'What?'

'What I mean,' she said, as though explaining it to a three-year-old, 'is that I need you to jump us up onto the palace roof. Can you do it?'

'I don't know…'

They'd skirted the edge of the building now and were standing at the back of the palace, between it and Rufus's house. Julia eyed the house carefully, but it seemed to be shut up for the night, just like every other residence in the Blue. Still, she could feel the fear prickling at the back of her neck.

They would come back for Marcella later, but right now Julia and Lucas had another reason to be in this alley.

Julia had seen it from her room in that house: the flat gutter lying between the pointed roofs of the palace. She knew it started here, in this alley, and she was willing to bet that if they could just get up there then it would take them straight to the courtyard garden where she'd met Claudia on her first and only visit to the palace.

It had only been a few weeks ago, and here she was with stitches in her neck again, but it still felt as though she'd come back into the Blue a different person from the one who had walked out. The new Julia wouldn't baulk at breaking into the palace just because it was teeming with guards. She was going to help Claudia escape this time, and then they could both be free.

Then she spotted it.

'There,' she whispered, pointing up at the flattened edge of the roof several storeys above them. 'Can you jump up there?'

Lucas still looked uncertain.

'I've seen you jumping into trees that are higher than that,' Julia said. 'I've seen the other Nobles jumping up to the tallest roofs in this city. The Secundus said you were the fastest they had. Was he wrong?'

'Sneaky,' Lucas smiled. 'Trying to provoke my pride.'

'Is it working?'

'I shouldn't think so,' said a voice from the shadows. A horribly familiar and unwelcome voice. 'Lucas doesn't have any pride, do you? I shouldn't be surprised to see you've come crawling back here, but I confess I am.'

Julia should probably have been frightened – she'd thought she would be – but instead the sight of his face just made her very, very angry.

'Didn't your friend Lorelei tell you that we were on our way?' she said sweetly.

Rufus smiled, showing his teeth.

'Why, Julia,' he said. 'Whatever can you mean? I'd hate to think you were implying that I, the son of the Empress, would ever be involved with rebels. For my own Attendant to make such an accusation–'

'She's not yours,' Lucas said, through gritted teeth.

'Then that isn't my name on her cheek?'

'It shouldn't have been,' Lucas said, taking two steps forwards. 'Not when my silver's in her ear.'

Rufus took two steps of his own. 'Even after you'd deserted her?'

'You know I didn't have a choice. You made sure I didn't have a choice.'

'Lucas,' Julia said, but he ignored her.

'You asked Lorelei to do it, didn't you?' he said. 'You asked her to send me away.'

Rufus laughed. 'Because you're such a threat to me? Don't be ridiculous.'

'Lucas…'

He ignored her again, his attention firmly focussed on Rufus.

'So Julia being assigned to you,' Lucas said. 'That was just an accident, was it? You didn't ask Lorelei to do that?'

'We don't have time for this, Lucas,' said Julia.

Rufus took another step forwards, until his face was barely a foot distant from Lucas's.

'You think I really want your discards?' he said, snarling the words.

Lucas opened his mouth to reply, but Julia had run out of patience. Neither of them was paying the slightest bit of attention to her, probably because neither of them actually considered her a threat. In the circumstances, it wasn't difficult to take a moment to sight the crossbow correctly so the bolt hit Rufus right in the centre of his eye.

Julia took some satisfaction from the fact that when he fell, he landed right in a bucket of miscellaneous filth that someone had left out in the alley.

'Lucas,' she said, in a tone of chilling calm. 'We. Do not. Have time. For this.'

He gaped at her for a moment, but regained his composure quickly enough to give Rufus's unconscious body a quick kick.

Julia rolled her eyes.

'Ready?' he asked.

'I have been ready for some several minutes now.'

He looked chastened as he scooped Julia into his arms and leapt up to the roof. He was beaming when he set her down though, like a puppy who expected a treat for performing a trick.

'Yes,' Julia said, 'well done. Now come on.'

They were in luck. The gutter ran straight between the palace roofs to the butterfly-filled courtyard Julia remembered, although since it was still full dark there were only a few moths flitting around the light that spilled through cracks in the shutters.

But someone was still awake.

When Lucas had jumped them down into the garden, it became clear that the light was coming from the kitchen, the same room in which Julia had met the King on her last visit. The King, who liked to stay up late and watch the fire.

But when she pushed open the door, the figure sitting in front of the flames wasn't the King, but Claudia.

They stared at each other for a second, then Claudia's face crumpled. Julia went to her.

Their embrace was strong, tearful and loud, as they each tried to cram weeks' worth of news into the first few minutes of their reunion. Claudia listened to Julia's warning about the approaching army with surprising stoicism, as though it didn't really matter to her. After all that they'd suffered during the Contamination and the carnage afterwards, perhaps fear had simply become normality for her.

But she did want to hear about Julia's parents.

'You didn't find them?' she said.

Julia let her expression reply for her, because she didn't want to say the words aloud.

'I'm sorry,' said Claudia, but her tone told Julia this was the result she'd expected. There was a hint of an *I told you so* beneath the words. That riled Julia enough for her to push back.

'I'm not giving up. I'm going back out there, it's just that right now we've got bigger problems.'

'They abandoned you, Jules. When are you going to abandon them too?'

'Can we please talk about my parental issues later? Didn't you hear me? There's an army on the way, and we need the King. Can you take us to him?'

Claudia winced.

'We can't leave the palace during curfew,' she said, 'but after that I think you'd better come to the temple.'

'The temple?' Lucas said, at the same time that Julia said, 'Curfew?'

'For the palace staff. The gong strikes in the morning,' Claudia said, looking out of the open door towards the lightening sky. 'It won't be too long now.'

Cam had already been on the ground for too long.

With all the Red Shirts thundering through the undergrowth around him, he had no chance if he couldn't get back up to his feet, but there was something wrong with his legs.

'Cam!'

The shout came from his right, somewhere behind the wall of rushing bodies that surged past him towards the other Invicti.

'I'm here!'

Tommy was by his side in moments, holding out a vial of blood.

'Snatched it from one of them. Drink up and then come the fuck on. We've got work to do.'

'Where's Felix?'

'Drink!'

He did as he was told while Tommy held off the Red Shirts, but when he got to his feet again he still couldn't see Felix.

'Did they take him?'

Three Red Shirts barrelled into him then, taking him to the ground. They were all enhanced by blood consumption, but then so was Cam and he was much more experienced. It took about ten seconds for him to put them all out of commission.

When he turned back Tommy had gone.

After downing a couple more attackers, Cam saw that the Secundus was already on the other side of the brawling bodies, ducking and weaving through the Red Shirts. It wasn't until he emerged with his hands full of blood vials that Cam realised he'd been busily snatching them from the belts of the falling and fallen soldiers.

Clever plan.

The Invicti were going to need that blood, because each of them was fighting about twenty of the Red Shirts. What was strange was that the army seemed intent on bringing the Invicti down, rather than on getting past them into the city.

Which was when the truth hit Cam, at the same moment a fist hit his cheek.

The Red Shirts who were attacking them could only be part of the army. The rest must be following behind, which meant it wouldn't be long before the Invicti were overwhelmed.

As though they weren't struggling enough already.

'Hurry up, Tommy!' Cam yelled as he pulled out his knife and dragged it through the circle of Red Shirts surrounding him.

Until the rest of the Invicti started fighting on even terms, Cam had no hope of escaping the melee to find Felix. As soon as Tommy got those vials to the others, the tide of the battle was going to change.

Finally, they'd have a level playing field.

Or so Cam had thought.

Tommy came to him first, speeding to his side to press a handful of vials into his palm.

'Go left!' he shouted, just milliseconds before he headed right with a handful of his own.

Cam ran. Now that he was able to run at Silver speed, he was the fastest thing in the vicinity. The Red Shirts stumbled as they moved, as though their brains were still trying to catch up with their feet, but Cam was a thing of beauty as he jinked and flowed under arms, over heads and through legs to reach the Invicti with the precious gifts he held in his hand.

Adewale was the first he reached, and it was a good thing too because he was already down on one knee as he tried to push away the Red Shirts. They must have zeroed in on his dark head standing tall above the others, because he was completely surrounded.

Cam jumped straight over the top of the soldiers and landed next to Adewale in the circle. Adewale didn't seem to register Cam's presence until Cam had already cut through half of the Red Shirts, but he understood the purpose of the vial Cam had already pushed into his hand.

It took effect fast.

Next Cam found Zita, who was kicking out at one Red Shirt while she chewed on another one's ear. It was completely gratuitous, because she was never going to incapacitate him that way, but Zita often seemed to lose control in the heat of battle. After Cam had handed her the vial, she could really let loose.

He turned away before the violence became too gruesome and went to find his next targets: Gul and Linh, covering each others' back on the far side of the seething mass of fighters.

Cam had intended to take Gul's place after handing him a vial, but three Red Shirts grabbed Cam from behind before he could get into position. They must have been watching him, because they snatched for the contents of his hand, grasping for the last vials.

'No!' Linh yelled, lunging forward with her knife to give Gul the seconds he needed to crack his vial open and drink its contents down.

But the result was not what Cam had expected.

Gul had already taken a few scratches in the fight: a graze to the cheek, a gash in his side, and various lacerations across his hands from punching through the bodies of the Red Shirts. They were nothing more than minor inconveniences to a Silver, but in the seconds after he'd drunk from the vial he fell to the ground clutching at the wound across his stomach.

The circle of fighters around them became still. They could see the blood pouring from Gul's wounds and they knew what it meant. They were no longer trying to pry the little bottles from Cam's hands.

He opened his fist and dropped them to the ground, smashing them into the dirt with his heel.

'Ditch the bottles!' one of the Red Shirts cried to his fellow soldiers. 'They're fucking contaminated!'

Not all of them, because that wasn't how Lorelei worked. She'd left most of them clean, but having just a few contaminated ones sprinkled in amongst the others...

There was the malice in it.

The Invicti had seen the Red Shirts loaded with the vials before. They had expected them, even though it seemed stupid in hindsight that the soldiers would take bottles into battle when they were themselves fully charged, because in effect they were just arming their enemies with blood. But Tommy had taken the bait, and after the first couple of vials had worked as expected he'd had no reason to doubt them. The Invicti had trusted their contents without thinking about the fact that it was the enemy who controlled them, even if the grunts were unaware of the burdens they carried.

Now all that blood was rendered useless, because they couldn't tell what was pure and what was not.

That was when the battle changed.

The Invicti were left only half powered, but the Red Shirts became more unified, knowing they couldn't rely on using the vials to heal themselves and must now rely on each other instead. Worse than that, they were resentful at being tricked, and they turned that resentment on the Invicti. Specifically, the Invicti who hadn't managed to secure uncontaminated blood vials, or those who were now too weak to defend themselves.

Like Gul.

Linh had swept him up into her arms and was trying to carry him out of the melee, but the Red Shirts were catching at her legs and shoulders, dragging her back down.

They'd already piled on top of Cam. Hands closed around every part of his body as they pulled him away from Linh so they could chase her down.

Because Gul was the one they were really after. Their fervour was so high that it was as though Gul had been responsible for the contamination himself, as though they could undo the fact that they had been betrayed by rubbing him out of existence. He was the symbol for that traitorous contamination now, simply because he'd had the bad luck to drink the vial that had contained it.

They ran him down, and then they ground him down, stamping him into the earth in the same way that Cam had stamped on the vials.

Now that he was human, he wasn't going to rise from that.

They turned on Linh next.

This wasn't the same rabble of Red Shirts they had been scuffling with earlier in the battle. The heat of their anger gave them unity of purpose that made them move together like the Weepers did, as a collective rather than as single units. It made them into a blade.

They attacked together but then, just as abruptly, they stopped together too.

A whistle had cut through the cries that surrounded them. The Red Shirts turned towards it like meerkats detecting predators, then they were gone, disappearing en masse towards the Blue. Suddenly the forest felt very empty indeed.

'Shit,' someone groaned.

The Invicti were surrounded by carnage. Trees had been pushed to the edges of the area in which they had fought, making a clearing where there had been none before. The ground was coated with blood, but the most surprising thing was the number of bodies that now littered the ground. Cam had thought he'd been taking down a lot of Red Shirts, but it wasn't until the ones who were still standing had cleared out that he could actually count them. There were so many lying in the leaf litter that it was a wonder there had been any left to go on to the Blue.

But the Red Shirts weren't the only ones who had fallen. There was Gul, but also Aaron, who'd been turned human by a contaminated vial, but had managed to escape mortal injury. He was lying against a tree stump nursing what looked to be a broken arm.

That wasn't what drew Cam's attention though, because over on the other side of the new clearing, up in the branches of a beech tree, he could see Felix and Emmy waiting.

He nearly broke down then and there.

They'd failed to stop the Red Shirts, the un-enhanced half of them were badly injured, and they'd lost Gul, but all Cam could feel in that moment was blessed, pure relief at seeing Felix safe and sound.

He could only pray that the King was ready for the army, because in just a few more minutes it would be on its way into the Blue.

When Claudia finally managed to sneak them out of the palace, they found the temple cold and empty.

Well, almost empty.

'No,' Julia said as she ran up to the dais. 'No! How did this happen?'

The King was right back in the place where she'd first seen him. The gilding had already covered most of his skin. If she watched very closely she could almost see the metallic line creeping up towards his fingertips.

'We found him on the floor by the fire a few days after you left,' Claudia said. 'He'd been getting quieter every day, spending less time out of his rooms, then he must have just collapsed. We couldn't wake him up.'

'So you just put him back here?'

'The Empress did. Things have been a bit different since you left.'

Julia looked back at his golden curls and remembered what it had been like to see them move. They didn't yet look as though they were the solid stone they had once seemed – though she wasn't prepared to touch them to find out – but the air in the temple was draughty enough that at least a few tendrils should have been swaying free.

She looked at Lucas.

'What are we going to do now?'

'There's nothing we can do. We wait for the army to come, and hope that our side wins.'

Julia shook her head. It wasn't enough.

'I need to get Claudia out of here,' she said, 'and we need to fetch Marcella. We can go into the Red together and–'

'I don't want to leave,' Claudia interrupted. 'Jules, we talked about this before you left. I'm happy here.'

'It doesn't matter anyway,' Lucas said, 'because it's too late. I'm betting it won't be long before the army gets here. You don't want to be trying to get out while they're trying to get in.'

'So what?' Julia said. 'We're just going to hide in here?'

Lucas smiled. 'You know me better than that. You've got your weapons?'

Julia checked her belt, counting the knives and crossbow bolts slotted around her hips.

'Yes,' she said. 'You've got enough blood?'

'More than.'

'Then let's go and take down this army. Claud, stay and look after the King.'

Julia turned to follow Lucas up the aisle to the door, but Claudia grabbed her by the wrist and held her back.

'Whoa,' she said. 'Hey. You're not leaving me here with the body. You can't just leave me behind.'

Before Julia could argue about it, the doors of the temple slammed open and Viv came running through them.

'Dammit,' she said, heading straight for the dais without even acknowledging the others. 'I thought you said he was awake?'

'He was,' said Julia.

'Until?'

'A few weeks ago,' said Claudia.

'Well,' Viv said, throwing herself down into one of the pews, 'that's the end of that, then. The army's on its way. Once it gets through the Invicti, the Blue will belong to Lorelei.'

The Invicti had no choice but to leave Aaron behind. With the horses gone, either exhausted by the ride or scared away by the fighting, the only way to take him to the city would have been by carrying him, but they didn't have enough runners to do that.

A few of them had struck lucky with the blood vials before they'd discovered the subterfuge – Tommy, Cam, Naia, Adewale and Zita – but that left Linh, Konrad, Darius and Bartek who'd need the others to carry them to the city at Silver speed, because that was the only way they were going to catch up with the Red Shirts.

Linh didn't want to leave Gul's body behind, but she would. No one had even suggested that she shouldn't come along for the final battle, least of all her, despite the tears that were running freely down her cheeks. She would see this thing to its end now.

And then, of course, there was Emmy.

She should have been able to fight, because she'd been feeding from Felix for days now. She should have been able to run too, providing one more vehicle for the downed Invicti, but instead she was falling asleep up against a tree.

She would need to be carried too.

If they took her at all.

'Something's wrong,' Felix said to Cam.

He was sitting at Emmy's side, as he had throughout the battle. Her wrist was in his hand, his fingers pressed against her pulse.

Cam's stomach dropped.

'What is it?' he said, as though he couldn't already guess what Felix was going to say.

'She's fading.'

'Shit. Then we need to get her to the King, and we need to do it now.'

'Are you sure he's still in the city?'

Cam wasn't sure of anything anymore, but Sol was their last remaining hope. If he wasn't ready to fight back the Red Shirts, then the battle for the Blue was already over.

But he could barely admit that to himself, so he wasn't going to say it out loud.

'Yes,' he said instead. 'I'm sure.'

'Then we'd better get going.'

'Mmm.'

Felix brushed the dirt from his hands and scooped Emmy up into his arms.

'Shame I'm not Silver anymore,' he said.

'Mmm,' Cam murmured again.

Felix stopped walking.

'What?' he said.

Tommy yelled, 'Get your arse over here, Cam!'

He held a finger up to Tommy, asking him for a moment of time, then turned back to Felix.

'Felix, I…' Cam rubbed at the back of his neck.

'Hurry the fuck up!' Naia shouted.

'Felix, I'm not taking you in there. I'm sorry. If they're still trying to capture you, or kill you, then the city is the last place you should be right now. I'm sorry, but I need you to stay here with Aaron.'

'I can look after myself,' Felix said, raising an eyebrow.

'Against five of their Tacitum, yes. Against tens of their Red Shirts? I'd be worried.'

'So you're leaving me behind again?'

Cam sighed.

'Will you wait?' he asked.

There was a long pause, then Felix sighed too. He handed Emmy over to Cam, along with a bottle of blood he'd prepared for her.

'I'll always wait.'

The gong rang out even through the heavy doors of the temple. It could have been a call to battle, summoning the remaining guards to fight for the protection of the Blue, but it sounded more like an invitation.

Lorelei was opening the gates and letting the army in.

'Can't we do something?' Lucas said.

'You can try if you want,' Viv said, 'but I won't. I've got other things to protect besides this city.'

She had stretched her legs out along the pew, rubbing her back as she shifted in the seat. Julia realised belatedly that she must be pregnant.

No wonder the Secundus had sent her on ahead.

'You're staying here then?' Julia said.

'I don't have much choice.'

'So what should we do?'

Viv looked up at Julia, her face softening as though she knew Julia wouldn't like what she was about to say.

'Honestly? I think you should stay here too. If the army makes it to the city, then the Invicti have already lost. If Emmy's in the same state as him,' she nodded towards the King, 'then we're out of last hopes.'

'We can't be,' said Lucas.

'Do you really want my advice?' Viv said.

There was a long pause before he replied.

'Yes,' he said eventually.

'Then you contaminate Julia and her friend, and the three of you get the hell out of here the moment the army reaches the square. Go out into the Red before Lorelei turns this city into an abattoir.'

Julia and Lucas looked at each other.

'I'm serious,' Viv said to him. 'If you care about them at all, and if you girls care about your lives at all, then get out while you still can. She'll ruin this place. It might not have been perfect, but she'll have you both in cages by the end of the day.'

'I don't want to leave our home,' Claudia whispered.

'I'm sorry, but it's not your home anymore, sweetheart. Please, I'm begging you: run.'

Julia looked at her best friend. She could see the pain in her eyes, but it was fast turning into resolve. Viv had manage to persuade her of the danger where Julia had failed.

She'd do this if she had to.

'Alright, then?' Julia said to her.

'Alright.'

'And what about you, Lucas?'

But he wasn't paying attention to Julia. She was about to berate him for that when she realised that he was staring at the back of the temple, towards the dais where the King was lying encased in gold.

Except he wasn't, not anymore. His skin was quickly regaining its colour as the metallic sheen drained away from him, as though the sun was hiding its face behind a cloud.

Viv had seen it too, because she was on her feet now and fast approaching the pedestal.

'Sol?' she said. 'Are you awake? Are you really awake?'

He opened his eyes. When he finally spoke, the words seemed to arrive from a great distance.

'She is here.'

20

They came from both sides of the square, the Queen from the south and the King from the temple in the north. They seemed to grow taller with every step, more iridescent, as though they were the only creatures in the world who were giving out power rather than sucking it in.

Cam had watched the change coming over Emmy as they'd neared the city. As soon as they'd stepped over the boundary line, her eyes had lit up and her chin had lifted from her collarbone. By the time they'd reached the tumbledown buildings in the outskirts, she'd been walking on her own. Once they'd entered the city proper, she'd no longer needed guidance from the Invicti.

She'd never been to the place before, but she'd still headed towards the square like a bloodhound following a scent. Or, more accurately, a leash, because it was the bond stretched between her and Sol that had pulled her on.

The Red Shirts were waiting in the square. Lorelei's Red Shirts, because she was there too with the former Invicti who had betrayed their comrades in arms to join her side.

At least the real Invicti had already managed to thin their numbers a little.

But no one was looking at them, because everyone had turned to watch Emmy's approach.

She was smiling, a grim smile of dangerous delight. It was a smile that said she knew there was vengeance to be had here, and she was going to take her fill. Her eyes fixed on Lorelei.

'I recognise you,' she said, so softly that Cam wasn't sure Lorelei would have been able to hear it all the way across the square.

Whether she heard the words or not, she unsheathed two curved blades from her belt, spinning them around her thumbs for a couple of turns before catching them in her palms.

Emmy laughed again, more loudly this time, and flexed her fingers by her sides as though she were unsheathing her own weapons.

'The blood, Cam,' she said.

'What?'

He hadn't been listening properly, because he'd just spotted the King standing on the steps of the temple behind Lorelei.

He was staring. Cam could see the gold in his ice-blue eyes from here, calling out to the gold in Emmy's, dragging them towards each other as the bond tried to snap them back into their proper places.

But the Red Shirts were in the way.

'Cam,' Emmy said again.

He turned to her to see that she was gesturing at him impatiently, holding her hand out towards him.

'The blood?' he said.

'The bottle of blood Felix gave you. Come on, I want to try a thing.'

Cam was a little concerned, but he pulled it out of his pack nonetheless and handed it over.

'Oh, don't look at me like that,' she said. 'Just watch. It's going to be fun.'

But the dark smile was taking over her face now, tugging it into grotesquerie. She pulled the cork out of the bottle and took a swig of it, as though to demonstrate that it was uncontaminated.

Which, of course, it wasn't. It was Felix's blood.

'Remember when Laila did this back at the club in London?' she said, then she poured the rest of the bottle over her head, slicking the blood over her skin so it covered every visible inch of her. 'Let's see if it has the same effect on a bunch of blood-hungry soldiers, shall we?'

She moved then, fast. Instead of waiting for the Red Shirts to come to her, she ploughed straight into the centre of the crowd.

They didn't see the trap.

To start with they crumpled in on top of her, but a couple of seconds later they fell back outwards again, moving more slowly now, staggering into their fellow soldiers as they tried to grapple their way out of the crush. They were replaced by others who repeated the motion, who were replaced by others, and then others, until the scene resembled a detonation in slow motion.

A detonation of contamination, because Emmy had now managed to turn a good half of the Red Shirts human without making a single offensive move.

She always had loved to use blood as a weapon.

Julia and the others had left Viv behind and followed the King out of the temple, but no further. Julia was confident with her weapons, but not confident enough to walk out into a blazing mass of Nobles with just a few bits of metal and some pointy sticks between her and a draining.

She'd led Claudia and Lucas up onto the roof of a nearby building using a side staircase and a little creative climbing, and now they had a clear view of the whole square.

At least the Servers seemed to be staying locked up in their homes. The streets were deserted, shutters barred and doors firmly shut. The residents of the Blue had seen enough disturbances over the past months to know the signs, and to know when they should stay indoors.

All of them except Julia, of course.

She unholstered her crossbow.

'Well, that's fine for you,' Claudia said. 'But what are we going to do?'

Julia looked over at Lucas, who was sizing up the battle.

'I could go down there,' he said.

'I've got a better idea,' said Julia. 'Do you think you could get in and out of the guardhouse without being seen?'

'Probably.'

'I found this,' she waved the crossbow, 'on the first floor in a pile of others. Do you think—'

Lucas had already gone. He was back seconds later with an armful of bows and an entire bagful of bolts and arrows.

Claudia whistled as she took one of the weapons from him.

'I've always wanted to have a play with one of these,' she said.

Julia grinned.

'Try it,' she said. 'You'll love it.'

'Shit,' Naia yelled as something narrowly missed her shoulder. 'What was that?'

'Back up, I think,' said Cam, pointing towards a rooftop on the northern edge of the square.

Naia squinted.

'Well, it would be good if they could try fucking aiming.'

She stopped complaining when one of the Red Shirts took the next arrow through the throat, giving her time to put him down.

'Alright, then,' she said. 'Back up. I like it.'

The Invicti had charged the remaining Red Shirts the moment that Emmy had finished deploying the blood. Assisted by the bowmen, the Invicti were cutting a swathe through them. The ones who were still Silver were falling like trees while their newly-human comrades were running out of the square and back into the Red, but Lorelei and her traitors were standing firm.

That was where the real fight was going to be, because there were only nine Invicti left, ten if you counted Lucas, but there were at least thirty guards with Lorelei. Taking down three Red Shirts each might not have been a problem, but taking out three of their former comrades? That was a different matter.

They'd trained together, lived together and fought together over hundreds of years, and now they were squaring off for the sake of Lorelei's little takeover plan.

From the looks on their faces, Cam guessed that some of the traitors weren't too comfortable with that either, although Eveline looked as though she were having the time of her life. So, for that matter, did Lorelei.

'Run away then, you fucking cowards!' she screamed after the retreating Red Shirts. 'Let the grown ups talk.'

It was clear that, despite her words, she wasn't in the mood for conversation. She brandished her knives and led the charge, with Eveline and Tiberius at her side.

Carmen was quicker than the rest of the traitors, breaking away to head off Naia and Adewale, who'd used the last of their speed in an attempt to circle around and come at the guards from behind. But Lorelei's fighters had clearly loaded up on their own supply of uncontaminated blood, because a few had segued effortlessly into motion to join Carmen, who was already dragging Adewale to the ground.

Then Cam lost track of the fighting, because Lorelei and Eveline were slamming into him.

Lorelei lunged at Cam with one of her blades, but Emmy was between them before Cam even registered the attack. She twisted the knife out of Lorelei's hand with a grip so tight it drove her fingers into Lorelei's wrist, snapping the bones and tendons.

'You fucking bitch,' Lorelei snarled. 'You're supposed to be dead. Charles should have fucking killed you.'

'Do you want to know how I killed him?' Emmy said with eerie calm as she wrapped her empty hand around Lorelei's throat. 'I could show you if you like. There's something about the feeling of the flesh breaking between my fingers.'

That was all Cam heard before he took Eveline's knife in his stomach.

He had let himself get distracted by Lorelei and Emmy. He still hadn't quite got used to the idea that Emmy, the damaged creature they'd rescued in the Red, was perfectly capable of looking after herself now. Despite her birdlike frame, she was more than strong enough to fight her own battles.

Cam had been neglecting his.

'You were always such a soft touch for her,' Eveline sneered as she kicked his legs out from under him. 'Some of us haven't forgotten where she came from. The blood *matters*.'

It took a moment for Cam to understand what she was getting at, particularly as he was distracted by the hole in his side, but when he put the pieces together he couldn't stop himself from laughing through the pain.

'That's what this is about?' he said, rolling up to his knees. 'You're still sore that Sol chose her for his queen? Because she was human rather than Silver? Are you kidding me?'

She drew back her leg to kick Cam in the stomach, but he caught her foot and used it to pull her over onto her back.

'Do you know what kind of blood matters?' he said as he straddled her arms against her torso, pinning her to the paving.

Emmy was still standing right next to him, so it took only a split-second to rub his fingers against her blood-stained sleeve then shove them between Eveline's lips.

'Contaminated,' he said, then smiled as he crouched back on his haunches and watched her change, because there was poetry in it. She'd have to work hard to retain her snobbery against humans when she was one herself.

It was only then that Cam registered the silence. While he'd been fighting Eveline, the battle in the square had been a distant rush of speed and blood and brutal noises. Now there was nothing but stillness, filled with heavy tension.

The King was standing on the other side of the square in his customary battle armour of blood and gore. The bodies of the traitors lay strewn around him. He'd toppled them all, leaving them crushed, cleaved and incapacitated.

But he wasn't the only weapon on the field.

Cam was crouched in Emmy's shadow as she lifted Lorelei by the throat. The Invicti were frozen around her as they watched, waiting to see what kind of queen they'd brought back from the Red.

Then Emmy twisted her wrist. There was a sickening crack as Lorelei's vertebrae snapped apart, but still her eyes glared daggers at Emmy and her lips formed the shape of curses that her body couldn't voice. Her mouth continued to move even as Emmy closed her grip; even as she sank one finger after another through the skin; even as blood rained down onto Cam.

'Ems,' Cam said, but it was too late.

The Queen had already licked the last of the contaminated blood from her lips and spat it into Lorelei's eye.

Then she closed her fist.

Emmy had gone chasing after the stragglers as soon as Lorelei's corpse hit the ground. She hadn't waited to speak to Sol. She hadn't even acknowledged him; she'd just turned away from the unclosed distance between them and left it incomplete.

That worried Cam.

She was still so sharp and brittle. She'd just returned from centuries of being separated from the love of her life, and even the bond hadn't been enough to keep her by his side while there were still enemies around for her to run down.

Maybe it was easier for her to fight than it was for her to admit that she was hurting.

At least Sol seemed to be his usual, stoic self.

'Would someone like to tell me what that was about?' he said.

'Lorelei was a traitor,' said Tommy, slipping smoothly into his role as Secundus as though it hadn't been hundreds of years since he'd last seen the King. 'As was Eveline.'

'And Alistair and Carmen and Tiberius,' said Zita.

'Don't forget Laila,' Cam added.

'Ah,' Sol said, 'I'm not certain that Laila can take any joy in life when she is not betraying someone. I assume that her guards have remained inside the palace with her?'

'Not sure, Primus,' said Tommy, using Sol's old title.

Naia kicked at one of the now-cured soldiers that she and Konrad had formed up into a neat little line across the square. Eveline was amongst them, glaring at Cam.

'Well?' Naia said to the man she'd pulled out of the row. 'Where are Laila's guards?'

'Mostly here,' he said, looking around at the gore coating the square. 'A couple inside, I think.'

Adewale and Darius fetched them out, and they swore fealty to the King on the spot. Most of the traitors swore fealty to him in fact, possibly because they'd just seen him go through the rest of the guards like a blade through water.

It was easy to forget what legends meant when they were enshrined in stories, and that was what the King had always been to most of the guards: a story. They didn't remember the Fall, or the Revelation, or the wars before that. All they'd known was a children's story that they'd assumed must have been exaggerated.

But Sol was no exaggeration.

Neither was Emmy, striding into battle with her fingers flexing as though they itched to sink into flesh.

These were the monarchs of the Silver. These were the nightmares that had kept the rest of their kind at bay after the Revelation, because they offered their society some kind of stability.

But they themselves were far from stable. They were dear to Cam, but unpredictable, and as he watched the Invicti affirm their fealty to Sol one after another, he couldn't help but wonder whether this might all have been a terrible mistake.

Sol seemed satisfied with his diminished guard, but to Cam the bedraggled dregs of their squad was a sad sight. Yes, they'd fought the army and won. Yes, they'd brought Emmy back to the Blue and woken Sol from his stasis, for the second time. And yes, they'd seen off Lorelei and her rebels, so Felix would be safe for the time being.

It wouldn't last, though.

Not all of their enemies were dead. The traitors were down, but not contained. The Red Shirts were compromised, but not neutralised. And as Sol had received oaths from his Invicti, Laila had watched the scene from the palace steps, saying not a single word.

With so few of them left to defend the Blue, it was going to take a miracle for them to hold it for long.

Up on the rooftops, Julia had watched Lucas swear his fealty to a King he'd only just met. That seemed a little short-sighted to her, but she got the impression that saying no hadn't really been an option.

She couldn't help but remember what Viv had said to her out in the Red, back when Julia had still thought she was the Queen.

Don't make the mistake of thinking that our king would be your saviour.

She understood that now.

She and Claudia had fought for the Nobles, had risked their lives for them, but all that had changed from the humans' perspective was the identity of the hand on the whip. All of this effort had been for nothing.

Claudia would stay here, because she believed she was happy in her servitude, and Julia would contaminate herself and go back to the Red to live in the trees, because anything was better than having the name of her master stamped on her cheek.

As though summoned by her thoughts, Lucas jumped up from the square and landed beside her.

'Where's Claudia?' he asked.

'Gone back to the palace. She wanted to see if she could help. You know, lots of wounded Silver.'

That grated on Julia, the fact that her friend had dug herself so deep into this place that she didn't even need to be asked for her blood anymore. She'd gone as though she'd thought it was a privilege to serve, as though Julia would have been harming her if she'd taken the opportunity away from her.

But that was exactly what she wanted to do.

'Stay,' he said.

'You know I can't.'

'Why? Because you want to find the parents who abandoned you? Claudia's right about them, and I'm asking you: please stay with me. Not forever. Just for a little while, until it's safe for the Invicti to leave the city again. Then I'll come with you, and we can go wherever you like.'

She shook her head.

'You want me to stay in a place where I'll never be more than a slave. I can't do that, Lucas. Don't ask me to do that.'

Julia's cheek burned as she felt Lucas staring at the mark on her skin. It had nearly faded now, but it was still there: the reminder that for as long as she was in the city she would always be owned.

'You don't belong to him,' Lucas said.

'Because I belong to you? Is that what you're going to tell me?'

Lucas looked pained at that, his brow furrowing into lines of displeasure.

'Of course not,' he said. 'Is that what you think? You think I want to go backwards, to the way things were before we even left this place? That's not how it's going to work, Julia. I don't want you to stay in the Blue so you'll be my Attendant. I want you to live with me. I want to tell you fairytales you don't believe and make plans with you while we cook dinner together, like we used to. I'd just like to be able to spend some time together that doesn't involve us fighting for our lives.'

'Sounds a bit dull,' Julia said with a little smile.

'Not forever,' he smiled back. 'Just for a while.'

Julia took a step closer to him and looked up into his eyes in a way that she hadn't done since the last night they'd spent together in the Blue. All those days in the Red had been filled with embraces and glances that had felt accidental, or snatched, but this was a deliberate connection that she was forging between the two of them.

She reached up and gently touched his cheek, tracing the new lines of stubble on his jaw, which itself seemed squarer than it had once been.

'Do I know you anymore?' she asked.

He caught her hand and held it there, pressing it against his cheek.

'I know you,' he said. 'You may have been my Attendant once, but that's not who you are to me. You're Julia. You're the person who taught me how much more fun everything is when you share it. You're fierce, and adventurous, and a little bit terrifying when you're angry, and that was all before you turned into a crossbow-shooting, knife-wielding maniac.'

'Watch it,' she warned, reaching back to tap the stock of the bow that was still hanging from her belt. 'I know how to use this thing.'

'I know you do.'

When she brought her hand back around it found Lucas's waist. She let it stay there, because it felt natural to reach out to him now. After all the distance between them in the Red, she'd needed to come back here before she'd felt she could pull him back towards her, even if he wasn't quite the same as he had been before.

'Your eyes look strange without the silver,' she said. 'Especially at night. I remember the fire shining off them when we were in your garden.'

Lucas looked away for a second, as though he were ashamed of the change.

'It's better this way,' he said. 'I can walk around in the Red and the Blue as much as I like.'

'Will you show me them?' she whispered.

'Julia…'

'No one's watching except me. You don't have to hide it.'

He shifted his feet a little and dropped their clasped hands from his cheek.

'What's wrong?' she asked, because he wasn't looking at her anymore.

'What if…' he said, then he stopped himself, pushing his hair back from his face. When he spoke again, his eyes were fixed on Julia's.

'What if you're the person I need to hide them from?'

The air suddenly felt very still and silent. It hung around them in sheets that seemed to block out the rest of the world.

'Say something,' he whispered.

'I don't know what you're telling me.'

'Yes, you do.'

Yes, she did.

Silvering.

The magic that happened when the Nobles fell in love. She'd thought it was just a fairytale, and Lucas hadn't been so sure himself, but he'd still told her the story of when the King had fallen in love with the Queen. The silver in the whites of the King's eyes had extended into the irises, writing his love there for everyone to see. And when she'd loved him back, the silver had turned gold.

She'd heard the stories, and she'd seen enough golden eyes over the past week that she knew they were true.

She could think of no other reason why Lucas would be hiding his eyes from her now.

'Show me,' she said.

'Why?'

She couldn't admit the truth. She couldn't stand there and admit to him that she was so unsure of her own feelings that she didn't know whether his eyes would be silver or gold.

Surely silver. She liked him well enough, she knew that much, but this wasn't love, was it?

This couldn't be love.

Maybe he hadn't even silvered. Maybe he was ashamed of that. Maybe he didn't want her to know the truth.

'Show me,' she said again.

It didn't happen quickly. It started in the whites, the filaments threading their way from the sides of his eyes to the centre until they reached the rich brown of his irises.

They didn't stop there. They broke like rivers dividing into streams then into tiny rivulets, turning the brown into burnt honey cracked with heat. When the strands reached his pupils they split into rings of iridescence that circled the jet centre of his eyes, and then the movement stopped.

They were silver.

He had silvered.

For her.

She stood and she stared, because she couldn't think of a thing to say.

'I'm sorry,' he said. 'This is why I didn't want to show you.'

'You're sorry?'

'It's too much, I know. The silver in your ear, the silver in my eyes…'

She probably should have been scared by it, or intimidated at least. Lucas seemed to expect that she would be, but when she examined her feelings she could only conclude that her heart was racing for entirely different reasons.

'No,' she whispered.

'No what?'

'Stop talking.'

She pushed herself up onto her tiptoes and kissed him. For a second he froze, his lips motionless beneath hers, but then his arms wrapped around her and his fingers started tickling through her hair. Even when they eventually drew their lips apart, they couldn't seem to let go of each other.

'So will you stay?' Lucas whispered, his mouth so close that it moved over hers as he spoke.

Julia considered it.

Maybe it was the place that changed them. Maybe they only made sense together here. Maybe this was the only place where they could build their little paradise, surrounded by the broken buildings of the Blue.

'Alright,' she said as the beginning of a smile pulled at her lips. 'For now.'

Down in the square, the Invicti were on clean-up duty again, because once the conscious prisoners had been dealt with they still had to worry about the rest. It seemed as though it had been only days since Cam was waist-deep in Weeper bodies from the Contamination and now here he was again, only this time it was Silver bodies instead.

They'd all recover, or most of them anyway. The Invicti would hold them in the city on starvation rations until they could be persuaded to join Sol's cause, which probably wouldn't take long. The majority of them were young and had been spoiled by unfettered access to uncontaminated humans. They'd sign up pretty fast when they realised Sol was their only dealer.

Viv and Bartek had been sent to retrieve the uncontaminated humans that had been left behind by the army, assuming that there were any still alive in the Red. There had been more Weeper calls that afternoon than were usual this close to the city, so Cam wasn't hopeful.

'Is this the last of them?' Tommy asked Cam.

'Except for the ones that ran off into the Red,' he said, poking through the bodies with his toe.

'Well, they can stay there.'

'Because you're staying here?'

'Of course. Aren't you?'

Cam genuinely had no idea what he was going to do with himself.

'Maybe,' he said. 'Maybe I've been living in the wild too long.'

He smiled as he spoke, so Tommy would think he was just kidding, but he wasn't sure it had been a joke.

The Blue was somewhere he had always thought of as home without it ever actually feeling like home. The city was here, the people were here, and now Emmy was here too, but Felix wasn't. He'd be ejected if he ever set foot in the place, just as surely as the newly-human soldiers would be ejected shortly for their contaminated blood.

After all, that was the basis on which the Blue was founded.

Safe within, wild without.

But things in the Blue were feeling pretty wild right now.

The army was bothering him too. There had been so many of them, particularly when added to the numbers they'd faced in the mountains when they'd rescued Emmy. The total was so big that it scared him, because the Silver just didn't multiply like that. Whatever they had been doing in the mountains, the Invicti hadn't got to the bottom of it yet and until they had, it still felt like a threat.

How was it possible for Charles to have made that many Silver?

Cam would have asked Tommy about that, but then Emmy walked back into the square, and the moment was too large to interrupt.

It was as though she'd put the savage part of herself away by running it through the lines of the retreating Red Shirts. She'd walked across the square earlier and had only seen the fight, but now she was seeing Sol. Based on the transformation in her attitude, an onlooker might have thought she was seeing him for the first time that day. She might have been a completely different person.

Her face was already pinched with tears by the time she reached him. She pressed her forehead against his as he took her in his arms. Cam had to look away from the anguished relief that was etched on his king's face.

Sol had noticed the change too, then.

Time may not have changed them much physically, but the years apart had done their own kind of damage. They were different now. If Sol had changed even half as much as Emmy, then they might as well be strangers, tied together by a bond that had been forged by other people.

Cam couldn't predict how things would turn out now that they were reunited. They could save the city, or they could tear it apart around them.

He had no control over that.

But still, this was it: the fruition of his centuries of searching and starving and stretching until he was ready to break. This was what he had prayed for through all those years alone.

The King and Queen, together once more.

But Cam wasn't on his own anymore either, so he left the others to finish the clean up and began making his way back towards the Red.

He didn't want to keep Felix waiting.

In the forests of the Red, Cam wasn't the only one looking for Felix.

Two men stood behind a felled tree and watched as Felix and Aaron bickered quietly about what to do with Gul's body.

'See the eyes?' the first one said.

The second nodded. 'Just like he said. That blue.'

'That same blue.'

They watched a little while longer, but they could already hear the Invicti coming back this way to clear up their mess. It was time for them to leave.

But they wouldn't go far. Soon enough, they'd get the opportunity to make their move.

Epilogue

In the temple of the Blue, Emmy and Sol were finally alone.

She had insisted, dragging him into the nearest empty building.

He'd gone willingly, his half-smile twitching at the edges of his mouth as he anticipated a joyful and energetic reunion, but Emmy's intentions were quite different. She slammed the doors shut behind them, giving them some privacy, but that was where their designs diverged.

'Where is he?' she said.

Sol was a little taken aback by the vehemence of her tone.

'She said she'd take him to you,' the Queen went on. 'So where is he? She did reach you, didn't she?'

'To whom are you referring?' said the King.

'The woman. She took him from me to get him out of that place, to get him to you. Don't tell me she never reached you. I couldn't bear it, Sol. Everything I've done. *Everything* I've done has been for him.'

'Emilia,' Sol said, catching her face in gentle hands. 'My love. My queen. I have slept for almost as long as you have been missing. I don't understand what you're asking me.'

The silence that followed was long enough to fill the room, stretching into the cold, dark corners of the temple that had been the King's resting place for so many centuries.

'Sol,' she said, her voice trembling as uncertainty crept into her words, 'don't mess with me.'

'When have I ever?' he said, but the colour was already draining from Emmy's cheeks.

'No,' she muttered, then she doubled over, holding her stomach while her breath came fast and shallow. Her skin shone suddenly with sweat, despite the cool of the stone temple.

Sol took a step towards her.

'Emmy?'

'No,' she said, frantic now, her head shaking as she pounded her fists against Sol's chest and pushed him back against the wall. 'Don't tell me that! Don't tell me you don't have him. Solomon, where is our son?'

In the mountains of the Red, the remains of Charles's people were still licking their wounds when the messenger arrived from Charlestown.

Most of the Red Shirts still had dealings with the coastal town from time to time, so the face of the Silver who knocked at the stone door was not unfamiliar to them.

'You're not coming in,' the door guard said.

'You'll want to hear this,' the man replied.

'Because we're desperate now, is that what you think? You might have heard the news from the Blue, but we've still got fighters left. We don't need the likes of you.'

'Is that how you're going to play it, then? Like a wee numpty? Or are you going to invite me in and hear what I have to say?'

'You can't talk out here?' the guard said, taking a step closer.

'I want to talk to whoever's in charge, but I'm guessing you dinnae ken who that is now. Am I right?'

The silence that followed spoke for him.

'As I thought.'

'You can tell me,' the guard said.

The messenger laughed at that, more loudly than was warranted. It riled the guard enough for him to take a swing at the Scot, which was a stupid move. He was on his back in seconds with the messenger's blade at his throat.

'You can take them the message for me, then,' the Scot said. 'Can you do that? I wouldn't nod right now if I were you.'

'Yes,' the guard whispered.

'Then tell them this: we've got something they'll want. If you want in, then be quick about it. Sunset tomorrow, out by the mountain pass. Got it?'

The guard started to nod, then remembered the blade and whispered another, 'Yes.'

'Good lad.' The messenger sheathed his knife and started to walk back into the trees, but he hadn't got far when he turned around to yell back at the guard.

'By the way, this thing we've got, this thing I'm sure you're going to want?' He grinned. 'We've found the boy.'

If you enjoyed *The Silver Queen*, why not read *The Blood Prince*? It's the third and final book in the *Sovereign* trilogy, and it carries on right where *The Silver Queen* left off.

***

Join my Readers' Club and receive a FREE short story

www.josiejaffrey.com/subscribe

***

Please leave a review!

If you enjoyed *The Silver Queen*, I'd be so grateful if you would please review it. Book reviews can make a huge difference to the success of a novel, particularly those of self-published authors like me. If you have time to leave a review, even if it's just a sentence or two, then I'd really appreciate it.

***

Explore the rest of the Silverse…

This book is just one small part of the Silverse, a whole world of vampires that's waiting for you to explore. There are more novels, short stories, serialised story episodes, and even audio drama podcasts. They're all interrelated, although each series stands alone.

Find out more on my website at www.josiejaffrey.com

Acknowledgements

Uber thanks to Vicky and Zoe for their beta reading skills. This book is so much better than it would have been without your tough love.

Huge thanks to my family on both sides of the pond for their support.

Big thanks to Ali at Wallingford Bookshop for all the books and coffee.

And of course, above all, thank you to Max for being practically perfect in every way. You are utterly wonderful, even if I might imply otherwise by snarling at you while I'm editing my manuscripts.

CONTENT WARNINGS

General warnings:

Post-apocalyptic setting; humanity has been mostly wiped out by a virus that turns them into zombie-like creatures. Small communities of humans are isolated from the abandoned outside world, which is considered contaminated.

General warning for violence.

General warning for blood/gore, including blood drinking, description of injuries, zombie-like creatures, dead bodies.

One of the main settings is a city controlled by vampires where humans are considered servants/slaves. Issues of power disparity/ class divide/consent under slavery discussed briefly.

No racism, no homophobia (main character relationships are F/M and M/M), no ableism, no animal cruelty (other than calling an ornery horse a 'bastard'), no misogyny.

No sex; some kissing (teen appropriate).

Some swearing (up to and including 'fuck' but not frequent).

Specific warnings:

Blood drinking as sexual/pleasurable behaviour; sometimes violent (only off page).

A main character is temporarily, and side character permanently, under the control of a sadist; he injures them, keeps them locked in his house, and emotionally manipulates them.

Minor characters whose mouths have been sewn up.

www.ingramcontent.com/pod-product-compliance
Lightning Source LLC
Chambersburg PA
CBHW010551170726
48285CB00011B/2849